"I'M OVERWHELMED BY AN URGE TO MAKE A PASS AT YOU."

"That wouldn't be wise," Rainbow said, sounding breathless. She stared up at him from wide, mossy-green eyes. God, her eyes reminded him of some of the jungles he'd visited—cool, dark places under the canopy of trees, places where he'd always found peace.

"You're irresistible," he said, stepping closer so that they almost touched.

His cynical side reminded him that this was the woman he had called a fraud and a swindler. But the cynic got drowned in a sea of sensation. Jake wasn't thinking. He was experiencing, feeling, reveling in the moment—and all he knew was, even as he stepped over the edge of the precipice, he had never felt freer in his life.

His mouth found hers. Their tongues met in an ancient mating ritual, and honeyed heat spread through him.

Enthralled, he could only follow where need led him.

Other Avon Contemporary Romances by
Sue Civil-Brown

CARRIED AWAY
LETTING LOOSE

SUE CIVIL-BROWN

Chasing Rainbow

AVON BOOKS NEW YORK

This is a work of fiction. Names, characters, places, and incidents either are the product of the author's imagination or are used fictitiously. Any resemblance to actual events, locales, organizations, or persons, living or dead, is entirely coincidental and beyond the intent of either the author or the publisher.

AVON BOOKS, INC.
1350 Avenue of the Americas
New York, New York 10019

Copyright © 1999 by Susan Civil-Brown
Inside cover author photo by David Ewart Photography
Published by arrangement with the author
Visit our website at http://www.AvonBooks.com
Library of Congress Catalog Card Number: 98-93534
ISBN: 0-380-80060-8

First Avon Books Printing: February 1999

AVON TRADEMARK REG. U.S. PAT. OFF. AND IN OTHER COUNTRIES, MARCA REGISTRADA, HECHO EN U.S.A.

Printed in the U.S.A.

WCD   10   9   8   7   6   5   4   3   2   1

Prologue

"**W**E'VE GOT TO DO SOMETHING, LUCY."

Joe Krebbs had just returned from a visit to their old home, and he looked worried. Spirits were allowed to return and check on their loved ones from time to time, but Lucy tried to avoid it. The person she loved most was here with her now, and looking in on old friends only made her feel wistful.

But Joe went back occasionally, and from the way he looked right now, that might have been a mistake.

"What's wrong?" she asked gently. "I thought you were delighted that your nephew was finally moving into your old condo."

"I was. That's why I went back to check. I wanted to see how he was settling in, but I found something else. Sweetheart, our friends are in danger."

Lucy felt a shudder of fear pass through her. It had been a long time since she had felt any such thing, and the sensation was unpleasant, even in her present disincarnate state. "What do you mean?"

"Well," Joe said, "you know what happened to us. It's about to happen again. We've got to do something to warn them!"

"But how? It's not like we can pick up a phone and call them!"

Joe shook his head, staring off into the incredible blue sky of eternity. "There's a way. I know there's a way. All we need is a psychic."

"But nobody would listen!"

"I think," he said slowly, "that I know how to get their attention."

One

SOMEBODY WAS WATCHING HIM.

Jake Carpenter dropped the last of his boxes in the middle of the living room and looked around. Of course, no one was there. He shook his head a little, dismissing the sensation as the early stages of heat exhaustion.

Grabbing the towel he'd been using all morning, he wiped the sweat from his brow. He was a big, strong man, with dark hair and startling blue eyes. In his work as a petroleum geologist he had acclimated himself to some of the harshest climates in the world, but while Florida in August wasn't as hot as the jungle he'd recently left behind, it was at least as humid. He wished he'd bought some Gatorade to drink, and settled for a glass of water.

He looked around the two-bedroom condominium with its contrasting modern architecture and antique furnishings, letting the cool air conditioning wash over him, and found himself remembering the last time he'd been here. His uncle, Joe Krebbs, had been alive then, and the two of them had done some deep-sea fishing on Joe's boat.

But now Uncle Joe was dead, and the condo felt

empty. Jake stood there, feeling the deep well of sadness that filled him now whenever he thought of the man. He'd felt closer to his uncle than he had to his father, and Joe had been just about the only family he had left—except for a couple of cousins he preferred not to think about.

Well, he told himself, that was the way life was. People you cared about eventually moved on, one way or another—which was why it rarely paid to invest in intangibles. The only constant he'd been able to find in life was science. When he held a drilling core sample in his hands, he was holding rocks that had endured for millennia. Living rocks that whispered their stories to him and that would whisper their stories to generations to come.

Braced by the reminder of what really mattered, he bent to heft the box and carry it into the second bedroom, which he planned to use for a study.

But then it came again, the neck-prickling certainty that he was being watched. Straightening quickly, he whirled around—and saw that no one was there. More than once over the years that ability to know he was being watched had saved him from thugs on dark, dangerous streets around the world, or from snakes and tigers in the jungles. It unnerved him to realize he'd been mistaken.

But after a moment, he shrugged the feeling off, though it wouldn't quite go away, and returned to moving and unpacking.

"I'm sorry, Joe," he heard himself saying to the empty air, "but I think I'm going to have to rearrange some furniture." As soon as he spoke, he felt embarrassed. Joe would hardly care now how the furniture was arranged—if Joe could even hear him, and with the certainty of a scientist, Jake believed he could not.

Even if there was an afterlife—a possibility Jake

found hard to stomach—Joe wouldn't care about earthly things now. And why, he wondered, had he begun to think about such things, anyway? Since Joe's death, such questions had occurred to him often, and they made him uneasy.

Brushing that thought aside, along with the feeling that he was being watched, he carried the box into the second bedroom, now devoid of the guest furnishings his uncle had installed there so long ago. There had been a queen-size bed, a dresser, a rocking chair, and some blue curtains, but they were now in the master bedroom.

Jake had stayed in the guest room on his visits, and the furnishings had a sentimental attachment for him, so he had decided to use them as his own. The big wooden bed that had belonged to his uncle had gone into storage, along with the other items that had once filled the room. Hard-headed realist or not, Jake couldn't bring himself to sleep in his uncle's bed.

In his entire life, except for his years in college, when he had decorated an off-campus room in early Goodwill, Jake had never had either a permanent home or any furniture to call his own. It felt odd now to step into a room full of pieces he had bought himself over the past couple of days—a desk, a desktop computer, a comfortable executive chair, a credenza, bookshelves, and a file cabinet.

The curtains hung by his uncle had been taken down, leaving only the white mini-blinds, giving the room the businesslike atmosphere he wanted it to have.

Here, surrounded by his books and his research notes, he hoped to write a textbook about petroleum geology. And maybe, if he had time, he would write a memoir of his experiences in the field.

He set the box on the desk and ripped it open.

Field notes. Carefully he lifted the file folders containing research notebooks and loose papers out and put them in the file cabinet, filing them according to the system he had been using for years. When he had emptied the box, he cut the tape on its underside and folded it flat, stacking it with others leaning against one wall.

He was just going back to the living room for another box when he heard a tentative knock at the door. He went to answer it and found himself looking down at a slender, beautiful gray-haired woman with a complexion as fresh as any debutante's.

She smiled up at him and handed him a flyer. "Hello, Jake," she said. "Do you remember me? I'm Nellie Blair. I was a good friend of your uncle's."

"Nice to see you again, Mrs. Blair." He looked down at the flyer, something about a condo association meeting this evening.

"You might want to come," Nellie said, indicating the flyer. "You've been nominated for association president."

Jake was startled. "Me? Why? I'm just moving in."

"Well, your uncle was president, you know. For a long time. We thought it might be a nice gesture."

"But . . ." Jake trailed off, trying to marshal his objections.

"Besides," Nellie said with a friendly smile, "you're the youngest person in the building. We figure you're up to it."

Before he could say anything else, Nellie had patted his hand in a maternal fashion and strode down the hall to the elevator. As the doors opened to admit her, she gave him a friendly wave, then stepped in and vanished.

Jake looked at the flyer, shook his head, and closed the door. President of the condo association? No thanks. Hell, there were more handicapped slots in the parking lot than regular ones, and the average age of the building's residents was rumored to be sixty-five. These people needed someone in their own age group who would understand their needs.

And, he decided, the only graceful way to decline would be not to go to the meeting at all. That would certainly make it clear that he didn't want the position, and there wouldn't be a lot of awkward questions to answer.

That decided, he returned to his unpacking. It was going to be nice living here until he took another contract abroad. Or so he told himself. Sun, sea, and sand—and a building full of people so old that they couldn't possibly get up to any mischief, let alone make horrendous amounts of noise, exactly the kind of retreat he was looking for.

Rainbow Moonglow laid out the tarot cards in her favorite T pattern, then hesitated before turning them over. The sun streamed in through the bay window of her little cottage near the beach, drenching the green plants she was growing on the shelf there.

As a psychic, she used the tarot cards a great deal, but she didn't endow them with any magical powers. To her they were simply a way to focus her psychic abilities and intuition. She might as well have used a crystal ball, a bowl of water with a few drops of oil in it, or one of her mother's many crystals, but she had always felt an affinity for the tarot deck. Something about the images on the cards seemed to nudge her unconscious.

Today she was doing a reading for herself, largely because she'd been plagued by a prescient sense that something momentous was about to happen in her life.

And for once she was surprisingly reluctant to explore the feeling and try to pinpoint it more closely.

Sighing, she reached out and turned over the first card: Death.

Well, naturally, she thought. She'd been feeling a major change was about to occur. She should have expected to turn up this card first. There was no new information in that.

Then, in rapid succession, she turned up the Hermit and Strength. So, she was living a solitary existence and she needed to keep her head and her sense of balance in whatever change was about to occur.

She sat back a little, brushing her long dark hair over her shoulders, and studied the three Major Arcana cards she had turned up. It was unusual, though not impossible, to turn up three Major cards in succession, and she felt uneasy. The sense that something important was coalescing around her was confirmed by those cards.

The Hermit really troubled her, though. She didn't think she lived a solitary life, although if she were to be brutally honest about it, she *did* tend to keep people at a distance, mainly because they were either so uncomfortable with or so doubtful of her psychic abilities.

Reaching out, she turned another card, and was relieved when it was one of the Minor Arcana, the Six of Wands, reversed. Confusion. Anxiety. Maybe embarrassment. Well, that would be nothing new. Any psychic who hadn't felt those things was a fraud.

This wasn't helping at all, she thought suddenly, and gathered up the cards, replacing them in the deck. They were going to tell her nothing she didn't already know.

The problem was with her. She was afraid of the change that was coming.

Suppressing yet another sigh, she rose from the

table and went to look out the window at the brilliant August day. A swim, she decided, would be the ideal distraction from her worries, and with no readings scheduled with her regulars, this was the perfect opportunity. And that, she decided, was exactly what she was going to do.

Just as she started for her bedroom to change into her swimsuit, the doorbell rang. She wasn't expecting anyone, and her few friends all had jobs and businesses that kept them occupied even during the slow days of August. Someone must have noticed the discreet sign in her front window advertising tarot readings. She hesitated, feeling truly reluctant to do a reading for someone else when she was feeling so much at odds with herself.

At last she decided it would be unkind not to answer the door. So many of the people who came to her were sincerely troubled and had nowhere else to turn.

On her doorstep she found an elderly couple who looked vaguely familiar. The man was tall and thin, with salt-and-pepper hair, and the woman wore the permed blue halo so popular with her age group. They were dressed casually, in shorts and sandals and straw hats, looking ready for the beach.

"Miss Moonglow," said the man, with a courtly little bow of his head. "I'm Ellis Webster, and this is my wife, Pat. We live over at the Paradise Towers. Could we have a few minutes of your time?"

Rainbow smiled and invited them in, offering them seats in her living room, all the while hoping that they were here to seek donations for charity rather than ask for a reading.

"We've been sent by our condo association to ask for your help," Ellis Webster explained.

"My help?" She couldn't imagine what she would have to offer to a condo association—unless, perhaps, they wanted to use her as a fortuneteller for some fundraising scheme. If that was the case, she would give them a firm refusal.

The couple exchanged looks, as if deciding who would take on the unpleasant task of telling her what they needed. Rainbow folded her hands and waited patiently.

Finally the Websters seemed to reach some sort of silent agreement. Pat turned to her and began to speak.

"This is really difficult to explain, Miss Moonglow. I personally am not inclined to . . . believe in ghosts."

"Ghosts?"

"Ghosts," Pat repeated. "We seem to have them in the building."

Rainbow *did* believe in ghosts—after all, her mother communicated with them on a regular basis. Still, she was surprised. This was not at all what she had expected to hear. Finally she said, "Are you sure?"

"A few of us are," Ellis said a little sourly. "I'm reserving judgment myself. But some people have seen them, and it's the general feeling in the association that we have to do something about them. Folks are becoming quite distraught and uneasy."

"Uneasy?" Pat repeated. "*Scared* is what they are, Ellis. *Terrified.* And one of these days someone is going to turn around and see one of these ghosts and have a heart attack."

"Which is why," Ellis continued in the same sour tone, "we need to do *something* about it. Liability, you see."

"Liability?" Rainbow repeated blankly. That was not a term she had ever heard applied to a ghost before.

"Liability," Ellis repeated. "If one of our residents

suffers harm because of these ghosts, and the association has done nothing to get rid of them, we could be sued."

"Oh, dear," Rainbow said, even as she felt a bubble of amusement. It was too easy to imagine the look on a judge's face if he heard that the condo was being sued because they hadn't done anything to get rid of a ghost.

"I agree it sounds ridiculous," Ellis said, "but people sue over everything these days. Even if it were dismissed, it would be expensive. We don't have that kind of money, and I'd be very surprised if our association insurance would cover it."

"So would I," Rainbow agreed, permitting a small smile to show. "Hauntings probably fall under acts of God."

"Most likely." Ellis looked as if the idea didn't sit well with him at all. "I *said* we should get better insurance."

Pat reached out and touched his hand. "You did, dear. I remember it. But I'm afraid this time it wouldn't make any difference. I've never heard of a policy for hauntings."

"Lloyds might have covered it," he said gloomily. "Well, it's too late now. We have to do something to protect ourselves. And that's where you come in, Miss Moonglow."

"I had a feeling it might be."

Pat smiled at her. "We—the association, that is—feel that a seance might help. You're a well-respected psychic here in Paradise Beach, and if you come and say we don't have ghosts, everyone will have to believe it."

"But what if there *are* ghosts?"

Ellis reflected distaste, while Pat merely looked resigned and asked, "Then you can do something to help get rid of them, surely?"

"That would depend on the ghosts, I'm afraid."

"But I've heard that ghosts come back because they have unfinished business."

"Sometimes."

"If we could find out what it is and help them resolve it, they'd go away, wouldn't they?"

"Probably. If that's what's going on." Rainbow wished her mother weren't at sea on a cruise. This was Roxy's end of the business. Rainbow never dealt with the spirit world, if she could avoid it.

"We have to try," Ellis said firmly, looking as if he hated to say it.

"Oh, I'm willing," said Rainbow. In fact, she was intrigued. This could be interesting, ghosts or no ghosts. It might even be the pick-me-up she needed when she was feeling so out of sorts. "But you have to understand, I can't guarantee anything. That I won't find ghosts, or that I can do anything to encourage them to move on if I do. There are no guarantees in this business."

Ellis finally smiled. "Miss Moonglow, if you made any promises, I'd think you were an utter charlatan."

Rainbow stiffened a little. "I am *not* a charlatan."

"I didn't say you were. Quite the contrary, in fact. I'm sure you believe fully in what you do."

But in truth, he didn't. It was as obvious to Rainbow as if it had been written on the wall. She smothered a sigh and looked away, giving herself some space to think and allow her intuitions to come to the fore.

This could be very messy and unpleasant for her, she realized, whether or not she found ghosts. Either way the condo residents were apt to be unhappy with her. On the other hand, if there really *were* ghosts over there, she couldn't abide the thought that the spirits might be unhappy and trapped.

"I'll do it," she said finally, looking at the Websters again. "But with two stipulations."

"And they are?" Ellis asked.

"First, no one outside the condo membership is to know about it. If anyone whispers a word of this outside the building, especially to the press, I'll withdraw immediately."

Ellis looked surprised, but nodded. "Very well. I don't think any of us wants the news to get out that the building is haunted and that we've hired a psychic."

"Which leads me to my other stipulation. I don't want to be paid for this."

"Oh, now really," Ellis began. He plainly didn't like the idea.

Rainbow, however, was insistent. She didn't want to be accused of cheating elderly people out of their money. "No pay," she repeated, "of *any* kind. No flowers, no food, no gifts, no money."

Ellis started to object again, but his wife cut him off. "That's all right," Pat said. She smiled at Rainbow. "Ellis is a businessman. He likes to have contracts and written agreements. But I think we can all do without that this time, Ellis."

"But the association won't have any proof that it made an attempt to exorcize the ghosts!"

"But everyone involved will know that we have," she assured him. "That's good enough."

But Rainbow felt it important to make something clear. "I don't exorcize ghosts," she said firmly. "If you want an exorcism, you'll need a clergyman."

Ellis didn't like that, either. "We have people of all faiths living there! They might be offended."

"Some of them are going to be offended by a seance," Pat pointed out reasonably. "If it doesn't work, we'll get a minister or a rabbi, or both. One step at a time, Ellis. It's nearly impossible to get a minister to do an exorcism these days. A seance is the simplest and easiest way to start dealing with this problem."

"One other proviso," Rainbow said. "I may not do a seance. I may just attempt to glean impressions. And the whole matter might not be settled with one attempt. It'll all depend on what I find."

Ellis nearly rolled his eyes. "I don't believe this! Surely there's a right way and a wrong way to do this, some series of steps that you have to follow."

Rainbow almost felt sorry for him. She'd met many people like him, and they all hated to hear what she was about to say. "I have to follow my intuition, Mr. Webster. That's the only formula I have."

Ellis Webster looked as if he found the idea unpalatable, but to Rainbow's relief, he didn't try to argue with her. She promised to come by that evening to speak with the association, then walked the Websters to the door.

Moments later she was wondering if the major change she had been anticipating had just walked through the door.

Joe Krebbs chuckled as he looked over the edge of his cloud. Sitting beside him, Lucinda worked on some embroidery, her needle flashing in the perpetual sunlight.

She would vastly have preferred an overstuffed wingchair to sit on, but Joe was enamored of the whole cloud idea, and she was indulging him. Clichéd though it was, Joe had always longed to float around on a cloud and play a golden harp. He'd tired of the harp a long time ago, and Lucy was hoping he'd soon get tired of floating on a cloud so that she could have an ordinary living room with comfortable chairs.

But she loved Joe with her whole heart, and she wanted his afterlife to be perfect, so she plumped up a little bit of cloud-stuff behind her for a backrest and reached for another shimmering thread.

"What's so funny, Joe?" she asked placidly, working ruby thread into gleaming white fabric stretched over a golden hoop.

"It's not funny, exactly," he answered, his chin propped in his hand. "Actually, it's what we were hoping to happen. But poor Ellis looks like he just swallowed a lemon."

"I take it he asked Rainbow to investigate us?"

"Yup."

"Poor girl."

"Poor *girl*? Why? This is what she does for a living."

"Well, she'll have to deal with all the doubting Thomases down there."

"Rainbow's been dealing with them all her life. She'll manage."

"I certainly hope so. I just wish there were a better way to do this."

"I don't know of one. We'll just have to keep things hopping until we get a chance to put the message through."

Lucy put aside her embroidery. Almost at once it dissolved into cloud-stuff.

"Your nephew's not married, is he?"

Joe looked at her. "Jake? No, not even involved." Suddenly his eyes sparkled. "Lucy, you wouldn't!"

She gave him a smile. "Rainbow deserves *something* for all her trouble, don't you think?"

Joe's answering laugh bounced from cloud to cloud.

Two

WEARING A GREEN BUSINESS SUIT THAT BROUGHT OUT the mossy green of her eyes, Rainbow sat at the back of the room and watched the condo association meeting. Given the time of year, a surprising number of the owners were present, nearly sixty in all. Apparently quite a few snowbirds—winter residents—had flown down in order to vote for the new association president. Rainbow had no idea who Jake Carpenter was, but he had evidently decided not to come to the meeting.

"Which just goes to show," said a man in yellow Bermuda shorts, orange polo shirt, sandals, and white socks, "that he doesn't care."

Rainbow was inclined to agree. How had this man gotten nominated for the post if he didn't come to meetings?

"He's just moving in," said a woman with champagne-colored hair that had been teased into a puffy rat's nest. Her makeup was thick and bright, and only served to emphasize the ruin age had made of her face. "He hasn't even had time to unpack yet."

The man in the orange shirt waved a hand. "That

just proves what I'm saying. He hasn't *lived* here. He doesn't know anything about us or our building."

"He visited Joe all the time," said another woman, who was decked out in a flowery flowing caftan. "Lots of us know him, and he knows us. And it would be a nice gesture to Joe."

"Joe's dead," said the man in orange. "The last thing he's concerned with now is the condo association."

"I wouldn't be too sure," piped up a small, bird-like woman.

A strange silence fell over the group. Rainbow looked around curiously, but no one turned her way and all she could see were the backs of heads.

"Look," said a man finally. Rainbow recognized him as Bill Dunlop, an elderly man with whom she had struck up a conversation at the library. Since then they had chatted several times on the street, and once she had had coffee with him and his wife in a nearby café. "We've all been complaining that we can't keep up with the job. The average age in this building is sixty-three. But he's a young man. He'll have the energy to do the job."

A murmur of agreement rose from the group.

"And if he doesn't?" someone asked.

"We'll deal with that if it happens," Bill said. "It's possible under our rules to replace him any time a majority of members wants to hold a new election. And I don't see anybody else here volunteering for the job."

"Certainly not me," said Ellis Webster from the dais. "One year was enough. There's a lot of work involved, and all the president gets in return is flak. Are we sure we want to do this to Jake?"

"It's easier to do it to someone who isn't here," a man near the front said. A laugh passed through the room, but when the vote was taken, Jake Carpenter was elected in absentia.

"Since Jake isn't here," Ellis said, "I move we continue the meeting under the old administration so we can deal with a matter of great importance. I'll pass the reins to him first thing in the morning."

The motion was seconded and passed. Rainbow felt a twinge of sympathy for the unknown Jake Carpenter. Judging by the way everyone else seemed to feel about the job, the poor man was probably in for a terrible year.

"Now," said Ellis, "let's move on to the haunting."

An uneasy silence filled the room once again, then was broken by a couple of nervous laughs.

"I feel pretty much the same," Ellis said. "But I'm aware the vast majority of our permanent residents are concerned. For those of you who've just arrived in town, let me explain briefly. Over the past couple of weeks, a number of our residents have been startled—even terrified—by inexplicable apparitions in their apartments and the hallways. I'm going to turn the floor over to some of them right now, so they can tell you what's been going on. Olive Herschfeld will speak first."

A plump woman with iron-gray hair walked to the front of the room and turned to the group. She was clearly nervous, and her attempt at a pleasant smile was wobbly. So was her voice.

"It had to be a ghost," she said. "I don't know what else it could be. I was standing in my living room Friday night when suddenly the air in the corner near the fireplace started to shimmer and turn all white. And it couldn't have been lights from outside because all my curtains were closed. All I know is, it sort of looked like the shape of a person. And the room turned as cold as the inside of my refrigerator. I don't mind telling you, I was scared *out of my wits*. I don't think I've ever been so frightened. Zach will tell you I was terrified."

"That's right." A short, lean man stood up. "I was in the bathroom and she started screaming. I didn't see what she saw, but I felt the room was like ice."

"Thank you, Olive," Ellis said. "Next we'll hear from Nellie Blair."

The pretty woman took her place in front of them. "I don't know what it was," she said apologetically. "I never believed in ghosts. But . . . something was out there on my balcony with me when I was watering my ferns. I could feel it so strongly. . . ." She shook her head. "Whatever it was, I didn't see it, but I felt it. And then it splashed water in my face."

"That might have been the wind, Nellie," someone said.

"No, it wasn't the wind. The wind was blowing the other way. But that wasn't the only time."

Rainbow looked around the room, listening with one ear, but equally interested in the responses from those gathered. A surprising number appeared to be on the edge of their seats, listening intently. Only a few looked bored or embarrassed.

"It was in my bedroom," Nellie said. "I have a vase of dried flowers on my bedside table. A friend gave them to me, you know, before she passed on. Anyway, I went in to get my hat and the flowers were out of the vase, on the floor. The vase wasn't even tipped over. So I put them back in the vase and went out for my walk. When I came back, the flowers were on the floor again. I thought maybe somebody was playing a terrible joke on me, but who? I live alone. Anyway, I put the flowers back, and again they were on the floor. It happened three more times. Once while I was sleeping. They were in the vase when I went to bed, and on the floor when I woke up. I'm a light sleeper, and if anybody had come into my bedroom, I would have heard them."

She shook her head, looking sad and a little worried. "It scares me, you know? I don't know what's worse, a ghost, or somebody playing a mean joke. I put the flowers away in a closet, but that doesn't make me feel safe."

There were more stories of a similar nature, of figures dimly seen in the elevator and hallways, of items being moved or played with when no one was around. It sounded like a haunting to Rainbow.

Then it was her turn to go before the group. She was pleasantly surprised at how many of the women's faces she recognized. Many of them had come to her at one time or another for a reading.

She explained what she would do and repeated her stipulations about not being paid, and about her activities not being mentioned outside the group. She braced herself for the usual complaints that she was a fraud, and that what she did was all balderdash, but was surprised when no one objected.

"What's to object to?" asked one man finally. "It costs nothing, we won't get any bad publicity out of it, and maybe it will help."

A murmur of agreement passed through the room.

Ellis turned to her. "So when can you start?" he asked.

"Tonight," she decided on the spot. "I'll start tonight."

"What do you need?"

"Just the unit numbers where things have happened. I'll wander around and get a feeling for the place, if that's okay."

"How will we find out what you learn?" Olive asked.

Rainbow hesitated. She hadn't considered that.

"Well, I guess I can write you letters about it as I go."

"That would be a good idea," Ellis agreed. "I'll copy them and put one in every mailbox."

"What about a seance?" Nellie asked.

"Not unless I'm sure it's necessary," Rainbow answered with a smile. "If it is, I'll let you all know so you can attend."

A half-hour later, reinforced with tea and cookies, and armed with a list of the places people had experienced problems, Rainbow set out to see what she could learn.

Jake answered his door with heavy reluctance. It was nine-thirty in the evening, and he still hadn't made full adjustment to the change of time zone. He was spending a lot of time feeling half-awake and out of sorts, and the sensation of being watched kept troubling him. Hell, he was even beginning to wonder if he should see a doctor about it.

He'd spent most of the evening in his office, trying to organize an outline for his book. The packing boxes in the living room and bedroom remained untouched, but he'd felt a need to do something really productive. As long as his office was set up, he could deal with the rest of it a bit at a time.

Like right now, he thought wearily, as he went to answer the door.

He expected to see Nellie Blair or one of her elderly cohorts. Instead, he was surprised to see a beautiful young woman with eyes the color of tree moss and long, silky dark hair that made him think of Indonesia. Did this mean he wasn't the only youthful resident in the building? He suddenly found himself hoping so.

"Yes?" he asked.

She smiled and offered her hand. "Mr. Carpenter, I'm Rainbow Moonglow."

"Excuse me?" It was as if she were speaking another language, and his fogged brain couldn't sort out the words.

"My name," she repeated slowly, "is Rainbow Moonglow."

It was an impossible name—strange, unusual, totally incredible—and he was instantly enchanted. And also instantly leery.

"Is that a stage name?" he asked, wondering if this lovely woman with the sweet, innocent face could be some kind of exotic dancer.

She laughed as if she was used to the question. "No, I'm afraid not. It's on my birth certificate."

"Oh." He wished he could sweep the fog out of his head, because he had the definite impression that he was acting stupidly and responding as slowly as if his last alert brain cells were mired in molasses. "It's a nice name," he managed finally.

"But one that takes some getting used to. Listen, I'm sorry to disturb you, but since you're president of the condo association—"

"I'm *what?*" he interrupted, as astonishment suddenly kicked a few dozen more brain cells into gear.

Her smile widened. "I guess they haven't told you yet. You were elected association president tonight."

"But I wasn't even at the meeting!" He was beginning to feel sandbagged—or as if he had stepped off the edge of reality into a strange world.

"I know," she said sympathetically.

"How can they do that?" This was unbelievable. "Don't I have *anything* to say about it?"

A little laugh escaped her, and her eyes danced merrily. "Well, they thought it would be easier to elect you when you weren't here."

"Obviously." He looked glumly at her. "Were you party to this?"

She shook her head. "I don't live here. No, my hands are clean on this one."

"Well, I'll have to resign. I don't know anything about this place."

"That might be an advantage," she told him. "Besides, Mr. Carpenter, these are all elderly people. They really would appreciate your help."

"I'm not a charity organization." He almost snapped the words, and as soon as he did, he wished he could snatch them back. Rainbow Moonglow looked as if she were somehow disappointed in him.

"It wouldn't hurt to try," she said gently.

Maybe not, he thought irritably. As long as this woman with the green doe eyes didn't look at him that way again. And as soon as he had *that* thought, he became convinced that fatigue had made him stark staring mad. What did he care what some strange woman thought of him, even if she did have beautiful eyes? Beautiful *strange* eyes, he amended. Eyes that seemed to see right through to his soul. Another fanciful thought, and it made him even more irritable.

"Is that what you came to tell me?" he asked. "That I've been sandbagged by a bunch of old coots?"

The smile returned to her eyes and danced around her mouth. "Well, not exactly."

Someone down the hall opened a door and leaned out. "Could you please take your conversation inside?" asked an old woman. "I'm trying to sleep."

"Sorry," Jake said automatically, thinking he'd like to be doing the same thing. Stepping aside, he motioned Rainbow into his apartment and closed the door.

The place was a mess, he realized suddenly. Boxes were scattered everywhere, along with the towel he'd been using to mop his brow, and packing paper he still hadn't gathered up. And of course, all the dust from nearly a year of being unoccupied.

"You really haven't unpacked," Rainbow commented, as she took the chair he indicated. "One of the ladies downstairs said that was why you didn't come to the meeting."

He sat on the couch facing her. "I didn't come because I didn't want to be elected."

"Oh." Her smile deepened. "That was a mistake. I don't think they'd have elected you if you'd come to the meeting and kicked and screamed."

"Probably not." He sighed and passed his hand over his face, trying to wipe away the fatigue. "I'm sorry. I must seem awfully dense, but I'm still recovering from jet lag and I'm exhausted."

"I don't want to keep you. I just felt, since you're the president now, that I had a duty to tell you that I'm going to be working on the haunts."

Now Jake became absolutely sure that he was having some bizarre dream. People in real life weren't named Rainbow Moonglow, and they didn't say they were "working on the haunts."

He sat back on the couch, feeling its reassuring solidity, and closed his eyes a moment. He wasn't dreaming; of that he was reasonably certain. It only *felt* like a dream, possibly because he was so fatigued.

Nevertheless, he half-expected that when he opened his eyes, the beautiful young woman with the tempting figure would be gone, and he'd find himself all alone in the messy apartment.

But she was still there, still sitting across from him in his uncle's easy chair, her knees primly together, her hands folded. Since she wasn't going to go away, he had a feeling that neither would this business about haunts.

"I don't believe in ghosts," he said finally.

"Neither do most people."

Well, at least she wasn't totally disconnected from reality, although he felt *he* was. "What I'm trying to say is, I don't understand why you're here."

"Because you're president of the association. I thought you should know what I'm going to be doing. The association asked me to look into the haunts."

"*What* haunts?"

"There have been some apparitions and cold spots, and some movement of objects when no one was around. It warrants investigation."

"Why? Because some person is telling tall tales?"

"More than one person is telling these 'tales,' Mr. Carpenter. The residents are very uneasy."

"And just what is your role?"

"I'm a psychic."

"Oh." To say he was disappointed would have been an understatement. That this beautiful young woman should be a fraud struck him as thoroughly disgusting. Those wide, innocent eyes hid the heart of a huckster. "So, these people are frightened, and you're going to take advantage of them."

She looked as if he had just slapped her. "I'm going to do no such thing!"

"Spare me." He rose and walked to the door, throwing it open. "So-called psychics are a dime a dozen in this state, every one of them making a living off the grief and loneliness of old people. Take a hike, Miss Rainbow Moonglow. And you can be sure of one thing: no matter what it takes, I'm going to see that you don't swindle these people out of whatever little life savings they have left!"

She opened her mouth, as if to argue with him,

but then closed it, pressing her lips together. Back stiff, head high, she walked past him and stepped into the hallway.

He closed the door in her face, turning the deadbolt with noisy finality.

Joe looked at Lucy and spoke. "Yes, Jake certainly *does* seem taken with Rainbow, doesn't he?"

Lucy smiled to herself, and just kept on stitching. "You'll see," was all she said.

Joe figured that even *two* eternities weren't going to be enough to understand the workings of the female mind.

Rainbow stood in the hallway for several minutes, feeling angry and offended. What a nasty man! He was leaping to conclusions about her based on nothing but misapprehensions. She had the worst urge to kick his door until he came back to open it, then tell him exactly what she thought of him.

But she didn't behave that way under any circumstances, not even these. What did it matter what he thought of her? The only thing that mattered was what she could do for these frightened people, and she was going to do it come hell or high water or Jake Carpenter.

Her chin set, she marched down the hallway to the elevator and punched the button. The doors opened almost immediately. Stepping inside, she pushed the button for the ground floor, then sagged as her anger deserted her.

It hurt, she realized. She didn't know Jake Carpenter from Adam, yet his opinion of her *had* hurt—even though he couldn't possibly know her well enough to *have* an opinion.

And she'd thought she had long since grown past

being concerned with the opinions of people she didn't know . . .

Worse, on her walk-through of the building, she hadn't sensed anything at all. Either her psychic powers were out of whack tonight, or nothing was going on. At least, nothing ghostly.

Except in Jake Carpenter's apartment. There she had felt a definite presence, a sense of warmth and love and even humor.

Whatever ghosts were dwelling with Jake, they were the kind anyone would like to have around. She might have mentioned them if he'd given her the chance. But considering his reaction to her, it was better to say nothing about it.

At home, she kicked off her shoes and exchanged her stifling suit for white shorts and a yellow T-shirt. A walk on the darkened beach would be nice, she thought longingly, but the beaches closed just after sunset—although she supposed the worst that could happen was that one of the local police officers would ask her to walk elsewhere.

Sighing, she gave up the idea and made herself a cup of tea instead. She took it out into her garden behind the cottage, her little garden with its high privacy fence and its profusion of tropical blooms. The flowers scented the night air, even though the plants were beginning to look a little wilted as they always did in the August heat.

Sitting in the near-dark, with only the soft light of the moon and the yellow glow from a lamp inside to light the night, she drank her tea and wondered why she felt as if she were on the cusp of something important.

The night was muggy and unusually still. The sea breeze which had blown all day had died, and the land breeze hadn't yet begun to send its cooling

breath toward the sea. Not even the highest frond
stirred on a nearby Washingtonia palm.

Finally, feeling sticky and hot, Rainbow carried
her cup into the house and let the air conditioning
dry her damp skin.

Just as she was about to dump the dregs of her
tea into the sink, she hesitated. Then, following a
custom she had learned from her mother as a child,
she turned the cup upside down on its saucer. She
turned it three times, then lifted it and looked into
the leaves in the bottom of the cup.

The leaves seemed to unlock a door in her mind
that the cards had earlier failed to open. Looking
down at them, she saw that the winds of change
were already blowing through her life.

Nothing would ever again be the same.

Rainbow was just falling into an uneasy sleep
when the phone rang. Reaching out blindly with one
hand, she found the receiver and put it to her ear.

"Oops," said the smiling voice of her beloved Uncle Gene, "I keep forgetting the time difference. Did
I wake you?"

"You know perfectly well you did." But Rainbow
was already smiling and pushing herself up higher
on the pillow. "You're just a night owl, Uncle Gene.
You can't get used to the fact that I'm not."

"Well, it's really not that late out there, Rainy. It's
not even midnight."

She glanced at the glowing numerals of the clock
on her bedside table. "Not quite by three minutes.
But that's okay. You know I always love to hear
from you."

"Of course you do! How could you not? I'm an
exciting, lovable old rogue, aren't I?"

"You don't need me to tell you that," Rainbow

said, her voice full of laughter and love. "You've worked very hard on your image."

"So I have. Image is everything, dear child." He paused. "You know I don't go in for all this stuff you and your mother do."

"I know."

"Not that I disbelieve it, Rainy. You and Roxy have both taken my breath away on more than one occasion. But I don't seem to be afflicted with the family psychic abilities to any great degree."

"Lucky you," Rainbow said with uncharacteristic bitterness.

There was a brief silence from the other end of the phone, then Gene said, "I knew it."

"Knew what?"

"Even I, the most psychically disabled member of the family, occasionally have twinges. I knew something was wrong. I kept getting an overwhelming urge to call you."

"Nothing's wrong, Uncle Gene. Really. I just had an unpleasant encounter this evening."

"An unpleasant encounter having to do with your abilities? Give me the name of the swine, and I'll straighten him out."

Moody as she was feeling, Rainbow couldn't help but laugh. "It's not that big a deal."

"Of course it is! It must be. If it weren't a big deal, you wouldn't have been so upset that I was able to pick up on it. Tell me what happened."

"Nothing, really. A local condo association asked me to look into some haunts in their building. Then their new president accused me of trying to bilk all the elderly residents out of their life savings."

"He did, did he? Well, clearly he doesn't know you."

"No, he doesn't," Rainbow agreed.

"Why are you taking it so much to heart?"

"I don't know."

"Hmm." Gene paused a moment. "Can you pick me up at the airport tomorrow afternoon?"

"Of course I can. Are you coming for a visit?"

"Well, not exactly. I agreed to be a spokesman for an environmental group out there, but they don't need me to film the ads until late next week. I might as well combine business with pleasure and visit you and Dawn."

"Dawn went on a cruise with Roxy."

"Your mother went on a cruise? I didn't think she was the type."

"She got hired to do a seance at sea."

That made Gene chuckle. "Now that *does* sound like Roxy. Well, I can visit them when they get back. In the meantime, I'll have you all to myself."

Rainbow smiled into the phone. "Sounds like a plan."

She hung up the phone and rolled over, hugging her pillow and smiling into the dark with pleasure. She loved it when Gene came to visit. He was always full of amazing stories drawn from his twenty years as a CIA agent, and from his second career as an actor.

Sometimes she envied him the exciting life he'd led. He'd traveled widely, and although he never spoke of such things, she suspected he'd had some hair-raising adventures. But he was inclined to dismiss his CIA career with a shrug and the comment that he'd "done his time in the three-piece-suit gig."

He was always vague about what exactly he'd done for the CIA, and that vagueness had filled Rainbow's head with all sorts of excited imaginings. She knew there were things he could have done for the organization other than spy, but in her heart she believed he must have been a covert operative. If he hadn't been, wouldn't he have said so?

This time, she promised herself, she was going to get the truth out of him.

And maybe, she thought, the change she had been anticipating was nothing but Gene's impending visit.

It was a comforting notion, and she carried it with her into her dreams.

Three

JAKE SLEPT THROUGH HIS ALARM AND WAS AWAK-
ened finally around ten in the morning by the sound
of his doorbell. Dragging himself out of bed, he
pulled on a pair of jeans and staggered to the door,
half-hoping it was that witchy little psychic again so
he could give her another piece of his mind.

It was not such a welcome sight. Two older men,
both of whom he vaguely recognized, stood there
with hand trucks stacked with cardboard document
boxes.

"Good morning," said the taller of the two. "I'm
Ellis Webster, and this is Abe Levinson. We've chatted in the past, when you were visiting Joe."

His sleepy brain made some sluggish connections,
and suddenly he remembered. "That's right. I think
I played shuffleboard with you."

The men looked pleased. "That's right," said Ellis.
"I didn't think you'd remember."

"You beat me soundly, too, as I recall."

The older man waved a deprecating hand. "I had
the advantage of a lot of practice. Listen, would you
mind if we brought these boxes in?"

Jake automatically stepped back, letting them

32

wheel the hand trucks in, wondering even as he did it, why. "What is this?"

"Association records. You were elected president last night."

Jake was suddenly wide awake. "I wanted to talk to someone about that."

"Where do you want these?" Abe asked. "In the spare room?" He headed that way without awaiting instructions.

"About this election—"

"It's quite an honor, isn't it?" Ellis asked, as he wheeled his truck into the office. "You don't have to tell me how flattered you are."

Flattered? Jake stood where he was, wondering why every conversation he'd had in the last two days seemed to be coming at him sideways.

A minute later, the two men reemerged from the office. Abe paused to shake his hand.

"We really appreciate you taking this on," he said warmly.

"But—"

Ellis interrupted. "It's not a terrible job," he said. "Not even especially hard. I'm the outgoing president, you know. I'll be glad to help you all I can, so don't hesitate to call me if you have any questions."

Faced with that, Jake couldn't quite bring himself to say that he didn't want to be president and they could take all the boxes back where they came from.

"And don't worry about the hauntings," Ellis said on his way out. "We've already taken care of that problem."

The hauntings. Jake had to do something about *that* before things got out of hand. Suddenly galvanized, he hurried to the bedroom to dress.

He'd never gotten around to unpacking anything last night, so he had to tear through boxes in search of fresh clothes and underwear. At last he found a pair of khaki shorts that weren't too rumpled, underwear, and a blue polo shirt that would lose its wrinkles in a few minutes of wear. The only shoes he had were work boots, so he laced them up over a pair of socks, thinking that he probably needed to go shopping for something more suitable for his new home.

The kitchen was bare, of course. He'd ordered out for pizza last night—and how he'd missed pizza whenever he was out of the country!—but he'd been too tired to deal with stocking his refrigerator. He'd better handle that today.

Five minutes later, feeling the morning sun on his cheek, he was driving to the Paradise Beach police station.

Going to the police about Rainbow Moonglow appeared to be his only legitimate option. He doubted he could persuade the residents that they were being taken, and he doubted he could persuade that little witch to back out when there was undoubtedly a lot of money at stake. That left the police as the only ones who could protect the elderly Towers residents. There was certainly nowhere else to turn.

He was just pulling into the police parking lot when a purple golf cart bearing an elderly woman with a crown of white hair turned off the street and followed him. It had always amused him that some people around here used golf carts instead of cars for transportation, and in spite of his cranky mood this morning, he got out of his car with a smile.

She looked at him sharply, her dark eyes taking in every detail. "I imagine you're Jake Carpenter," she said.

"Yes, ma'am." He was beginning to wonder if everyone in town knew who he was. He certainly couldn't remember having met this lady at the Towers.

"I thought so. You look a lot like your uncle."

He took that as a compliment. Even in his seventies, Joe had been a good-looking man. "Thank you."

"I'm Mary Todd," she said. "*Miss* Mary Todd. I was a friend of your uncle's."

"It's nice to meet you."

She cackled merrily. "That's a polite social lie, boy. Don't say it if you don't mean it."

"Polite social lies make the world go around."

"Only for small minds. Joe didn't think you had a small mind."

Jake found that he was enjoying Miss Todd's outspokenness hugely. This old woman was something else. "I guess that remains to be seen."

She laughed again, her dark eyes as bright as a bird of prey's. "You're going to do something about the ghosts, of course."

"Ghosts?" He wasn't willing to even admit he'd heard of them.

"You know perfectly well what ghosts I mean," she said tartly. "And now you're president of the condominium association, so that makes them your responsibility."

"I have to disagree with you, Miss Todd. Since I don't believe in ghosts, they can hardly be my responsibility."

"Hah! What a disappointment. You have a small mind, after all."

"No, I simply have a scientific, rational one."

"There's nothing rational about dismissing something simply because *you* haven't seen it."

He opened his mouth to argue with her, then thought better of it.

She pointed a finger at him. "Whatever you believe, my friends at the Towers are frightened.

You're president of the association, which means you *have* to do something about it."

"I *am* doing something about it."

"Humph. The Paradise Beach police may be damn good, but they aren't good enough to arrest a ghost!"

"What if it's *not* a ghost, Miss Todd?"

She paused, looking thoughtfully at him. "What do you mean?"

"What if someone is trying to frighten the residents?"

"Why on earth would anyone want to do that?"

"Oh, I don't know. Maybe to get them to sell cheap."

She frowned. "You know, I'd rather have it be ghosts. It would be so much more original."

Jake felt an impulse to laugh, but restrained it. He didn't want to offend this woman needlessly.

She wagged her finger at him again. "Just be sure you don't let your beliefs blind you, boy."

"My beliefs?"

"Your belief in science, to be precise. It's as blinding as any other belief, you know." With that, she turned her golf cart around and drove off.

Jake realized he was grinning like an idiot, and immediately sobered his face. Miss Mary Todd was a pistol, he thought. He actually hoped he had a chance to get to know her better.

Inside the police station, he asked the desk sergeant if he could speak to the fraud unit.

The sergeant, a plump man whose name tag identified him as "F. Parker," leaned over the high desk, resting on his elbows. "We don't have a 'fraud unit,' Mr. Carpenter," he said.

"Oh." Jake waited a moment, wondering how the hell everyone seemed to know who he was. He hadn't identified himself to this man, of that he was sure, but apparently F. Parker wasn't going to say another word, not even to tell him where he should go next. "Well, who would I see about a psychic who's trying to defraud people?"

"Have you been defrauded?"

"No, not me."

"A relative?"

"No."

"Then you don't have a complaint."

Jake restrained his impatience with difficulty. "Look, I'm the president of the Paradise Towers Condominium Association. Just before I was elected to office, the association hired a psychic to look into some reported hauntings."

F. Parker pursed his lips. "Why do you think a fraud is involved? Rainbow never defrauded anyone in her life."

Jake stared at him. Had he mentioned Rainbow Moonglow? No, of course he hadn't. This town must have a grapevine AT&T would have envied. "It's self-evident," he said.

"No, it's not. Rainbow never took money for anything she didn't do."

"She *can't* perform the service promised!"

"Why not?"

"Because there *are no ghosts*."

F. Parker sighed and shook his head. "Of course there are ghosts. Some good, solid citizens have seen them. And Rainbow would never take the job if she didn't believe they were there. That's good enough for me."

"Are you saying it's *legal* for a huckster to run around swindling elderly people out of their money?"

"No. But Rainbow isn't a huckster." The desk sergeant was beginning to look annoyed. "Look, sir, a great many people believe in mediums. A great many people believe in ghosts. If mediums provide the services promised their clients, they're doing nothing illegal, any more than a church is doing something illegal by holding out the hope of heaven if you follow its rules."

"But this is *different*."

"No, sir, it's not. That's what I'm trying to tell you."

"I refuse to accept that. I want to talk to your superior."

The sergeant suddenly smiled. "That might be a good idea. Wait here."

A couple of minutes later, the sergeant came back and escorted him to a rear office where the name plate announced, "B. Corrigan, Chief of Police." Parker knocked, then threw open the door and motioned for Jake to enter.

The chief, a man of about Jake's age, rose and came around his desk. "Sgt. Parker tells me you have a problem with a fraudulent medium, Mr. Carpenter."

"Yes, I do." At least this guy wasn't defending Rainbow before he had a chance to speak his piece.

"Have a seat, Mr. Carpenter, and tell me what's going on."

At last, Jake thought—someone who was actually going to listen to him. "I was just elected president of the Paradise Towers Condominium Association."

"Yes, I heard. Congratulations."

"Well, right about the time I learned they had elected me, I also learned they had hired a psychic to look for ghosts they think are haunting the building."

Corrigan nodded. "Rainbow Moonglow."

"You know all about this, then."

"I know that you think she's trying to defraud the residents. Can you tell me why?"

"Because she claims to be psychic!"

"Do you have proof that she isn't?"

"I don't need proof! She needs to prove that she *is*."

"Your residents seem to feel she's already done that. That's why they hired her."

"They've been deluded."

"I see." Corrigan tipped his chair back and looked up at the ceiling. "Apparently you don't know your neighbors very well yet."

"What I know is they're elderly. It's all too easy for some swindler to take advantage of them."

Corrigan's gaze was disapproving as it fixed on Jake's face. "*Elderly* and *senile* are not synonymous, Mr. Carpenter. Basically you're telling me that because your neighbors are old, they're fools."

"I don't believe I said that."

"You implied it."

Jake wanted to grind his teeth. Was everybody in this town exceptionally obtuse? "Look, Corrigan, these people have started seeing ghosts, and they've turned to a psychic for help. That's grounds enough to question their competence."

"In your view, perhaps. Not in mine. What's more, the psychic they've called upon is a well-respected member of the community."

"I don't believe this. What she's doing ought to be illegal."

"But it's not. Nor is it really your concern. They're adults, capable of making such decisions for themselves."

"But I don't want to see them hurt."

"That's admirable, but there isn't anything you can do about it."

"And what about these so-called ghosts?"

"What about them?" Corrigan smiled faintly. "It's not illegal for a ghost to haunt, the last I heard."

"But what if they're not ghosts? What if someone is trying to scare the residents to get them out of the building? To scare them into selling cheaply?"

"There are much easier ways to do that than to stage a haunting."

"So you're just going to ignore the possibility?" Jake began to wonder exactly when it was he had stepped off the bus into a different reality. All of this was beginning to take on the proportions of a nightmare.

"Of course I won't ignore the possibility. But I'd need some kind of evidence to launch an investigation. Right now all I have is your speculation, and pardon me for saying so, it's no more credible than the ghost stories. Less, in fact. At least the ghosts have multiple witnesses."

Everybody in this town was a lunatic, Jake decided, as he walked back out into the hot Florida sun. They all needed to be locked up for their own safety. Maybe the sun had addled their brains.

Or maybe it had addled his. Maybe he had suffered heat stroke when he was carrying his belongings into the building yesterday, and he was lost in some comatose dream.

But the sun felt too hot and real—and Rainbow Moonglow certainly wasn't a figment of his imagination. Not when he ran into her at the produce section at the grocery store.

"Don't buy that tomato," a woman's voice said from beside him. "See, it's been bruised by people squeezing it."

He looked over and saw Rainbow, looking good enough to eat in an orange top and lime shorts. She tempted him like a cool, refreshing dessert. "Oh," he said, sounding stupid enough to make him want to cringe.

She smiled, a pleasant smile that was totally unexpected, considering the way they had separated last night. "Here, take this one. It's the right color, and nice and firm. How many do you want?"

"Three." He loved tomatoes and hadn't eaten many in the last couple of years. Before he could say anything more, she had selected three and dropped them into his plastic bag.

"These are vine-ripened local tomatoes," she told him. "You'll enjoy them." Then, with another devastating smile, she turned away and went back to filling her own cart with lettuce, cucumbers, green peppers, and broccoli.

Jake stared at her, suddenly feeling as awkward as any fifteen-year-old boy who had been foolish enough to think he was a grownup. Rainbow Moonglow was a beautiful woman, but it wasn't only her beauty that was disturbing him.

He was annoyed that she could be so pleasant to him after what he had said last night. He was annoyed that she looked so beautiful when she by rights ought to look like an old hag. Weren't fortunetellers always old hags?

But most of all, he was annoyed that she had gotten the upper hand by the simple expedient of being courteous—while he had lost the high ground by behaving like a boor.

Forcing himself to ignore her, he finished filling bags with bean sprouts, snow peas, bok choy, ginger root, lettuce, green peppers, and fresh spinach. After only a few days here, he was already beginning to crave the vegetables that had been a large part of his diet the past few years. Hamburgers and fries no longer tasted like heaven to him.

Unfortunately, when he finished, Rainbow Moonglow was still there, checking out the cantaloupes. Gritting his teeth, he marched his cart past her, managing to say a taut "Thank you" as he passed by.

"You're welcome," she said in a friendly tone.

He darted around the corner into another aisle and told himself to stop behaving like a jerk. Certainly he'd lived in enough foreign countries that he knew how to live with beliefs he found strange or ridiculous. And certainly he knew enough about being the stranger in town not to go around offending everyone simply because their beliefs were different. Miss Rainbow Moonglow was obviously a well-respected and well-liked member of this little community, and apparently people around here believed in table-knocking, mind-reading, ghost-hunting, ectoplasm-producing mediums. It wouldn't be wise to start an open war with one before he even knew the lay of the land.

Cripes, didn't anybody in this country eat short-grain rice? His eyes scanned three shelves full of rice, all of it long-grain. He preferred the sticky short grain rice served in Asia, which he found more flavorful.

"Are you having trouble finding something?"

Damn it, the Moonglow woman was back, looking at him across her cart with that same pleasant smile.

"Short-grain rice," he managed to say.

"Oh, it's here somewhere." She came to stand beside him and look at the shelves. "I prefer it myself, but it's not always in stock, so I buy several packages when I can find it."

"I'll keep that in mind." Why was he finding it so difficult to be civil? He decided it must have to do with the fact that she was beautiful and she smelled good, and he hadn't been with a woman in . . . well, never mind. He didn't want to think about that. Not now.

"Oh, look," she said. "They've filled the space for the short-grain rice with long-grain. They'll never re-order it if the space is full." She reached out and began moving packages of rice to their proper place. "I'll be happy to give you some rice," she continued. "I have four or five bags at home and you're certainly welcome to one."

He didn't want to accept; he didn't want to be in her debt. On the other hand, he didn't want to eat long-grain rice. But pride won out. "I'll manage with the long-grain."

She turned toward him, the hint of a laugh in her eyes and around her soft lips. "Don't cut off your nose to spite your face, Mr. Carpenter. It's only a seventy-eight-cent bag of rice. I promise not to hold it over your head."

"I didn't mean—" But he couldn't bring himself to lie.

"Of course you did." Her smile never wavered. Returning to her cart, she gave him a little wave and walked down the aisle, disappearing around the corner.

Left to look with disfavor at the long-grain rice, he knew that was exactly what he deserved for turning down a neighborly offer. Shaking his head at his own stupidity, and wondering why he suddenly seemed unable to relax and go with the flow, the way he usually did in a strange place, he picked up a half-pound bag of rice and made a mental note to speak to the manager.

He didn't see Rainbow again in the store, and for some reason that left him feeling even more irritated.

It had to be jet lag, he decided. There could be no other reason that *everything* was irritating him so much.

Rainbow was carrying her groceries into her cottage when Mary Todd drove up in her purple golf cart. Leaning heavily on her cane, Mary climbed out of the cart and grabbed a plastic bag of groceries to carry into the house.

"It's all right, Mary," Rainbow said swiftly. "I can manage."

"I know you can," the older woman said tartly. "But so can *I*. What did you do, shop for a month? There's an awful lot here."

"My uncle Gene is coming for a visit."

Mary followed her into the cool house. "Is that what put the color in your cheeks? I was wondering if it had anything to do with Joe Krebbs's nephew."

"Jake Carpenter?" Rainbow set the bags on the counter and faced Mary, aware that her cheeks were growing pink with the thought of Jake. "He's a singularly unpleasant man."

"He's a singularly *misled* young man," Mary corrected. She placed her bag beside the others and turned for the door. "Come on, come on, you don't want food sitting in this heat any longer than necessary."

Rainbow trotted obediently after her and scooped up another four bags. Mary picked up a package of three rolls of paper towels and followed Rainbow back inside.

"Would you like something cold to drink?"

"Iced tea, if you have it," Mary requested, as she settled on a chair at the dinette in the corner.

Rainbow poured two glasses and gave one to Mary at the table. Then she started unpacking the groceries and putting them away. "What did you mean, that Jake is misled?"

"Oh, he believes too much in science and not enough in other things. Do you know what he told me this morning? He thinks someone may be staging the hauntings to scare people."

Rainbow faced her, a box of cornstarch in one hand and a bottle of soy sauce in the other. Gene loved her Chinese cooking. "Why would anyone want to do that?"

"He suggested that someone might be trying to frighten the residents into selling cheaply." Mary cocked her head, her dark eyes bright and observant. "It's a possibility, you know."

"Yes." Rainbow returned to putting the food away, moving swiftly to get to the meat, fish, and frozen items. "I was thinking about that this morning. When I went through the complex last night, I didn't sense anything at all."

Mary pursed her lips. "Is that unusual?"

"I don't know." Rainbow gave her a small smile. "This isn't exactly my forte."

"What about calling your mother?"

"She's at sea and won't be back for a couple of weeks."

"How unfortunate. Do you think you've bitten off more than you can chew?"

Rainbow shook her head. "Not really. If there's something there, I'll sense it. I know that for a fact. What I meant was that I don't know if it's possible to feel nothing at all when there's a haunting."

"I suppose if ghosts exist, then perhaps they can come and go as they choose."

Rainbow shrugged and joined Mary at the table. Everything that needed refrigeration was put away; she felt the rest could wait. "Apparently there are some hauntings where the ghosts seemed to be trapped, almost as if they can't move on to their new existences. I hear there are other kinds where the dead merely want to communicate something to someone left behind. In those cases I suppose it's possible I wouldn't always sense something. But I really don't know for certain."

"Hmm. What can you do about it?"

"Well, I'll go back again tomorrow and see if I can

sense anything. If not, I guess I'll have to try to hold a seance."

"That'll certainly raise Jake Carpenter's hackles."

Rainbow shrugged. "Too bad. He doesn't really have anything to say about it, as long as the other residents want me to try."

Mary chuckled gleefully. "You go, girl!"

The slang sounded so odd coming out of Mary's mouth that Rainbow found herself laughing.

But Mary had a word of warning. "Don't let that young man intimidate you. Don't let him get away with it. He's sadly in need of a good shaking up."

"Then he may get one," Rainbow said firmly. "I agreed to do this, and I'm not going to let anyone stop me. But how did you hear about it? I asked the residents not to tell anyone what I was doing."

Mary assumed a mysterious smile. "Very little in this community escapes me, gal. Very little."

And with that, Rainbow had to be content.

Gene Holder looked like every woman's dream of the dashing older man, which was undoubtedly why he'd found a second career in Hollywood. Even at sixty, Gene was certainly handsome, with a tall, lean build, gray hair, and a face carved just enough by the wind and elements to look interesting. He was also a rogue.

Rainbow often wondered how her uncle had ever survived working for a government agency. Nothing about him seemed amenable to being a nameless, faceless, gray-suited clone, or to working undercover. When he came through the gate at Tampa International Airport, he was wearing a straw hat, sunglasses, a T-shirt that proclaimed "I'm the guy your mother warned you about," and a pair of tennis shorts that showed off an excellent pair of legs.

Gene was vain about those legs, possibly his only vanity.

Rainbow threw her arms around him and laughed when he lifted her off her feet and swung her around. "Uncle Gene!" she said with real delight. "Oh, how good it is to see you!"

"You're a sight for sore eyes, Rainy. Now get me out of here before the woman in the pink pantsuit finds me again."

Rainbow's eyes sparkled with laughter as she looked up at him. "Another admirer?"

He put his hand over his heart. "I'm irresistible, I know, but it can be a royal pain in the butt sometimes. She chewed my ear all the way from Los Angeles about her grandchildren, her ex-husband, the divorce settlement, her bursitis, her delicate stomach, and everything that's wrong with the world."

"Poor Uncle Gene."

While they walked swiftly down the concourse toward the tram, Gene kept stealing looks over his shoulder. "It didn't really bother me until she insisted on telling me the details of her gall bladder surgery." He shook his head. "I'm not squeamish, Rainy. Hell, I've had bullets dug out of me with nothing but a couple of shots of whiskey to dull the pain—"

Rainbow looked up at him in shock. "You're kidding!"

His green eyes, so very like hers, twinkled a little as they returned her look. "I'm not kidding. It was a long time ago, sweetie, nearly forty years—and needs must when the devil drives. Plus, it makes a great story for the ladies. But not for *this* woman. Anyway, I'm not squeamish, but—" He broke off and shook his head. "It was the stomach pump part that got to me. The gory description of the tube running down her throat and the—well, never mind.

I'm sure you don't want to hear about it either."

"Not really."

The woman in pink hadn't caught up to them when the tram departed for the main terminal.

"You're safe," Rainbow said.

"Not yet. There's still the baggage carousel."

When they reached the baggage claim area, they found chairs from which they could see the carousel and sat together.

"Tell me about this fellow who thinks you're a fraud," Gene said.

"I've decided to ignore it. He just seems to be an unpleasant person."

"Really?"

She felt a burst of irritation. She hated it when Gene started reading between the lines. "Don't say it that way, Uncle Gene, as if you think I'm lying."

"I don't think you're lying to *me*," he said, a sparkle in his eye. "You might be guilty of deluding yourself, however."

"Well, I'm not. He's an irritating, nasty man, and the only thing to do is ignore it."

"Possibly. You *do* seem to be having a rather strong reaction to a mere idiot." He looked toward the carousel and sighed impatiently. "If they don't hurry up and that woman finds me, I'm going to make this airline sorry they ever sold her a ticket."

Rainbow didn't believe him. Gene often liked to speak extravagantly, but she'd never seen him do anything to hurt another soul. "She won't bother you again. You're with *me* now."

"I just wish I hadn't checked my bags. We could already be on our way."

"Aren't you overreacting? All she can do is talk to you."

"Her voice sounds like a buzz saw—whine,

whine, whine. My ears are still hurting. Oh, damn, there she is."

Rainbow turned in time to see the woman in the pink pantsuit coming down the escalator. She was a very attractive woman of about fifty, and all of a sudden Rainbow had a sneaking suspicion that her uncle wasn't innocent in all this. She looked at him.

"What did you do, make a pass at her?"

He shifted uneasily. "Not exactly."

"*Not exactly?* You're saying you encouraged the poor woman, and now you're trying to duck responsibility for her interest?"

"I'm saying that I was wrong to be interested in the first place. There is nothing interesting about her."

"Which is why you should get to know people before you make a pass." Rainbow shook her head. "I'm disappointed in you, Uncle Gene. Thinking with your hormones at your age."

He gave her a sour look. "I maybe be sixty, but I'm still alive and *male*. All my hormones are intact. It's a damn shame the woman's package is deceptive."

Rainbow looked away, hiding her amusement. Gene Holder would be a rake until the day he died—a day which she hoped was in the very distant future. "Just watch your behavior in Paradise Beach. I have to live in that town."

"My dear, I promise to be on my best behavior."

The first suitcases showed up on the carousel, and much to Gene's relief, they belonged to the woman in pink. She picked them up and departed without a glance in his direction.

"Saved!" he whispered.

"You could hardly have been more obvious about avoiding her."

"Naturally. I wanted no further misunderstanding."

His bags weren't far behind the woman's, and they made their way to the elevator, and from there to the fifth level of the parking garage where Rainbow's car was parked.

"You know, Uncle Gene, it's not just a matter of me being embarrassed to have a sixty-year-old uncle who acts like he's twenty."

Gene looked at her as she unlocked her trunk for his suitcases. "No?"

"No. You have to consider that you might have hurt that woman's feelings."

"I don't know her well enough to hurt her feelings."

"That's a good excuse, I suppose, but if you ask me, she must have been hurt by the way you seemed to be interested and then ran away like she was the Gorgon."

He cocked his head and smiled faintly. "You always did have a kind heart."

Not really, Rainbow thought as she climbed into the car. Not when she could think murderous thoughts about a certain Jake Carpenter. For all her protests that she was going to ignore it, the fact was, she could have cheerfully tied him to the railroad tracks and watched him beg for mercy.

That satisfying image put a smile on her face as she turned the car toward home.

Four

GENE WENT FOR A SWIM IN THE GULF BEFORE DIN-
ner. He owned a house on the California coast, and
Rainbow always found it amusing how eager he was
to swim in the Gulf of Mexico.

"The water's warmer," he told her, "and the
waves aren't usually as big. It's a more user-friendly
experience."

After he showered off the salt-water and changed
into shorts and a T-shirt that claimed "Divers do it
deeper," they ate steak and salad on Rainy's little
patio, amid the flowering azaleas, hibiscus, and bou-
gainvillea.

"I'm afraid I'm going to have to go out for a couple of hours after dinner," Rainbow told him. "I
promised to check on that haunting at the Towers,
and I really ought to get going on it."

"I thought you checked it out last night."

"I did, but I didn't sense anything then. I'd like to
go back and try again."

"No problem," he said with a smile that left her
feeling uneasy, though she couldn't say why. "I'll
tag along. Who knows, I might meet a ravishing
widow."

"Uncle Gene, you promised you'd behave!"

He held up a hand. "I will. I'm a man of my word, but I'm a romantic, too, Rainy. I'm still waiting for the woman who will sweep me off my feet. Who knows? She might be living at the Towers, just waiting for me to appear."

Rainbow didn't know whether to be amused or concerned. Generally speaking, the only way to deal with Gene was to be amused. Anything else only led to frustration. "If you see someone interesting, just don't make any passes until you've gotten a chance to know her."

Again he laid his hand over his heart. "I've learned my lesson."

"Right," Rainbow said drily. "At this late date."

Gene feigned a hurt expression. "I pride myself on being an old dog who *can* learn new tricks."

"Well, come along if you want to, but I'd appreciate it if you'd wear a different shirt. This is business, after all, and some people might consider that a little bit too suggestive."

"I'll take care of it," he assured her. Five minutes later he reappeared, wearing a red T-shirt that announced, "Dead bungee jumpers come with no strings attached." When he saw the look on her face, he spread his hands and said, "Hey, at least it's honest."

"Where do you find these shirts?"

"Neat, aren't they? And comfortable, too. Nobody's ever going to get me into a tie again."

"Not even the lady of your dreams?"

He shook his head. "I'll get married in a safari shirt. Or maybe a Nehru jacket."

"If you ever get married."

"The woman of my dreams won't expect me to wear ties, Rainy. That's the whole point, isn't it? To find someone who doesn't want you to change."

She had to admit he was right. But then, Gene was like that. Amid all his outrageousness were pearls of genuine wisdom. Before they left, she put a bag of short-grain rice into her straw shoulder bag. Gene raised an eyebrow, but didn't say anything.

She had called ahead earlier that morning, making arrangements to visit the affected condos that evening. Their first stop was with the Herschfelds, Olive and Zach, in their ground-floor unit.

Tonight Olive was wearing a black caftan that showed off her iron-gray hair beautifully. Her husband was wearing stained white overalls that looked as if he'd just been working.

"My boat is having engine trouble," he said, by way of explanation. "I'll just go wash up."

Olive offered them iced tea and lemonade. Gene, dripping charm, said he'd love some lemonade. Rainbow declined. "I just need to walk around a little, Mrs. Herschfeld, and get the feeling of the place. Like I did last night."

"Go right ahead," Olive said.

"I'll keep Olive company," Gene promised Rainbow. She didn't like the gleam in his eye, but consoled herself with the knowledge that Zach Herschfeld was just in the next room.

Rainbow stood for several minutes at the sliding glass doors that opened onto the patio, watching the steady rhythm of the waves as they rolled toward shore, seeking the inner stillness that was necessary to what she did. It would have been easier if she hadn't been so aware of her uncle and Olive murmuring in the background, and hadn't been so worried that Gene would charm his way into some serious trouble.

But after a while, the sound of their voices seemed to fade, and the rhythm of the sea entered her, making her feel relaxed and somehow removed from everything around her, as if she were floating gently.

Little by little she began to feel a presence, as if there were another person in the room with her, Olive, and Gene. She turned slowly, not wanting to disturb her mood, and saw that Zach had not yet rejoined them. No, she sensed him still in the other part of the unit, could feel the gentle flow of his thoughts as he followed the routine task of cleaning up.

She felt Olive and Gene, too, felt the surprisingly bright flow of their mutual interest. But that was all right, she decided, as she let herself absorb the feeling. There was nothing in that she needed to worry about. Apparently her uncle was keeping his promise.

She turned a little more, toward the fireplace, and felt herself drawn toward it, to the corner beside it. Here, she thought, feeling a cold draft snake over her skin. *Here.* She felt sadness and loss and a totally unexpected sense of amusement. Amusement? From a ghost?

An instant later the feeling was gone.

Blinking as if she were waking from a long sleep, Rainbow looked at Olive and her uncle.

"It's here," she said.

They stopped talking immediately and looked at her.

"Really?" Olive looked uneasily at the corner. "It's here right now?"

Rainbow shook her head. "Just for a few moments. It's gone now."

"Thank goodness! Live and let live, I always say, but ghosts don't belong in our world!"

Gene regarded her almost soberly. "What did you learn?"

"Nothing much. I felt sadness, loss . . . and a sense of humor."

"Humor?" Olive looked shocked.

"I'm afraid so," Rainbow said. "It's certainly not an angry ghost. At least, not judging by what I felt here." She looked at Olive. "You don't need to be afraid of it, Mrs. Herschfeld. It doesn't mean any harm to you. In fact, I'd be surprised if it comes back again. I got the feeling it just wanted us to know it was around."

Olive regarded the corner of her living room with distaste. "Fine. Let it go bother someone else. Please."

"I can't say for certain that it will," Rainbow told her, "but that's the impression I got."

A few minutes later she and her uncle were on their way to Nellie Blair's apartment.

"You need to lighten up, Rainy," he told his niece. "Break out of that little shell you're in and enjoy life more."

She pressed the button for the elevator and looked at him. "That's easy for you to say, Uncle Gene. You don't have to fight to get people to take you seriously."

He looked sadly at her. "Why on earth would I want anyone to take me seriously?"

"You do, as an actor."

"Actually, my acting career took off only after I *stopped* being so serious about myself. My dear, you used to be such a happy, carefree child. Now I find you living alone and worrying about silly things like how people might react to my T-shirts. And back there, you didn't even want to take a few minutes to enjoy Olive and Zach."

She felt stung. "That's because I'm *working*. Besides, I was intruding on them and I wanted to get out of their way as quickly as possible."

He shook his head. "Dear child, that's where you're wrong. Olive and Zach would have really

liked it if you'd stayed a little while to chat with
them. They were *enjoying* your visit, and they'd have
enjoyed it a whole lot more if you'd relaxed a little
bit."

"I'll keep that in mind."

Gene sighed, reading the hurt in her face. "I'm not
criticizing you, Rainy. Just suggesting you should
have more fun."

"I have lots of fun," she lied stoutly.

"I don't think you've had any real fun since Walter broke off your engagement because—what was
it he said?"

"I creeped him out," Rainbow replied stonily. "I
was too weird to be around."

"You were never weird," Gene said firmly. "But
trying to be perfect and so straitlaced isn't going to
convince anyone that you *aren't* weird, you know."

Rainbow looked to one side, swallowing a sigh. "I
know."

Gene reached out and touched her cheek. "You
need to learn to love yourself, Rainy."

She blinked back an errant tear and gave him a
crooked smile. "And you need to go back to being
the outrageous Gene we all know and love, so I can
get on with my work."

He studied her a moment. "So be it. You should
have let me wear the T-shirt I had on earlier. Olive
would have loved it."

"Probably. But Mrs. Blair might not."

"What is taking that damn elevator so long?"
Gene asked, punching the button again. As soon as
he did, the doors opened, revealing a sweating,
plump, balding man in his middle fifties who was
accompanied by a large chair on a hand truck.

"Sorry," the man said, trying to turn the chair
around so he could pull it out of the elevator. "This
thing is giving me fits."

"Let me help," Gene offered. "I'm Gene Holder, and this is my niece, Rainy Moonglow."

The man nodded to them both and wiped his brow with his forearm. "Thanks. I appreciate it. I've been meaning to get rid of this damn thing—"

Rainbow felt a wave of ice wash over her and she was suddenly dizzy. Stepping to one side, she leaned against the wall and fought for balance. *Something was wrong.*

Gene stepped into the elevator, and helped the man pull the chair around. Moments later the two of them were pushing it toward the back entrance, probably to leave it beside the trash bin.

As they walked away, Rainbow felt the ice drain from her body and the world stabilize once more. Still, she leaned back against the wall, afraid the sensation might overwhelm her again.

But no, it was gone. The world was back to normal, the hallway once again seventy-eight degrees. Even the dizziness had vanished as if it had never been.

Gene returned a few minutes later. "Are you all right?" he asked. "You look pale."

"I'm fine. But I'm not so sure about that man."

He raised one eyebrow. "Harvey Little? What did he do?"

"Not a thing. I just felt . . . death around him."

Gene shook his head. "That wouldn't be surprising, given the shape he's in. The man needs to work out, or something. He was gasping like a beached fish by the time we got the chair into the parking lot." He patted his hard stomach with satisfaction. "Five miles a day makes all the difference."

Rainbow couldn't help laughing, but she looked back toward the door where Harvey Little had disappeared.

"Don't say anything to him, Rainy," Gene said

gently. "There's nothing you can do about it."

"I suppose not. It's just that . . . I'm not sure what I felt was *him*. Not exactly."

Gene punched the elevator button again, and this time the doors slid open immediately. They stepped in.

"The ghost?" he asked.

"Maybe. Maybe not." She shook her head. "It wasn't very clear, I'm afraid."

"What floor?"

"Eight."

He leaned back against the handicap railing and folded his arms as the elevator rose. "Remember that time your high school principal had a heart attack?"

She nodded. She would never forget it. All morning long, anytime she had been near the man, she had felt cold, dark waves of nausea and dizziness wash over her. By the time she had been sure it was related to him, it was too late.

"And remember how it felt after he died?"

She nodded again. "All light, as if a terrible dark pressure was gone."

"And what did you say when you told me about it?"

"That I'd never be afraid of death again, if that's how it felt."

He nodded. "So if it's Harvey's time, it won't be long before he's feeling a whole lot better. But there's nothing you can do to change what's going to happen."

"I know, but I might have warned him." That was the most troubling part of being psychic, deciding whether or not to raise issues. "I would have said something to him—maybe he'd go to the hospital?— but I wasn't sure it was him."

"Maybe not. But if it *is* him and he doesn't have

the sense to get himself to a doctor, nothing you say will change anything."

She knew he was right; long ago she had discovered that people who didn't ask for her help didn't want it and wouldn't listen. In fact, they could get downright nasty about it.

Nellie Blair was eagerly awaiting their arrival and seemed impatient to get the introductions behind them—except when Gene, ever the gallant, bowed over her hand. Nellie blushed and Gene smiled his winningest smile. Rainbow gave him a warning look.

"I couldn't wait for you to get here," Nellie said finally, leading them farther into the apartment. "It happened again!"

"What happened?" Rainbow asked. She looked around, half expecting to see something, but all she saw were the cool beiges and blues of Nellie's decor.

"It was the ghost," the older woman said. "I'm sure of it. Remember I told you I had to put the vase of silk flowers away because the flowers kept ending up on the floor?"

Rainbow nodded.

"Well, when I came home from Tampa this afternoon, the vase and flowers were right back on my bedside table—and I had left them in the hall closet in a box!"

"Wow!" said Gene, looking suitably impressed.

Rainbow began to wish she hadn't agreed to take this case. This went far beyond anything she had dealt with before. In the past, she'd sense presences, cold spots, and even moods from spirits, but other than one event at a seance led by her mother, she'd never had to deal with moving objects. If these ghosts were actually moving things around to this degree, she was in over her head.

All of a sudden she remembered what Mary Todd

had said about Jake Carpenter's suspicions. "You're sure no one was in here while you were away?"

Nellie was surprised and a little offended. "No one else has a key!"

"Not even the maintenance staff?"

"Of course not! No more than anyone else would have a key to *your* house, Rainbow. I *own* this unit. No one comes in here unless I open the door to them."

Rainbow nodded. "I had to ask, Mrs. Blair. You can understand that."

"I suppose." She shook her head. "Jake Carpenter asked me the same questions a little while ago when I told him what had happened. I didn't expect to hear them from *you*. He seems to think this is a hoax."

"Well, I can't say I've ever seen a haunting like this before," Rainbow admitted. "I've heard of them, though, which is why I'm not as sure as he is that this is a hoax."

Mollified, Nellie relaxed. "I think it's a message. A friend gave me those flowers just before she died. It seems very important that they continue to be disturbed."

"You might be right. May I go into your bedroom?"

"Be my guest. Would you like anything to drink, Mr. Holder?"

Rainbow half listened to her uncle working his charm on Nellie Blair while she walked into the bedroom. Nellie had one of the larger, nicer units, with both a living room balcony and a bedroom balcony, and a spectacular view of the sunset over the Gulf. Vermilion ribbons of cloud stretched across the evening sky, while the sun's fiery globe hovered just above the dark teal of the water. That view alone was almost enough to make Rainbow think about trading her cottage for one of these units.

And there was the mauve vase filled with dusty rose silk flowers. She knew it the instant she saw it. At some level, her mind detected some sort of psychic impression in the air around it. She wasn't a psychometrist—someone who received all kinds of information by touching objects—but she reached out for the vase anyway, seeking a stronger impression.

Just before her fingers touched it, the vase slid away.

Rainbow, hardly daring to believe what she had just seen, stared at the vase and saw how the silk flowers were nodding gently, disturbed by the recent movement. Excitement began to bubble up in her.

Once again she reached out, and once again the vase danced away, staying just out of reach. All of a sudden she laughed and said, "This is so *cool!*"

An instant later, she was joined by her uncle and Nellie. "What?" they asked eagerly. "What?"

"When I reached out for the vase, it moved away," she told them, still smiling. "Twice. It's just so *cool.*"

Once again she reached out, but this time the vase didn't twitch.

"Wouldn't you know it?" she said in disappointment. "But really, it moved twice."

"I believe you," Gene said.

"So do I," Nellie agreed. "After all, the darn thing's been dumping itself on my floor for days now. And it managed to walk from the closet back to the table. Why *wouldn't* it move when you reached for it?"

As her hand closed around the vase, Rainbow felt something. Laughter. Gentle amusement. Sorrow. Untimely death. Wistfulness.

"Lucy," she said aloud.

"Oh my God!" Nellie clapped a hand over her mouth, and was suddenly blinking back tears.

"Do you know her?" Rainbow asked.

Nellie nodded, speechless.

"It's not the same as what I felt in Mrs. Herschfeld's apartment, though," Rainbow said, holding the vase in both hands now. "It's a different presence."

"We have *two* ghosts?" Nellie looked shocked.

"That's the feeling I get. Neither one is angry, but both are a little sad. Sad, yet amused." She looked down at the vase in her hand. "These ghosts are enjoying this haunting, I think."

Nellie nodded eagerly, her eyes pleading for more.

"I sense untimely violent death—"

"Oh, it was awful," Nellie said, finding her voice. "So sad!"

"Great loss," Rainbow continued, lost in the sensations. "Purpose. There is a purpose . . . no, there may be more than one purpose to the hauntings. Yes, more than one." She started to put the vase down, but just then she was hit by one more strong impression. "Lucy wants you to know she's happy now."

Mrs. Blair was no longer able to hold back tears. Reaching out, she took the vase and cradled it like a baby. "I won't put the vase away again, Lucy," she said. "I promise. It'll stay right here beside my bed."

She raised her eyes to Rainbow. "It's okay if Lucy wants to haunt my apartment. She was my dearest friend . . ."

"What happened?" Gene inquired, "if you don't mind my asking."

"Not at all. She and Joe Carpenter—that's Jake's

uncle—went out on his boat one day last fall and something went wrong. The Coast Guard thinks the engine caught fire or blew up or something. There was just a little debris left."

Nellie polished the glass vase with the tail of her shirt and put it back on the night table. "If she wants to dump the flowers every day, that's all right by me."

"I think," Rainbow said gently, "that she just wanted you to know she was here."

Nellie nodded, fighting back more tears. "I can't thank you enough for telling me that, Rainbow. It means so much."

"So," Gene asked a few minutes later as they headed back to the elevator, "haunting solved?"

"Not by a long shot. There's something more going on. I can feel it."

"Mmm. Are we done for now?"

"I just need to make one quick stop on six. It'll only take a couple of minutes."

"I'm not complaining, you know." He gave her a smile. "I've been enjoying myself."

Rainbow looked up at him, feeling a surge of love. It would be nice, she thought, if the entire world were populated by people like her Uncle Gene—instead of people like Jake Carpenter.

She supposed she was being a fool to do this, but she had said she would, and whether he liked it or not, she kept her promises.

When they reached his door, she knocked, then pulled the bag of rice out of her purse.

"What's that?" Gene asked. "A lethal weapon?"

"Why would I be carrying a weapon?"

"Something tells me this is Jake Carpenter's apartment."

"What makes you think that?"

"The determined look on your face."

Just then, the door opened and Jake looked out at them. "You!" he said. Clearly he wasn't pleased.

"Now look," Gene said, "it wouldn't kill you to be polite to my niece."

"It doesn't matter, Uncle Gene," Rainbow said.

"Yes it does!"

"Who the hell are *you*?" Jake asked.

"I'm Gene Holder, Rainbow's uncle. And whether or not you believe Rainy has psychic abilities is irrelevant. She has done nothing to harm *you*. The very least you can do is treat her with the same common civility you'd show a stranger on the street."

"She's not a stranger on the street," Jake retorted. "She's a stranger knocking on my door, who just woke me up from the first decent sleep I've been able to get since I left Indonesia."

Rainbow stepped between the two men, hoping to deflect further argument. She was never comfortable with this kind of confrontation. "Look, I'm sorry. I just wanted to give you the rice I promised this morning." She thrust it at him, and he took it.

Jake looked down at the bag in his hand. "I wish you hadn't done that."

"Of course you do," she said sweetly. "You want to believe I'm a witch who doesn't have a decent bone in her body. Sorry to disappoint you."

"Rainy..." Gene said, somewhere between laughter and dismay.

"I never said you were a witch," Jake pointed out.

"No, you said I was a swindler. A huckster. I'd rather be a witch. Good night."

"Just wait a minute. Look... I'm sorry I've been such a boor. But I really don't believe in all that psychic crap."

"Fine. Did I ask you to?"

Jake looked from her to Gene, as if he thought another man might have some advice to help him out here. Gene shrugged, looking amused.

It was, however, Rainbow who spoke next, and the words that came out of her mouth surprised even her. "Joe says you should lighten up."

The effect was instantaneous. Jake's face paled, and then he slammed the door in her face.

Confused, Rainbow looked at her uncle. "What did I say?"

"You said Joe said he should lighten up."

"Oh. Joe?"

Gene shook his head. "Rainy, Rainy, you're still slipping up at times. You're not supposed to blurt your impressions without preparation, remember? Joe. Remember what Nellie said? Joe Carpenter was Jake's uncle."

Rainbow was appalled. To think she had let something like that slip past her guard, and to that man of all people!

Just then, Jake's door flew open again, and he put the package of rice back in her hands. "Keep your damn rice!"

"No," Rainbow shot back, throwing it into the apartment, "*you* keep it."

She turned and started marching away, head high. She didn't care whether Gene followed her.

"And leave my uncle out of this sham!" Jake called after her.

This time Rainbow had the last word. "That'll be hard to do if he wants to get involved!" To her great satisfaction, the elevator door opened the instant she pressed the button. She stepped inside, escaping that nasty man.

Gene was still standing by the door. When Jake looked at him, he said very quietly, "She *is* psychic, you know. And it's not at all fun."

"It's all a hoax."

Gene shook his head. "Nobody keeps playing a

hoax when it leaves her alone and crying into her pillow at night." He turned away and headed for the elevator.

"Say," Jake called a moment later. "Aren't you Gene Holder?"

"I thought that's what I told you."

"I mean, aren't you *the* Gene Holder? Didn't I see you in the movie *Cutty's Last Hours*?"

Gene paused to nod. "Yes, you did."

"I like your work."

"Thank you." He hesitated. "Would you like to play a round of golf tomorrow?"

"I'm rusty."

"Good, that means I'll stand a chance of beating you. Say eight o'clock? I'll meet you out front."

But Jake was still suspicious. "Why?"

"I'd like to hear more about your theory of what's going on around here."

"How did you hear about that?"

"Mary Todd told Rainy. It's a small town, Jake. You might keep that in mind. I'll see you in the morning."

This time when Jake's door closed, it did so quietly.

Five

"**Y**OU ASKED HIM TO PLAY GOLF?" RAINBOW LOOKED at her uncle as if he'd lost his mind.

"I certainly did." They were sitting in her kitchen, sharing an early breakfast of bagels and melon.

"But Uncle Gene, he hates me!"

"He misunderstands you. I might be able to do something about that."

Rainbow shook her head and wondered why she felt so betrayed. There was no reason on earth to think her uncle should be limited in his friendships by her dislike of people. She certainly wasn't childish enough to feel that way.

"Besides," Gene continued, "you really shook him with your reference to his uncle."

"I didn't mean to do that."

"I know. But perhaps I can . . . deal with it."

"I don't see any reason to deal with it. The man is convinced I'm a fake, and nothing is going to change his mind."

"I wouldn't be so sure of that, my dear."

Rainbow repressed an urge to snort, and instead sipped her orange juice while she collected her thoughts. "You remember Walter," she said finally.

67

"Convincing him I was really psychic only made him decide I was creepy. Just leave it alone, Uncle Gene. Jake Carpenter doesn't matter."

"Perhaps."

Gene let the subject go, but Rainbow wasn't at all sure she'd heard the end of it. Gene couldn't seem to understand that her circle of friends was very small and very select precisely because she was psychic. In the first place, she couldn't be easily misled about what people thought of her. In the second, those who believed in her powers too often found her "creepy," and those who didn't believe scorned her for being a fake. She didn't know a whole lot of people who were willing to leave her abilities out of the friendship equation.

Although since coming to Paradise Beach ten years ago, she'd found more acceptance than she'd enjoyed elsewhere, largely because the town was small enough that most people were able to realize that she wasn't cheating her clients. Or at least to accept that her clients felt she wasn't cheating them. Even the chief of police had dated her a couple of times a few years ago.

But like so many of her romantic relationships, it had died on the vine before really blossoming. Men just couldn't stomach the idea of being in a relationship with a woman who consulted tarot cards and relied on her intuition as completely as her brains. It made them seriously uncomfortable.

Gene departed twenty minutes later, leaving Rainbow to gaze sadly out the window and wonder why she couldn't just have been like other people.

"Rainy?" Gene's voice called her from the front of the house.

It was nearly one o'clock, and Rainbow had had a surprisingly busy morning, with one scheduled reading and three unexpected walk-ins. Her stomach was just beginning to rumble its demand for lunch, and she was trying to decide what to make for the two of them. Smiling, she hurried out from her reading room to greet her uncle.

And stopped dead when she saw Jake Carpenter standing beside him in the living room.

"I invited Jake for lunch," her uncle said. "If you don't want to fix something, I thought we could all go out together."

Rainy looked at her uncle as if he had just sprouted horns. He *knew* what she thought about Jake, yet he had still invited him to her house. She considered giving him a good shake for his audacity, but decided he'd just turn it into a hug. After all, he was bigger and stronger. "Jake doesn't want to have lunch with me, Uncle Gene."

"That's not what *he* said."

She glared at him, then looked at Jake who appeared to be feeling both uncomfortable and awkward. "We got off to a bad start," the impossible man said. "I thought maybe we could mend our fences."

"Mend our fences?" Her voice was full of disbelief.

"Rainy . . ." Gene started to say, trying to forestall her.

But she was not about to be forestalled. Whether she wanted to admit it to herself or not, this man had hurt her, and she'd spent the better part of two days stewing about it and mentally rehearsing all the things she would like to say to him. She was going to have her say. Now.

"No, Uncle Gene," she said firmly. "This man has told me what he thinks of me and has closed his door in my face twice. And now you expect me to go out to lunch with him?"

"It's the civilized thing to do," Gene said. "Adults try to work out their differences."

"This is a difference that cannot be worked out. This man thinks I'm a fraud, a huckster, a swindler of elderly people! His mind is so irrevocably closed that a ray of intellectual illumination couldn't possibly penetrate it!"

Gene started to smile. "You have a way with words, my dear."

But Jake shifted uneasily and said, "I may have jumped to conclusions."

"Jumped! That's an understatement. You took off like a rocket! And you didn't even give me a chance to answer your charges!"

Jake appeared to brace himself. "You're right, I didn't. And your uncle convinced me that I was wrong about you. I may not believe that what you do is possible, but that doesn't mean you aren't sincere."

"Well, thank you very much," she said acidly. "Your approval means more than I can say."

Jake looked at Gene, who shrugged as if to say, "You made the problem, not me."

"Look," Jake said after a moment. "I already apologized once for being a boor. My only excuse is that I was exhausted and suffering from jet lag. I'm not usually so brutish."

Rainbow looked at her uncle, wondering why he had put her in this difficult position. After their second encounter last night, she really wasn't inclined to accept Jake's apology, although, she admitted unhappily, Jake *had* been trying to apologize last night when she had blurted that thing about Joe. And his reaction to that, given the beliefs he was beginning with, was perfectly understandable.

"Apology accepted," she finally said, reluctantly.

"Good." Gene beamed at them both. "So now we can go out and get some lunch?"

She nodded.

"Let me just change," Gene said. "It'll only take a minute." He was wearing plus-fours—knickers—and a polo shirt, suitable for golf but not for lunch on the beach.

Left alone with Jake, Rainbow hardly knew what to say or do. He stood there, just inside her door, looking entirely too attractive in khaki slacks, deck shoes, and an open-throated blue shirt—and she *hated* feeling that attraction.

She spoke. "I'm sorry I blurted what I did about your uncle last night. I'm usually more cautious."

His face darkened a little. "You won't manipulate me by mentioning Joe."

"Is that what you think? That I was trying to manipulate you?" The urge to slap him was growing again.

"Why else did you say that?"

"Oh, I don't know. How about I just suddenly had this very strong impression, and I announced it?"

His expression said he didn't believe her.

Rainbow shook her head. "You really don't get it, do you? I don't use my talent to manipulate people. What's more, I usually don't blurt out stupid things like I did last night because all it does is make people feel even more suspicious of me. It certainly doesn't make anyone more likely to believe me. Look how *you* reacted."

He nodded slowly, as if he were actually considering what she was saying.

Well, close-minded though he was, apparently he could be reasoned with—which might not be a good thing, she found herself thinking glumly. When he was unreasonable, at least she could continue to dislike him. This new side of him was somehow even more threatening.

"What worries me," he said finally, "is that while you're ghost hunting, the residents aren't looking for more rational explanations of what's going on."

"You mean that someone might be trying to scare them out of their homes?"

"It's a possibility, yes."

She shook her head. "I know what I felt when I was there last night."

"You're saying there definitely are ghosts?" He looked as if the words tasted sour on his tongue.

"Yes, I am. There are. I felt it in Olive Herschfeld's apartment, in Nellie Blair's apartment, and in *yours*."

"Mine?" He got the strangest look on his face, and for once Rainbow would have given a great deal to know what he was thinking.

"Yes, yours. Don't worry about it, though. You're apparently deaf to it, and anyway, whatever it is is benevolent."

"Benevolent." He repeated the word almost woodenly. "Then I won't worry about it."

Which, she thought reluctantly, had probably been difficult for him to say, given his totally incredulous approach to the subject.

"Are we ready?" Gene emerged from the guest room, once again clad in tennis shorts and a green T-shirt that said, "You never really learn to swear until you learn to play golf."

They went up the beach a little way to a small restaurant with a view of the water. The lunch rush was nearly over, so they were able to get a table by the window without difficulty. Rainbow busied herself with the menu, preferring to let Gene and Jake do most of the talking. After all, anytime she said anything to Jake, they got into an argument. After they ordered, however, talk once again turned to events at the condo building.

"I'm afraid I don't really know the residents that well," Jake said. "I used to visit my uncle maybe once a year, but I rarely stayed more than a week at a time. I played shuffleboard with some of them, and met them in the hallways. I got to know a few of Joe's closer friends when we all went fishing together, but basically I don't know anyone that well."

"That'll change," Gene said. "Where did you live before?"

"Oh, all over the world."

"Really? What do you do?"

"I'm a petroleum geologist."

Rainbow found herself listening with more interest than she wanted to as Jake continued.

"I go where the work is, and a lot of it is overseas. I spent a couple of years on the North Sea and in Alaska, some time in the Middle East, and most recently I was in Indonesia."

"No wonder you had jet lag."

Jake smiled at both of them. When he smiled, Rainbow thought, he was more than just an attractive man. His whole face became warm and appealing. She looked away, unhappy with her reaction.

"I'm not sure it was just jet lag," Jake said. "It might have been partly culture shock. I seem to go through it every time I'm out of the country for a long time, living with local people. Somehow it's easier to go overseas and immerse myself in a totally foreign culture than it is to come home and discover that what ought to be familiar isn't."

Gene nodded. "I've had a taste of that myself at times."

"Really? When you were on location?"

He shook his head. "Actually, in a past life I

worked for the federal government. I spent some time overseas."

"But he won't tell you anything about it," Rainbow said, retaliating sweetly for Gene's getting her involved in this lunch. "He was with the CIA."

Gene shot her a look. His past affiliation was not something he liked to advertise.

Jake looked at her uncle with renewed interest. "Really? I bet you have some war stories to tell."

Gene shrugged.

"He had a bullet dug out of him once without anesthetic," Rainbow said.

This time Gene glared at her, and she couldn't help laughing.

"I'll get even with you," her uncle said.

"Too late. I'm getting even with *you*."

"I figured as much."

Jake looked from one to the other. "What for?"

Rainbow favored him with a smile. "It's a long story. I wonder what's taking lunch so long?"

Just as she spoke, a waitress brought their meals. Rainbow had chosen her favorite seafood salad. Gene, as usual, thumbed his nose at cholesterol counts and was dining on fried grouper. Jake had ordered broiled cod on a bed of rice.

"Have you ever traveled overseas?" Jake asked her.

"No, I'm afraid not. I've spent most of my life in Florida."

"Do you want to travel?"

"I'd love to, but so far I haven't been able to afford it. Besides, I wouldn't want to go alone, which means I'd have to find a friend who wanted to go to the same places." Nor was she comfortable talking about herself. "Are you going to stay here permanently?"

"For a year, at least."

"I didn't know there was any petroleum around here."

"I'm planning to write a book."

"Really? About what?"

"Petroleum geology."

She grimaced.

"Hey," he said, laughing. "It's not *that* dull! It's actually quite fascinating. The rocks tell stories, and there's always a new one to read. Over the years, I've branched my studies out from geology to paleontology, and now reading a core sample can be like reading a good book."

"Sort of like what Rainy does with her talent," Gene remarked.

Rainbow wished he hadn't redirected the conversation, and shot him another look. Gene simply smiled at her.

"How do you mean?" Jake asked.

"Well, you can read things in stones that other people can't see. It took training, perseverence, hard work, and a lot of talent. Rainy does the same thing. The only difference is that her art isn't considered a science—yet. But if you were to ask the average man on the street about the things you read in rocks, you might as well be talking about magic."

"With one big difference."

"Of course," Gene said equitably. "You have the religion of science behind you."

Jake surprised Rainbow by laughing. "You know, that's almost exactly what an old lady said to me yesterday. She said that my belief in science was as blinding as any other belief."

Gene nodded. "It can be. If you let it. Who was this elderly lady? I'd like to meet her. She sounds like a woman after my own heart."

"A Miss Mary Todd. She drives a purple golf cart,

and she isn't reluctant to stick her nose in wherever she wants."

"Miss Todd," Rainy said, "is one of our most prominent local citizens. She's a real dear."

"With a tart tongue," Jake added. "But I liked the old girl."

Of course, thought Rainbow. Mary Todd didn't have psychic powers. She looked down at her salad and speared a piece of tomato with her fork.

Gene finished his lunch a little before the other two and suddenly rose from the table, tossing down a couple of twenties. "My treat," he said. "I just remembered an appointment."

"An appointment?" Rainbow asked, feeling her heart sink.

"You're not the only reason I came to Florida, my dear." He gave her a brilliant smile. "Jake will see you home. Won't you, Jake?"

"Sure. I'd be delighted."

Yeah, right, thought Rainbow, looking down at her plate again to hide her scowl. Damn Gene and his machinations! Maybe *he* was the one she ought to tie to the railroad tracks.

"I like your uncle," Jake said when Gene had gone.

"I do, too. Sometimes. But he's a rogue and there's never any telling what he might do next."

"You mean like abandoning you to my mercies?"

She looked up, feeling her cheeks heat with embarrassment that her uncle's ploy had been so obvious, and found Jake smiling at her. It wasn't a casual smile, but something . . . warmer. Friendlier. Almost sympathetic. "He drives me nuts sometimes," she admitted.

"He means well. I think he'd really like it if you and I managed to bury the hatchet."

"How are we supposed to do that? We have a fundamental disagreement."

He put his fork down. "I didn't believe the witch doctors in some of the places I lived, but I didn't go around insulting them, or the people who had faith in them. I should never have said what I said to you, and I can't apologize enough. I don't have to believe your abilities are real to admit that you're sincere."

She regarded him suspiciously. "Can you change your convictions that easily?"

"I haven't changed any."

"You believe I'm a fraud."

He shook his head. "No, Rainbow, I don't. Like I said before, I think it's possible you really believe in what you're doing."

"So in essence, you've decided I'm not a fraud, but I'm certifiably crazy."

"I didn't say that!"

"What's the difference?" She tossed her napkin down and rose, giving him a brittle smile. "I'm not hungry anymore. I think I'll go home."

She headed for the door, head high and back stiff. Enough, she thought. She'd had enough of this. She'd tried to be polite to the man yesterday, and for her trouble had gotten her rice handed back and the door closed in her face. Now all of a sudden today she was supposed to forget all that and be willing to accept that he thought she wasn't a bad person, just a deluded one. Well, to hell with him!

She decided to walk back along the beach and paused at the bottom of the stairs from the boardwalk over the dunes to remove her sandals. She had only taken two steps in her bare feet when Jake caught up with her.

"It's a beautiful day," he remarked.

"It's hot and muggy." Never mind that the sea

breeze was blowing and actually making it rather pleasant.

"The sun is awfully strong. Aren't you afraid of getting a burn?"

"I always wear sun block."

"Oh."

She kept walking as fast as she could, and he kept pace right beside her. Clearly he was not going to vanish, no matter how hard she wished the sand would open up and swallow him.

"Look, Rainy—"

"Nobody calls me Rainy except my family!"

"Excuse me. *Rainbow*. Listen, I'm really sorry you took me wrong. I don't think you're crazy."

"No?" She turned and faced him with flashing eyes. "Just deluded?"

He shook his head. "No more deluded than people who go to church."

"How magnanimous of you!"

He waved a hand almost helplessly. "I can't seem to say anything right to you! What I mean is, you were raised to believe all of this. Your mother's psychic, right? Well it's only natural that you would believe the same thing. And I was raised not to believe in it, so it's only natural that I don't."

"Which leaves us poles apart on one of the central issues of my life."

He nodded. "Yes, it does. But that doesn't mean we can't be friends. Nor does it mean that I can't respect your beliefs."

She looked past him, squinting into the sun that glared off the aquamarine waves, listening to the steady roar of the surf and the raucous cries of gulls. Why was she being so difficult about this, she wondered? She was ordinarily more inclined to go with the flow, to let things wash over her like those waves out there, and then steadily seep away.

This man had been doing his best to smooth things between them, and she had been doing her best to prevent it. There had to be a reason she was being so contrary, but she had a feeling she wouldn't like the answers.

She looked up at him, noting the squint lines around his eyes and the way his mouth seemed to express an almost deferential hope. He had a very expressive mouth.

So here they were, acting more like two kids on a schoolyard, than adults. Or rather, she was.

She sighed, the sound lost in the pounding of the surf. "Why should we want to be friends?" she asked, and this time there was no truculence in her tone.

"Because we have a common goal?"

"We do?"

He nodded. "We both want to resolve the problem at Paradise Towers. We have different ideas about what the problem really is, but we both want to fix it. And I can't help feeling we'd both do better if we cooperated."

"How?"

"I'm not really sure. All I know is, I've started chatting with some of my neighbors, and they're *all* very concerned about what's going on. You've been saying the same thing. They're uneasy, and some are really frightened, and understandably so. Whether the problem is supernatural or earthly, it's hard to feel safe in your home when someone or something can get in and out of it at will."

Rainbow nodded. "Exactly."

"So see? We agree on that much. I went to the chief of police about it, but he said he needed proof that someone was trying to scare the residents. Which, I guess, pretty much leaves you and me to work the problem."

"But why do you want to work with me if you think I'm way off course?"

He shrugged. "Because as difficult as it is for me to admit it, you may *not* be off course."

Rainbow nearly gaped at him. "Are you allowing that there might be ghosts?"

"Not exactly. I'm allowing that some of the residents *believe* there are ghosts. And if there's no earthly explanation for what's going on, then you're probably the only cure. I'm a great believer in the power of conviction. I once saw a man die because he believed he was under a curse."

Rainy nodded slowly, thinking about what he had just said.

"Hey," he continued, "it's a scientific fact that some thirty percent of the time people are cured of illness simply by faith in their doctors. Or faith in a pill, even if it's a placebo. If these people believe they have ghosts, and believe you can solve the problem, you probably can, and I'm not going to stand in the way."

So he'd found a scientific reason to accept what she was doing. Rainbow decided she could live with that, even if she didn't fully agree with it. Besides, she was aware of the so-called placebo effect, and she couldn't deny it played a role.

"So how do we work together?" she asked finally.

"All we have to do is share information, whatever we learn as we go along. You may hear things from the residents that are useful to me, or vice versa. Pooling our resources seems like the most intelligent way to battle the problem."

She nodded. "All right. It certainly can't hurt."

They started walking along the sand again, this time more slowly. The subtropical sun was at its height, blazingly hot on the skin despite the steady breeze.

They passed by a heavy man who was stretched out on a beach towel, his skin already looking an unhealthy red. He wasn't going to enjoy the rest of his vacation if he didn't watch it, Rainbow thought. He must be from up north. Far up north. Too many visitors failed to appreciate how fast they could burn at this latitude.

Two little children, greasy with sun screen, were building a lopsided castle in the sand. Their mother lay nearby, reading a paperback novel. A jogger passed them, kicking up little fountains of sand with his bare feet.

"It's so peaceful out here," Jake remarked. "I suppose it's jammed during tourist season?"

"Busier, but not crowded. I don't think I've ever seen the beach really crowded, unless there's something special happening, and then the crowding is limited to the area right around the event."

"That's good. I've been having all kinds of visions of the horrors of the season."

"Well, if you want to get anywhere, it *will* take longer, especially along the boulevard. Traffic is pretty much bumper-to-bumper during the season."

"I'll keep that in mind."

"Everything takes longer when the tourists are here, though. Checkout lines get longer, for one thing, and you have to wait at most restaurants if you go out for dinner, especially on weekends. Everyone tries to cope, but by spring tempers are getting a little frayed."

"That's understandable."

By the time they reached her cottage, Rainbow was hot and thirsty and wanted nothing so much as a tall glass of iced tea. She asked Jake if he'd like to join her, and he accepted with a smile.

She served it in her "green room," a small greenhouse she had added to her cottage that opened off the living room into a sunny spot in her garden. It was full of plants that needed a gentler climate than those outside, and made it possible to enjoy the garden in air-conditioned comfort.

"I like this room," Jake said as he joined her at the white cast-iron table. "It's great."

"Especially in the heat of the summer," Rainbow agreed. "It's like having a private corner of paradise."

"It seems you're quite the gardener."

"I try. It makes me feel so peaceful to tend to my plants, and I get a lot of joy out of watching them grow. I suppose some people would feel overwhelmed by how many I have."

"I don't. I like them." He drank half his glass of iced tea before he spoke again. "I have to admit, I have no idea where to start looking for someone who would want to scare people out of the Towers."

"Me either," Rainbow said. "I suppose we could talk to some real estate agents to see if anyone has expressed an interest in the property."

"That's a good idea. In fact, that's a *great* idea." He brightened considerably at the prospect of having something useful to do, and Rainbow felt an inkling of genuine liking for him. "If developers are looking around, real estate agents should have heard something."

"You'd think so." She hesitated a moment. "Have you heard what's been happening to Nellie Blair?"

"Something about a poltergeist? I haven't heard the details."

"A friend gave her a vase of silk flowers just before she died. Nellie originally complained that she couldn't keep the flowers in the vase. Every time she turned around, she'd find the flowers had been dumped on the floor, even though the vase was still upright."

Jake nodded. "That would make anyone uneasy."

"Considering Nellie's an elderly woman living alone, she's handling this remarkably well—better than *I* might. Anyway, she put the vase in the closet so she wouldn't be disturbed anymore."

"I'm surprised she didn't call the police."

"And tell them what?"

He nodded, giving her a rueful smile. "I see your point. Nothing else was disturbed?"

"Not a thing. Anyway, she came home yesterday and found the vase and flowers had been moved from the closet back to her bedside table."

"Good Lord! We need to check it for fingerprints."

Rainbow suddenly remembered Nellie taking the vase from her and felt her stomach sink with disappointment. "That won't work. She took it from me and polished it with the tail of her shirt while we were talking. Neither one of us was thinking about fingerprints."

"I've got to talk to her. If it happens again, she shouldn't touch it. We'll get the police to come and dust it."

"I guess."

He looked knowingly at her. "But you don't think the agent was a person, do you."

Rainbow shook her head. "I felt a presence in that room, Jake. You can laugh at me if you want."

"I'm not laughing. Remember, I said I respect what you believe."

She was still finding it difficult to accept that after the vehemence of his initial reaction. Although to be fair, his initial reaction had been born of an admirable desire to protect the other residents of the building. "Well, I felt a presence," she said firmly. "I even identified it by name, and Nellie recognized it as her friend's name. She said she wouldn't be bothered anymore by the flowers being dumped on the floor."

"We still need to investigate."

"Of course." Rainbow met his gaze straightly. "But I'll tell you right now, Jake, it's not going to happen again."

"You can't know that."

"Yes I can. The ghost simply wanted Nellie to know she was there, and that she was happy. There won't be any more trouble in Nellie's apartment."

"Well, that's fine, too. I'm not going to complain if the whole thing just goes away. I don't care who's right or wrong about this, I just want to be sure the residents are safe."

"Well, I'd be more positive of that if I hadn't felt a different presence in Olive Herschfeld's apartment."

She had to give Jake credit. He looked as if he were trying to swallow an apple whole, and about to choke on it, but when he finally spoke it was to say neutrally, "Really?"

Her initial reaction was to call him on his patent disbelief. But then she decided that if he could work so hard to keep their new peace agreement, the least she could do was gracefully ignore the things that danced across his expressive face. She needed a minute, though. Frankly, she had never known anyone to rile her as quickly as Jake Carpenter could. She didn't at all like this unexpected side of herself.

"It was a distinctly different presence," she said finally, keeping her own tone neutral. "A male presence."

"How would you—" He broke off. "No, I'm not going to ask that."

"Why not?" she asked, a trifle tartly. "You want to know how I can tell if a presence is male or female without seeing the obvious—er—signs."

"Well, yes."

She shrugged. "Men and women feel different psychically. I don't know why." Nor was she going to go any further than that. What was the point of trying to explain things he wouldn't believe anyway?

He was looking at her with a kind of perplexity, as if she were an interesting scientific problem—or a bug under a microscope. She had the strong feeling that this was going to be a rocky association no matter how hard they tried to get along.

She repressed a sigh and looked away, wishing it weren't so difficult to get acceptance. She didn't ask for belief; simple acceptance would do. But that too often seemed beyond the ability of the doubters.

"Have you ever . . ." He hesitated as if seeking his words with care, then continued, "Have you ever mistaken the sense of a living presence for a ghost?"

"What do you mean?"

He looked almost embarrassed to be discussing this, and it took him a minute to reformulate his question. "Well . . . I can almost swallow the possibility that you might sense that someone had been in a room a little while ago. I mean, there are so many ways we might detect that—smells, like perfume, or something moved around. I can easily credit that you might be more sensitive to these things than the rest of us. So I was just wondering if you might have detected that someone other than the Herschfelds had been in their apartment."

Again she felt a flare of impatience and quashed it. She could be offended by his determination to believe there was a logical, ordinary explanation for her extraordinary ability, or she could choose to accept it as honest inquiry. She decided to give him the benefit of the doubt—for now.

"No, I wasn't mistaking it. But I can't explain to you how I know the difference."

She could see him mentally throwing up his hands, but after a moment all he said was, "All right."

Just then her doorbell sounded. Rainbow was surprised to hear it, since it almost never worked. The salt air was forever corroding the electrical contacts and shorting them out.

"I guess I'd better be going," Jake said, rising. "I'm sure you have plenty to do. I'll nose around and see what I can find out, and let you know."

Rainbow was at once relieved and disappointed to end their conversation. The worst thing about Jake Carpenter, she decided suddenly, was that he made her feel so many contradictory things, not the least of them a strong sexual attraction.

Jake followed her to the door, standing to one side as she opened it.

Miss Mary Todd stood there, just about to press the bell again with the tip of her cane. "Ah, there you are," she said, her dark eyes gleaming with satisfaction. "And Jake Carpenter, too. My, my. Have I interrupted a powwow for peace?"

"I was just leaving," Jake said, leaving the pointed question unanswered.

"Good," said Mary. "Because you both have to come to the Towers at once. The ghosts have flipped their wigs!"

Six

"WE CAN ALL RIDE OVER ON MY GOLF CART," MARY suggested.

Jake looked at it. "Let's just go in my car. It's air conditioned."

Rainbow agreed. "It'll be cooler, Mary." Indeed, the humidity was almost stifling.

Mary shook her head. "I don't want to be without my wheels. You never know when you might need to make a quick getaway."

Rainbow grinned at her. "What have you been up to?"

Mary assumed an expression of innocence. "Absolutely nothing, gal. Remember who you're talking to. At my age, one never gets up to anything."

"Yeah, right," Rainbow said. "And the moon is made of green cheese."

"Have you been there?" Mary demanded. But there was a twinkle in her eye that prevented Rainbow from taking her seriously.

Rainbow suspected that Jake had difficulty restraining his amusement when Mary donned a custom-painted lavender motorcycle helmet with a dark visor over her snow-white coiffeur. He stopped looking amused when Mary accelerated her cart to thirty-five miles an hour, the highest posted speed limit in Paradise Beach.

He grimaced when she took a corner on two wheels, scattering some seagulls who had been dining on a pile of discarded french fries. The birds shrieked angrily as they took to the air, and a couple of them followed Mary down the road as if they wanted to attack the cart.

"Why didn't she just telephone?" he asked, as they rounded the corner after her. "She could get herself killed, driving that cart at this speed."

"I don't know," Rainbow replied. "Mary has her reasons, although they're not always clear to anyone else."

He shook his head. "If she rolls that thing, I don't think the helmet is going to be much help."

"At least she's wearing one."

The parking lot of the Towers was filled with residents, clustered together as if they were afraid. Mary rolled into their midst, scattering senior citizens in every direction before she came to a stop.

"The woman needs a keeper," Jake said, as he wheeled his Explorer into an empty spot safely away from the milling residents.

Rainbow climbed out of the car to hear someone saying, "For God's sake, Mary! You could have *killed* someone."

Mary, pulling her helmet off, shook her head. "Whether that would be a tragedy remains to be seen. But I do need to get my brakes checked. If I'm going to hit someone, it ought to be on purpose."

Nellie Blair spied Rainbow and called out to her. "Thank goodness you're here! The place is going haywire. The phones don't even work."

"What's happening?" she asked.

Nellie shook her head. "Things are floating all

over the place! We must have a whole crowd of ghosts!"

"I wonder," said Bill Dunlop, "if there's a word for a crowd of ghosts. Gaggle? I think I like gaggle of ghosts."

Olive Herschfeld frowned at him. "This isn't funny, Bill."

"I don't think it's funny at all," he told her. "I was trying to make a grilled cheese sandwich in my toaster oven, but the damn thing wouldn't hold still long enough for me to get the sandwich into it."

"You don't make a grilled cheese sandwich in an oven!" said a small woman in a muumuu. "You make it in a frying pan!"

Bill looked at her. "That wouldn't hold still, either!"

"I was trying to water my flowers," said another woman. "Every time I reached for it, the watering can danced away, and twice it spat at me!"

A chubby woman with a black streak of mascara running up her heavily rouged cheek complained, "It grabbed my makeup right out of my hand and smeared it on my face!"

Rainbow looked at Jake and read a mixture of doubt and curiosity on his face. "Is it happening all at once?" she asked.

A chorus of voices answered her: "Of course!" "Yes!" "You'd better believe it!"

"It seemed to start all at once," Ellis said, taking the role of spokesman. "We all came running out into the halls at about the same time, complaining that things were flying around our apartments."

"Is it still going on?"

"I don't know. Nobody's wanted to go back in and find out."

Rainbow looked at Jake. "I guess that explains why Mary didn't just call me."

"Apparently. Well, I'll go in and take a look."

"Not without me, you won't."

He shook his head. "It might be dangerous."

"Somehow I doubt it."

"Rainbow, if someone really *is* trying to scare the residents out of the building, they won't care if someone gets hurt."

"Scare us out?" This appalled question came from Abe Levinson. "Why would anyone want to do that?"

"Real estate," Mary said, tapping her cane on the ground for emphasis. "Amazing, what people will do for a piece of beachfront property. My own nephew tried to have me committed."

"But it's a ghost," said Nellie. "It *has* to be. No human being could make all of that happen at once. In one unit, maybe. But not in all of them."

"Ghosts!" said the man Rainbow had met on the elevator with her uncle. Harvey Little, she seemed to remember his name was. His tone was scornful. "What's the matter with you people? Are you all senile?"

Sixty pairs of eyes glared at him. Harvey was one of the youngest residents, but he was still old enough to know better.

"I think we should all go in there together," Zach Herschfeld said. "That way, if anyone is in there, we'll catch him."

"If he doesn't get out the door while we're all looking inside," Jake pointed out.

"We can watch the doors," a man said. "We only need a few of us to keep an eye out. But you won't be able to get in our units without keys."

"Oh, no," a woman in red said, "I didn't *bring* my key. I was so scared I just ran out!"

Jake looked at Rainbow. "The doors are like a hotel. They lock automatically."

Within a few minutes it was ascertained that a good quarter of the residents had abandoned ship without their keys.

"Senile," said Harvey Little. "What did I say?"

"Shut your damn mouth," shouted a tall man at the rear of the crowd. "Senility has nothing to do with it!"

"What would you know?" Little shouted back. "Your brain is so old it's got cobwebs!"

"What an obnoxious little man," Mary said loudly, poking him in the stomach with her cane.

"Don't you lay a hand on me," Little said. "I'll call the police."

Mary raised her cane until it was right between his eyes. "Yes, they'll certainly believe that an eighty-year-old woman attacked you."

"I have witnesses!"

"I didn't see a thing," said a man in a fuschia shirt and slacks.

A chorus of "Me neither" rose from other onlookers.

Mary Todd smiled. "You see? No one would believe it. Now, close your mouth and mind your manners. Children should be seen and not heard."

Laughter greeted her sally. Harvey Little turned so red that Rainbow feared he might be having a stroke, but he didn't say another word.

"Look," Ellis said, "while we're standing here squabbling, we don't know what's going on inside. Maybe everything's stopped. But if we don't get in there soon, we might never discover what's happening."

Rainbow turned and headed for the lobby doors. She wasn't afraid of ghosts, and she didn't particularly care whether anyone followed her. In fact, she thought it might be easier to detect what was going on if she didn't have nearly sixty people running around and gabbing.

Jake apparently had the same idea. He asked everyone to remain outside until he and Rainbow had had a chance to look around. Apparently the residents, who had already been treated to the ghosts' hijinks, weren't really all that eager to go back inside.

"I told you," said an anonymous man's voice behind them, "that we ought to have a master key for all the doors in the complex."

"There used to be one, back when the building was first built," someone else said. "But so many people have come and gone and changed the locks . . ."

"I don't like the idea that just anyone could get into my unit if they got hold of the master key," said Nellie Blair.

"It would have to be locked up, of course. But look what it's going to cost us now for a locksmith . . ."

Jake and Rainbow exchanged glances.

"Maybe," said someone else, "we can get a volume discount from the locksmith."

"Add that to your senior citizens' discount, and the locksmith would probably have to pay *you* to come out here," Mary said drily.

Jake and Rainbow stepped into the lobby and the doors closed behind them.

"They're going to be arguing the key issue for a while, it sounds like," Jake remarked.

"It's easier than talking about what they saw in here."

"Maybe so."

Rainbow paused in the lobby and closed her eyes, trying to let the atmosphere of the building seep into her. Everything was quiet now. Unusually quiet. If anything was still happening, it was happening silently.

Having Jake beside her made her feel edgy. She wanted to reach out and feel the building's silence, to find whatever might be inhabiting it, but all she could feel was the heat of Jake's presence, the awareness running along her nerve endings like a faint anxiety she couldn't shake. Somehow the man seemed to exude sex appeal with every breath he took, and she seemed to have receptors that were determined to note it.

Finally, feeling exasperated, she opened her eyes. "I need to walk around."

He nodded. "Me too. You might be able to sense what's going on from here, but *I* need to see it."

She gave him credit for managing to say that without sarcasm.

Just then the doors behind them opened. They turned to see a small squad of men entering the lobby, led by Colonel Jeremiah Albemarle.

The colonel owned a small cottage on the beach which hunkered between the Towers and the Sunset Hotel. Retired from the Welsh Fusiliers, he was a familiar sight to local residents because, in the early mornings he could always be found marching along the dunes with ramrod straightness as if in time to the tune "Men of Harlech."

He was a tall, slender man, with a bald head and a glorious white Spitfire mustache. Right now he was wearing khaki shorts, a safari shirt, and a pith helmet and looked ready to lead troops into the jungle. Tucked under his arm was a swagger stick.

He was leading a band of five men, the youngest of whom had to be at least seventy. They were armed with objects ranging from a string mop to a Dustbuster.

"I sent out a call for assistance to my veterans'

group," he said. "We can't let you do this alone. We're all combat veterans. We've been in these situations before."

Jake and Rainbow exchanged looks again. She wondered just exactly how much combat experience they'd had with ghosts, but she forebore saying so. Jake was not so courteous.

"I doubt you've had much experience with this kind of thing, Colonel."

"Pshaw," said Albemarle. "We've dealt with infiltrators before. I certainly have. Besides," he added, holding up a handful of keys, "you won't be able to get into any of the units without these."

Jake looked down at Rainbow. "Over the barrel," he said, sotto voce.

Rainbow decided to try. "Colonel, if these are ghosts, I'm sure you've had no experience dealing with them."

At least he didn't take umbrage. "Some of my best friends became ghosts," he said firmly. "Besides, Sergeant Fields here brought his Dustbuster to suck up the ectoplasm."

Jake rolled his eyes. Rainbow tried another tack. "I can't be disturbed," she told the colonel. "I have to be able to maintain absolute concentration."

He gave her a brisk nod. "We'll be silent. We'll begin with a two-by-two sweep on the ground floor. The others are watching the exterior doors. I'll post a man at each elevator and stairwell. Two of us will accompany you on the sweep to prevent anyone from slipping by. Men, be sure to check your targets; there may be civilians in here."

"Good thinking," Jake said, and sounded as if he really meant it.

And he probably did, Rainbow thought. Men always seemed to like military things. Running this like an army operation was bound to appeal to him.

Personally, she wished they'd all go play their games elsewhere and allow her to do her job.

Colonel Albemarle finished barking orders to his followers, looking as if he were enjoying himself immensely. The elderly men scattered, moving quietly, toward their assigned posts. Rainbow thought their slinking was a little overdone, but suppressed her amusement. Her mother had been right; men grew up but they never matured.

They went to the door of the first unit and began to try the keys that Albemarle was carrying. Unfortunately, the security-conscious residents hadn't indicated their unit numbers on the keys or key rings that filled the colonel's hands and pants pockets.

"This could take all day," Jake remarked from where he was leaning one shoulder against the wall with his arms folded.

"Nonsense," said Albemarle. "I'll be only a few moments."

Rainbow glanced at her watch and said, "Those people can't stand outside in the heat for long. Why don't I just tell them to come into the lobby? I'd hate for any of them to have heatstroke."

Jake hesitated, then nodded. "I guess nobody is going to threaten the whole crowd of them."

"If anybody's *in* the building," she couldn't resist adding. Her senses might be at less than their best, thanks to all the distraction, but she felt with absolute certainty that no one else—at least, no one else who was alive—was in the building. She could feel the emptiness around them, a psychic silence. If there had been ghosts here, they were gone now.

"I'll go out and tell them," she said after a moment, reigning the intensity of her concentration. "You go on. I'll follow in a minute."

"I don't want you to be all alone anywhere in this building," Jake said. "I don't want you at risk."

"I won't be." She smiled. "Believe me, there's no one but us in this building right now." Turning, she walked back to the door.

"Don't underestimate her, Carpenter," Colonel Albemarle said. "I have a strong respect for the sixth sense. I've known more than one man who knew he was going to die in battle the next day. And I've seen more than one of them as clear as I can see you—after they died."

The residents outside had taken matters into their own hands.

"This is ridiculous," said Tom Horner, a short wiry man with shaggy white hair. "We're all steaming like clams out here."

"Do *you* want to go back in there?" asked Abe Levinson. "I nearly got hit in the head by a flying teacup."

"Well, I'm going across the street to get something to drink."

"I've got a better idea," said Olive Herschfeld. "Why don't we take up a collection and ask the café to send some pitchers over, the way they do when we have a party?"

"Why don't we just *have* a party?" someone else suggested.

Everyone turned to look at him. "It wouldn't be appropriate," said Abe.

"What's inappropriate about it? The ghosts threw us out. We've been evicted! If the ghosts can have fun, why can't we?"

"That'll teach 'em," said Tom. "Let's show 'em they can't intimidate us!"

Up on his cloud, Joe looked down with a gleeful chuckle. Lucinda tried to hide her amusement. The last thing she'd admit was that she was beginning to have as much fun with this as Joe was. That spitting watering pot had been a beautiful touch, she thought with forgivable pride.

"I always told Yolanda she shouldn't wear so much makeup," she remarked.

"And you were right, Lucy. But smearing that mascara across her face?" He chuckled again. "Brilliant move."

"Maybe she'll be afraid to touch the stuff for a while," Lucinda said with satisfaction.

"She always did look like a hand-painted teapot."

"Don't be cruel, Joe."

He looked wounded. "Who, me?"

Lucinda shook her head and returned to watching events below. "We're not getting any closer to warning them," she reminded him.

"All in due course, my dear. All in due course." He grinned and wiggled his eyebrows. "But I sure did enjoy watching Mary put my nephew in his place."

By the time she stepped outside, Rainbow found a party in full swing. The café across the street was now ferrying over pitchers of lemonade and iced tea along with finger sandwiches to the Towers residents, who had moved to the side patio and were lounging at tables with umbrellas. Someone had found a portable radio and it was blaring country music for a group of seniors who were line-dancing on the shuffleboard court. They looked charmingly absurd in everything from caftans to Bermuda shorts, not exactly the usual garb for doing the Cotton Eye Joe.

Four men, with drinks in hand, had gone to the horseshoe pits and were pitching shoes while their wives kibitzed good-naturedly from the comfort of shaded chairs. One of the shoes flew too far and hit

Harvey Little in the shin, causing him to hop around on one foot and swear violently.

"Sorry, Harvey," said the man who had hit him, looking totally insincere.

A tiny woman wearing a flowered straw hat and skin-tight biker shorts wagged a stern finger at Harvey. "Watch your language, young man. You're in the presence of ladies."

Harvey swore even more loudly.

Waves of heat were rising from the parking lot, but shaded from the sun, with the sea breeze blowing briskly, none of the residents looked uncomfortable—with the exception of Harvey, who now sat on a chair to nurse his shin and glare.

Ellis Webster joined her. "We figured some of the association funds could be well spent on refreshment. Can't let the ghosts have all the fun. How's it going inside?"

"I don't know yet. Finding out which keys go to which doors is proving to be time consuming."

"Well, don't worry about us. One of the guys ran over to the liquor store to get a keg and some ice. This party probably won't end for hours. Would you like some lemonade?"

"Maybe after I've walked around inside a little. If anyone gets too warm, send them in to the lobby. Just don't send them alone."

"Wouldn't dream of it. But I doubt anyone will want to go in soon." He gestured to the festive atmosphere. "It's kind of nice, you know? Some of these folks never come to our building parties. Today they don't have any choice and they're finally getting to know their neighbors. If you run into a ghost, thank him for us, will you?"

Rainbow had to laugh.

Mary Todd, holding court in a shaded chaise

longue, halted Rainbow on her way back in. "What did you find out?"

"Nothing yet."

"Well, get back in there and do your thing, gal. Scare the bejesus out of that young man."

Rainbow shook her head. "I don't try to scare anyone, Mary."

"And that's where you make your mistake. Stop trying to be so ordinary. There's nothing ordinary about you, and there never will be. Revel in it!"

If only it were that easy, Rainbow thought as she went back inside.

The air-conditioned comfort of the lobby was welcome, sending a chill snaking along her spine as it dried the sheen of perspiration on her skin. They were coming to the time of year when she began to hate her home state. While the folks up north were looking forward to the cool days of autumn right around the corner, here they were looking forward to at least another two months of summer.

Then, shaking herself from the melancholy mood that seemed to be stealing up on her, she went to look for the others.

After looking at four apartments, none of which seemed to be at all disturbed, Jake was beginning to wonder if his neighbors had imagined the whole event. Rainbow rejoined them as they readied to take the elevator to the second floor, and he found himself surprisingly glad to see her.

If he could say nothing else, he could admit that Rainbow Moonglow was wonderful to look at, and so far she had never once managed to bore him.

Never boring. He thought about that, then tried to dismiss it as the result of his attraction to her, and tried to tell himself he wouldn't have found her half

so fascinating if she hadn't been so beautiful. So
sexy.

And she was definitely sexy. Every cell in his body
seemed to respond to her. He had the worst urge to
get his hands into her beautiful, silky-looking black
hair, the wildest desire to grab her and hug her close
until every one of her luscious curves was imprinted
on him.

Of course, she was a flake, but he could live with
that—at least in a friend. He wouldn't be able to
tolerate a deeper relationship with her, though.
Beautiful or not, she was still a flake, and he preferred his existence to be orderly and calm. He
couldn't imagine trying to share his life with someone who would actually consult tarot cards. His tolerant attitude would go up in smoke the first time
she told him they couldn't do something because her
cards said it wasn't auspicious.

In his younger days, when he'd been guided by
his hormones rather than his brain, he'd gone steady
with a girl who religiously read her horoscope every
day, and who agreed to date him only after she decided their horoscopes were compatible. Six months
of that had been enough to make him run for the
hills. He couldn't imagine what it would be like with
Rainbow, who probably not only believed in horoscopes but read the tarot and talked to ghosts. The
mere thought made him feel—well, squeamish, for
lack of a better word.

But she was definitely eye candy. He could spend
hours just looking at her, enjoying the way she
moved, craving her neat little figure, delighting in
the way her mossy green eyes could sparkle with
anger or become as quiet and peaceful as a pool in
the depths of the rainforest.

He told himself that making a truce with her was
the adult thing to do. Gene Holder had been right

about that. At least for now, until this matter was settled, they were bound to rub shoulders frequently, so it wouldn't hurt to get along.

But every other urge he felt toward her—primarily rather primitive ones having to do with an ardent desire to hold her close and explore all those lovely curves with his hands and his mouth—had to be ignored. She ought to wear a sign, he thought. One that said, "Dangerous Curves."

"They're having a party on the patio," she said, as she joined him, Colonel Albemarle, and a cadaverous-looking man named Roger Bartlett on the elevator.

"Who? The residents?"

She nodded, looking amused. "Someone went across the street to the café for drinks, and the men have broken out their sporting goods."

He was surprised. "They don't seem very worried."

"What's the point in worrying?" Bartlett asked. His voice was a deep bass, and he waved his Dustbuster for emphasis. "When you get to be our age, there's no time left to waste on it."

Rainbow favored him with a smile. "That's a good philosophy."

"Of course it is," he said. "Age *does* teach you something."

"I would think experience would teach a lot of things," Rainbow said placatingly.

Satisfied, Roger Bartlett subsided, holding the Dustbuster at his side.

The elevator doors opened onto the second floor. Colonel Albemarle stepped out first, using hand signals to direct his men along the hall. Rainbow glanced at Jake again and got the distinct impression that he was enjoying himself immensely.

The second key they tried opened the door they

stood before. Jake stepped through first, then swore as an icy deluge of water dropped on him from the ceiling.

Rainbow peeked quickly around the doorframe. When she saw him standing there dripping, her expression of concern changed rapidly to amusement. "What happened to you?"

"Damned if I know. Water came from the ceiling." He looked up, but couldn't see any dampness above him to indicated that there was some kind of leak. "Where the hell did it come from?"

"Probably from that watering can at your feet."

He looked down at it, and he was not amused. "It must have been rigged to dump on whoever came through the door."

"Really?" Rainbow entered the room, taking care not to step in the puddle. "Can you prove it?"

"I don't have to prove it. There's no other way that could have happened."

"Mm," she said noncommittally. She pointed past him. "I suppose somebody rigged that, too?"

He turned and gaped as he saw two hardbound books dancing in the air in the middle of the living room. "It *has* to be rigged," he said.

She turned to him, a smile on her lips and a challenge in her green eyes. "Prove it," she said.

He charged forward and snatched the books from midair. They came easily into his grasp, and he couldn't feel any resistance, as he was sure he would have if they'd been connected to strings or fishing line. Nor could he, no matter how hard he searched, find anything attached to the books.

"I suppose," Rainbow said drily from behind him, "these real estate sharks could have developed an antigravity machine of some kind. Although it seems such a waste to use it for something like this, when the government would probably pay billions for it."

He scowled at her and tossed the books on the sofa. This apartment was a mess, he admitted. It was obvious that small things had been tossed around the room, but nothing he picked up to examine appeared to have anything attached to it. Not even magnets, that might have given an antigravity effect. There *had* to be a way, he argued with himself.

"All right, Miss Smarty-Pants," he said to her, "tell me what's going on here."

She shrugged and smiled at him. "Some ghosts are having fun."

"But *why*?"

"I don't know. When they're ready they'll tell us, I suppose."

"Why don't you just call them on the psychic hotline?"

She looked hurt, and he kicked himself mentally. "I'm sorry," he said swiftly. "I didn't mean that. Honestly. I'm just frustrated."

She nodded, but he could see that he had just sacrificed the little blossom of trust he'd been nurturing in her.

What the hell did it matter? he asked himself, mentally throwing up his hands. Rainbow was not only a flake, she was a sensitive flake.

Just then she started to smile.

"What?" he asked. *"What?"*

"Joe says you need to brush up on your manners. You've spent too much time in the jungle."

As soon as she spoke, she clapped her hand over her mouth, looking appalled.

"Joe?" he said, looking like a bull ready to charge. "I told you not to pull that with me!"

"I'm sorry," she said. "I shouldn't have let that slip out."

All of a sudden, the watering pot lifted from the floor and dumped another deluge on Jake's head.

A helpless laugh escaped Rainbow. "Lucy agrees," she said, and walked out.

Behind her she heard Colonel Albemarle say, "Bring that Dustbuster over here, Sergeant Fields. There's ectoplasm in the area."

She couldn't hear Jake's response to that, but it didn't matter. He deserved to be dustbusted.

Seven

"LUCY AND JOE?" ASKED NELLIE.

Rainbow had joined the residents at their im-
promptu party, leaving Jake to explore the rest of
the building. "Those are the names I picked up on."

"Oh, dear," said Nellie, looking concerned and
sad.

"They seem to be happy, Nellie."

"That's not what I'm worried about."

"And rightly so," said Mary. She turned to Rainbow. "Come on, gal, you must remember the boat
explosion that killed two Towers residents nearly a
year ago."

Rainbow looked at her. "Yes, Nellie told me about
it."

"It's them." She tapped her cane forcefully on the
pavement to punctuate the word.

Rainbow turned her head, letting her gaze wander
out to sea. "Violent death. That might explain a lot."

"Of course it would," said Mary. "There's unfinished business here, and we need to find out what
it is."

Rainbow nodded slowly, letting her vision go out
of focus as she turned her attention inward. "I'm

afraid I don't really have any more than that."

"It was so sad," Nellie continued, her voice quavering as she fought back tears. "They were both my good friends. Joe planned that trip for days. He was going to take Lucy out and propose to her. He bought a ring and candles and a white tablecloth, and had a restaurant prepare special meals he could heat up on board. He was going to propose at sunset he said."

"I'm so sorry," Rainbow offered inadequately.

Nellie gave her a wavery smile. "Joe had never been married. He said Lucy was the woman who taught him to love. I just hope he gave her the ring before the boat exploded."

Mary patted Nellie's hand. "It's all right," she said. "They're together now. I have no doubt of it."

Nellie nodded.

"Why did the boat explode?" Rainbow asked. Nellie didn't know the details. Maybe Mary knew something Nellie didn't.

"No one knows," Mary answered, echoing what Nellie had said. "There wasn't enough of it left floating to tell, and the water was really deep. The Coast Guard put it down to poor engine maintenance."

Nellie shook her head. "I was never happy with that. Joe cared for that boat like a baby."

"Anything could have happened," Mary added. "A fitting broke. A hose split. If gas leaked from anywhere, the hold would have filled with fumes and a single spark would have been enough." She shook her head. "Accidents happen. Even on well-maintained boats."

"It was so tragic," Nellie said. "They were as happy as kids those last few months. Joe was like a man reborn. And I'd known Lucy ever since her husband died fifteen years before, and I never saw her as happy as she was those last months."

The summer afternoon was edging into evening, bringing no relief yet from the heat. Rainbow sipped her lemonade and looked out over the Gulf, battling a growing sense of fatigue and searching her memory for other impressions she had gleaned from the Towers ghosts. "If there's unfinished business," she said finally, "I didn't get a sense of it."

"Maybe Joe and Lucy just miss their friends," Mary said. "Maybe they've just come back for a visit."

That didn't feel exactly right to Rainbow, either, but she couldn't put her finger on why. Well, she'd have to go back in and check it out again—but not right now. Right now she was feeling too annoyed at Jake to tolerate seeing him. And to be honest, she was feeling annoyed with herself for being so attracted to a man who was so determinedly blind about what was going on right around him. Surely he couldn't honestly believe that watering can had been rigged by human agency to dump on him *twice*?

"I'll try again tomorrow," she told Nellie. "Maybe when things are calmer, I can get better impressions."

Mary arched an amused brow. "Jake Carpenter is proving to be a distraction, eh?"

"He's just so determined to believe some human is behind all this, but there's no way he can explain a watering can dumping itself on him not once, but twice! And after he moved."

"Twice?" Mary Todd chuckled with glee. "Oh, I wish I'd seen that!"

Rainbow saw movement from the corner of her eye and turned, half-expecting to see that Jake had finished his search of the building and was joining them. Instead, it was her Uncle Gene, dressed now in a pair of black shorts and a black T-shirt that said,

"A clear conscience is the sign of a bad memory."

He joined Rainbow and her companions, smiling genially and looking as dashing as always, though how he managed it in a T-shirt and shorts Rainbow could never say. He made a courtly bow over the hands of both Nellie and Mary, causing both women to blush and giggle like schoolgirls.

Which was exactly the effect he wanted, Rainbow thought. Gene never passed up a chance to wow the ladies.

"I hear there's been some sort of brouhaha here."

"Where'd you hear that?"

"It's all over town."

Great, thought Rainbow. The next thing she knew, the newspapers and TV would be here. She wanted no part of that.

"Don't worry," said her uncle. "I told them all that my niece would fix it."

"Oh, thank you so very much!"

He looked surprised. "What did I do?"

"I wanted to keep a low profile on this. I don't want the newspapers and TV accusing me of bilking elderly people."

"They won't," Nellie said. "You're not charging us anything."

"Still."

Mary shook her head. "You're too defensive, gal. You have a splendid talent, and you ought to be perfectly willing to display it. And to hell with those who don't believe."

"Easy for you to say, Mary."

"I suppose it is," Mary said tartly. "After all, I've lived my life the way I wanted, and consequences be damned. You see, child, everybody pays the piper. You might as well pay for the dance you *want*."

"Hear, hear," said Gene.

But she hadn't wanted this dance, Rainbow thought. Although that wasn't really true, she admitted after a moment. She had chosen to use her talents rather than simply let them lie fallow. So maybe she ought to stop apologizing for them and trying to avoid notice. Maybe she ought to—in the outdated phrase her mother loved so much—just let it all hang out.

Although, since Walter, she didn't seem as able to do that. He had hurt something essential in her, and even after all this time, she was still walking around with scars.

Nellie was telling Gene what had happened that day, and Rainbow was content to let her do the recounting. It was obvious to her that Nellie was attracted to Gene, and that Gene reciprocated. She felt a little uneasy about that, but there was always a chance one of these days he might get hooked and reeled in. It would be nice if he got reeled in here, where she would be able to see him frequently.

Unless, of course, he kept touting her private business to people all over town. She'd have to discuss that with him later.

"Twice?" Gene was saying with delight, as Nellie wrapped up the story. "The watering can dumped on him *twice?*" He hooted at the thought.

"He still thinks it was rigged," Rainbow remarked.

"Well, of course he does," Gene said. "That's his way of approaching life. He's sure there has to be a rational, logical, *tangible* reason for everything. That's his scientific training."

"Well, he needs a new premise," Rainbow said tartly.

"Perhaps," Gene agreed, smiling.

"He's not even being scientific about this. He's

jumping to conclusions based on his *beliefs*, not on the evidence at hand."

"So are you, my dear."

Rainbow looked at her uncle, feeling betrayed. Gene reached out and patted her hand.

"I'm not saying you're wrong. I'm simply pointing out that the two of you are coming from different belief systems. He's looking for something tangible to explain events. You're not, because you believe at the outset that there isn't one."

Rainbow looked away, feeling uncomfortable. Gene was right, she realized. She and Jake were having a clash of beliefs, and what was more, she wasn't giving his beliefs the same respect she was demanding for hers.

And what if Jake was right? What if there *was* a tangible cause for the haunting? What if the things flying all over the building had nothing to do with the ghosts she sensed? They could be entirely separate.

But no, she decided after a moment. She knew exactly what she had felt after that watering pot had dumped on Jake the second time. The sense of a slightly mischievous personality had been unmistakable.

Harvey Little came up to the table. "Are we ever going to be allowed back inside?"

Rainbow shrugged. "I don't see why you can't go back in if you want."

"This has been a ridiculous waste of time," he complained. "We've spent half the afternoon out here for no good reason. The building must have settled or something."

Nellie looked up at him. "Didn't you have all kinds of things flying around *your* unit, too?"

"I got banged on the head when some things fell off the shelf in my bathroom. They were probably ready to fall anyway." He shook his head. "I don't hold with this spook nonsense, and I don't think the association should be paying for an exorcism."

Rainbow started to speak, but Nellie beat her to the punch. "We're not paying for anything. And we're not having an exorcism. Ms. Moonglow is simply trying to figure out what's been going on."

"It'd make more sense to get somebody out here to find out what's wrong with the building! We're so close to the water, the foundation might be settling."

Ellis Webster joined them. "The building supports go all the way down to bedrock, Harvey. The place would have tipped over years ago otherwise."

"I still say something is wrong with the building, and it ought to be checked out before somebody gets killed. And this ghost nonsense!" He glared at Rainbow. "I know somebody who's capitalizing on a newspaper headline. And she may not be charging anything now, but when it gets worse, you'll all find yourselves over a barrel and paying her everything you've got!"

Rainbow bit her tongue with difficulty. She was definitely not going to defend herself to this unpleasant little man, but she did indulge a moment of fantasy in which he was a crawling insect she was spraying with a can of insecticide. No, a worm was better. She could definitely see Harvey Little as a worm. A worm she would put on her fishing hook and use for bait.

"Don't you talk to Rainbow that way," Nellie said, flaring. "You're a disgusting little man! You always think *everyone* is up to something unsavory."

"I do not!"

"Yes, you do! Only two months ago you said Ellis was stealing from the association funds, because it couldn't possibly cost twelve hundred dollars to repaint all the cast-iron patio furniture. Remember? Ellis had to show you the three estimates he got before you believed it was the best deal. And then there was the time—''

"Okay, okay," said Harvey. "So I'm suspicious . . . I'm just careful. What's wrong with that? There are sharks everywhere. Any so-called psychic could come to this place and drag up Joe Carpenter! It was in all the papers. Hell, I could do as good a job of gulling all of you as *she* is."

"She's not gulling anyone!"

"Right. Just don't expect to use any of *my* money for this nonsense!"

"Don't worry," Ellis said. "Nobody's money is going to be used."

Harvey spun on his heel and walked toward the building, and Nellie muttered, "I hope his *ceiling* falls on his head next time."

Gene was looking at Nellie with apparent admiration. "You were wonderful," he told her.

She blushed.

Gene leaned over and took her hand. "Will you have dinner with me tonight?"

Rainbow looked quickly away, feeling a sudden, inexplicable tightening of her throat. She couldn't help it. All her life long, she'd wished a man would look at her the way Gene was looking at Nellie right now.

Jake, Colonel Albemarle, and the rest of the men finished their exploration of the building. Jake hated to admit it, but Hank Fields had probably had more luck with his Dustbuster than he'd had. He hadn't found one thing out of place that he could prove had been put there by human agency. Nor had he found one thing that *couldn't* have been tossed around by some skilled troublemaker. He was no closer to solving the problem. In fact, all he had accomplished was making Rainbow angry again.

And that really bothered him, much as he hated to admit it. But he got so mad when she did her hocus-pocus using Joe. In fact, he resented the hell out of it.

Colonel Albemarle lined up his troops in the lobby and cleared his throat, signifying an intent to speak. The veterans all immediately assumed stiff postures of attention, broomsticks and mops held rigidly upright.

"Well done, men," Albemarle said. "We came when we were called, and we all performed proudly in the face of an enormous threat. We're involved in an unusual war here, one that will never make the history books. But while history records only the glowing highlights, it's the individual bravery of individuals that yields triumph rather than defeat. Today we were triumphant against a foe whose powers we cannot know."

He cleared his throat again. "I'd recommend a reconnaissance in preparation for future operations, but since we can't see the enemy, there's no way to know where they are or how well they're armed. We will have no way of knowing if they begin to creep back in the night, and the only sentries we'll have are the good residents of this building. It's a disadvantage, men, but one I'm sure we will deal with. Never let your weapons leave your side. You may need them at a moment's notice.

"And Fields, you be sure to take that Dustbuster far away before you empty it. Wouldn't want the rascals to come right back."

"Yes, sir!"

"Obviously," the colonel continued, "we can't be sure that we've removed the problem. It may be that the Dustbuster didn't get them all. Or it may be that once we empty the thing they'll just return. Unfortunately, I'm not all that familiar with ghost operations, so we'll just have to wait and see. However, it's been my experience that an enemy rarely concedes after a single battle.

"But whether or not we managed to remove the threat permanently, all of you are to be commended for the willingness to face an invisible foe. You marched forward with courage into the jaws of hell, and you emerged victorious!"

A cheer went up from the assembled men.

"The one thing we can say with absolute certainty is that our presence made Mr. Carpenter and Ms. Moonglow safer. Except for the incident with the watering pot, nothing happened." He paused for effect. "I doubt that would have been the case if we hadn't been here."

He scanned his ragtag squad and nodded approvingly. "I'm going to dismiss you now, but hold yourselves in readiness. We may well have to return."

Jake watched the men march away, thinking they all looked a lot prouder of themselves after the search than he felt. They'd done something good, after all, racing to the aid of their neighbors, however insanely. All Jake felt was that he had wasted an afternoon he could have spent working on his book and he hadn't accomplished a damn thing.

Except to hurt Rainbow again. Christ, he wished that woman didn't have such expressive eyes. He felt he could read every thought that passed through her head. He could certainly see it when he wounded her.

He wanted to retreat to his apartment, but the colonel had left him in charge of all the keys. They were scattered on a tabletop right now. Looking around, he found a decorative basket and dumped all the keys into it so he could carry them out to the residents.

Just then, Harvey Little came through the doors, looking mad enough to spit. Seeing Jake, he halted and waved. "They're all a bunch of damn fools!" he said. "Being led like a bunch of sheep by that charlatan."

"Now, wait—"

But Harvey wasn't waiting on anyone. "She hasn't said a *damn thing* she couldn't have found out from the newspapers, and they're eating it up like a bunch of gullible fools. Christ, if she told them all to walk into the Gulf, they'd probably do it!"

"I don't think—"

"I don't care *what* you think! I'm not going to have any part of this crap. Idiots! The building is probably settling. We need to have the foundation checked! Instead they hire a psychic!"

Jake watched him walk to the elevator, thinking that he really didn't like that man. On the other hand, what he said about the building settling bore some consideration.

As a geologist, that probably should have been his first thought. He was a little embarrassed that he had first looked for some kind of conspiracy where there was probably a more real, more threatening danger. If one of the building's bedrock supports had weakened, they were all in far more trouble than some real estate scam could do to them. He'd better call an engineering firm and make arrangements. But first he needed to check the structure for any visible cracking. That would probably show best on the outside of the building where things wouldn't be in the way.

Carrying the keys outside, he turned them over to Ellis Webster to return to the residents. It was a small revenge, to give the man the headache of sorting out all these keys. He held Ellis responsible for getting him into this mess; after all, it had probably been Ellis's idea to nominate him for association president.

Then, reluctantly, he looked at Rainbow.

In the evening sun, her eyes were dark and unreadable, like the surface of a still pool. Her face betrayed nothing.

"I'm sorry," he said. He wondered, a little wildly, if he was going to spend the rest of his life apologizing to this woman. "I was irritated at having the water dumped on me."

"Of course," she said. Her voice offered him nothing.

Ellis spoke. "Did you find anything?"

"Nothing but a minor mess that could have been caused by the building settling." Even as he said it, he felt guilty. No settling could have caused that watering can to levitate and dump on him. He watched Rainbow's reaction and felt a twinge when he realized she was disappointed in him.

Disappointed? What right did she have to be disappointed? But—and this really hurt—he was disappointed in himself. He was being dishonest. "Except for one thing," he said, the words feeling like lead in his mouth.

"What's that?" Ellis asked.

"The watering can that dumped on me. Settling couldn't explain that."

Rainbow gave him a big, wide, warm smile of approval, making him feel oddly lightheaded and exhilarated all at once. Oh, man, he'd better watch his step here.

Nellie Blair, too, smiled at him with approval. "So we're not all a bunch of senile old coots?"

"I would never say *that*," he assured her, appalled. "I never even *thought* it!"

"The boy has possibilities," Mary Todd remarked. "He'll get his head out of the sand yet."

Jake wasn't sure that was a compliment, but he let it pass. When Nellie and Ellis insisted he join them for some lemonade, he agreed readily enough. Somehow he wound up in the chair next to Rainbow.

"I really can't explain the watering can," he said, deciding that was the safest place to start. "God knows I tried. But the other things I saw—well, if the building were to settle suddenly, things would fly around a bit."

Instead of arguing with him, everyone nodded, even Rainbow. He had believed that she was fully committed to the idea of ghosts, to the point of explaining everything by their presence. But maybe, since he had been willing to admit he couldn't explain the watering can, she was willing to admit more than one agency might be at work here. Maybe she wasn't quite as flaky as he'd believed.

The thought gave him no comfort.

"That's what Harvey Little was saying," Ellis remarked, "but the building is supported on bedrock."

"But one of the pilings might be failing," Jake said. "If it is, we need to know before it gets worse."

"What a thought!" said Nellie. "I can't imagine living in the leaning tower of Paradise Beach."

"Is there anything we should look for?" Ellis asked.

"Cracks in the ceilings, walls, or floors. Cracks in the exterior of the building." Jake fell silent a moment, thinking about it. "But . . . it seems to me if the building were settling unequally, the elevators would be having some problem." He shook his head. "I don't know enough about architectural stresses. I'll need to talk to somebody who does."

"Well, you're the association president," Ellis said.

"Go ahead and do what you think is best."

Jake sensed an ally in Ellis, someone else who wasn't happy with the ghost idea. Maybe there were other residents who also weren't half daft. Although, he admitted, that wasn't really a fair characterization . . . these people were being faced with inexplicable phenomena. Why shouldn't they seek every explanation, including the most outrageous? After all, most of them probably weren't scientists.

He turned to look at Rainbow and felt his heart skip a beat. Her green eyes gleamed with the faintest amusement, but that isn't what made him catch his breath. No, it was the visual impact of a beautiful woman wearing a pretty seafoam green sundress that exposed smooth shoulders and just a hint of cleavage. It was the sight of perfectly formed calves, smooth and satiny, tinted just the faintest gold by the sun. Why, he found himself wondering, couldn't this woman have been normal?

Normal women didn't frighten him the way this one did. Normal women were known quantities who yielded to reason. This woman sat there looking mildly amused, displaying the kind of beauty that belonged on an artist's canvas, and wrapped in a layer of mystery he could never hope to penetrate because he could never share her belief system.

Down, boy, he told himself sternly, and looked quickly away from her.

"Well," said Gene, "Nellie and I are going to dinner. Do you want to change first?" he asked her.

"Where are we going?"

"Wherever you like."

"I know a good, casual seafood place up the boulevard," she suggested. "We can go as we are."

Gene smiled at her. "My kind of woman. I swore I was never going to wear a necktie again."

Nellie laughed. "There aren't many places around

here where you need one. The courthouse, maybe."

He laughed and rose, helping her out of her chair. Over his shoulder he said to Rainbow, "Don't wait up for me."

"I wouldn't dream of it," she answered drily.

"I need to go, too," Mary said. "I've got a bridge game." She headed for her golf cart, followed by Ellis Webster, who was worried about her brakes and offered to take a look at them for her.

Left alone at the table, Rainbow and Jake exchanged uncertain looks. Rainbow reached for her small purse, getting ready to leave.

"I'll drive you home," Jake said.

She shook her head. "I can walk. It really isn't that far."

"No, I'd like to take you. But first, would you mind coming up to my place for just a minute? I haven't checked it yet, and I'm wondering what it looks like."

"Sure." She gave him a smile. "Who knows? Maybe we'll find something there that proves it was all caused by humans."

Her response, far from reassuring him, seemed like a double-edged sword. Was she implying that he might have rigged something in his apartment to bolster his case, and wanted her there when he pretended to find it?

But he couldn't tell. And he didn't feel inclined to endure the wrath that would probably result if he came right out and asked her.

"I wonder," he said, as they stepped into the elevator, "what gave Colonel Albemarle and his cronies the idea that a Dustbuster would work on ghosts."

She gave him an amused look. "I take it you haven't seen *Ghostbusters*."

He was just unlocking his unit door when another

one of the residents stepped off the elevator. The
man spied him and came toward him with the look
of someone on a mission. He was a plump man with
very short legs, and he waddled like a duck as he
strode toward them.

"Just a minute, Carpenter," the man said.

Jake turned and waited.

"You're president of the association. I want to
know what you're going to do about the mess my
unit is in."

"Why should I do anything, Mr. Hanes?"

"Because this mess isn't my doing! It's the association's problem. There's something wrong with the
whole building. Whether it's ghosts or settling, I
don't care, but cleaning up should be the association's responsibility."

"Considering that everyone is in the same mess,
it makes more sense for each of us to do it ourselves," Jake replied reasonably enough.

"My wife isn't well! There's no way she can clean
it all up."

Rainbow opened her mouth, but Jake beat her to
the punch. "You look like you have two functioning
arms and two functioning legs. Do it *yourself.*"

The man's mouth drew into a thin line. "You have
no sense of responsibility, do you?"

Jake just looked at him.

"It's *your* fault we have this problem."

"How could it be my fault?"

"It's *your* uncle who's haunting this place! *You*
ought to repair the damage he's done."

Jake could feel his jaw setting. He looked down at
Rainbow, wondering what she had been saying and
to whom. Then he looked at his unpleasant neighbor
again and something strange came over him. When
he spoke, he had the oddest feeling that someone
else had taken control of his mouth.

"If my uncle's haunting this place," he said, "then he has a damn good reason. And you'd better be careful, or I'll sic him on you!"

The man's eyes widened, and he looked like a boiler ready to burst its seams. Evidently he thought better of exploding, however, because he turned sharply and stormed away to the elevator—if a duck could storm.

Rainbow looked up at Jake, and there was no mistaking the smile that danced in her eyes. "That was brilliant," she said. "You turned the tables on him beautifully."

"Which leads me to something else," he said firmly. "I want a word with you, Ms. Rainbow Moonglow. I want to know just what the hell you're telling people."

Turning, he shoved his key into the lock and opened his door.

Then he froze, looking with disbelief at his living room.

Eight

"My goodness!" Rainbow said in a hushed voice.

Jake didn't say anything at all; he simply stared.

Perched, upside down, in the middle of the ceiling, was his uncle's easy chair.

The two of them stood frozen on the threshold. Jake finally spoke in a hoarse voice. "Have you ever seen anything like this before?"

"No," Rainbow whispered, "but I don't know much about ghosts."

"No? Then how come you're supposed to be an authority?"

"You want the truth? My *mother* talks to ghosts. Me, I just read tarot cards and pick up psychic impressions."

Jake couldn't take his eyes from the chair, though it was difficult not to turn and look at Rainbow, to see if she was serious. "Talks to ghosts?"

"She's a trance channeler."

"Oh." He'd heard about that somewhere. If Rainbow's abilities strained his credulity to the breaking point, trance channeling was something he classified in the category of "How Dumb Can People Be?"

"I'd have asked her to handle this, except she's on a cruise right now."

"Oh," he said again. Any other words seemed pointless. "It has to be attached to the ceiling somehow," he said finally.

"It certainly wasn't put there by the building settling."

"Obviously." He wanted to kick himself. While he'd been running around checking on other people's units, his own had apparently been wide open to some jokester. That made him mad.

He stepped into the room, approaching the chair, but Rainbow grabbed his arm, halting him.

"We don't know if it's attached."

He looked at her. "Of course it's attached! I'm sorry, Rainbow, but I just don't see my uncle bench-pressing his easy chair."

"It was *his* chair?" That seemed to have significance for her.

"Purely coincidental," he said firmly. "Easier to hang from the ceiling than the sofa."

She looked dubious. "Even if it is attached," she said finally, "we don't know *how* it's attached. It could fall on you. We need to get help."

He had to admit she was right. That was a heavy chair, and if it fell on his head, he'd probably spend a good, long time in a body cast.

"I wish my mother were here," Rainbow said. "Well, not really. I mean, she can be difficult and embarrassing. But she'd find out what's going on here, even if it *is* just some lunatic prankster."

"She deals in living people, too?"

"Well, of course! Her guides answer people's questions all the time. They see more than we do, so the information is often useful."

"Really." He hoped the word was sufficiently noncommittal. With that chair hanging in the middle of his living room, he was suddenly reluctant to piss Rainbow off. He had the creepy feeling that maybe he was mistaken about what was going on here. And if he was, he didn't want any psychic getting angry enough to bean him with a La-Z-Boy.

Which was an absolutely insane thought for him to be having, he realized, but he was rapidly getting to that point. The peaceful life he'd envisioned having in Paradise Beach had yet to materialize. Putting out a well fire was beginning to sound like a picnic by comparison. There, at least, he would be in *control*.

"Look," he said after a moment, "I'm going to go stand on the couch and see if I can tell how that chair is attached."

She nodded. "Just don't get anywhere under it. *Please.*"

He wanted to kick himself for saying it, but he said it anyway. Giving her a big grin, he said, "Aw, gee, you really *do* care!"

Her cheeks colored. "Of course I care!" she snapped. "I'd care about anyone!"

"Right." He let his smile say otherwise, even though he was acting like a jerk. What the hell. Everyone around here was acting like a jerk. Why shouldn't *he?*

He edged around the chair and stepped up onto the sofa, trying to see if there were bolts or something else holding the chair to the ceiling. And of course, he couldn't see a damn thing. The legs of the chair seemed to be sitting as comfortably on the ceiling as they would have sat on the floor.

He reached out to give it a test push, but Rainbow stopped him with a cry.

"Don't!" she said. "If that thing falls off the ceiling it'll be damaged. It might even damage the floor."

He drew his hand back, acceding to her wisdom.

"I wish we had Colonel Albemarle's men right now. Four or five people ought to be able to handle that chair without too much trouble."

"Well, let's go get some help," Rainbow suggested. "There's a whole bunch of people down on the patio."

Jake jumped down from the couch and paused to look up at the chair. "They better not have put bolts in my ceiling," he grumbled.

"Well, like I said, there's one thing we can say for sure—that chair didn't get up there because the building settled."

He looked at her and saw again that faint glimmer of amusement in her gaze. She was enjoying herself, he realized. He wished he could say the same about himself.

Lucy looked at Joe, who was chuckling over Jake's response to the chair.

"Bolts!" Joe said, chortling. "As if I need to use anything like that."

"Maybe you should put the chair back down, Joe," Lucy said. "You're going to drive Jake nuts."

"That's exactly what the boy needs! Besides, I don't want him sitting in my favorite chair. Nobody sits in that chair but me."

"But you can't leave it on the ceiling forever—can you?"

Joe grinned at her. "Watch me, sweetie."

In spite of herself, Lucy started to laugh, too. It *was* funny, she thought. Besides, she was developing a real fondness for Rainbow, and it would be nice if they could help the young woman convince Jake that there was more to the world than met the eye. Getting into the spirit of the thing, she put the newspaper on the seat of the chair.

"Let him explain that one away," she said.

*   *   *

Rainbow and Jake returned to his unit with Ellis Webster, Zach Herschfeld, and Abe Levinson. Their three companions had been warned that the chair was on the ceiling, but that didn't keep them all from gaping as they hesitantly entered the apartment.

That's when Jake saw the newspaper. "How'd that get up there?" he asked.

"Beats me," said Rainbow.

"Well, enough is enough," Jake said. Striding forward, he stopped to one side of the chair and reached for the newspaper. It came free at his touch and he turned it over, trying to find some sign of glue. Nothing.

And again he felt the uneasy prickling at the base of his skull, the one he'd been having all too often since moving into his uncle's condo. He passed the newspaper to Rainbow, who examined it, too.

"Nothing," he said.

Her eyes wide, she looked at him and shook her head. "Maybe I need to see if I can get ahold of my mother. She knows a lot more about this than I do."

"Sure, why not?" said Jake, who was beginning to feel unreal. "The more the merrier. A few extra fruitcakes will only add spice."

He wanted to snatch the words back as soon as they escaped his mouth, but it was too late. It didn't matter anyway. Rainbow didn't look offended.

"She's a fruitcake, all right," she said. "But she's a knowledgable fruitcake."

The other three men were edging closer to the chair, all of them looking uneasy. Actually seeing a recliner on the ceiling was a little different from hearing about it, Jake supposed. They circled around it, looking at it from all angles, considering the problem.

"We'd better get some ladders," Ellis said.

Jake shook his head. "Not just yet. We don't dare try to pull it down while we're standing on ladders. If it won't come away, then we'll climb up to examine it more closely."

Everyone agreed with him, so the four men each grabbed one corner of the chair and pulled. It didn't budge. Jake and Zach, being the tallest of the crew, reached up to grab the chair at the bottom, but no matter how hard they pulled, it didn't start to come loose . . . not even when Jake did a pull up, adding his own weight to that of the chair.

"Well, if that doesn't beat all," said Abe Levinson.

"It *has* to be bolted up there," said Ellis.

"Try moving it to the side," Rainbow suggested. "If it's bolted it won't budge."

Jake shrugged and reached up, pushing on the chair. And as easily as if it were sliding over smooth ice or ball bearings, it moved. "Great," he said. "There goes the bolt idea."

Rainbow read the disgust on his face. She thought this was really exciting, but he obviously found it extremely annoying.

Jake pushed on the chair again, this time from a different direction, and it moved easily. "Maybe if I push it far enough, whatever is holding it up will give way."

"Maybe," said Ellis. "But we'd better help you, in case it starts to fall."

The men grabbed the chair again at the corners and started moving it around. It went everywhere they pushed it: to the side, around in circles, and all the way to the other side of the room. Nothing they did seemed to be working it free.

"Well, hell," Jake said finally, "I guess I'm just going to have to live with a chair on my ceiling."

Abe studied the chair. "I guess you could call it

modern art. It kind of makes a statement, doesn't it?"

"Yeah," said Zach. "The statement that ghosts are real."

Jake scowled. "I'm not ready to accept that."

"Maybe *you* aren't," Ellis answered, "but *I'm* getting closer to it with each passing minute." He looked at Rainbow. "That was Joe's chair. God help anyone else who sat in it."

She nodded in agreement. "I can feel the impression of Joe all around it," she said. "He's here right now."

"Then I'm getting out of here," Jake said. "Right now. I've had about all of the cockamamie crap I can take. The chair can stay there until hell freezes over."

"At least put it where it won't fall on anything," Rainbow suggested.

He obliged, giving the chair a shove that sent it into the corner across the room. "Come on, let's go," he said. "I need air and I need to be someplace where the earth is solid."

The three other men left them, talking among themselves and shaking their heads. Rainbow waited while Jake checked the rest of the apartment and found nothing amiss. Then, leaving the chair behind them on the ceiling, they went down.

"How about dinner?" Jake said, as they reached the parking lot. "My treat. I need somebody to tell me I'm not really losing my mind."

Rainbow hardly hesitated. Going home to eat dinner alone didn't sound half as interesting as dining with Jake, despite all his wrongheaded notions. Besides, she had the sneaky feeling he was beginning to come around to her way of seeing things, however reluctantly. Chairs on the ceiling could have that effect.

"Sure," she said. "I know just the place."

She directed him to the Paradise Beach Bar. It was getting near sunset, and from where they sat on the porch, they could see the Gulf of Mexico and the slowly lowering orb of the sun.

"It's not going to be much of a sunset," Rainbow remarked. "Not a cloud in the sky."

"I thought this was supposed to be the rainy season here."

"One of them. We sure could use some rain."

The menu ran mostly to sandwiches and appetizers. Jake ordered the club sandwich and Rainbow opted for an appetizer of chicken fingers and stuffed mushrooms. She treated herself to a fancy tropical cocktail that was a rainbow of colors with fruit sections around the rim of the glass. Jake wanted a more prosaic beer.

"Ah, that's good," he said, when he'd taken a long draft. "It can be really difficult to get plain old American lager overseas, and it's almost never this cold. Sometimes I used to dream about ice cubes. Glasses full of ice. *Mounds* of ice." He shook his head and gave her a grin. "Of course, when I was on the North Sea I used to dream about tropical beaches. It can be amazing, what you miss."

"I'll bet."

"When I was in the marines I was stationed for a year in Okinawa. The surprising thing about the place was that it had a continuing water shortage. Water was rationed, of course, and for days on end we weren't allowed to take showers. And when we got to take one, the water was cold. So I started dreaming about long, hot showers."

"How long were you in the marines?"

"Just four years. The GI Bill got me through college. I figure it was a more than fair trade."

"It sounds like you've lived just about everywhere."

He shook his head. "Not really. I've lived in a lot of places where they're looking for oil. And most of what I've seen has been drilling sites. Once we find the oil, I move on, take a new contract."

"So you don't work full time for an oil company?"

"I did at first. That's how I worked on the North Sea. Later I discovered I could do better as a consultant, especially since I seem to have a nose for the stuff. There are a lot of governments who want to find oil but don't want to invite a big oil company in. That's what I was doing in Indonesia."

"Will you be going back after you finish you book?" She found herself hoping not.

"I'm not sure. I'm getting tired of living out of a duffel bag. But I've got a whole year to figure that out." He sipped his beer and shook his head. "Besides, I've got a more pressing problem right now— a chair on my ceiling."

"That's really something, isn't it? I believe in ghosts, but I've never seen anything remotely like this. And I can't imagine how it could be happening, anyway. I mean, ghosts are incorporeal. They have no real substance."

"Not even ectoplasm?" he asked sarcastically.

"I've seen ectoplasm," she said, trying to keep the defensiveness out of her voice. "It really does exist."

He raised a hand as if to say, "Have it your way."

"But it couldn't do that, I'm sure," Rainbow continued. "I mean, it's barely there. It's this shimmery substance that you can almost see through. I've heard of apparitions looking as solid as you or me, but . . ." She trailed off, thinking for a moment. "This looks more like poltergeist activity than a standard haunting."

"Don't most of those poltergeist cases turn out to be kids playing tricks?"

"Some of them."

"Well, we don't have any kids in the building. And frankly, I can't imagine any possible way that chair can be hanging on my ceiling without being bolted there, but if it *were* bolted, it wouldn't move."

She nodded.

"On the other hand," he continued, "I'm not entirely ready to capitulate."

She had to smile at that. "I didn't think you were."

He sat back in his chair, returning her smile as he sipped at his beer again. The breeze was warm, the Gulf was beautiful, and the woman across from him was entrancing despite all her wackiness. Relaxation began to uncoil the tendrils of tension that had been tightening his muscles most of the day. Hell, he thought finally, so what if there were ghosts? Maybe he could live with the idea—as long as it didn't force itself down his throat.

"What about you?" he said.

"Me?"

"Well, I told you something about my background. What about yours?"

She flushed faintly and looked out to sea. "My background is—well, unconventional."

"I kind of thought so."

"My mother has always been, um . . . well, *unique*. She was living in a commune in the seventies when she had my sister and then me. I don't think she was ever sure who our fathers were."

"Oh."

Rainbow smiled faintly. "So we both got the made-up last name of Moonglow. Unfortunately, she left the commune while I was still in diapers, and being called 'Rainbow Moonglow' was something of a disadvantage."

"I never knew my father, either," Jake said sympathetically. "He died when I was young."

"At least you know his name."

"You've got a point. What's your sister's name?"

"Dawn."

"Dawn Moonglow." He shook his head. "Memorable. Is she psychic, too?"

"Not at all. Lucky Dawn. She works as a court reporter, and evenings and weekends she transcribes my mother's channeling sessions. She feels cheated that she's never had a psychic experience, but I keep telling her she's the lucky one."

"It's tough, huh?"

Her green eyes returned to his face. " 'Tough' isn't exactly the word I'd use. But it can make you quite an outcast when you know what other kids are thinking before they say it, or when you know what's going to happen before it does."

He nodded, not sure how to reply. In the first place, he didn't believe in such things, but even if he allowed their existence, there didn't seem to be any safe way to sympathize with a wacko for being a wacko . . . although Rainbow was a genuinely *nice* wacko.

"By the time I was in high school, I learned to hide it pretty well, so that wasn't as bad. I even managed to keep it mostly under wraps when I was going to college."

"Mostly?"

"Well, I had this terrible premonition that my roommate was going to get hurt if she went out with this guy she had just met. I didn't tell her because I didn't want her to think I was weird."

"I take it she got hurt?"

"He tried to rape her."

"That's awful."

"Anyway, the experience changed my mind about pretending I wasn't psychic. I mean, if I know something that can help people, I can't keep my mouth shut. It doesn't matter what it costs me, but if I say nothing I become a kind of accomplice, you know?"

He shook his head slowly. "I think you're being too hard on yourself, Rainbow. You didn't *make* that happen to your roommate. You didn't have anything to do with it."

"Except that I might have prevented it if I'd cared more about her than about myself."

"Maybe. If she'd listened to you. And maybe not. One of the things that bothers me about this psychic business is that it seems to imply the future is fixed, somehow. Instead of having numerous probabilities out there, you're saying that one particular thing is going to happen."

"Not at all. What I say is, if you do certain things, other things will happen. I believe I pick up on a likelihood at any given point in time, but if we change our actions it might never materialize."

"On the other hand, if the future *is* fixed, your roommate would have nearly gotten raped anyway. Say she listened to you and didn't go out with the guy. Who's to say he wouldn't have attacked her in some other place and at some other time?"

"No one can say that for certain."

"Of course not. So what's the point of premonitions?"

Rainbow gave a little laugh. "You're beginning to sound fatalistic here."

"I'm not really. I'm just arguing for the sake of arguing, I guess. I'm not comfortable with the whole idea of predicting the future."

"Neither am I, but I do it all the time. Sometimes I'm right, and sometimes I'm wrong. There aren't any guarantees."

He leaned forward, propping his elbows on the table. The sun's globe was riding the crest of the waves now, heavy, huge, and orange. The water sparkled with sharply contrasting shades of blue and lavender.

"What about tarot cards?" he asked. "You mentioned them. Do you think they really have some kind of magical power?"

"Of course not, but they act as a kind of focus for me. They're a means of organizing the impressions I get, a means of helping me concentrate. Sometimes I read tea leaves. A crystal ball would probably do the same thing. I'm just more comfortable with the cards because they represent various aspects of life and human nature, so when I look at one of them, I concentrate on the impressions I'm getting in that particular area of life for the person I'm reading for."

"Are you sure you're not just exceptionally good at reading people?"

One corner of her mouth lifted in acknowledgment. "I'm sure that's part of it. But that's not all of it. It couldn't be."

"Then why did you say your mother's an embarrassment?"

"I really shouldn't have said that."

"Why not? Everybody's been embarrassed by a parent at one time or another."

"But she doesn't embarrass me anymore. She can be wonderfully outrageous, and terribly dramatic, and sometimes even silly, but that's just the way she is. It was hard to live with at times when I was a kid. You know how that goes. Every kid wants June Cleaver for a mother. Instead, I had Mae West talking to ghosts."

He laughed at that, but it was a friendly laugh, and she didn't appear to take umbrage. "She sounds like quite a character."

"She is. I came to appreciate that she was also a wonderful mother. While other kids had June Cleaver, I had an ongoing adventure. And all the other kids forgot how weird we were when she threw a birthday party for us. They used to be just fabulous, with the whole backyard turned into a fantasy of one kind or another. She worked in the circus for a while before she joined the commune, and she had lots of friends there while I was growing up. I was the only kid in town who had acrobats or elephants or a sword swallower at my birthday parties."

"So for one day a year you didn't get snubbed?" he asked, almost gently.

"Actually, it was more than one day. For a couple of months before my birthday, everyone wanted to be my best friend."

"That wasn't very fair to *you*, was it?"

She shrugged one smooth shoulder. "I knew who my real friends were. And I wasn't above taking advantage of my mother's friends to bribe all the other kids to be nice to me for a while."

"It sounds like your mother loves you very much."

"Yes, she does. And she really *was* a good mother to me. It wasn't her fault that I wished she'd act like the other mothers at parent–teacher night. Or that she'd dress like other people. The problem wasn't Roxy, Jake. It was *me*."

"Don't be so hard on yourself. You were just acting like a normal kid. Even children who have perfectly average parents get embarrassed by them."

After they ate, they walked for a while on the darkening beach. When Jake reached out and took her hand, Rainbow didn't object. They might be poles apart, he found himself thinking, but surely they could find some common ground. With her small, delicate hand tucked in his, that suddenly seemed very important.

It grew even more important when they paused

to watch the moon rise between the buildings. He turned to look out over the water at the ribbon of silver moonlight and found himself facing Rainbow.

In that instant, the night stood still. The sound of the surf faded away and all he could hear was the heavy beating of his heart. He wanted her. He wanted her in ways he had never wanted a woman before. He wanted to take her right here on the damp sand, to fill the night with the magic he was sure they could create together. He wanted to hear her soft cries mix with the rhythms of the sea, wanted to find that oneness that could come only in the moments of deepest intimacy.

And it was only with the greatest effort he turned away and resumed their walk.

The gap between them seemed unbridgable.

Jake drove Rainbow home and dropped her off around nine o'clock. Gene was still out with Nellie Blair and Rainbow felt the silence of her cottage in a way she'd never noticed it before. In the past she'd always found it cozy and welcoming, but tonight it felt abandoned. Empty.

She wished Gene would come home but doubted she'd see him before midnight, if that early. So she decided it was a good time to try to put a call through to her mother on the cruise ship. Roxy would probably be busy entertaining guests, but Dawn might be available and could take a message.

It took nearly ten minutes for the operator to put the call through, and Rainbow was astonished to hear her mother's voice.

"What's wrong?" Roxy demanded, as soon as the connection was completed.

"Nothing, really, Mother. I'm fine. I thought you'd be working."

"I'm between shows right now. Why? Didn't you want to talk to me?"

"Of course I wanted to talk to you. I just didn't think I'd be able to."

"Then why'd you call?"

This was one of the reasons Rainbow didn't call her more often. Conversations usually wound up being fractured. "Because I wanted you to call me when you could."

"Oh. Well, Mustafa has been warning me that big events are about to happen in your life."

Mustafa was one of Roxy's spirit guides. Rainbow felt her heart jump nervously. "That's the impression I've been getting. Did he say what it was going to be?"

"No. He's being awfully coy about it. Said he isn't going to interfere, no matter what. I gather it's nothing bad, or he'd be sending out warnings like smoke signals."

"Red Feather is the one who uses smoke signals, Mother."

"Whatever. Anyway, why are you spending all this money to call me?"

"Well, I've got a ghost problem."

"In that cottage of yours? No way, not unless you killed Walter and buried him in the backyard."

Rainbow couldn't help laughing. "You know I'd never do anything like that."

"I can't see why not! If anyone deserves killing, it's Walter."

"Be that as it may, I'm not keen on spending the rest of my life in jail."

"No, I guess I can see that." Roxy sneezed. "Sorry, I'm allergic to something on this damn boat. It's a wonder I can even get into a trance." She sneezed again. "Well, if you haven't killed anyone, there's no reason you should have a ghost. Are you sure you aren't just suddenly developing new powers? I was about your age when my trancing started."

"No, no, Mother, the ghost isn't in my cottage."

"Well, that's good. Mustafa assured me that house was perfectly safe for you, and I'd have some words for him if it turned out he was wrong."

"Well, he wasn't."

"Good. I've got to check up on these guides of mine from time to time. Their sloppiness could ruin me, you know."

"I know, Mother. But about the ghosts—"

"Well, if they're not your ghosts, what's the problem?"

"They're not *my* ghosts. They're in a condominium building here in Paradise Beach."

"In a condo? That shows poor taste!"

"Regardless, the building's residents have asked me to help."

"Well, of course. That shows some common sense, at least."

"Maybe not. I'm in over my head."

Roxy fell silent a moment. "You know, I always felt you should develop your talents in another direction. Fortunetelling with tarot cards is a very seedy business, full of frauds."

"But—"

"You wouldn't be in over your head if you'd listened to me, Rainbow."

"Yes, Mother."

"But when do children ever listen to their mothers?"

"Rarely—or so you tell me."

Roxy laughed heartily. "I'm amazed I lived long enough to hear you admit it!"

"Well, I just did. But this call is costing me a fortune, so could we please get down to business?"

"This *is* business. I'm telling you that if you'd listened to me, you wouldn't be in over your head in your *business*."

Rainbow stifled a sigh. "Yes, Mother."

"You could at least try to sound like you truly agree with me when you say 'Yes, Mother.'"

"I'm trying."

"To get back to these ghosts—you really need to learn to stay on the point, Rainbow—what exactly are they doing?"

"Haunting the entire condo building, some sixty units. There's been a lot of poltergeist activity, but there are no children in the building." Paranormal research had established that poltergeists—ghosts which moved objects, started fires, and threw things—were most often associated with the presence of children in puberty.

"None?" Roxy sounded thoughtful. "That's very rare. What have you got so far?"

"A very strong impression of a couple who died in a violent accident nearly a year ago, and a chair that seems to be firmly attached to the ceiling."

"Really?" Roxy was suddenly almost breathless with excitement. "A chair on the ceiling?"

"Yes. When you push it, it moves around, but no amount of pulling will bring it down."

"Oh, my. Oh, my! This is wonderful! Actual physical proof! I'm transported with joy!"

"That's all very well, Mother, but believe me, the residents aren't. I don't know enough about this, or what to do about it, so if you could give me some advice—"

"Advice?" Roxy interrupted. "My dear Rainbow, you don't know enough about the subject to handle this, and nothing I tell you over the phone will give you enough information. So I'll do you one better. I'll be there tomorrow night."

Rainbow was astonished. "Tomorrow? But the cruise . . . your contract . . ."

"Hang the contract. I took this job only because I wanted to take a cruise. I thought it would be exotic and romantic. Instead I'm locked up in a place smaller than the average prison with a bunch of codgers who are even older and more senile than I am! I can't wait to get off this boat, and I don't care if they don't pay me a dime."

"But you're at sea!"

"We're docking in San Juan early in the morning. I'm going to jump ship and fly home. You need me, Rainbow, and I'm on my way. Dawn and I will call you from the airport when we get in, but don't worry about picking us up. I'll take a limo."

"But—"

But Roxy had already disconnected.

Rainbow stood with the receiver to her ear, listening to the dial tone, and wondering what she had just unleashed.

Nine

RAINBOW WAS ACTUALLY GLAD WHEN SHE SAW THE airport limo pull up in front of her cottage the next evening. She'd spent the entire day brooding—except for a scheduled reading and a walk-in—and thinking about the time she'd spent with Jake the preceding evening.

Something had happened when he had taken her hand while they walked on the beach, something that had left her feeling warm and happy and maudlin all at once. It was as if she'd tasted something she wanted and knew she could never have. Which was, of course, exactly what had happened.

Most of the time, she didn't mind living alone. There were advantages, of course. She was free to do as she chose, and she was responsible for no one but herself. Cooking for one was the pits, but she'd even gotten used to that.

But sometimes—sometimes she ached with loneliness, the kind no friend or relative could assuage.

Today had been one of those days, and she'd found herself trying to recapture the feeling she had had last night when Jake had held her hand. She had felt excitement and yearning, of course, but she had also felt acceptance.

Which was absolutely ridiculous, she kept telling herself. Look how Jake had reacted to the whole idea of her psychic powers. He would *never* accept her.

At least he was more honest than Walter had been. Walter had initially greeted her assertion of psychic abilities with an indulgent smile. Later, when she always knew what he wanted for dinner before he even got in the door, he dismissed it as coincidence, and "thinking alike."

But finally there had come the day she told him he was going to receive a job offer from a major brokerage firm. He'd laughed it off, telling her not to take herself so seriously. He hadn't even applied for a job there.

When he got home that night, he hadn't been laughing. He'd taken the job offer, which had been exactly what she had predicted, but he had also ended their relationship.

"You're too creepy, Rainbow," he'd told her, among other unkind things.

But the sight of her mother sailing up the walk with her purple caftan flying and the matching turban askew on her orange hair brought the first genuine smile of the day to Rainbow's lips. Her sister Dawn was right behind their mother, her chunky body clad in the customary mannish business suit. Dawn had gone even more overboard than Rainbow in trying to dress conservatively, so much that she was as odd looking in her own way as their mother.

"My baby," Roxy said, reaching out to embrace her and surround her in a cloud of lavender perfume.

Rainbow felt tears prickle her eyes as her mother's arms closed around her, holding her tight and rocking her gently. It occurred to her that she was never going to be too old for her mother's love to comfort her.

They moved inside, lugging the luggage, and Rainbow started making the inevitable pot of tea. Dawn doffed her jacket, revealing a surprisingly pretty beige shell. Roxy ditched her turban and finger-combed her thinning hair.

"It was awful," she said forcefully. "Just awful! The seasickness was bad enough, but being cooped up with a bunch of people who think the height of excitement is dining at the captain's table was more than I could take."

"They're just not our kind of people, Mother," Dawn remarked.

"Certainly not! Look at me. I'm nearly seventy-three, but I only feel fifty. I always say you're as young as you feel. These folks should have been decaying corpses years ago!"

Rainbow smothered a laughed. "Don't be unkind."

"I'm not being unkind. I have nothing against the elderly. A lot of people would put *me* in that class. But this group—well, it was a wonder they didn't all have nurses to help them around. One woman came to me for a reading and then had chest pains—chest pains!—when Mustafa spoke to her. What did she think was going to happen if she asked questions from a trance channeler?"

"It can be shocking, how different you sound and look when one of your guides is speaking," Rainbow said.

"Well, of course! That's how it's supposed to be."

"The woman *was* rather frail, Mother," Dawn said.

"If she was that frail, she shouldn't have been on that ship! Good heavens, they had to have a helicopter come get her and take her to a hospital."

"It could have happened to anyone," Dawn argued. "These things can't be predicted."

"Hmph." Roxy scowled at her and looked over at the stove. "Is that tea ever going to be ready?"

"The water will boil eventually," Rainbow said.

Just then her doorbell rang. Excusing herself, she went to answer it.

Jake stood there, hands in the pockets of his khaki shorts. "Hi," he said, looking as if he wasn't quite sure what he was doing there.

Then, behind her, Rainbow heard her mother say with great satisfaction, "Aha! I knew it!"

With a sinking sensation in the pit of her stomach, Rainbow looked over her shoulder. Roxy was grinning like a cat that had just caught a canary.

"Introduce me," Roxy said, marching forward, her caftan billowing around her like the sails of a Roman galley. "I knew there was a man in the picture somewhere."

"Ah," said Jake, in a tone that made Rainbow's head swing around to look at him. "I take it this is your mother."

Rainbow stood between them, thinking that this was going to be one of those terrible collisions, like the ones that happened when atoms crashed in a linear accelerator. There would be an explosion, and pieces would fly everywhere.

"Rainbow's apparently lost her voice," Roxy said. "I'm her mother, Roxy Resnick."

"Pleased to meet you, ma'am. Rainbow's told me a lot about you."

"None of it very flattering, I bet. I've always embarrassed her." Roxy stuck out a plump hand and Jake shook it.

"I'm Jake Carpenter," he said. "Rainbow and I are working together on the haunting over at Paradise Towers."

Roxy frowned. "You don't have a psychic's aura."

"I'm not psychic," Jake said, looking uncomfortable, "but I'm the guy with the chair on his ceiling."

"How apropos," Roxy said. "I can't think of a better place to put a chair on a ceiling than in the home of a nonbeliever."

Jake actually grinned. "It does seem to make a statement."

"Loud and clear, I should think." Roxy favored him with a smile. "Come in, come in. We were just about to have tea. And afterward, if you're a very good boy, I may read your tea leaves."

"That would be . . . interesting."

Life was tough enough, Rainbow thought with a sinking heart, without bringing Roxy Resnick, medium extraordinaire, into contact with Jake Carpenter, realist extraordinaire. She could already see storm clouds on the horizon.

Jake and Dawn exchanged pleasant greetings, then everyone gathered at the breakfast bar in the kitchen. Rainbow poured boiling water into the teapot and set it on the counter to steep. She had bought a box of the glazed chocolate doughnuts her mother loved, and she placed a half-dozen of them on a plate, passing out napkins to everyone.

"Now, sit while the tea steeps," Roxy ordered, "and tell me what's been going on."

Jake and Rainbow looked at one another, each clearly hoping the other would begin the tale.

"I'm not sure, exactly," Jake said, proving he had more guts than Rainbow. "Odd things have been reported. Items flying through the air, mainly. I haven't ruled out human inducement, or even the building settling."

"But then," said Roxy, "there's the chair on the ceiling."

Jake looked rueful. "Yes," he said, "there *is* the chair on the ceiling."

"You're sure it's not bolted there?"

"It moves when I push it, but it won't come down." He shrugged a shoulder and looked at Rainbow. "I tried to work today, but every few minutes I had to come out of my office and look at that chair, to be sure it was still there. At one point I found myself lying on the couch looking up at it, just waiting for something to happen." He shook his head. "I must be losing it."

"Actually," said Roxy in her best I'm-giving-a-lecture voice, "that's a perfectly normal response to a miracle."

"I'm not ready to label it a miracle."

"Of course you're not." Roxy favored him with an indulgent smile. "What do you do for a living?"

"Mother—"

"I'm a petroleum geologist," Jake answered.

"Ah! A scientist. Well, of course this is giving you serious difficulty. It seems to fly in the face of all known physical laws."

"Exactly!" Jake looked like a man who'd at last found another sane person on the planet.

Rainbow looked at her mother, wondering how Roxy managed to do it. Even Walter had liked her and had never felt "creeped out" by her. Now Jake appeared about to become another Roxy Resnick conquest.

"Have you ever been married?" Roxy asked.

"Mother!" Rainbow was appalled. Surely Roxy wasn't going to vet Jake as a potential mate.

But Jake suddenly grinned, as if he were enjoying himself hugely. The wicked sparkle in his eyes made Rainbow uneasy.

"No, I've never been married," he said. "Have you?"

"Once, long ago," Roxy said. "Morris Feldman, the novelist."

"Really?"

"He was a dear soul, but we just weren't meant for one another. And after Morris, well . . . no one else could quite measure up." Roxy looked at him sharply. "Are you too critical?"

"I like to think I'm a clear thinker."

She stabbed a finger at him. "You're evading my question, young man. You called my daughter a fraud. Is that your usual method of dealing with people?"

"Obviously not. I haven't called you one yet."

Rainbow held her breath, sure that her mother would erupt, but Roxy startled her with a hearty laugh.

Needing something to do, Rainbow poured tea for everyone and passed around the milk and sugar. Roxy bit into a doughnut with obvious relish and a few comments on the rubber chicken that seemed to have been a staple on the cruise. Dawn looked at Rainbow and rolled her eyes.

"I saw that," Roxy said to her.

Dawn shrugged. "From the moment we set foot on that boat, all you did was complain."

"There was plenty to complain about. I can't imagine why anyone would pay hundreds of dollars to have such a miserable time." She turned to Jake. "Don't ever take a cruise."

"I wasn't planning to."

Just then Rainbow heard her front door open. Moments later Gene, wearing a purple T-shirt that said, "My other shirt is in the wash," entered the kitchen.

"Gene!" Roxy shrieked. "Rainbow didn't tell me you were here!"

"Sorry to disappoint you, Roxy." He smiled at them all, dropped a kiss on Rainbow's and Dawn's cheeks, and gave Roxy a hug that she claimed was going to shatter her spine. Then he shook hands with Jake.

"Well, well," he said, "isn't this cozy?"

"We're just getting to know Jake," Roxy said.

"Cross examining him, you mean." He took a doughnut and looked at Jake. "Did she ask you what you *do?*"

"Yes." The corner of Jake's mouth lifted with humor.

"And whether you've ever been *married?*"

"We got to that."

"And how much you *make?*"

Jake shook his head. "We haven't discussed that yet."

Gene clucked his tongue and shook his head at Roxy. "You're falling down on the job, Rox. You should have had that out of him by the third sentence."

"It's none of my business," she replied with a sniff.

"Mm. I never knew that to stop you."

"Besides," she said airily, "Mustafa already told me."

Jake looked startled.

"Mother," Rainbow said swiftly, "please don't . . ."

"Why not?" Roxy demanded. "He may as well know us, warts and all, right from the start. It saves misunderstanding later—which you should have learned from Walter."

"Please," said Jake, "will somebody *please* tell me about Walter?"

Four pairs of eyes fixed on him. "Why?" Roxy demanded.

"Because he's been mentioned to me several times, and my curiosity is killing me. I'm envisioning a cross between Genghis Khan and Dracula."

Rainbow wanted to die. The last subject she wanted her family to discuss with Jake was Walter.

Roxy ignored her daughter's pained expression. "Is this just idle curiosity?" she demanded.

Jake grinned. "Probably. How could it be anything else when I don't know Walter?"

Roxy laughed, and Gene looked amused. Dawn and Rainbow exchanged glances of commiseration.

Rainbow spoke. "This really isn't appropriate, Mother."

"Mothers know best," Roxy replied with a dismissing wave of one plump beringed hand. "*Walter*," she said, in a disapproving tone that might well have been applied to a mass murderer, "was Rainbow's fiancé."

"Was?" he asked.

"Was," Roxy repeated.

Jake looked at Rainbow, and she was surprised by the gentle sympathy she saw in his face. "I guess," he said, "that Rainbow should be the one who tells me about him, then. And only if she wants to."

Rainbow gave him a grateful smile.

"Nonsense," said Roxy. "She can't *possibly* be objective."

"Neither can you, Mother," Rainbow said.

"Yes I can. I wasn't nearly as distressed by the breakup as you were. In fact, I wasn't distressed at all. That man was no good for you. The only thing I wonder about is why you were never able to see that yourself! Love is blind, I suppose."

Rainbow sighed and looked down into her teacup. There was no stopping Roxy, once she got rolling.

Gene tried to intervene. "Really, Rox, you shouldn't embarrass Rainy this way."

"How could I possibly embarrass her by saying that her former fiancé was a toad? It's not as if Rainbow did anything wrong!"

"Certainly," Gene said, "but . . ."

Roxy waved him to silence. "The man *was* a toad. Of course, that wasn't immediately apparent. All his warts were hidden in his mind. On the surface he appeared to be quite a nice young man. Well-mannered, handsome, successful."

"A stockbroker," Gene said.

"Well, not exactly," said Dawn, who had a tendency to be a stickler for details, probably as result of her experience in the courtroom. "He worked for a large brokerage as an analyst."

"Whatever," said Roxy, with a frown at Dawn. "He made money with other people's money. I personally think that can lead to a certain weakness of character in some people, you know. They are perfectly willing to take risks with other people's assets. There's something about that that troubles me."

"People in Walter's profession are often very ethical, Rox," Gene said mildly. "They tend to lose their jobs and go to prison if they aren't."

"There are ethics, and then there are ethics," Roxy said. "Be that as it may, this young prince was certainly a toad in disguise."

"Toad," Dawn agreed with an emphatic nod.

"This toad," Roxy continued, "wooed my daughter with great determination—until he had her where he wanted her. Reminded me rather of a predator, now that I think of it. Toads don't lure their prey, do they?"

"I'm sure I don't know," Jake said, the faintest hint of a laugh in his voice. He looked at Rainbow, and she saw the amusement there, warm and friendly amusement, as if he were really enjoying her mother.

Resigned, Rainbow sighed and waited for the rest of the tale to be told in Roxy's inimitable fashion, with detours every few paragraphs as she digressed into conversational byways.

"Well, I still think he was a toad," Roxy decided. "This toad, as it were, got engaged to my daughter and then proceeded to take advantage of her."

Rainbow looked sharply at her mother, wondering what the woman could possibly be thinking. Walter hadn't taken advantage of her.

"As soon as the ring was on her finger, he moved in with her. Now, I didn't object to that. After all, that's what people who love each other do, and I've never been very impressed with all that crap about waiting for marriage. In fact," Roxy said with a flourish of her hand, "I simply can't think of anything more appalling than putting two virgins into bed together on their wedding night! The blind leading the blind, if you ask me."

Rainbow flushed and stared fixedly at her tea, unwilling to see Jake's response to that pronouncement.

"All right," said Gene drily, "we understand that you didn't object to Walter simply because he moved in with your daughter."

"Certainly not," said Roxy. "What I objected to was the way he used her. Rainbow had her own business back then, too, you know. She saw clients all day, and quite often in the evenings and on weekends. This . . . this toad didn't seem to mind her working, but he contributed absolutely nothing to the household expenses once he moved in—I told you, Rainbow, that that wasn't right!"

"Yes, Mother." She wanted to sink right through the floor, just vanish and be swallowed up by the sandbar beneath her house.

"Well," Roxy continued, "Rainbow felt that it was better that way. She wasn't beholden, she said. It gave her freedom. Yes, certainly it gave her freedom.

Freedom to cook all the meals, and do all the laundry and cleaning, because poor, dear Walter was exhausted after a day of slaving in the financial mines."

"He *was* a toad," Jake commented.

"Exactly," Roxy said approvingly. "But of course, Rainbow didn't ditch him. He ditched *her*."

"But why?"

"Well, all along he'd been treating her psychic abilities as if they were some amusing child's game. Patting her on the head like a puppy," Roxy said sourly, "until she made a prediction he couldn't ignore. Then he said she was too creepy, and he moved out."

"Definitely a toad," Jake said, with even more emphasis than before.

"Well, you seem to be a little better," Roxy observed bluntly. "At least you're not claiming to be creeped out by the chair on the ceiling."

"Creepy isn't the word I'd use. Perplexing is more like it. What's creepy is . . . well, I hate to say this out loud, because I'm not real comfortable with the feeling."

Roxy leaned forward avidly, and even Rainbow watched him intently.

He shrugged. "I keep getting the feeling I'm being watched."

"Ooooh," said Roxy with delight.

"Really?" Intrigued, Rainbow forgot about the grief her mother was putting her through. "How often?"

"It comes and goes, but it's been pretty persistent since I moved in."

Roxy looked at Rainbow. "He's got a touch of ability, doesn't he?"

"Maybe."

Jake looked uncomfortable. "I don't know about

that. I mean—well, I always know when someone's watching me, but I don't think the feeling is that uncommon. Most people seem to sense it. This is different only because there's nobody there."

Rainbow felt her opinion of Jake rise two or three notches. It couldn't have been easy for him to admit he was feeling watched, particularly to this crew, with their automatic bias about the probable source of the feeling.

"I wasn't going to say anything about it to anyone," Jake said. "But then there's that chair on my ceiling."

"It does kind of make it interesting," Gene remarked. "The feeling could be dismissed, but not with the chair hanging up there."

"Joe's chair," Rainbow said quietly, and Jake's blue eyes met hers, conveying a whole mixture of conflicting feelings.

"Joe's chair," he agreed quietly.

"Well, that does it," said Roxy. "I have to go see this chair right now."

Jake took Roxy and Dawn in his car, and Gene rode with Rainbow in hers. It was nearing sunset, and the sky was streaked with vermilion clouds.

"Where were you all day?" Rainbow asked her uncle.

"Well, I had to film a spot for that environmental group this morning. I actually had to stand in the middle of a bunch of alligators."

"I'd have been scared to death!"

"Nah," he said with a grin. "They'd been fed right before filming, and none of them seemed to want to move a muscle. Besides, I'm bigger than anything in their usual diet."

"I still would have been scared. I like alligators, but in their proper place."

"Well, they'd have a proper place if people would stop draining wetlands to build new houses."

"True."

"And after the filming, Nellie and I had lunch together and then went to the mall. It was too damn hot to do anything outside."

She glanced at him. "Nellie, hm?"

"Now, don't go getting any ideas. I just met the woman. She likes my T-shirts, though."

"That's a definite mark in her favor."

"I certainly think so."

"You would," Rainbow said on a laugh.

The condominium parking lot was full, and it looked as if most of the residents were out on the side patio. When they stepped out of their cars, they could smell the delicious odors of a barbeque.

"I wonder if the ghosts are flipping out again," Rainbow said, as they got out of the car.

"No, this was a scheduled event," Gene said. "Nellie invited me, but I thought I ought to come home and spend a few minutes with you before I dashed out again."

Rainbow looked at him with amusement. "Really, Uncle Gene, I'm a big girl. I won't be crushed just because you prefer Nellie's company to mine."

Gene winced. "I deserved that."

But Rainbow went off into a peal of laughter that let him know she'd only been teasing. They joined the other three and crossed the parking lot toward the building entrance.

Nellie saw Gene and waved him over.

"I'll be back in a few minutes," he called to her.

"Bring everyone along with you," Nellie called back. "We need some fresh faces."

Paradise Towers was rarely noisy, but tonight it was utterly silent. If any of the residents remained indoors, they must have been reading or sleeping.

The elevator carried them up to Jake's floor.

"If the building were settling," Gene remarked, "at least if it were settling enough to throw things around, the elevator wouldn't be working."

"That's what *I* thought," Jake agreed, "but I contacted an engineering firm anyway. They'll be out tomorrow to look it over. Better safe than sorry."

"It's a waste of money," Roxy said bluntly. "If my daughter says this place is haunted, it's haunted."

"Not everyone agrees with you, Mother," Rainbow said drily.

Roxy shrugged. "So what? People have been disagreeing with me my entire life. It hasn't kept me from being *right*."

From the corner of her eye, Rainbow saw Jake struggle to suppress a grin. She certainly couldn't blame him. Roxy could be utterly outrageous.

At the door to Jake's apartment, they eagerly clustered around. In fact, Jake was the only one who didn't seem eager. Rainbow noted the way he hesitated before putting his key in the lock.

He caught her watching him and gave her a rueful grin. "I can't make up my mind what I want more— to find the chair still on the ceiling, or to find it back where it belongs."

She nodded sympathetically, and without stopping to think about it, reached out to lay a reassuring hand on his arm.

As she did, she saw the leap of fire in his gaze. She snatched her hand back as if she'd been burned. He shouldn't be able to make her feel like this with a simple look. He shouldn't be able to deprive her of breath and turn her knees to water, and start a pagan drumbeat in her blood!

She tore her gaze from his and forced herself to look down at his hand and the key that still hesitated right in front of the lock.

He shoved it in, turned it, and pushed the door open. Reaching in, he flipped a switch, filling the living room with light, then stepped back to let the others enter before him.

"My heavens!" Roxy exclaimed in a tone of utter ecstasy, "this is *wonderful*."

Rainbow, peering over her mother's shoulder, saw that a floor lamp had joined the chair on the ceiling.

"Oh, come on," Jake said, crowding in behind them. "Not another one!"

All of a sudden the door of the apartment slammed shut behind them and all the lights went out.

Ten

For a long moment, no one moved, or even breathed. Then a babble of voices broke out and people started bumping into one another as they tried to move.

"Everybody hold still," Jake said. "I know where there's a flashlight."

He eased his way past Rainbow and Roxy, then held his hands in front of him as he tried to remember the exact layout of the furniture.

"Why is it so dark in here?" Dawn asked. "There ought at least to be light from the windows."

"The curtains are closed," Jake replied.

"Why?" demanded Roxy.

"Because," Jake explained, with just the faintest hint of exasperation in his voice, "this unit has a beautiful view of the Gulf."

A moment passed before Roxy said, "What in the world does he mean by that?"

"It has a western exposure, Mother," Rainbow explained. "The sun must make it unbearably hot in here in the late afternoon."

"Oh."

"This place cooks like an oven if I don't draw the

curtains," Jake said, then swore. "Damn! How did that table get there?"

Just then the lights came back on, and the five of them blinked in the sudden brilliance. Jake stood in the middle of the living room, his shins against a coffee table that appeared to have moved three feet in the few brief moments of darkness.

"Oh!" said Roxy, "this is wonderful! *Wonderful!*"

"That's a matter of opinion," Jake said irritably. "Furniture moving in the dark is *not* something I'd call wonderful."

But Roxy ignored him, sailing into the center of the room with her hands clasped in delight. "I've never seen anything like this!" she said. "Never! Imagine the forces it must take to keep a chair *and* a lamp on the ceiling."

"The lamp's a new addition," Rainbow said, approaching it cautiously.

"It sure wasn't up there when I left earlier," Jake admitted. He looked almost glum as he stared at the dangling furnishings.

"Remarkable," said Gene, his voice lacking its customary amusement. "Has anyone taken pictures?"

"Who'd believe them?" Dawn said prosaically. "Those could be fastened to the ceiling by bolts or something. That's what everyone would believe."

"You don't need engineers," Roxy said, turning to Jake, her eyes alight. "You need the Association for Psychical Research."

"I don't think so," Jake said, looking horrified.

"Don't be so narrow-minded," Roxy scolded. "Can your science explain this?"

"Not yet," Jake said.

"And it never will, unless it takes an open mind on the subject."

"It's true," Rainbow told Jake. "Here we have evidence of something that can't be explained by ordinary physical laws. It deserves further examination."

Jake gave her a half smile. "Even if I brought in a team of scientists, could anyone guarantee that chair and lamp would still be on the ceiling by the time they arrive? Murphy's Law, you know."

"He's probably right, Rainbow," Roxy said. "It's a message meant for him, anyway."

"For me?" Jake looked uncertainly at the chair.

"Well, of course," Roxy said tartly. "It's on *your* ceiling! It certainly isn't directed at the Secretary General of the United Nations!"

"Oh."

Gene, meanwhile, had crossed the room, and now gave the chair a gentle nudge. As if it were on skates, it sailed a few feet across the ceiling. "Fascinating," he remarked. "Absolutely fascinating."

He gave the lamp a little nudge, and it too sailed across the room, stopping beside the chair.

"Well," said Gene, "it certainly isn't bolted or glued in place. Now, a large magnet on the floor above . . ."

Jake came over to stand beside the chair, shaking his head. "Imagine how big it would have to be. And I doubt there's enough metal in the chair for a magnet overcome the pull of gravity anyway."

"You're probably right." Gene poked at the chair again, putting it back out of the way in its corner. Jake pushed the lamp and it stopped in its original position beside the chair.

"You know," Gene said, "it's interesting the way that lamp always stops next to the chair."

"Yeah."

"We need videotape," Dawn said suddenly, "videotape of the chair and lamp moving. That'd be proof."

Jake shook his head. "I don't know if I want proof of this."

Rainbow looked at him in amazement. "Why not? A tape would prove we haven't all lost our minds."

"It'd prove nothing except that someone found a way to rig this setup. Or that someone knows how to do special effects."

"Oh."

Roxy and Dawn sat on the couch. Jake and Gene stayed where they were, studying the chair.

"What does Mustafa say, Mother?" Rainbow asked.

"He's being suspiciously quiet—which probably means he's up to something."

"What could Mustafa possibly be up to?"

"I don't know." Roxy shrugged as if it were of no consequence, but Rainbow didn't believe it for a minute.

"Who is Mustafa?" Jake asked.

"One of my guides." Roxy twitched her caftan with one hand, and reached up to straighten her turban. "He's usually very helpful."

"He's usually very talkative," Dawn said bluntly. "Getting him to be quiet is the problem most of the time."

Jake looked uneasily from the ceiling chair to Roxy. "I'm having trouble with this," he said. "Somebody help me here."

"How can we?" Roxy asked. "If you don't believe, you don't believe. If I tell you a ghost put that chair on your ceiling, and that my spirit guide is refusing to discuss the matter, what are you going to do with that? Ignore it? Probably."

"I don't know. I don't seem to know anything anymore." Jake sat with a thump on the wing chair and put his chin in his hand.

Rainbow started to feel sorry for him. This had to

be very trying, after all. It was so alien to everything he believed.

"Now, don't get into a funk," Roxy said, in her usual perfunctory manner.

Jake straightened. "I'm not, I'm thinking."

"I wouldn't blame you if you got into a funk," Roxy said magnanimously. "It's . . . overwhelming."

Jake snorted and looked at the chair. "Actually, I'm underwhelmed. Just for the sake of argument, if that chair really *is* a message, what's it *saying?*"

Roxy shrugged. "It would be helpful, I suppose, if the ghost had written a note."

Almost in spite of himself, Jake felt a smile began to creep across his face. "That's asking for a bit much, isn't it? I mean, here we have a chair and a lamp on the ceiling, and we're asking for *notes?*"

Roxy waved a hand. "Why not? It never hurts to ask. Besides, ghosts are the most annoying creatures. They never do anything in a straightforward manner."

Rainbow spoke. "What isn't straightforward about a chair on the ceiling? How much clearer and more believable can you get if you want to send a message that ghosts are here?"

"True," said Roxy.

Jake looked as if he'd just swallowed something unpleasant. "Still," he said finally, "if there's any other message, it's escaping me."

Rainbow turned to him. "Then you admit there are ghosts here?"

Jake hesitated, then shook his head. "I'll allow I'm reluctantly considering the possibility, but I won't be convinced until I'm absolutely positive there's no other explanation."

"Such as?"

"Oh, I don't know. What about a gravitational anomaly?"

"Then why aren't you floating beside the chair?" Rainbow countered.

He gave her a sour look as Gene chuckled.

"She's got you there," Gene said.

Jake nodded and gave Rainbow a look of respect. "You don't leap to conclusions, do you?"

"No." She smiled too brightly. "In spite of your initial impression, I *can* be a critical thinker."

"I never said you weren't!"

"Right. However, I *do* think critically, I *did* go to college, and the only difference between the way you and I think is that I allow a greater range of possibilities than you do."

"Still," he argued, "I'm not convinced there isn't an explanation that fits within the laws of physics."

"The laws of physics don't necessarily rule out paranormal experiences," Rainbow shot back. "The problem with science is that by emphasizing experimentation as the only way to prove anything, it totally disregards eyewitness reports! Look at ball lightning."

"What about ball lightning?"

"It's been reported throughout recorded history, but since science can't duplicate it in a laboratory, they're still arguing about whether it really exists! Well, it's the same with paranormal experiences. An extraordinary number of people claim to have them, but science shrugs it off, pointing to the fact that these people can't duplicate the experience in a laboratory setting. So? Nobody is claiming that paranormal experience is as reliable or commonplace as speech, and most laboratory testing overlooks the emotional factor that exists in most paranormal events."

He spread his hands, not exactly agreeing, but not exactly disagreeing, either.

"Then," Rainbow continued, on a roll now, "we

have that magician what's-his-name who claims that because he can reproduce a paranormal event through ordinary means, it indicates that it was nothing but a fraud to begin with. That's the worst case of faulty logic I've ever encountered!"

Jake nodded. "I have to agree with you there."

"Why?" Roxy asked.

"It's quite simple, Mother. Finding one way of reproducing a result does not mean its the *only* way. Consider. If I throw a soccer ball into the net, does that necessarily mean someone else couldn't *kick* it into the net? Or conversely, just because I didn't— or couldn't—kick the ball into the net, does that mean no one else could?"

Roxy nodded, impressed. Gene applauded silently.

"You're right," Jake said. "You're absolutely right. You know I don't believe in paranormal events, but I've always been troubled that scientists have fallen prey to that kind of thinking."

"When they do that," Rainbow finished off roundly, "they're not being scientific. They're being *debunkers*. And they're clothing their personal prejudices in the religion of science."

Jake nodded. "I'll grant you that much," he said with a crooked smile. "However, the chair is still on my ceiling, and I'm damned if I know why."

"Well that's a step forward," Joe said to Lucinda. She was reclining on their cloud, juggling fluffy little balls of cloud-stuff. "He's at least beginning to consider other possibilities."

Lucy sighed, wishing Joe would get over his fascination with being on a cloud. She wanted that wing chair more than ever, and tossing balls of cloud-stuff was an act of desperation. "Can we get a regular living room, Joe?"

"Why?" He looked at her, momentarily distracted from Jake. "All my life I believed when I died I'd float on clouds."

"I know, dear, but . . . well, it's such a cliché."

He laughed. "I know—I love it." Then he sobered. "Just a little longer, Lucy? If you really want a regular living room, we'll do that next, okay?"

She felt her heart melt at his boyish eagerness. "All right, dear." She tossed a ball of cloud-stuff in the air and willed it to stay suspended. It did. She could wait a little longer for her easy chair, she decided.

Joe returned his attention to Jake. "The boy is getting a real shock here, Lucy. He needs it."

"I still don't know why you think it's so important," she said. One of her balls landed on Joe's back. He didn't notice, and it vanished instantly. Lucinda tossed the rest of her balls away and rolled over to look at Joe. "I thought you wanted justice. We're not getting any closer to that at all."

He flashed her a grin. "First things first, my love." He touched her chin gently. "When he starts to believe, everything else will fall into place. You'll see."

Lucinda shook her head. "I have a bad feeling about this, Joe. So far, all you've really managed to do with this is introduce Gene and Nellie. And pardon me, but I don't think that's such a good idea. He's a ladies' man. He'll love her and leave her, and she'll be worse off than ever."

"Well, that was an unexpected side effect," he admitted. "I never imagined that. For heaven's sake, Lucy, he was all the way in California when I started this."

"Mmm." Lucy picked up a handful of cloud-stuff and threw it at him. "And what about Rainbow? She likes Jake, but they're never going to find common ground. They're too different in outlook. They may have an affair, but it'll never last. He'll never be able to live with her psychic abilities, and she'll be hurt all over again."

"I'm working on that."

"That's what worries me." She sighed and looked down from their cloud. "I guess it's time for me to empty a watering pot on Gene's head—before Nellie gets in any deeper."

"You want me to put a chair on her ceiling, too?"

She frowned at him. "You've already done quite enough, Joe. It's time for me to start mending things."

He shook his head. "Careful, sweetheart. Some things here are happening of their own accord, and I'm not sure we should interfere too much."

"You should have thought of that before you started!"

Joe sighed and looked dubious, but he'd never yet been able to keep Lucy from doing something once her mind was made up.

As her family was getting ready to return home, Rainbow looked at Jake. "You never did say why you came over this evening."

He looked uncomfortable, glancing at Gene, Roxy, and Dawn, all of whom were clearly listening intently while pretending not to. "I, um, thought you might want to go for a walk on the beach."

"Oh, well my mother and sister just arrived—"

"Of course she wants to go," Roxy said, "and we don't mind in the least, do we? Rainbow, give your keys to Gene. He can drive us home."

"But I haven't figured out where everyone is going to sleep."

Roxy clucked her tongue. "I've been a mother a long time, my dear. We'll sort it out by the time you get home. I *do* remember how to make up a bed, you know."

Gene took the keys from Rainbow, giving her a wink. "Outmaneuvered, my dear."

She scowled at him, but he was already ushering the other two women from the apartment. Then they were alone—except for the ghosts, of course, a presence Rainbow could sense but not get a firm handle on.

"I'm sorry," Jake said. "I didn't mean to put you on the spot. If you'd really rather go home, I'll drive you."

She was touched by his uncertainty, and his willingness to offer her an escape. Walter had been very different, assuming from the outset that he was God's gift to her, and that he was always right. Insecure herself, she had initially liked his confidence, although it had begun to wear a little thin toward the end.

"I really *would* like to walk on the beach," she admitted. "I just don't like being maneuvered."

"Sorry about that."

"Oh, I didn't mean you. I meant my mother." She shrugged and smiled. "I ought to be used to it by now. But let's get out of here. I don't feel—alone."

He looked almost sheepish. "I *do* feel like I'm being watched again."

"We are. I just wish I could figure out what they want."

"They?"

"Two of them. A man and a woman." She didn't offer any more because he was getting that "Oh, God, I want to get away from this" look, and right now she didn't want to deal with it either. Not the ghosts, not the furnishings on the ceiling, not her mother nor her uncle, and nothing remotely related to the paranormal. For just a little while, she wanted everything to be *normal.*

For a little while, she wanted to forget that there was a gulf so wide and deep between her and Jake that not even his forbearance could bridge it. For a little while she wanted to be an ordinary woman, just like every other woman in the world.

Jake left a light on and locked the apartment behind them. "I wonder what I'll find on the ceiling when I get back," he joked.

"I don't even want to think about it," Rainbow said honestly.

"Neither do I," he admitted. "It's as if there's this great big stumbling block in my brain, and I keep banging my shins on it."

She nodded, understanding exactly what he meant.

Their escape to the beach was not quite so easy, though. Downstairs, the patio party was still in full swing. Gene, Roxy, and Dawn had joined the crowd, and everyone else seemed to want Jake and Rainbow to join in, too.

It took a few minutes, but they finally made their escape, leaving behind a lot of knowing looks. Rainbow took off her sandals and they walked across the white sand down to the water's edge. The moon hung high in the east, dappling the water with silver. The waves were gentle tonight, the roar of the surf muted. Far out on the water they could see the lights of a day-cruise ship heading toward harbor.

"Have you ever taken one of those day cruises?" Jake asked her.

"No, never. Most of them are for gambling, and I don't have any interest."

"Still, I hear they provide good food and music."

"I imagine so." She shrugged. "I don't know. I just never thought it would be exciting to ride a boat out past the twelve-mile limit so I could eat and drink while other people spend hours gambling. Does it appeal to you?"

He smiled, his teeth glinting white in the moonlight. "Being away from everyone and everything appeals to me. The longer I live in that building, the more I feel the urge."

"Are your neighbors bothering you?"

"Not exactly. But being president of the association means I'm seeing more of some of them than I'd like. I was envisioning this quiet year of writing my book. Instead, I'm worrying about finding engineering firms, and whether the building's plumbing needs an update, and whether Elsie Murchison ought to be able to hang flowerboxes on her balcony railing."

"Can she?"

He shook his head. "Strictly forbidden by the covenants. She may never speak to me again."

"That's a shame."

"Oh, I don't know." He laughed and shook his head. "There are worse things I can imagine than that woman never speaking to me again. She's a born pain in the you-know-what."

Rainbow laughed, too, but the laughter died as he reached out and took her hand, depriving her instantly of breath.

For an instant she felt almost stunned at how good it felt to have her hand tucked in his, how warm and dry the callused skin of his palm was. That simple touch caused a soft, melting feeling to spread throughout her entire body. Never had she felt so soft inside.

Together they started walking south along the water's edge, toward the quieter, darker end of the beach.

"It's a beautiful night," he remarked.

"Yes." She couldn't have said any more, simply because she was having trouble inhaling.

"I love the breeze here at night," he continued. "It's so cool and dry, coming off the land."

"Yes."

He squeezed her hand, driving the last breath from her body. "The sea turtles should be hatching soon. I hope I get to see it."

She didn't reply. It seemed more important to concentrate on putting one foot in front of the other in the cool, damp sand. It seemed more important to let the warmth spread from his palm throughout her entire body.

He continued, "Someone told me the reason they don't allow outside lights at night on the sea side of the building is because of the turtles."

She nodded, and finally managed to draw a full breath. She hoped he didn't hear the faint tremor in her voice. "Sea turtles tend to lay their eggs on dark beaches. If there's too much light, they go back out to sea. If the turtles nest, the babies hatch at night, and when they do, they head for the brightest horizon. Back when there were no people, that was the sea. Unfortunately, even if the buildings have no light on the backside, there's still too much light from town. It confuses the hatchlings and they head the wrong way."

"That's sad."

"At least people are trying," she said. Pointing to an area of beach that was staked off and surrounded on three sides by mesh, she continued, "That's a turtle's nest right there. The mesh is there to encouraged the hatchlings to head toward the water."

"That's a great idea."

"Unfortunately, only one out of a thousand hatchlings will survive to adulthood." She shook her head sadly. "And of course, with each passing year, their habitat grows smaller."

"Somehow I don't think we can make people give up their beachfront homes."

"Of course not. But there's probably a lot we could do."

"Such as?"

"Turn off all the unnecessary lights at night, instead of keeping the place lit up like the World's Fair. Be more careful with beach renourishment, so we don't make the sand inhospitable for nesting. There are probably dozens of things; I'm no expert. But I did see a turtle lay her eggs once. And a few years ago, I actually saw the hatchlings crawl out of a nest."

"I'd really like to see that."

"Come down here every night and watch that nest. You might have to stay out until all hours for a while, but you'll get to see it."

"Maybe I will. Would you like to watch with me?"

She caught her breath, and nearly missed a step. "Um . . . I'll think about it."

He squeezed her hand again, and this time she squeezed back. The sand was cool, damp, and sensuous beneath her feet, and the breeze tossed her hair, causing it to caress her cheeks and neck.

And inevitably she found herself wishing it were Jake who was caressing her with gentle, suggestive touches. He was such an attractive man with his sun-bronzed skin and his blue eyes, but it was his smile that really melted her. When he smiled, his entire face smiled, creasing the corners of his eyes in a way she found irresistible.

She was surprised that he wanted to spend time with her, given their differences of opinion on matters she considered extremely important, but right now she didn't want to worry about it. All she wanted to think about was how beautiful the evening was, and how good it felt to be strolling along the beach with her hand in his.

She knew she was taking a risk by allowing herself to feel these things. Disappointment would follow; it always did. But the risk was exhilarating anyway, the emotional equivalent of the time she had gone parasailing and had felt like a seagull soaring high above the beach and the swimmers below.

They found a hole of darkness created by the shadow of a building that blocked the streetlights behind it. Only the moon touched them here with its silvery glow. The surf pounded its steady rhythm, sealing them off from the other sounds of the world.

Jake paused with Rainbow beside him. When he turned to face her, she knew what was coming. It was too soon, some little voice in her head warned her, even as her heart leapt with eagerness. But it would always been too soon for the two of them, she argued back—always. There would never be a right time or a right place when they were poles apart in what they believed.

This was a moment stolen out of time, and she was entitled to it. Why shouldn't she take what life offered if she was willing to pay the price for it later?

And it had been so long, so very long, since the last time a man had wanted to hold her and kiss her. When she was younger, men had been more eager to touch her, and she had been more willing to accept their advances. But with time, she had become more particular, and so had the men near her age. Since Walter there had been no one, and even her dates with the chief of police had been platonic rather than romantic.

But tonight was romantic. The moon, the sea, the

sand, and the cocoon of shadows conspired to make the night magic.

And Jake. His face was shadowed, but his eyes gleamed. He stepped closer and she could feel his warmth beckoning to her across the gentle breeze. Unconsciously she tipped her head back, signaling her welcome. She wanted this; oh, how she wanted this! Her heart beat rapidly even as she felt her insides liquefy.

He reached out, wrapping his arms around her, giving her an astonishing impression of his leashed strength, and then she was pressed to the hard breadth of his chest, feeling his solidity like an anchor as the world around them vanished.

He murmured something, but his words were lost in the pounding of the surf and the pounding of her pulse in her veins. His head bowed, a mysterious and entrancing mask of shadows and silvery light from the moon, coming closer.

She felt as if she hovered on the brink of some dangerous and exciting journey. Her breath caught in her throat, and a thrill very like fear shot through her. Then his lips found hers, drowning her in a sea of sensation.

Warm and firm, his mouth found hers, caressing gently, tasting sweetly. Her hands lifted, clinging to his shoulders, and her head fell back as she surrendered to a kiss so exquisite she could hardly believe it was real.

He was so hard and warm against her, and his strong hands caressed her back gently, seeming to cherish her. Every nerve ending in her body awoke, soaking up sensation, storing it up, savoring it. It had been so long . . . so long . . . so long.

He deepened the kiss, running his tongue along the crease between her lips until she opened to him, inviting him in. Then his tongue tangled with hers, at first teasing and taunting, and then settling into a rhythm that made her knees go weak. A heaviness filled her center, a slow, warm, pulsing weight that drove her to press even closer.

His shoulders beneath her hands were hard and powerful, and her palms joined the play, running over them, measuring them, loving them. One of his hands slipped down her back until it cupped her bottom and pressed her even more firmly against him, sending a sharp thrill of delight to her very center.

Yes, oh yes! She felt as if she had been lifted on the waves, and they were rocking her gently, lifting her higher and higher. The ache between her thighs was growing harder, compelling her, driving everything else from her mind. With just a kiss . . . just a kiss . . .

And then he was gone. He lifted his mouth from hers and tilted his head back, looking straight up at the heavens, his mouth open and his eyes closed.

But he didn't let go of her. He held her, steadying her as she struggled to find her way back to reality. Little by little she became aware of the sand beneath her feet, of the stars wheeling overhead, and the pounding of the surf was no longer inside her.

And she was once again on the beach with a man she hardly knew, held more intimately to him than seemed wise. Fear pierced her, and suddenly she felt as if she were standing alone on a cold, windy precipice. She considered stepping back, trying to regain her distance as well as her space, but then he looked down at her and smiled.

"Wow!" he said.

Rainbow felt herself smiling back at him, and suddenly everything was okay. She was no longer alone in the world into which his touch had catapulted

her. He had come there with her, and somehow that
made her feel so much safer.

He released her with obvious reluctance, pausing
to drop a gentle kiss on her cheek. For an instant she
hoped he was going to sweep her up into another
embrace, but it was not to be. He gave her another
soft kiss, this one on her lower lip, then seemed to
shake himself.

He stepped back, still smiling, and took her hand
again. They started walking, this time heading toward her house.

"I like your mother," he said, clearly trying to find
a safe avenue of conversation.

"She can be a pill."

"I imagine so." He shook his head and gave a low
chuckle, the sound barely audible above the surf.
"Still, she's fun and opinionated. I guess you never
have to wonder where you stand with her."

"That's a fact."

"My father died when I was very young," he said.
"My mom had to work, and Uncle Joe was more of
a father to me than an uncle. I really miss him."

It was on the tip of her tongue to tell him that Joe
was watching over him, but she bit the words back.
And that, she thought unhappily, was the whole reason it was foolish to let this man kiss her. If she
couldn't tell him things like that for fear of upsetting
him, there was absolutely no hope for them, other
than as friends.

Sorrow hovered around her, but it was a familiar
sorrow, and she brushed it aside. There was no
point, she told herself, mooning over things that
would never be hers.

Paradise Beach was a small community, and the
distance between the Towers and her home was an
easy walk, even on the sand. They said little, but that
didn't surprise Rainbow. He must feel the gaping

distance between them as surely as she did.

At her door, he bent and brushed a light kiss on her cheek, released her hand, and said good night.

Rainbow didn't wait to watch him walk away. She had watched too many men walk away in her life and refused to watch again. Inside, she leaned back against the door, listening to the sounds of the silent house and the faint clatter of palm fronds in the breeze outside.

Straightening her shoulders, she walked toward the kitchen to make herself some tea.

She was alone again except for her family. She ought to be used to that by now.

Jake walked home, enjoying the balmy breeze and the rustle of the wind in the trees that lined the street. He was used to feeling alone—hell, he had years of experience at it, ever since he'd taken his first oil job—but he wasn't used to feeling lonely.

Tonight he felt lonely, and he knew Rainbow was the cause of it. Oh, she hadn't intended to be, but she was anyway. First there was her family, so wonderfully close, from what he'd seen of them tonight. He had no family at all anymore, and he missed it more than he wanted to think about.

And then there was Rainbow, as far out of his reach as if she were cased in glass and living on another planet. He shouldn't have kissed her. It had done nothing but show him exactly how much was beyond his reach.

But she had felt so good and so right in his arms. Something inside him had seemed to uncoil and relax into the delicious sea of desire she'd awakened in him, and he'd never had that feeling before, as if he had never before been totally able to let go.

The feeling was as enticing as the passion she awoke in him, and he was genuinely sorry that he'd never know it again. But to go any further with her would be to trifle with her, because the gaping chasm between them was unbridgeable, and they both knew it.

He didn't want to go back to his empty apartment with the chair on the ceiling, and he didn't want to go back to the feeling of being watched by unseen eyes.

Much as he hated to admit it, he really *was* beginning to wonder if Joe were lingering in the apartment, keeping an eye on things.

It wasn't that he didn't believe in an afterlife, because he did. But he had a whole lot of trouble believing that people who had died would bother to linger on earth, disturbing the living and hanging things from ceilings. To his way of thinking, once you moved on, you moved on. There was no reason Joe should want to come back and mix things up, let alone be able to. Life and death were separate universes; and they weren't supposed to collide.

Which was maybe a very narrow view, he admitted to himself. If there was life after death, then why *shouldn't* the dead be able to communicate with those they had left behind?

But if Joe was trying to communicate, he wasn't doing a very good job of it. The chair on the ceiling, while being both shocking and fascinating, said nothing.

Except that maybe Joe *was* there. And maybe that's all Joe wanted him to know. Maybe it was the ghostly version of the good-night hug Joe used to give him when he was a child. Maybe it was just Joe's crazy way of saying, "I love you and I'm still around."

He could live with that. Although he could live with it a whole lot better if the furniture would come down off the ceiling.

He managed to get back into his unit without running into any of the residents, a feat he was beginning to consider a major triumph. Since he had been elected association president, he couldn't stick his head out the door without being bearded for a conversation or a complaint.

He shouldn't feel bad about that, he reminded himself. It was better to know his neighbors than be a stranger in the building, and most of them seemed like genuinely nice people.

But he was used to a certain degree of mental privacy, and he didn't feel like he was getting it here. Oh, well.

Inside the apartment, he stood leaning against the closed door. The light was out. Hadn't they left it on? It was definitely out now, and the curtains were open. He was sure they'd been closed. Through the uncovered window, he could see his balcony, the shadowy shapes of the furniture out there, and the moon.

The moon was huge now as it sank toward the water, a silver orb that seemed to hold a smiling face. The Man in the Moon. His uncle said that as a child Jake had talked to the Man in the Moon, carrying on entire conversations with it.

As he stood there, Jake found himself wondering what had happened to that fanciful child. When had he become so mired in realism that he could no longer feel the magic?

He had felt magic tonight, though, in his embrace with Rainbow. It should have exhilarated him, but instead it scared him to death.

There be dragons . . . he felt as if he were standing on the very edge of the world, in danger of tumbling off.

Shaking off the melancholy mood, he flipped the

light switch and stood stunned. The end table was
now on the ceiling.

"Christ, Joe," he heard himself say, "what the hell
are you up to *now*?"

Eleven

JAKE WAS NOT IN THE BEST OF MOODS WHEN HE WOKE
in the morning. He had spent the night tossing and
turning, and fighting with the bedclothes and his pillow. He felt as if he'd been in a boxing match, with
the remnants of a nightmare preying on his mind.
He had dreamed of falling down a deep, dark well,
becoming smaller and smaller until he vanished.

The first word out of his mouth was a curse, and
that was unusual. He was typically a bright, cheerful
riser, but this morning he felt ornery enough to chew
nails.

And he didn't want to go into his living room. He
avoided it for as long as he could, delaying in the
shower until the water ran cold, and brushing his
teeth until his gums felt raw—but finally he had to
face it. Dressed, he put his hand on the doorknob
and offered a silent but heartfelt prayer that his living room would be back to normal.

In fact, if he had any wish at all, it was that the
whole mess would go away and he could convince
himself it had been some kind of temporary mental
aberration resulting from jet lag and culture shock.

Yet he knew that wasn't going to happen.

With a sigh, he opened the door, then groaned.

Not only were the chair and the lamp on the ceiling, but the end table had remained from last night still bearing its load of magazines as well as Joe's pipe rack, tobacco cannister and ashtray. At least nothing new had been added since he'd turned on the light last night.

He stood in the bedroom doorway, surveying the insanity his life had become, and tried to decide on the best course of action.

He could always move out, of course, but he doubted he'd find anything on the beach to rent long term. Tourist season was right around the corner, and everything was probably booked from the first of October.

Or he could stay right here and try to deal with furniture on his ceiling and the increasingly likely possibility that Joe was trying to tell him something from beyond the grave.

Neither option was palatable.

He went into the small galley kitchen to make coffee, and froze when he saw Joe's favorite mug sitting beside the coffeepot, as if waiting to be filled. That mug had been in the cupboard last night. Of that he was absolutely sure.

He stared at the mug and accepted the inevitable.

"Okay, Joe," he said aloud. "You win. I believe it's you doing this. God knows how or why. So if you're trying to tell me something, you'd better find a clearer way to do it. And in the meantime, I'd appreciate it if you'd put the furniture back where it belongs."

Nothing changed. Of course, he hadn't expected it to. That was the whole problem with this. Weird things were happening, but they were happening in such a way that he couldn't really trust them. Now, if the furniture had moved back, he'd have been able to believe beyond any shadow of a doubt that Joe *was* behind this.

But the stuff was still on the ceiling, and he was left in his quandary without answers.

Mentally throwing up his hands, he started to make coffee.

"You know, Joe, this is spectacular," he said to the empty apartment. "I'm impressed. Really. And it's so very much like you to do something spectacular when simple handwriting on the wall would be far more effective!"

Although, he found himself admitting, he'd have been more likely to dismiss a signed, handwritten note on the wall. He couldn't dismiss furniture on his ceiling.

"Okay," he said. There was a knock at the door, and he put down the coffee cannister and went to answer it. "Okay," he said again to the living room, "you have my attention, damn it! *Now let me know what you want.*"

He flung the door open and found Trixie Martins standing there. Trixie was one of the residents he had lately come to recognize from encounters in the hallways. She was about seventy and plainly proud of her bustline, since she always wore tight knit tops in loud colors and push-up bras. Jake found himself continually trying not to stare at her remarkable bust, which always preceded her like the prow of a ship.

This morning she was wearing a shocking pink T-shirt over her impressive bosom, tight white leggings, high-heeled white sandals, and enough makeup to have decorated the entire female population of the building. Her hair, as usual, was lacquered into a high champagne blond beehive, reminiscent of a long-ago fashion trend.

"Hi, Jake," she said. For all her odd looks, Trixie

was a genuinely nice person, as far as he could tell. She gave him a warm smile that went a long way toward canceling her tawdry fashion taste. "Do you have company? I heard you talking." She tried to peer around him.

"Oh, I was just talking to myself," he said, trying not to open the door wide enough to let her see how matters had progressed in his living room. "Bad habit."

"Oh." She gave a nervous little laugh and backed up a step, which gave him room to breathe without bumping into her prow—er, bust.

"How are you?" he asked, holding the door so that little more than his head was visible. He felt like a jerk doing it, because it seemed so unfriendly. "Is something up?"

"My neighbor. All night." She rolled her eyes dramatically. "He was pounding on the walls. In fact, it sounded like he was throwing things. Anyway, he kept me up most of the night, and when I complained to him this morning, he slammed the door in my face." She rose on tiptoe, trying to see past him into the living room.

Jake straightened a little, blocking her view. "Not very nice."

She shook her head. "Anyway, I thought you could have a word with him. We have strict rules about noise, you know. And while I can live with his TV and stereo in the daytime, banging on walls and shouting in the middle of the night just can't be overlooked." Now she crouched a little, trying to see between his ear and shoulder.

He lifted his shoulder toward his ear, doing what he thought was a passable imitation of Quasimodo. "No, of course it can't." He stifled a sigh, feeling more like a school principal than a condo association president. "I'll have a word with him, Trixie. Who is it?"

"Harvey Little. Thank you, Jake." She started to turn away, then paused to ask, "Have you learned anything more about what's been going on around here? The haunting, I mean?"

He shook his head and banged his cheek on the edge of the door. "We're still looking into it. I have engineers coming today."

She nodded. "Well, I hope you get the furniture off your ceiling."

Jake watched her sashay away, realizing glumly that the whole building knew about the mess in his apartment and he needn't even have tried to conceal it.

He closed the door and stared at his ceiling. "Come on, Joe. Cut it out!"

But nothing moved. And everybody, Trixie included, seemed to be a lot more blasé about the tableau on his ceiling than he was. Maybe he should just learn to shrug it off.

After he had a cup of coffee and a bagel, he went to speak to Harvey Little, resigned to feeling like a jerk yet again. All the building's occupants were adults, he told himself. Why did they need *him* to handle things like this? What he should have done was tell Trixie to call the cops the next time Harvey decided to hold a boxing match in his living room.

Well, it was too late now.

He had to pound on Harvey's door three times before he finally heard the lock turn.

Little poked his head out through a narrow crack. The man looked awful, Jake thought. Bleary-eyed, as if he'd just come off a binge, with dark circles under his eyes.

"Whaddya want?" Little demanded truculently.

"Sorry to bother you," Jake said, as pleasantly as

he could manage, "but I had some complaints about noise from your unit last night."

The shorter man scowled at him. "I wasn't making no noise!"

"That's not what I hear. Something about it sounding like you were banging on walls."

"It wasn't me!" Harvey said furiously. "It was them! All freaking night long—bang, bang, bang! I figured Al was beating that damn broad up!"

Jake felt the corners of his mouth turn down with distaste. "Let me see if I have this straight. You thought your neighbor was beating his wife, but you didn't call the police?"

Harvey's frown deepened. "Ain't none of *my* business. Besides, I got no use for cops. Anyway, that bitch deserves it! Always poking her nose in where it doesn't belong, ya know? Always sticking them damn bazoombas of hers in a guy's face. Now, maybe I'd'a wanted to look at 'em fifty years ago, but the broad's at least seventy if she's a day!"

Jake had heard enough. Smiling coldly, he said conversationally, "You're a jerk, Little. And don't make any more noise at night, or you'll have to deal with me."

Little glared at him and slammed the door loudly. The crack sounded almost like a gunshot in the carpeted hallway.

Just then, the door of the Martins' unit opened and Trixie looked out. "What did he say?" she asked Jake.

"He claims *you* were the ones making the noise."

She shook her head. "You can ask Al. All we were doing was trying to sleep."

"I believe you, Trixie."

She leaned out further and gave Little's door a sour look. "I can't imagine why he moved into a condo. He should have found himself a mountaintop somewhere and become a hermit!"

Jake didn't answer; he didn't want to get involved in taking sides in a disagreement between owners. "Well, let me know if there's any more trouble. Or better yet, call the police when it's happening. They'll straighten him out."

"I think I will!" With that, Trixie closed her own door with a bang. This second crack caused the two doors on the other side of the hall to open, and curious faces peered out.

"It's nothing," Jake said. "Did anyone hear any noise from over here last night?"

Both residents shook their heads.

"What kind of noise?" asked one, a small elderly man with a face like a bassethound.

"Banging," Jake answered. "Banging on walls."

"Oh. Well, maybe," said the man. "I thought it was the water pipes. They do funny things sometimes."

"I'm deaf," said the other resident, a plump, grandmotherly woman in a pink housecoat. "I don't hear a thing without my hearing aids, and I don't wear them to bed."

"Well, if any noise bothers you, will you let me know?"

They both nodded agreeably.

"Say," said the elderly man, stepping further into the hallway, "when are we going to have the seance?"

"Seance?" Jake was surprised. "I didn't know we were going to have one."

"Well, I thought that was the whole idea of bringing in this Moonshine woman."

"Moonglow," Jake corrected him automatically. "Her name is Moonglow."

"Silly name."

"It's a *lovely* name," said the woman in the pink housecoat, leaning further out of her door. "Rainbow Moonglow. And she's a very nice, pleasant young woman. I go to her all the time for readings. She told me once that my cat was starting to get sick and I ought to take her to the vet. I'm *so* glad I listened. Buttons had a kidney tumor, and the vet was able to remove it before it did any damage."

Jake listened to this with reservations, figuring that the woman had subconsciously suspected something was wrong with her cat, and Rainbow had subconsciously picked up on the concern. Nothing paranormal in that.

"That's nothing," said the man dismissively. "When my wife died fifteen years ago, the day after the funeral, I saw her standing in front of me as plain as I see you!" He gave Jake a challenging look. "And I didn't imagine it!"

"Of course not," said the woman in pink. "Lots of people see their loved ones after they pass on. I'm quite sure they come back to let us know they're all right."

The old man cackled. "I think Martha came back to let me know she was watching me. She always used to say that if I ever married again, she'd haunt me."

Jake spoke. "Did you marry again?"

Another cackle. "Hell no! Do you think I want that woman haunting me?"

Almost in spite of himself, Jake grinned.

The old man's eyes were bright with humor. "Wasn't a woman ever born who could take old Martha's place, and that's a fact. Martha wouldn't let her."

The woman in pink clucked disapprovingly, but Jake laughed.

"About this seance," the old man continued, "I

have my doubts about these things. I mean, it's one thing for Martha to come back to tweak me, but it's another to think some total stranger could communicate with her at will, you know?"

Jake nodded; indeed he did. "Well, we'll just have to see if it comes to that. I have an engineering firm coming to look at the building today to ensure we aren't having some kind of physical problem that could be causing the events we've seen."

The old man shook his head. "The building might shake, son, but I don't think it'll throw things all over the place—not without falling down around our heads."

Nor could it put furniture on the ceiling, Jake thought as he walked away. He was beginning to feel like a man clinging to straws, and the straws were slipping through his fingers.

"We need to hold a seance," Roxy said over breakfast.

Rainbow nodded. She hadn't slept well last night, though, for thinking about the kiss she and Jake had shared on the beach, and this morning she felt seriously cranky. Wisely she tried to keep her mouth shut and bury herself in the paper.

Roxy was clad in a lavender bathrobe and a lavender nightcap edged with lavender lace. At some point in her career as a trance channeler, one of her guides had told her that purple was a color that favored her. Since then, Roxy wore purple in its every hue and shade and never wore anything else. Rainbow kept waiting for the day Roxy would stop using that outrageous orange dye on her hair and start dying her thinning mop to match her wardrobe. At least it wouldn't clash as outrageously as that orange did.

And Roxy's hair really *did* look orange. As orange

as the carrot juice in Rainbow's glass. Long ago, her mother had been a natural redhead, but like most redheads, the color had started fading by the time she was in her thirties. By the time she was fifty, Roxy had become violently allergic to henna, and had started resorting to other dyes, with the current result.

"Carrot juice," Roxy said with a sniff, failing to heed the warning signs about Rainbow's mood. "Here we are in Florida! You could at least drink orange juice."

"I do sometimes," Rainbow said, as pleasantly as she could manage. "This morning I felt like something different."

"You're not turning into one of those health food freaks, are you? I've been eating steak and eggs and bacon my entire life, and I'm as healthy as a fifty-year-old."

"No, Mother."

"Good." Roxy fell silent as she bit into one of the leftover chocolate doughnuts. Rainbow couldn't bear to watch. The thought of all that sugar first thing in the morning made her stomach turn over.

"So when are we going to hold the seance?" Roxy asked.

"I'll have to see what I can arrange."

"Let's not waste too much time! My clients will be expecting me back by the end of next week."

"You could always drive up here, if necessary, Mother. It's less than an hour from Sarasota."

"But I shouldn't *have* to," Roxy pointed out.

Just then, Dawn entered the kitchen. Today she was wearing a relaxed outfit of dark slacks and a man's button-down blue Oxford shirt. "Oh, God, Mother, not a doughnut for breakfast! You'll be in a rotten mood before lunch when your blood sugar plunges!"

Roxy ignored her. "I've been feeding myself for seventy years," she told Rainbow. "I'm still capable of fending for myself."

"*You* don't have to put *up* with you," Dawn said, opening the refrigerator. "Is there any more carrot juice, Rainy?"

"It's in the juicer by the stove."

"Not you, too!" Roxy said, appalled.

Dawn shrugged. "One of us has to be sensible."

"Appalling word, sensible." Roxy sniffed disapprovingly. "You always had too much sense for your own good, Dawn."

"Probably." Dawn lived with their mother, and was so used to this kind of conversation that it hardly touched her.

"I'm trying to convince Rainbow that we need to have a seance."

"Well, of course," Dawn said equably, sitting at the island beside Rainbow. "It's your stock in trade. Naturally you think it's necessary."

Roxy pursed her lips. "You're becoming entirely too disrespectful, Dawn."

Dawn shrugged one of her broad shoulders. "That's a matter of opinion. And for what it's worth, in *my* opinion you should let Rainy decide what needs to be done here. It's *her* case, after all."

Rainbow bit her lip, reluctant to admit she'd called her mother because she *didn't* know what to do. But of course, Roxy had already figured that out.

"I second that," Gene said, appearing in the doorway wearing a T-shirt that announced, "Snow is God's way of telling the world to hush." "Rainy makes the decisions, and when she decides she needs you to hold a seance, she'll say so. In the meantime . . . what does anyone know?"

"Well," said Roxy, ready as always to leap to center stage, "we know that there's a ghost called Joe and a ghost called Lucinda." She favored Rainbow with a smile. "That's what you said, isn't it?"

Rainbow nodded.

"We also know that Joe is trying to send a message to Jake. Hardly surprising," Roxy said firmly, "considering that that young man is entirely too delusional."

"Delusional?" Rainbow said, experiencing a strong urge to leap to Jake's defense. "What in the world do you mean by that?"

Roxy waved a plump, beringed hand. "Why, science, of course! He's deluded by science. He thinks science has all the answers. Now, I ask you, is that a rational attitude, considering how many things in this world are unexplained?"

No one answered her. No one really wanted the lecture.

Roxy looked disappointed but continued sans lecture. "Joe obviously wants his nephew to know that there's more to this world. Why else would he put the furniture on the ceiling?"

"Oh, I don't know," said Gene. "Maybe he's bored!"

Roxy sniffed at him. "The afterlife is never boring, Gene. My guides have said so."

"Then why do they spend so much time talking through you? I'd think they'd have better things to do."

Roxy looked down her nose at him, no mean feat, considering that she was seated while he was standing. "They *choose* to speak through me. It amuses them."

"Then life on the other side must be as exciting as watching grass grow."

Roxy sniffed again and turned her back on him. "Brothers. They can be so annoying!"

Gene shrugged, giving Rainbow a grin over the

top of Roxy's head. "The engineers are coming to inspect the building today," he said. "I think we ought to be there."

Roxy frowned over her shoulder at him. "Why ever would we want to do that? They're not going to find anything useful."

"Maybe. Maybe not. But if they do, how foolish are you going to look if you don't know about it and pursue this ghost thing."

"Really, Gene, mother should have suffocated you at birth."

He laughed. "I'm not saying you're wrong, Roxy—you know that. I've had too many close encounters with your abilities to discount them. But . . . what if they find something? We should certainly know about it."

"He's right, Mother," Dawn said.

Roxy sighed. "Very well. But I promise you, they're going to find nothing at all. This is one of the most spectacular hauntings ever, and we're going to be a part of it." She suddenly looked rapturous again, contemplating the excitement of coming events.

But just as suddenly, she frowned at Rainbow. "You really shouldn't wear black, Rainbow. It makes you look all washed out. Bold colors, my dear. How many times do I have to tell you?"

Rainbow lifted her juice glass to her mouth and drank, swallowing a dozen possible retorts in the process. She should never have called Roxy about this mess at the Towers, she thought. In fact, she should never have gotten involved at all.

Now her whole life was disordered. Her house was full of relatives, and Jake . . . well, she didn't want to think about Jake. It was akin to contemplating suicide: nothing good could possibly come of it.

Dawn touched her arm. "What say we go for a swim, Rainy? Just the two of us."

Rainbow seized the offered escape. "Absolutely. How about right now?"

"Not now!" Roxy said, appalled. "You just ate. You have to wait an hour—"

Rainbow smiled at her mother. "Sorry. That's an old wives' tale. Shall we go, Dawn?"

"Nobody ever listens to me!" Roxy wailed to Gene, as her daughters went to change.

"Maybe," Rainbow heard Gene say, as she walked away, "that's because you try to exert too much control. They're grown up now, Roxy."

"Of course they're grown up now! But I'm still their mother!"

Shaking her head with a smile, Rainbow closed her bedroom door behind her.

Jake glanced at his watch and saw that there was plenty of time before the engineers were due, so he decided to take a swim. At least while he was in the water, at this time of day, there was little chance any of the building's residents would collar him to complain about something. Most preferred to enjoy the beach either in the very early hours or in the late evening, when the sun wasn't as strong.

Twenty minutes later, he was strolling along the water's edge in his bathing suit and a T-shirt, carrying a towel. He was heading north, in the general direction of Rainbow's house, and some part of him acknowledged a wistful hope that he might run into her.

It was unlikely, and he was uneasy with the wish because it reminded him of the days of his youth, when he hung around on the street corner near a girl's house in the hope she might decide to take a walk. He'd wasted a lot of time that way over Betsy

Miller and had finally reached the inescapable conclusion that Betsy never left the house unless she was in the company of her parents or her friends.

Now here he was, at the advanced age of thirty-eight, acting much as he had at sixteen. Scary. Funny but scary.

Then he caught his breath and froze as he saw the woman in the scarlet maillot. There was no mistaking that long black hair, even at this distance, nor the chunky figure of Dawn Moonglow beside her. The women were spreading out towels in the sand, talking and laughing.

For the longest time he couldn't move. He had the insane feeling that his wish had brought Rainbow to the beach, and the even more insane feeling that this was destiny.

Hoo boy, he was losing it.

He told himself to turn around, to head the other way. Rainbow was off limits. Getting any closer to her would only mean they'd both eventually have regrets.

But his feet apparently had plans of their own, because even as his brain was ordering him to turn around, he found himself walking forward . . . and the closer he got to Rainbow, the faster his heart seemed to beat.

Dawn saw him coming and said something to Rainbow, her words lost in the sounds of the surf and the cries of the seagulls wheeling overhead. Rainbow turned and smiled, and Jake felt the world stand still.

She was gorgeous. Exquisite. A creation of beauty and light. Jake, who ordinarily waxed as poetic as the ordinary scientist, which was to say not at all, found himself having insane thoughts about scarlet against milky skin, about long, dark tresses blowing in the breeze.

The suit hugged her figure lovingly, leaving little to the imagination, but Jake's imagination was suddenly running at top speed with what it had. Hers was a neat figure, the kind he had always thought of as perfect—gently curved, sweetly endowed but not exaggerated. Her hips were gently rounded, not the flat boyish hips women seemed to prize these days. Her legs seemed to go on forever, long, trim, and firm. Her breasts were not the overlarge melons in the dreams of puerile men, but instead, firm mounds that would just fill his hands. He could easily imagine how they would feel in his palms.

He paused, hoping his tongue wasn't hanging out. It had been a lifetime since the simple sight of a woman had affected him this way.

Warning klaxons were sounding in his brain, cautioning him that with each step he took toward her he was walking ever deeper into quicksand. This woman was the stuff of his dreams and fantasies, a vision with as much mystery and beauty as a star-strewn night sky.

Help.

Then Dawn waved him over and he found himself walking toward the women again, feeling almost as if he were attached to a line they were reeling in. He didn't like the helpless feeling and wondered wildly if Rainbow also practiced magic. Maybe she had cast some kind of spell that had deprived him of will and common sense.

And then he didn't care, because he was standing just two feet away from her and she was smiling shyly, blushing faintly as his eyes devoured her.

"I think I'll just go for a swim," Dawn said drily, after a minute during which Rainbow and Jake had simply stared at one another and said nothing. Neither of them heard her, or noticed when she walked away.

"Hi," Rainbow said finally.

"Hi," he answered, his voice so husky it sounded strange.

Her blush deepened, and the sight caused his groin to throb. He felt a blush beginning to stain his own cheeks, as he wondered what his body was revealing. Thank goodness she kept her eyes on his face.

Rainbow's color heightened even more. "We came down to take a swim," she said inanely.

But it didn't sound inane to him. In fact, it struck him as a brilliant conversational gambit. "So did I," he said with equal brilliance, his gaze never wavering from her face.

"Will you—will you join us?"

"Sure." God, he realized with a sudden sense of panic, he was being reduced to monosyllables, his brain having utterly disconnected itself from his tongue. He had to think of something to say, something that would keep her from turning her back and walking into the water—although he confessed an ardent desire to see how she looked when that maillot was wet and her nipples were puckered from the chill of the water. With a jerk he yanked his thoughts back from that looming precipice and tried to think of something—anything!—sensible to say.

"Um . . . the engineers are coming in a couple of hours."

She nodded. "I know."

Why had he never before noticed what a pretty smile she had, and how beautiful her teeth were? "I, uh, don't have a lot of hope, though."

She shook her head. "Me neither."

"The furniture," he explained.

"Right. The furniture."

Forcing himself to take a deep breath, he dragged his gaze from her and nailed it to the sparkling waters, letting the calming sight of the aquamarine waves cool his overheating brain. Rainbow in a bathing suit was lethal to his peace of mind. He *had* to stay away from this woman.

"We plan to come over when the engineers arrive," Rainbow offered. "To hear what they have to say."

His gaze snapped back to her like a rubber band stretched too tight. He was drowning in her nearness, and he didn't give a damn. What he wanted—what he *really* wanted—was to drag her off to some private place and discover if she felt and tasted as tempting as she looked. Christ, it was the caveman response, and all of a sudden he was in sympathy with the hairy barbarians who'd carried clubs and dragged women off. It would be so *easy* to do right now.

Her cheeks were nearly as red as her maillot now, and he wondered wildly if she was reading his mind. She was psychic, after all. Maybe he was an open book to her. His face burned as he considered the primitive level of his current thinking.

He struggled for something safe to say. "Uh . . . they're coming around one o'clock."

She nodded. "I know. We'll be there."

Something else, he thought. There had to be something else he could say to keep this conversation going. "One of the residents complained to me this morning."

"Really? About what? More ghost stuff?"

"I don't know." The sun was hot on his shoulders, almost as hot as his blood. Only with great effort did he keep his gaze from trailing downward over Rainbow's luscious curves. "She said her neighbor was banging on the wall last night. And he said *she* was doing it."

Rainbow suggested, "Probably the ghosts. Knock-

ing on the walls is a common poltergeist phenomenon."

She sounded so intelligent, he thought. No woman
had ever sounded as intelligent. She was so sure, so
confident of her knowledge in an area that—he admitted it to himself even in his current state of hazy
passion—he was terrified of.

"Maybe . . . maybe you'd like to check it out?" he
suggested.

"I'd love to. But after my swim, okay?"

He nodded, dry of words and empty of conversation.

"Come on," she said, giving him a brilliant smile.
She reached out and took his hand. "Let's get wet."

He pulled off his T-shirt, dropped his towel on the
sand, and followed her into the chilly water like a
puppy on a leash.

Oh, God, he had it bad. It had come over him like
a hurricane blowing in off the Gulf, swallowing him
in the wild winds of a passion stronger than anything he had ever felt.

She must be a witch, he decided, as the water
reached his hips and he began to bob with the movement of the waves. She was a witch and had put
him under some spell.

And he was in no hurry to find a cure.

He watched as she lifted her arms and used a
rubber band to put her hair into a ponytail, and then,
as if she knew what he was waiting for, she sank
into the water, disappearing from sight, only to rise
upward again like a mermaid, shedding silvery riv-
ulets of water.

And nothing was left to his imagination any
longer. Her nipples were hard, ripe as berries for
plucking, and he had the worst urge to free them
from the confines of the Spandex so he could take
them into his mouth and taste their sweetness.

A sudden splash of cold salt water from the side startled him and dragged him back from the edge. He turned swiftly and found Dawn grinning at him.

"Down, boy," she said, and splashed him again.

His face suddenly felt sunburned, and he dived quickly into the cool Gulf water, swimming away from Temptation and her annoying sister.

What he ought to do, he told himself as the salt water washed away his embarrassment and desire, was pack a suitcase and get the hell out of Dodge.

Before it was too late.

Twelve

DAWN SAID, "IF YOU'D BEEN OUT THERE ALONE, AND it hadn't been broad daylight, Jake would have grabbed you."

Rainbow felt another blush stain her cheeks. She and her sister, wearing terrycloth coverups over their suits, were walking back to the cottage. "Don't exaggerate, Dawn."

"I'm not exaggerating. That man is so hot for you he can hardly restrain himself."

"He's a gentleman."

"In broad daylight."

Rainbow swatted her sister with her damp towel. "Cut it out, Dawn."

"Why? It's obvious you'd like him to grab you. I just thought you should know the feeling's mutual."

"So?" Rainbow kept her gaze fastened on the sandy path that passed for a sidewalk here as they walked between beachfront cottages that looked as if they'd been transplanted from some small fishing town in New England. "It's just a sexual attraction, Dawn. It's meaningless."

"A great many meaningful relationships have started with sexual attraction."

"Well, this is one relationship that can never be meaningful."

"Because of your psychic abilities, you mean?"

Rainbow gave a brief nod, wishing her sister would drop this subject. The mere thought of Jake was beginning to make her irritable.

"Well, just because Walter was a toad doesn't mean this guy is," Dawn said sensibly. "You can't be a nun for the rest of your life."

"Why not? I like my life just fine."

"Ah, but *fine* is a long way from *great*, and I have a feeling Jake could make your life *great*."

"Not if he thinks I'm a fraud and a swindler."

"He's backed off of that."

"Yeah, right. Maybe his hormones are getting in the way of his brain."

Dawn started to laugh, but when Rainbow shot her a nasty look, she turned it quickly into a cough. "Everything has to start somewhere, Rainy."

"But hormones wear off. And then we'd be right back to where we started, him with his scientific superiority, and me just a swindler and a fraud."

"So have a fling."

Rainbow stopped walking and gaped at her sister. "You're kidding!"

Dawn shrugged. "Hey, if a man ever looked at me the way Jake Carpenter was looking at you, I'd jump in with both feet. Opportunities like him don't come knocking every day, even for beautiful women like you."

Rainbow felt a surge of sympathy for her sister. As far as she knew, Dawn had never had a romantic relationship. Men seemed to look right through her, which really wasn't fair, because although she was chunky and dressed mannishly, she had one of the nicest personalities and sweetest temperaments of anybody walking the earth. She deserved to be loved more than most people.

"Dawn—"

Dawn silenced her with a wave of her hand. "Don't say it, Rainy. I got over it a long time ago, and I'm content. I just hate to see you miss an opportunity because you're afraid."

"But I have every *reason* to be afraid!"

"So does a skydiver, but he doesn't want to miss the experience. You've built a shell around yourself, Rainy. You need to break out of it."

"Setting myself up for another emotional catastrophe is hardly likely to accomplish that."

Dawn sighed and started trudging toward the cottage again. "Maybe," she said. "Maybe."

But Rainbow was more disturbed than she wanted to admit. Dawn was now the second person—Gene was the first—who'd suggested she was afraid and hiding in a shell. She didn't think of herself that way at all. No, she saw herself as having gained some wisdom so that she was now sensibly cautious.

And it *was* sensible to be cautious. Only a fool would step into the path of a moving car, and she put men in the category of dangerous vehicles which could run her down if she wasn't careful.

On the other hand, whispered that nagging little voice in her brain that always put in its two cents at precisely the wrong time, even though cars are dangerous, you get into one and drive it all the time.

But it's not the same, she argued back. Not the same at all. Getting *into* one and stepping in front of one were not the same thing. When she got into one, she was in the driver's seat.

And with Jake, she could never be the driver. She sensed that with an instinct so deep it defied logic. With Jake she would be on a roller coaster ride blindfolded, with no idea where the track might sud-

denly vanish and fling her into the air without even
a parachute to break her fall.

No sensible person would do such a thing.

The engineers arrived punctually at one. Most of
the Towers residents were out on the patio to greet
them, as were Rainbow and her family. Mary Todd
drove up in her golf cart just a few seconds after the
engineers, with her beau, Ted Wannamaker, in tow.
Ted, a distinguished-looking man of about seventy,
had the resigned look of a someone going to the gal-
lows.

"Ted doesn't believe in ghosts," Mary announced
to Jake. "You should get along well with him, Jake.
The two of you think alike."

Jake and Ted exchanged looks, not quite sure how
to interpret this remark.

"The things I do," Ted said finally, "to convince
Mary I really *am* devoted. Apparently now it's a
ghost hunt."

"The place is haunted," Mary said with a sharp
rap of her cane on the pavement. She turned to Jake.
"I hear you have furniture on your ceiling."

Jake gave up and shrugged. "It was there the last
time I looked."

"Bolted?" Ted asked with genuine interest. "Why
did you put it there?"

"I didn't put it there. And no, it's not bolted. I
don't know *what's* holding it up there."

"Well, something must be holding it there," Ted
said reasonably.

Jake felt a surge of frustration but bit back an annoyed response.

"Of course something is holding it up there,"
Mary said sharply. "Something *supernatural*."

"Oh, really," said Ted disbelievingly.

Jake shrugged off his irritation. Why should he be

irritated at Ted Wannamaker, who was simply making the same assumptions he had made himself? "You're welcome to come take a look at it," he said. "Nearly everyone else in the world has had a go at it."

Ted nodded. "I think I will, if you don't mind. Mary's absolutely convinced that something here will convince me that ghosts really do exist. She's made me promise to try to keep an open mind."

Mary snorted. "Your mind has been closed for at least forty years."

"On this subject, perhaps." Ted gave her an affectionate smile.

Just then Gene joined the group. Mary at once took advantage of the presence of another distinguished-looking man near her age, and looped her arm through Gene's. She introduced Gene and Ted, then said with a coy bat of her eyelashes, "Gene is a movie actor."

Gene looked down at her with an amused smile. "They need ladies in Hollywood who are as beautiful as you, Mary."

Mary gave an almost girlish laugh, while Ted's pleasant smile faded to a frown. "Flattery will get you anything, Gene."

"I'll keep that in mind." Lifting her hand from his forearm, Gene kissed it.

Rainbow, watching, wanted to growl in disgust. Nellie Blair, sitting only a few feet away, looked dismayed. Seeing her expression, Rainbow decided that enough was enough.

Marching over, she took Gene's other arm. "Uncle Gene, could I have a word with you, please?"

He looked down at her. "In a minute, Rainy."

"No. *Right now.*"

He arched a brow, looking faintly amused. Then he turned, excusing himself to Mary, Ted, and Jake.

"That was rude, Rainy," he said, when they had moved a distance from the others.

"So was what you were doing! Did you see Nellie's face? She looked as if her heart were breaking. Now, if you want to play ladies' man, I suggest you go back to California to do it. While you're here, kindly remember that this is a small town and I have to live in it, and confine your tomcatting to women who are experienced enough to handle it!"

"Tomcatting!" Gene pressed a hand to his heart. "I'm wounded."

"Bull," Rainbow said bluntly.

"Besides, it wasn't my fault. I just wanted to meet Ted. It was Mary who turned it into something else, and I was just playing along. She wants to make Ted jealous, you know."

"I don't care who started it! You've been dating Nellie, and she deserves a certain amount of respect from you!"

"Well, of course!" Gene hesitated a moment, looking past his niece to where Nellie sat, her face pointedly turned the other way. "All right, all right. I didn't mean for this to happen, though, so don't blame me just because I was being gallant."

"Being gallant means considering the feelings of the woman to whom you've been paying special attention for the last few days!"

Gene sighed and gave her a faint smile. "You're right, of course, my dear. But it was just so tempting to play the game with Mary."

"Well, you've done considerably more damage than making Ted Wannamaker jealous. Besides, he's known Mary his entire life and has probably seen her play this game a million times."

"That doesn't mean the game doesn't still work." Gene patted her hand, then walked over to sit beside Nellie. Rainbow watched him speak to Nellie, and after a few moments, the woman's head lifted and she began to smile again.

Of course, Rainbow reminded herself, she may have just made a big mistake by sending Gene back to Nellie. If he decided to ride off into the sunset in his usual style, Nellie might only wind up being hurt worse than if the relationship broke off right now.

The three engineers, who had been standing in a huddled knot beside their van, began to unload their equipment. Jake strode over to help them, as did a number of his neighbors.

They were an interesting crowd, Rainbow thought, as she watched from a distance. Two of the men had hair below their shoulders, and looked as if they might have escaped from a commune back in the sixties. They wore cutoffs and T-shirts that Gene probably would have been proud of.

One shirt said, "Engineers do it carefully." The other said, "Long live slide rules." That in spite of the fact that the fellow had at least two calculators hanging from his belt.

The third man looked like a stereotypical nerd. Tall and thin with thick glasses, he wore rumpled khaki slacks and a white shirt that was buttoned to the throat. In his breast pocket was a plastic protector full of pens and mechanical pencils.

The nerd seemed to be in charge of the group. He supervised the removal of the equipment to the lobby, then stood with a clipboard, checking off items as they were set down.

"Okay," he said finally, his voice reedy. "Everything's here." He turned to Jake. "You say the events have been happening throughout the building?"

Jake nodded. "I have to point out, though, that the elevators are still working."

"Hmm."

"Cool," said one of the long-haired guys.

"And," Jake continued, "I haven't been able to find any signs of settling around the foundation. No cracks or anything."

"Hmm," said the nerd again. "But it was a sudden shift?"

"Well, I don't *know* that it was a shift," Jake said. "I mean, I can't say for sure the building moved. But everything started flying around at about the same time."

Those who had crowded into the lobby with them bobbed their heads in unison, looking like a flock of strange tropical birds.

"Did it *feel* as if anything were moving?" the nerd asked.

"Only the stuff that was flying in the air," one resident called out. Again everyone nodded.

"Hmm. Is anybody's door sticking?"

All the heads shook.

"Hmm."

Rainbow, along with Roxy and Dawn, stood nearby and listened to the exchange. Turning her head slightly, she found Jake looking straight at her. Why had she never realized just how warm blue eyes could be? Her heart skipped a little beat.

"This may take a while," the nerd said. "If things were flying around, I'd expect there to be some obvious structural damage. At the very least, doors should be sticking or refusing to close."

"Maybe the whole building's falling into a sink-hole," Abe Levinson said.

"That wouldn't explain the furniture on Jake's ceiling," Bill Dunlop argued.

Jake wondered if he should just give guided tours of his living room. Maybe he could charge a dollar a pop until he had enough to buy himself a new recliner.

The hippie with the slide rule T-shirt looked at Jake. "There's furniture on your ceiling?"

Jake swallowed a sigh and nodded.

"Like, too totally cool, dude!"

The other hippie nodded.

"You wouldn't think so if *you* had to live with it."

"No, man," the guy said, "you gotta think of the possibilities!"

The nerd cleared his throat. "That's what we're here to check out," he said, with a frown to Slide Rule.

"Aw, man," said Slide Rule, "you know no building settling is going to put furniture on the ceiling."

"Exactly!" said Roxy, swimming forward, her turban slipping to one side and her royal purple caftan billowing around her. "That's what *I've* been saying."

The nerd frowned at her. "Excuse me, madam, but we're here to check out the building. If there's furniture on the ceiling, there has to be a good, logical reason for it, and we'll find it."

"Hah!" said Roxy, folding her arms.

"I'm with her, man."

Nerd shook his head. "Just do your job, Evans. Just do your job. The furniture is probably bolted or affixed with some kind of adhesive."

"It isn't *affixed* with anything," Roxy said. "It *moves.*"

Rainbow felt amusement curve her lips as she listened to the discussion. Roxy never gave ground when she believed she was right. Rainbow, on the other hand, was usually inclined to let things lie, and let people believe what they chose—unless, of course, they called her a fraud.

The doors of the lobby opened to admit Colonel Albemarle, decked out in his customary khakis and pith helmet, and carrying both his swagger stick and a Dustbuster. Behind him came his squad of five men, all of them armed with Dustbusters.

"We saw the gathering outside," he announced, touching his swagger stick to the brim of his helmet. "Thought you might be having another run-in with the ghosts."

The nerd frankly gaped, but Slide Rule grinned with evident appreciation.

"Let me guess," said Slide Rule. "The vacuums are for the ghosts."

"Yes, of course," said Albemarle. "Who might you be?"

"We," said the nerd, recovering from his evident shock, "are the engineers who are here to check out the building."

"Ah," said Albemarle. "Well, you won't find anything. Fields here sucked up the bounders last time we were here." He turned to Jake. "Unless the rascals have returned?"

Jake didn't quite know how to answer that. He seriously doubted that the ghosts had been vacuumed away—assuming there *were* any ghosts. After all, the furniture was still moving itself to his ceiling.

"They're still here, Colonel," said Pat Webster. "They're moving the furniture in Jake's apartment."

Thank you very much! Jake thought. Yes, he really needed a band of old men armed with Dustbusters running around in his apartment trying to vacuum up the ghosts.

"They are?" said Trixie Martins. "They are, really? Maybe that's what I heard banging all night. Maybe it wasn't Harvey Little at all."

"Don't be ridiculous," said Harvey, who'd been trying to remain inconspicuous behind a fern. "There aren't any ghosts in *my* apartment!"

"Then you *were* banging on the walls all night!"

"I was not!"

"*Were too!*"

"*Was not!*"

"Please!" Jake shouted, holding up his hands. "Let's not turn this into a playground fight. These men are here to see if the building's settling, and I suggest we let them get on with it. As for the banging on the walls, maybe it was the water pipes."

The nerd shook his head. "I don't think so. That has a very distinctive sound, you know. One wouldn't mistake it for somebody banging on the walls."

"Well, I wasn't banging on anything!" Harvey declared, pushing a fern frond away from his face. "She was the one who was banging all night!"

Trixie gasped. "I did no such thing! But rest assured, next time you decide to throw things around, I'm calling the police!"

He glared at her. "So am I!"

"But don't you see?" Roxy said, clasping her hands ecstatically, "it's a common poltergeist phenomenon!"

"What do chickens have to do with it?" demanded a man in a red shirt.

"Chickens?" Roxy looked confused. "I didn't say anything about chickens!"

"You were talking about poultry!"

"No, no, no! *Poltergeists*. A particularly mischievous and noisy type of ghost!"

Rainbow spoke. "But there are no adolescents in the building, Mother."

"Hah. You could fool me."

Slide Rule looked at Roxy. "Hey, I get it. These poltergeists only happen when there's a teenager in the house, right?"

Roxy beamed at him. "Right. Usually, that is. There have been reports of them appearing otherwise, though."

Rainbow shook her head. "Not really, mother. There is always an unusually high level of unreleased sexual tension involved, and that usually means adolescents."

"Sexual tension?" said a man in a black polo shirt. "Are you suggesting that this building is full of sexually frustrated people? I don't think I like that!"

"Oh, good heavens, no," said Roxy. "All you need is *one* person to generate the phenomenon. Besides, it's doubtful a poltergeist is really a ghost. It's more of a telekinetic phenomenon."

"A what?"

"Telekinesis," Roxy said. "You know, a person is moving things around or making noises through paranormal abilities. Not a ghost at all."

A number of people were beginning to look at each other uneasily, and Rainbow decided this could get unpleasant if neighbors started suspecting one another of being the cause of this problem.

"No, mother, this is not a poltergeist," she said firmly. "We already know that. We've already sensed the presence of Lucy and Joe."

The room suddenly grew quiet as every eye fixed on her.

"Lucy and Joe?" Murmurs passed through the crowd.

Jake wanted to grind his teeth. Even as he was seriously beginning to wonder if Joe might have something to do with what was going on in his apartment, he didn't like the idea of Rainbow telling the whole world. It seemed—well, he couldn't say exactly *what* it seemed. Disrespectful, perhaps? Whatever, it bothered him. He didn't want the whole building talking about his uncle this way.

"But my dear," Roxy said, "there might be more than two sources for the phenomena. This building is a veritable hotbed of psychic activity. There could be any number of things happening at once."

Rainbow shook her head firmly. "I've been

through the entire building. It's Lucy and Joe."

"It can't be," snapped Harvey Little. Forgetting he held the fern frond, he let go of it and it snapped back, hitting him in the face. He jumped, then stormed out from behind the plant. "It can't be them!" he insisted. "They're dead!"

"Which is entirely the point," said Roxy, undaunted. "How else would they be ghosts?"

"I've never heard anything so ridiculous in my life," Little said sourly. "What a bunch of senile old fools you are."

Angry words of disagreement came his way from every direction, but he ignored them. "You're a bunch of loonies, that's all I have to say!"

With that, he stomped his way to the elevators.

Disapproving silence followed him until the elevator doors closed.

"What a thoroughly disagreeable man," Roxy said.

"He certainly seems distressed by the idea that it could be Lucy and Joe," Mary Todd remarked, "which seems like a rather strong reaction, when you consider he moved here only a couple of weeks before they died."

"I don't think he's reacting to their identity," Gene said. "He just doesn't like the idea of ghosts."

"I don't fully agree with you," Mary said. "The idea of ghosts is so much more . . . disturbing, if you know their identity."

"I'll give you that," Gene agreed.

Jake would, too, but he didn't say it. He had to admit, though, it would probably be easier to believe a strange ghost was putting furniture on his ceiling than that it was Joe.

"The man needs to mellow," said Slide Rule. "He's going to give himself a heart attack."

Nerd spoke. "Could we *please* get down to business here?"

"Sure, man," said Slide Rule. "Keep your shirt on."

"I wasn't going to take it off."

Slide Rule rolled his eyes. "You know, man, you're the kind of dude who, like, gives a bad name to engineers."

"No," said the nerd, "*you're* the kind who give us a bad name. Sloppy work, sloppy dress, sloppy language . . ."

"Hang loose, man. I get the job done."

"So let's get on with it. Now!"

The engineers marched away with their bags of equipment—or rather, the nerd marched and the other two straggled along behind.

Colonel Albemarle cleared his throat again. "Men," he said, "I think it might be good to scout the building once more. And it would be wise to keep at least one Dustbuster turned on at all times."

"The batteries will run down, sir," said one of his men, a short, stout guy with hair turned an interesting shade of green from dye.

"Then we'll run them one at a time, but see that at least one is turned on. We wouldn't want any of the little buggers slipping around us."

They marched off and Jake turned to Rainbow, lifting an eloquent brow.

She didn't know how to respond. She thought that Colonel Albemarle was definitely out of touch with reality, but his delusion was harmless. Besides, facing the unknown, who was to say what would really work?

Although in her experience with spirits, they really weren't likely to be impressed by a vacuum cleaner, large *or* small.

Roxy spoke. "Mustafa must be rolling on the floor with laughter."

"If there *is* a floor in heaven, Mother," Dawn said.

Roxy arched a plucked eyebrow at her. "I'm not at all sure he's in heaven, Dawn."

Dawn's eyes widened. "You don't think he's in the *other* place!"

"Of course not! I wouldn't associate with such types!"

"But—"

Roxy shook her head. "I'm convinced there must be some other place, a sort of halfway house for those spirits who still have business here."

Rainbow had trouble smothering a grin at the thought of a heavenly halfway house full of people who still wanted to make trouble on earth.

Jake joined them, greeting Roxy and Dawn with a warm smile, and giving Rainbow a smoldering look that raised the lobby temperature at least ten degrees. Or so she felt, wishing she could fan herself.

"The engineers will be at this for hours," he said. "I'd invite you up to my place, but I'm not sure I still have anything to offer you to sit on."

"Why?" Rainbow asked. "Has something else levitated?"

"God knows. I'm getting so I'm afraid to open my door and look. Last night an end table moved up to join the chair and lamp, complete with magazines and Joe's pipes and tobacco."

"Oh, my!" said Roxy, her eyes alight. "This is so incredibly wonderful."

He gave her a wry look. "That's a matter of opinion, Roxy."

"Oh, I'm sure it's a major inconvenience for you, but it's just so remarkable to see such a display."

"I'll grant you that."

She favored him with an indulgent smile. "So you *are* coming around to our way of thinking."

"I'm rapidly getting to the point of believing almost anything if it will get the furniture off my ceiling!" He turned to Rainbow. "In fact," he said, "I'd be very grateful if you'd come up to my place, Rainbow, and see if you can pick up any clearer impressions about what is going on."

Astonished, she simply stared at him.

"Well, if she won't do it, *I* will," Roxy said.

Dawn stepped down hard on her mother's foot. "You weren't asked, Mother. Let Rainbow go."

Comprehension dawned on Roxy's face. "Ouch! Oh. Yes, of course."

Rainbow felt color stain her cheeks again. Drat! It had been such a long time since *anyone* had been able to make her blush the way Jake could with a simple look. She wanted to turn to her mother and defuse the moment by inviting her to come along, but Dawn intervened again.

"We'll just wait down here—won't we, Mother?"

"Yes, of course!" Roxy beamed at Jake and her daughter.

"Thank you," Jake said with remarkable composure, considering what had just been implied. "Rainbow?"

She felt she ought to say no. The temperature was rising rapidly, and she didn't think it was because the air conditioning had gone out. This man was dangerous to her, and she really ought to avoid him.

"Yes," she said, much to her dismay, and then felt a pleasurable shiver pass through her as he took her hand.

Under the watchful eyes of the Towers residents and her family, he led her toward the elevator.

"Yee-ha!" cried Joe with satisfaction. "It's working, Lucy! It's working!"

Lucy nodded. "That part of it. But what about the rest, Joe? What about *justice?*"

"I'm getting to that." Joe propped his chin in his

hand, beaming down on his nephew. "Ha!" he said again with delight. "The boy's finally coming to his senses."

"Or losing them," Lucy said fondly.

He grinned at her. "Losing them, then. It sure was fun, wasn't it, Lucy?"

A soft smile lighted her face. "It still *is*."

Joe's expression softened and he reached out to take her hand. "You bet, Luce, you bet. I can't imagine anything better."

She smiled and nestled her head on his shoulder. "Me, neither," she said.

"I'm just sorry it took me so long to find you."

"It's okay," she told him. "We have forever now."

"Yep." He glanced down at Jake, then decided to let the boy handle things himself. Right now, he just wanted to gaze into Lucy's eyes and feel at peace with her and everything else.

It just kept getting better and better, he thought, and sent a prayer of thanksgiving winging on its way.

Better and better.

Thirteen

THE FURNITURE WAS STILL ON THE CEILING, BUT nothing new had been added, much to Jake's relief. He closed the door behind them, then stuffed his hands in his pockets so he wouldn't reach out and grab Rainbow.

She walked into the middle of the living room and closed her eyes, clearly listening to her inner voices, or whatever they were.

He didn't know what he expected from her. If she started talking about Joe, chances were he wouldn't believe her anyway. But he was rapidly getting to the point of being willing to take any help, no matter how outlandish, if it would just return his life to normal. If a witch doctor walked through the door right now, he would probably agree to drink some smelly repulsive green potion, if only it was promised to return reality to its usual parameters.

Hell, he was getting to the point of *sending* for one of the witch doctors he'd met on his travels. They were all sensible men and women, usually exceptionally intelligent, and except for their rather strange theologies, utterly down-to-earth and practical.

And so was Rainbow, he admitted to himself, as he watched her stand still and silent. Except for her belief in the paranormal, she was as bright and realistic a woman as he'd ever met.

Maybe she wasn't a crackpot, after all. Maybe the distance between him and her was no wider than the gulf between differing faiths.

And there was always the possibility that she was right. Every time he looked at the furniture on his ceiling, he certainly had to wonder.

He hadn't yet closed the curtains, and sunlight was streaming through the windows. Beyond Rainbow he could see the cloudless blue sky and the small dark dots of seagulls on their perennial search for food. A pelican flew by, drifting on a thermal, looking prehistoric with its huge bill and immense wingspan. Unlike most birds of prey, pelicans had puppy-dog eyes, and this one seemed to be sadly glancing through the windows at the humans as it soared by.

Rainbow turned toward him, giving him a rueful smile, and spreading her hands. "I can't sense anything at all," she said apologetically.

"You mean Joe's not here?"

"*Nobody's* here."

For some reason that brought a huge smile to his face. "So we're alone?"

"Completely."

His smile broadened until his cheeks ached. "That's the best news I've heard in a while."

Her expression grew doubtful, and he felt he ought to reassure her somehow, but there didn't seem to be any good way to do that when he was feeling such a strong urge to pounce.

"Jake?" Her expression became concerned. "Is something wrong?"

"Not a damn thing," he said bluntly. In two long

steps, he crossed the room to her. Looking down into
her eyes, he felt as if the whole damn world could
go hang and he'd never miss it. "I'm being overwhelmed by an urge to make a pass at you."

Her eyes widened, but not from fright, and he
took heart. "That wouldn't be wise," she said,
sounding breathless.

"Hell, it's never wise. But sometimes it's totally
irresistible."

She caught her breath and continued to stare up
at him from wide, mossy-green eyes. God, her eyes
reminded him of some of the jungles he'd visited,
reminded him of the cool, dark places under the canopy of ancient trees, places where he'd always found
peace.

"Irresistible?" she repeated on a swiftly indrawn
breath.

"Irresistible," he said, stepping closer so that they
almost touched. *"You're* irresistible."

"Oh . . ." She expelled the word on a soft sigh.

Jake felt his heart leap as he realized he hadn't
offended her with his honesty. The irritating, cynical
side of him remembered that if he was going to be
honest, maybe he should be honest enough to admit
that this was the woman who only a few short days
ago he'd called a fraud and a swindler. It suggested
he also ought to consider he was thinking with his
small head rather than his large one.

But the cynic got drowned in a sea of sensation as
Jake stepped even closer to Rainbow. He saw a flare
in her eyes, but he couldn't tell what it was. All he
knew was that she didn't back away.

She wanted this as much as he did.

Exultation lifted him on a huge wave, and ran-
domly firing cells in his brain summoned images of
how she had looked earlier in that red maillot. Of

how her breasts had looked as if she had risen like some mythical creature from the sea.

The simple fact was, he wasn't thinking at all. He was experiencing, feeling, reveling in the moment—and all he knew was that even as he stepped over the edge of the precipice, he had never felt freer in his life.

She came into his embrace, warm, soft, and willing, her woman's body molding to him as if she had been created for him. In an instant he tumbled headlong and took flight.

His mouth found hers, hot and wet. Their tongues met in an ancient mating ritual, and honeyed heat spread through him, making him feel heavy and languorous.

Fear stabbed him as his desire surged far more quickly than anything he had known before. This was more than he had bargained for when he had given in to the impulse to hold her and kiss her. Not since his youth had he been passion's slave, and he felt a momentary panic as he realized he was on the edge of losing control.

But not even panic could stop what he was feeling with Rainbow in his arms. He could no more let go of her now than he could have fought his way free of a riptide.

Enthralled, he could only follow where need led him.

He felt her shiver against him and recognized it as a reflection of his own apprehension over what was happening, but then she melted even more closely to him, and he felt her arms close around his waist, holding him tightly, as if he were an anchor—as if she were afraid he might let her go.

Her arms were small, slender, a woman's gentle arms, but now they hugged him close with surprising strength, and he felt something in him respond in the same way a plant responded to rain. He needed this. God, it had been so long since a woman had held him as if she really wanted him, and the wonder that filled him was as strong as the passion that drove him.

He needed her.

Needing her, and giving in to his need, he let his body seek all that it wanted. His hands wandered from her back to her waist, then down to her softly rounded bottom, where they took hold, lifting her into him, holding her as close as he could get her to the cradle of his hips.

The rhythm that was pounding in his blood was echoed in his hips as he pressed himself to her again and again. Each press of his body to hers was sheer torture and sheer delight. He began to resent the layers of clothing that separated them, wanted to rip away the zipper of his slacks that bit into him each time he rubbed against her.

Somehow—he was never quite clear how it happened—they were lying on the couch, she beneath him, he between her thighs. He could feel her hips responding to the rhythm of his, arching upward, as if she wanted more and more of him.

Her shirt came untucked, and as if it had a mind of its own, his hand slid up beneath it. When his fingers crossed the smooth, warm skin of her midriff, he felt as if electric shocks were leaping from her through him to his groin. Had a woman's skin ever felt more wonderful?

But then his hand found her breast, covered in something silky. She filled his palm and against it he could feel the hardening point of her nipple. Perfect. She was perfect. Gently he squeezed her, and she moaned in response, arching sharply against him and telling him just how much she liked his touch.

Gently, gently, he rubbed his palm over her, enjoying the sounds she made, enjoying the way she felt to him, loving the way she bucked against him, every bit as needy as he.

More. He needed more. He needed everything, and he needed it with Rainbow.

His pulse was loud in his ears. He could hear nothing but its rapid hammering and the gasping sounds of his breath—her breath?—could feel nothing but the yielding, yearning softness of Rainbow beneath him.

He ground himself against her, forgetting finesse in his absolute need. Her fingers dug into his back, biting through his shirt, goading him onward.

"Jake . . ."

He thought he heard her sigh his name. The sound seemed to reach across the ages from a time he couldn't remember except as a feeling. As if he had been searching through lifetime after lifetime for this one voice, this one woman . . .

Then, all of a sudden, he felt he was being watched. A chilly trickle of uneasiness ran through him, cooling him a little. Just enough that he was suddenly conscious of who he was, who she was, and what they were doing.

He had a horrifying, humiliating image of himself acting like a rutting animal, springing upon a woman he hardly knew and doing things with her that . . . well . . .

He lifted his head, dragging in a ragged gasp of air and looking down at her, hoping she didn't feel the same embarrassment. He would never forgive himself if he had humiliated her by his behavior.

Her green eyes opened slowly, hazily, and looked at him questioningly. And then, as he watched, full awareness returned and painful color flooded her cheeks. She closed her eyes and turned her face away.

"Oh, my God," she whispered.

He didn't know what to do. For the first time in nearly twenty years, he was totally at a loss. His body was aching, throbbing, demanding surcease, but his mind was screaming that if he didn't stop now, she was going to hate him and he was going to hate himself.

But there didn't seem to be any graceful way out.

He drew another couple of ragged breaths, trying to kick-start his brain into some semblance of working order. Heat was still pooled in his groin, and it wouldn't take much to send him over the edge again. He held himself stiffly, afraid that the least little movement would be more than he could bear.

"Rainy . . ." He murmured her name, silently pleading with her to look at him.

She didn't respond but just drew a ragged little breath that sounded as if she were near tears. Oh, God, he thought, not *that*. He was terrified at the idea that he might have caused her to cry.

"Honey, please . . . look at me."

She bit her lower lip, then slowly turned her head until she faced him. Her eyes opened and he could see the glistening of tears there.

"I'm sorry," he said. "I'm sorry. I don't know what came over me . . ."

She astonished him then by giving him a wavery smile. "It's okay," she whispered. "It's okay."

He groaned, a sound more like a helpless laugh. "*Nothing* is okay now." Groaning again, he rolled off her, landing on his back on the floor with a thud. Staring up at the ceiling that had become a no-man's-land of strange events, he clasped his hands behind his head and drew calming breaths.

"I lied," he said finally.

"About what?"

"What came over me. I know exactly what came over me." It seemed like the time for bluntness. "I was out of my head with wanting you. My brain exited the room right about the time I felt you against me. I'm sorry. I usually have more control than that."

She rolled onto her side and looked down at him. Her eyes were dry now, and he wondered what she was feeling. "You weren't the only one who lost control," she said gently.

"That doesn't make what I did any more excusable." He gave her a rueful smile. "I don't usually come on like gangbusters."

A small smile curved her mouth. "I don't usually give in quite so fast."

Suddenly concerned that she not think he was misjudging her, he reached up and touched her cheek. "I know you don't."

"How could you know that?"

"Because I know *you*. At least a little. Well enough to know you don't give yourself cheaply or easily."

That eased a subtle tension in her face and told him he had managed to ease at least a part of her distress. Relief allowed him to relax.

"But I gotta say," he admitted frankly, "not once in my entire life has a woman gone to my head as fast as you did."

Another blush stained her cheeks, but she smiled. "You don't have to soothe my ego."

"I'm not trying to. I'm trying to soothe my own. Losing control is not something I'm proud of, so naturally, it has to be *your* fault."

"Oh." A little laugh escaped her, and at last her smile reached her eyes. "I can live with that."

"I figured you might be able to." He gave her a grin. "You know, when I was sixteen and acted like an animal, I didn't feel quite so embarrassed."

"Ah, but when I was sixteen, I didn't feel quite so flattered when a guy acted like an animal."

A laugh exploded out of him, then faded away. He looked at her seriously. "I want you more than I've ever wanted a woman. But it's not enough, is it?"

Looking almost sad, she shook her head.

"I didn't think so." He returned his attention to the ceiling. "You know, Joe's handiwork is kind of interesting from this angle."

She readily accepted the change of subject. "How so?"

"It makes me feel like I'm floating, to lie here and look at furniture. Try it."

So she lay on her back on the couch and looked at the chair, table, and lamp on the ceiling. "You're right," she said after a moment. "It feels like I'm lying on the ceiling."

"Neat, huh?"

Silence enveloped them for several minutes, and the last tension seeped out of the room.

"Rainy?"

"Hmm?"

"Do you feel Joe now?"

A few seconds passed before she answered. "Yes," she said finally. "I do."

"I thought so. Crazy as it makes me feel to admit it, sometimes I can feel him. And right now I get the feeling he's pleased."

"Yes, I think so."

"Well, I guess I'd be pleased, too, if I were a ghost and I'd managed to put three pieces of furniture on the ceiling."

"It *is* spectacular."

He hesitated, afraid to ask, afraid of the answer. "But what does he want?"

Rainbow was silent for a couple of minutes that seemed endless. "There's something he wants you to know," she said finally, her voice sounding almost dreamy. "It's important. But I'm sorry, Jake. I don't know what it is."

He sighed. "Well, I guess he'll get around to letting me know when he's ready."

"I imagine so."

They lay there for a long time, staring at the furniture, neither of them realizing what an amazing conversation they had just had.

"They've been up there too long," Roxy said.

She, Dawn and Gene were sitting with Mary Todd, Ted Wannamaker, and Nellie Blair in the lobby at an octagonal table covered in green baize. Gene had suggested playing rummy, but no one else had seemed interested. Most of the others had drifted off to follow their own pursuits when they realized that nothing exciting was likely to happen for a while.

"Who?" Gene asked, knowing perfectly well to whom she referred. "The Dustbuster Brigade?"

"No, of course not," Roxy said impatiently. "I'm talking about Rainy and Jake. They've been up in his apartment entirely too long."

"It's none of your business, Mother," Dawn said.

"Of course it's my business! She's my daughter and she left me here while she went up to a man's apartment. A man who, I might point out, is still a virtual stranger. For all any of us knows, he could be a serial killer. I hear they're very charming."

"Oh, Mother," Dawn said in disgust, while Gene sent an amused look to Nellie, and Ted and Mary exchanged humorous glances.

Roxy straightened her purple turban, which was tilting precariously over one ear. "Well," she said to

Dawn, "how do *you* know he isn't some unsavory character?"

"I'm sure he's exactly what he says he is."

"But how are you sure?"

Nellie spoke. "He's exactly what he says he is, Roxy. I knew his uncle for years, and Jake has come to visit from time to time."

"Mmph," said Roxy, unwilling to be soothed. "I can't believe she just walked off like that, after I interrupted my cruise to come to her aid!"

"Mother, you were looking for any conceivable excuse to get off that boat," Dawn said drily. "Although telling the cruise company that your daughter had been in a terrible accident was going a little far, don't you think?"

"Well, they wanted to know what kind of emergency it was. I could hardly say she was working on a haunting. They *never* would have understood *that*."

"Probably not," Gene agreed gravely.

"Oh, do be quiet, Gene! You've been impossible ever since you got out of diapers!"

Roxy looked toward the elevators again, drumming her extravagantly manicured nails on the table. "She's going to get into trouble," she said in a doomsday tone. "Even if he isn't an ax murderer, nothing good can come of this."

"He seems very nice," Dawn said.

"He is," Gene agreed.

Roxy clucked her tongue impatiently. "You hardly know him any better than I do. After Walter—"

"He's not Walter," Dawn said flatly. "And what's more, Walter never looked at her the way Jake does, and Rainy never looked at Walter the way she looks at him."

"That's what worries me! I'm not *blind*. Walter was a mere thunderstorm in Rainy's life. This young man could well turn out to be a force five hurricane.''

No one seemed to have any easy reply to that. Several minutes passed while Roxy tapped her toe impatiently and drummed her fingers. Finally she said, "I'm going up there."

Mary spoke. "Don't be ridiculous. The gal is thirty-something, which entitles her to make her own mistakes."

"You don't understand! You're not a mother—"

Mary snorted. "It doesn't take a mother to understand that you're doing the gal absolutely no good if you feed her distrust of men!"

"Hear, hear," said Gene, clapping his hands in approval. Nellie beamed at him.

"Traitor!" Roxy accused her brother. "Have you no heart? Don't you care what happens to Rainbow?"

"Of course I care," Gene replied. "I care every bit as much as you do."

"You couldn't possibly. You're not her mother!"

Gene sighed. "You know, Roxy, I held that little girl when she was an infant. I babysat her for weeks at a time while you were off—what was it you called it? Oh, yes, *doing your own thing*. How many times did Dawn and Rainbow stay with me when I was able to take vacation? I'll readily admit that I didn't spend as much time with the girls as you did, but I also lay claim to some very *parental* feelings where they're concerned. I was certainly the only father figure they ever had."

Roxy sniffed. "Are you saying I was a bad mother?"

"Nothing of the sort! I *am* saying, however, that I'm the closest thing they ever had to a father, and that gives me some rights. Mary is quite right. Don't feed her fear. If you do, you'll only turn it into a prison."

"It's already a prison," Dawn said. "She's terrified of Jake. Terrified of even allowing him to be a friend."

"That's good," said Roxy. "I don't want her to be hurt."

"None of us wants her to be hurt," Gene said. "But sometimes that's the price you pay if you don't want to live in a cage."

"It's true," Nellie said. "Years ago, when my husband had his first heart attack, I absolutely panicked about losing him. I was living in terror of something that hadn't even happened yet. One afternoon, I was talking to my daughter, and said how awful it was to know I had nothing left to look forward to except losing him. And you know what she said to me? She said, 'Mom, if we're to be perfectly honest, that's all any of us has to look forward to at any time in our lives.' "

Gene reached out and took her hand, squeezing it gently. "Did it help?"

Nellie nodded. "It was a surprising help. Because she was right, of course. That's all any of us has to look forward to, and if you let that cloud whatever days you have left, then you might as well give up right now. You have to risk the pain in order to find the joy. And as it happened, Mort and I had another twenty years together."

"But this is different," Roxy complained.

"No, it isn't," Mary said. "No pain, no gain."

Gene chuckled and Mary winked at him.

But Roxy had apparently given up any thought of chasing her daughter down. Though she kept staring disapprovingly at the elevators, she made no move to get out of her chair.

"You don't understand," she said presently.

"Rainbow hasn't been the same since Walter walked out on her."

"No, she hasn't," Gene agreed. "She's become cautious."

"She's *afraid*," Dawn said. "She hasn't really let anyone get close to her since then."

"So I'm worrying needlessly," Roxy decided.

"Actually, you're worrying about the wrong thing," Gene argued. "You should be worrying that she won't take risks anymore."

Roxy frowned at him, but said nothing.

Just then Colonel Albemarle and his Dustbuster squad emerged from the elevators. The colonel marched over to them and touched his swagger stick to his pith helmet. "We've completed our sweep of the hallways and public areas," he assured them. "If there was anything there, we've got it."

Mary Todd arched an eyebrow at him. "And whatever are you going to do with whatever you've got, Colonel?"

He gave her a courteous nod. "Sergeant Fields will take the vacuums to an isolated area in Manatee County and dispose of the contents."

"Mm. And how do you suppose the residents of Manatee County will feel about that?"

"As I said, Miss Todd, the contents will be disposed of in an *isolated* area."

"One hopes."

"I promise you, we are endeavoring to ensure that no one else will suffer from these rascals."

"That's good to know," Mary said drily. "Well, don't let us detain you."

"My pleasure, ma'am. I just wanted to assure you that the public areas are now safe."

Mary fluttered her eyelashes. "I do declare, I feel ever so much better!"

Beaming, the colonel and his squad departed.

"Mary," Ted chided gently, "how could you tease him that way?"

"I did no such thing, Ted. All I was doing was playing along. What did you expect me to say? That he's totally nuts and he and his Dustbusters need to be locked up?"

"You didn't have to turn all southern belle on him."

"I *am* a southern belle, Ted. Age hasn't revoked my license to act like a ninny to inflate some poor male's ego."

Gene grinned at Ted. "You'd better look out."

Ted shrugged. "I'm immune. She hasn't treated me like a stupid male in years, anyway."

Mary gave him an arch look. "Are you *sure*?"

He gave her a crooked smile. "You certainly haven't tried to inflate my ego in at least fifty years."

"Your ego has always been hardy enough. You don't need anyone to inflate it."

"I think I'm wounded."

"Ha!" said Mary, unsympathetically.

Ted looked at Gene. "You see? But I suppose this is all a man can expect when he dangles after a woman for fifty years."

"Fifty-four years," Mary said.

"I beg your pardon. Fifty-four years."

"And I *am* letting you take me out to dinner tonight," she reminded him.

"Yes, of course. How could I have forgotten? I am *so* honored." But his eyes were twinkling as he looked fondly at Mary. "A southern belle must have her southern beau, after all."

And surprising everyone, Mary actually blushed.

Rainbow found it surprisingly peaceful to lie on Jake's couch, staring up at nothing in particular, letting the quiet wash over her, while he lay on the floor beside her. A sense of Joe's presence was still there, but it was gentle and faint, troubling her not at all. To her psychic self, there was a sense of vaguely heard voices in the ether, but nothing that made any particular sense, something like the babbling of many voices in a faraway crowd.

She felt as if she could stay like this forever.

Jake stirred. "I guess we'd better go downstairs. The gossips in this building already have enough to talk about."

"I guess so," she agreed reluctantly.

She sat up and swung her legs to the floor. Jake was sitting cross-legged, looking at her with a smile.

"Reality intrudes," he remarked.

"Always," she agreed, with a touch of unusual bitterness.

His smile faded. "I'm sorry," he said. "I didn't mean to make you feel bad."

With effort, she shrugged away the mood. "I'm fine. Just tired, I guess." What she didn't want to do was admit just how discontented she was feeling. It was hard now to remember that only a short while ago she had been perfectly content with her life as it was. Now all she seemed to be aware of was what it lacked.

And that was foolish. Happiness came from making others happy, not from seeking it for oneself. She knew that.

She found a smile somewhere and offered it to Jake. "Really," she said again. "I'm fine."

In one smooth movement, he rose to his feet and offered a hand to help her up. "Well, let's go face all the knowing looks. Maybe we shook take separate elevators down."

His wry suggestion drew a laugh from her. "My mother's probably annoyed over the way I left her in the lobby."

He shrugged. "She's grown up. She'll get over it."

"You don't know my mother."

He grinned. "Ah, but I know your Uncle Gene. He'll calm her down."

When they emerged in the lobby, they saw that almost everyone had disappeared, except for the group gathered at the octagonal card table. Six pairs of eyes fixed on them as soon as the elevator doors opened and there was no mistaking the curiosity in them.

"I suggest," Jake said under his breath, "that we take the tack that you were seeking psychic impressions."

"Easy enough to do."

Fixing a smile on her face, hoping she didn't blush, Rainbow walked forward, aware that Jake was right behind her. Somehow, knowing that made her feel able to face anything.

"Well?" said Roxy, looking suspiciously from her to Jake.

"I get a faint impression that Joe is hanging around Jake's unit," Rainbow answered easily, "but I can't tell why."

Roxy looked surprised, as if she wasn't expecting to hear that at all. Good, thought Rainbow. There were some things she didn't want to share with her mother.

But Roxy was never one to let a conversation get out of her control. "I still think we need to hold a seance."

Rainbow hesitated. She was coming to that conclusion herself, but for some reason it made her unhappy.

"Mother," said Dawn, "I told you, it has to be Rainbow's decision. Besides, if your guides are being silent on this issue, a seance is hardly likely to do anything except give them an opportunity to play their games with us."

"They play games?" Mary asked.

"Oh, yes," said Roxy. "Sometimes they act like a bunch of mischievous children. Red Feather takes particular pride in being difficult."

"He's still trying to get even with white people," Dawn explained. "He never misses an opportunity to remind us how we wronged the Indians."

"Oh," said Mary, at a loss for one of the few times in her outspoken life.

"And Mustafa just refuses to talk at all," Dawn continued.

"I never realized that it could be so difficult," Mary said.

"Oh, you just don't know," Roxy said, sensing a sympathetic audience. "Most people have absolutely no idea just how difficult it is to communicate with the spirit world!"

"But I thought you did it on a regular basis . . ."

"Well, of course," Roxy said proudly. "And quite well, I might add. But when my guides want to be difficult, there's certainly nothing I can do about it."

"No, there isn't," Dawn said firmly. "And if we hold a seance when your guides aren't feeling co-operative, we're apt to hear a whole bunch of stuff most of the attendees don't want to hear in public."

"Really?" said Mary, beginning to look truly interested. "What kind of stuff?"

"Oh, secrets," Dawn said vaguely. "There are times when they seem absolutely bound and determined to embarrass people."

"Oh," said Mary, her dark eyes gleaming. "A seance sounds like just the thing."

Everyone looked at her in surprise.

"Well," she said, "it would certainly be interesting!"

"Mary!" Ted said disapprovingly.

She grinned wickedly at him. "Just what kind of secrets do you suppose all these old farts could have? The real contents of their wills?"

"Mary . . ."

She shook her head, silencing him. "My dear, darling Teddy, you just never understood, did you? The only way to live is to live dangerously! Otherwise the boredom will kill you."

He leaned toward her, and the look he gave her was dead serious. "If you really believed that, my dear, you wouldn't have kept me dangling after you all these years."

Mary cocked her head. "Is that how you see it? My dearest Teddy, if I had wanted safety, I would have married you—and how dull we both would have become!"

She turned to Roxy. "I have a group of friends I'd really like you to meet. Such a pity you don't live here. I'd love to ask you to join our little club."

Ted raised his eyes to heaven, a gesture that had the effect of gaining Roxy's full attention.

"Would you like to hold a little seance for us?" Mary asked sweetly. "We'd be happy to pay your fee."

Ted frowned at her, and that somehow seemed to make up Roxy's mind. "I'd be delighted to," she said.

Rainbow had the feeling that something truly unfortunate had just been set afoot, but she didn't know how to stop it.

"Tomorrow night," Mary said. "I'll summon the group. Seven o'clock?"

"Yes," Roxy agreed. "That'll be fine." The two women began to discuss the details.

Jake looked down at Rainbow. "Why don't we go out to dinner tonight?"

Rainbow looked up at him, wondering what he could be thinking of. Hadn't they just agreed that mere sexual attraction wasn't enough? Although the sexual attraction she felt for him could hardly be described as *mere*. "Actually," she said, "I was thinking about spending the evening trying to read the cards for myself." She braced herself for a disbelieving look and was rather surprised when she didn't get one.

"I'm a little confused myself," he admitted. "I can understand why you want to do a reading. But perhaps afterward?"

Rainbow felt torn. On one hand, she very much wanted to go out with Jake. On the other, she had no doubt it would be the most reckless thing she could possibly do. But then she remembered what Mary had just said about living dangerously or dying of boredom. "Yes," she said, ignoring the sudden arrival of a flock of butterflies in her stomach. "That would be nice."

"Great!" He beamed at her.

"What's great?" Roxy demanded, suddenly tuning into their conversation.

Rainbow lifted her chin. "I'm going out with Jake for dinner this evening."

Roxy looked as if she were about to argue, but then jumped as Gene kicked her beneath the table.

"That's great," Gene said, beaming. "I'll take your mother, Dawn, and Nellie out to dinner then myself. There's this really neat place up the beach."

Just then Harvey Little emerged from his hiding place behind the fern and scuttled across the lobby to the elevators.

"Well," said Mary, when the elevator doors had closed after him, "what do you suppose he was up to?"

"He was just sitting there," Nellie said.

Mary shook her head. "I don't think so. There was something furtive about the way he looked."

"Did you think so?" Gene said. But his gaze had grown thoughtful in a way that told Rainbow he wasn't ignoring Mary's suspicion.

"What does it matter?" Nellie asked. "We weren't discussing anything of importance."

"Dinner and a seance," Gene said.

"You see?" said Roxy. "Nothing that should interest anyone except us!"

But Gene didn't look so sure, and Rainbow found herself wondering uneasily what Gene thought Harvey Little might have to do with all this.

Joe smiled at Lucinda. "You see, my dear? It's all beginning to come together. Jake and Rainbow are going out to dinner, and that revolting little man is beginning to get nervous. What do you think?"

"I think," she said, "we ought to beat on Harvey's wall again tonight."

"Great idea, Luce," Joe said with a grin. "Great idea."

"But on the other side this time. I don't want to keep Trixie awake again."

"Oh, why not?" Joe asked. "She'll only call the police."

A slow smile spread across Lucy's face. She was really beginning to get into this little scheme of theirs. "Oh, I do like the sound of that. By all means, let's keep Trixie awake."

Satisfied, they resumed their watch over their old friends.

Fourteen

MUCH TO EVERYONE'S DISMAY, THE ENGINEERS REfused to say anything about the state of the building. They had taken their measurements, they said, and inspected the property. Now they needed to go back to the office, evaluate their data, and prepare a report. That might take a week or more.

At least, that's what the nerd said. Slide Rule, however, leaned over to Jake as they were leaving. "The building's okay, man," he said quietly. "You better check out the ghost idea."

Jake watched them leave with a glum feeling of inevitability. So much for that hypothesis. Rainbow, on the other hand, apparently wasn't the least dismayed by this news. Of course not; she had expected it.

At least she didn't gloat. She didn't even send him a significant look. He could have forgiven her for saying "I told you so," but she had more dignity than that. She simply suggested they meet at seven, and he, having nothing else to say, agreed.

He watched Rainbow leave with her family and decided to spend the rest of the afternoon working on his book. Anything was better than brooding about events—and about Rainbow.

All the way home, Gene kept Roxy busy talking about everything under the sun except Jake, for which Rainbow was grateful. She knew her mother well enough to guess that Roxy wanted to say a whole lot about her disappearance upstairs with Jake. Roxy always had an opinion on everything, and what's more, felt that as a mother she was entitled to it.

Right now, Rainbow didn't want to hear it. Yes, she was being a jerk and taking a big risk, but she didn't need a lecture. Certainly not from her mother, who was capable of turning a molehill into a mountain in a matter of seconds.

No sooner did they get home than a woman knocked on the door seeking a reading. Rainbow gladly invited her in. After that, she had two scheduled appointments, and by then there was just enough time to do a reading for herself and get ready for dinner with Jake.

But as was usual of late, the cards told her nothing useful. It was as if her psychic powers had developed a big blind spot, and the feeling made her uncomfortable. At the very least, she expected to get some sense of the direction events were taking, but the cards mocked her with their silence, or with her inability to interpret them usefully. Either way, it was disconcerting.

Giving up at last, and accepting the fact that she was going to have to face her immediate future in the same ignorance as most people in the world, she went to dress.

Of course, Roxy felt she shouldn't dress up. Paradise Beach was a relaxed community where the comfort of tourists generally dictated the dress codes. But Rainbow felt differently. Going out to dinner was a special event and deserved something more than shorts and a T-shirt.

She selected an emerald green cotton dress with a fitted bodice and flared skirt, and white sandals. She passed on pantyhose, though. In this climate, at this time of year, wearing them would have been lunacy.

By the time she emerged from her bedroom, Gene had already hustled the rest of the family away, so she didn't have to bear her mother's comments about how she had chosen to dress. She realized that Roxy was just being protective, but she also figured that at thirty-something, she was entitled to make her own stupid mistakes without her mother's intervention.

And this was a stupid mistake, she thought, as she waited for Jake. Nothing good could come from it, and she began to wonder if she wasn't just acting like a stubborn horse and taking the bit between her teeth when common sense dictated she ought to head the other way.

It wasn't just stubbornness that was goading her, she realized. There was also an element of wistful hope. Stupid, irrepressible hope. Jake had proved to be tolerant of her psychic abilities, far more tolerant than she'd have expected after their first encounter. And that tolerance was leading her down the proverbial primrose path, drawing her along with the merest whiff of hope.

Because she liked Jake Carpenter very much. And while she still rankled at his initial assessment of her, she also respected him for it. He certainly didn't stand to lose a thing if she proved to be a fraud, so he had been protecting the other residents of the building, people who at that time were strangers to him. How could she not respect that?

She also respected his willingness to be tolerant—although she had to admit that she wanted more than tolerance from a man—and would have to have it in order to develop a serious relationship.

These very lucid thoughts were almost enough to make her run to her bedroom, strip off her dress, change into shorts, call Jake, and tell him to forget it.

But it was too late. Even as she started to turn and run from the danger, it pulled up in front of her house. Her heart hammered like a trapped animal's as she watched Jake climb out of his car and walk up to her door.

When the bell rang, for an instant she couldn't move. If she didn't answer it, he'd go away eventually—and probably never speak to her again.

And it was that last thought that galvanized her, causing her to open the door and smile at him. She couldn't bear the thought of him never speaking to her again.

"Hi," he said. His gaze traveled over her with blatant appreciation. "Wow!"

He had changed, too, she noted, and was now wearing an open-throated blue shirt and blue slacks that somehow made him look taller, and that emphasized the breadth of his shoulders and the narrowness of his hips. Every cell in her body suddenly remembered their earlier embrace, as if she were imprinted forever with the memory of his contours.

"You look good enough to eat," he said appreciatively, and then reddened to the roots of his hair. "I shouldn't have said it that way," he said swiftly, but her sudden laughter drowned his words.

"It's okay," she said, taking his arm. And it was. To hell with everything, she thought, feeling wild with exhilaration. If all she could have was tonight, she was going to have it all.

He took her to one of the nicer seafood restaurants a long way up the beach, past the condos and hotels.

They had to wait for the drawbridge at John's Pass while a day-cruise boat passed beneath them, along with an assortment of smaller boats coming back to harbor for the night.

The restaurant he had chosen was on the Intracoastal Waterway, with a view of homebound sailboats from the windows of the back dining room.

"I figured this was far enough away that we're not likely to run into anyone from the Towers," he told her with a smile.

She smiled back, but wondered if he thought he was protecting them somehow, or if he just didn't want to be seen with her. The last suspicion was unworthy, she realized immediately. He hadn't seemed to care who might hear when he'd asked her out.

So he wanted to be alone with her. The understanding gave her a delicious feeling, and suddenly the evening was alive and alight with beauty.

They dined on shrimp and crab as daylight gave way to twilight and then night. Unlike so many places on the beach, this restaurant didn't hurry its customers along, but gave them plenty of time to enjoy fine dining—and one another's company. By the time they reached dessert, they felt they had learned a lot about one another.

That was when Rainbow really noticed the man at the table behind Jake. He was dining alone, and the first few times their eyes locked, she had thought it was accidental. By the time she was drinking her liqueur, she knew he was staring at her.

He was an older man with steel-gray hair, dressed in slacks and a white shirt. Ordinary looking, she thought, except for blue eyes as exceptional as Jake's. She gave him a smile and a nod, and saw him smile and nod in return. Then she gave her attention to her reflection in the window glass, hoping the man would have the courtesy to direct his attention elsewhere.

When she looked again, the man was gone.

When they were driving home, Jake said, "I'd like to spend a little more time with you. I'd suggest your place, but . . . well . . ."

She laughed, feeling a little giddy. "I have an excess of relatives there."

"There is that," he agreed, flashing her a smile. "And my place has furniture on the ceiling."

"I vote for the furniture."

Oh, Rainbow, she thought, as soon as she spoke. *This is so dangerous!* Time alone with Jake would probably bring a repeat of what had happened that afternoon. Why else did he want to be alone with her?

And she must never forget that men viewed sexual matters differently. What would for him be a mere interlude might for her be a major catastrophe.

But she wanted him. Desperately. Deep down inside her was a burning desire that had been heightened in his arms that afternoon. She no longer merely felt an attraction, she felt a compelling *need* to be with him. She assured herself she was old enough to handle this, old enough to have a one-night stand without being crushed by it, but deep inside she feared that wasn't true.

Her body, however, wasn't listening, and right now her brain was so awash in anticipation of his touch that she wasn't thinking any too clearly. Tomorrow seemed a long way away, and tonight seemed to be all that mattered.

Amazingly enough, they managed to make it across the parking lot, through the lobby, and into the elevator without running into anyone. Rainbow felt a little like she had back in her college days when she'd sneaked her boyfriend into the dorm after curfew. The wild exhilaration in her was growing, consuming her with its addictive excitement.

When the elevator reached Jake's floor, he poked his head out to make sure the coast was clear, then they darted across the hallway and into his unit. Once the door was closed behind them, Rainbow started to laugh, and Jake joined her.

He leaned against the door and gave her a cock-eyed grin. "I feel like I'm living with thirty pairs of parents."

That sent Rainbow into fresh laughter. "Really?" she said, wiping tears from her eyes.

"Really. Nearly every morning, someone knocks on my door to ask if I've had breakfast. Three times in the past week, women have brought me plates of cookies or brownies. Four times they've brought me casseroles because bachelors can't be bothered to cook."

"Did they say that?"

He nodded. "In so many words. I've been asked if I need help doing my laundry, one lady offered to sew a button back on for me when it popped off my shirt the other day, and I've received all kinds of advice on how to wax the kitchen floor and what works best for cleaning windows."

"Wow!"

His grin broadened. "Actually, it's kind of touching. But I sure as hell don't want their advice on my love life."

Rainbow's smile became crooked. "No, I think we can mess that up well enough on our own."

His smile faded. "I'm sorry, Rainbow. You're right. This is foolhardy, and I'm old enough to know better."

"So am I."

That having been said and agreed to, they stood looking at one another in obvious yearning until finally Jake groaned and reached for Rainbow. A little murmur escaped her as her eyes closed and she leaned into his embrace.

Not again, Jake promised himself. He was not going to let this get out of hand again. He was going to control himself, take it slowly, let it build gently . . .

But the feel of her gentle curves pressed against him were the most powerful aphrodisiac he'd ever known. Just a kiss, he promised himself. Just one kiss . . .

Her face was pressed to his shirt front, and her arms wound their way around his waist. She clung to him as if she never wanted to let go. Then, almost as if she were reading his mind, she tilted her face upward. Her eyes remained closed, but her soft, slightly parted lips seemed to beg for his kiss.

He couldn't have said no if his life depended on it. Slowly, reminding himself to be gentle, to take his time, to restrain his wild need for her, he brushed the lightest of butterfly kisses on her lips.

Another murmur escaped her, and her hold on him tightened, demanding more. A surge of wonder and triumph filled him as he realized his feelings were returned in full measure.

But he had made a promise, and it bound him as tightly as any chain. He kissed her again, allowing his tongue one longing foray into the warm, welcoming depths of her mouth, allowing his body one long, lingering taste of her pressed to him, then he gently broke away.

It wasn't easy. Every cell in his body was screaming for her now, but he had promised. He almost cried out from the pain of it when he let her go.

They stood there looking at one another for a minute, then Jake pushed himself away from the door and headed for the kitchen. "Would you like something to drink? I've got coffee, tea, juice, and milk. Nothing alcoholic, I'm afraid. I have no evil designs on you."

"What, no designs?" she said, in mock disappointment.

He paused and looked over his shoulder, wiggling his eyebrows melodramatically. "I didn't say that. I have plenty of designs, just no evil ones."

She decided it was safest to leave that untouched. "I'd like some ice water, please."

"Wouldn't you know? I offer the woman a whole list of drinks and she picks the one thing I didn't mention."

But he was smiling as he walked around the corner into the kitchen.

Rainbow sat on the couch and noticed a small gold-framed photograph that hadn't been there earlier. Idly curious, she picked it up, then felt a shiver of shock as she recognized the face.

Jake came back around the corner with two glasses of ice water and saw what she was holding. "I wonder how the devil that got out here," he said. "I keep it in the bedroom."

Rainbow jerked her head around and looked at him. "Who *is* this man? He was staring at me in the restaurant and it was making me uncomfortable."

Jake froze in midstep. "Who was staring at you?"

"This man," she said, pointing at the picture. "He was even dressed the same. Is he a friend of yours?" That would explain why he was watching her.

Jake put the glasses down on the coffee table and looked at her. "Are you sure you aren't mistaken?"

"Of course I'm sure. He was sitting at the table right behind you, and he kept staring at me. Finally I just stared right back. Then he nodded and smiled, and when I looked again, he'd left." She shook her head. "I was glad when he was gone. It's unnerving to be watched that way."

"You couldn't have seen him."

Irritation stirred in her. "Why not?" she demanded. "It was *him*. I have perfectly good eyesight, and an excellent memory for faces. Who is he? Is someone following you?"

Jake bent over and took the photo from her. "You're mistaken," he said flatly.

She jumped to her feet. "I am *not*. I saw him as clearly as I see you right now. Ooh, you're impossible, Jake! Before you even knew me you were calling me a fraud and a swindler, and now you're telling me I didn't see what I saw!" She snatched up her purse and started toward the door.

"You men are impossible!" she stormed. "All of you! You treat women like idiots and fools. *You're* the only ones who ever know anything! And you don't even have the courtesy to hide your superior attitudes!"

"Wait! I'll drive you home."

She turned and glared at him. "I would walk barefoot on hot coals rather than endure one more minute of your insufferable company!"

"Rainbow . . ."

But she was already gone, slamming his door behind her.

He stood alone in the living room, the slam echoing like a gunshot. What had he said? Maybe it wasn't so much what he'd said but the way he'd said it. He looked down at the picture, feeling the shock she'd given him when she'd told him she'd seen this man in the restaurant.

It was Joe, and Joe was dead. She couldn't possibly have seen him. She *had* to be mistaken. But he wanted to question her more closely about it, and now she was gone.

"Shit!" he said, and threw the photo onto the couch. "Women!" All he had wanted was more information, but instead she'd taken offense. Well, she could just go hang.

Besides, he told himself after a moment, maybe she had seen the photograph and decided to use it. If a man had been staring at her at the restaurant, why hadn't she said anything so he could deal with it? Why hadn't this come out until now, when she saw Joe's picture?

Easy. He had been right in the first place. Rainbow Moonglow *was* a fraud.

Lucinda looked at Joe. "Now you've done it, Joe. You never, ever should have done that!"

"I thought he was coming around! You heard what he said earlier."

"He hadn't come around *that* much," Lucy pointed out.

"I guess not. This is harder than I thought it would be."

"Just look at them," Lucy said sadly. "Jake's convinced Rainbow is lying to him, and her heart is broken."

"I know. I know." Joe groaned. "Lucy, you've got to help me! I'm out of ideas, and I can't leave things like this."

Lucy wasn't at all sure they ought to do anything more, not after the mess they'd made of things already, but she didn't say so. Instead, she patted Joe's shoulder and desperately tried to think of something.

Rainbow kicked off her sandals, picked them up in one hand, and put her feet in the warm sand. A moonlit walk along the beach would soothe her, she decided. Besides, it was safer to walk here than along the busy boulevard at this time of night.

She passed palms and some dunes covered with sea oats on her way to the water's edge, then turned toward her home.

Men! she thought again, with angry disgust. Damn them and their superior attitudes. Damn them, damn them, damn them! And damn Jake Carpenter in particular.

An angry tear rolled down her cheek and she wiped it away. They were all alike. Walter had been the worst of the lot, but they were all the same. At least she hadn't known Jake long enough to feel *really* hurt by what he had done.

Yeah, right.

Another tear rolled down her cheek, and angrily she wiped it away. She was not going to waste tears on that man. She wasn't even going to waste another thought on him. He wasn't worth it. Thank goodness she had discovered what he was really like before they'd had sex. Otherwise she would not only have felt angry, but she'd have felt cheapened.

And wasn't that just like a man, to be willing to pretend anything just to get a woman into bed? Jake's "tolerance" of her beliefs had been nothing but a sham designed to lower her guard. Even the things he had said that afternoon about Joe and the furniture on his ceiling had probably been lies intended to soften her up for tonight.

She made a growling sound of frustration and kicked a broken seashell out of the way. Years ago it had been possible to walk these beaches and collect gorgeous shells, but these days the sand was picked so clean there was nothing left worth the effort of bending over. She kicked another shell and stopped walking, turning to face the sea. The foam on the waves almost seemed to glow in the moonlight, and the waves were dappled with silver. It was beautiful out there, but somehow tonight the beauty couldn't work its usual peaceful magic on her. Tonight, peace eluded her completely.

She stepped closer to the water and let the warm waves lap over her toes, feeling herself sink slowly deeper into the sand. That was what had been happening to her with Jake, she thought. She had been slowly sinking in deeper as his attentions had lapped at her resolve.

At her age, she should have known better.

She stayed there a long time, while the stars wheeled overhead and the moon sank steadily toward the horizon. She didn't want to go home and face her family's questions, but she didn't want to be out here after the moon set.

Sighing, she turned again and began to walk home. It was life, she told herself. It was just life. But she was never again going to allow a man to get so close.

The waves were strengthening, heralding a storm somewhere out at sea. She climbed higher on the broad expanse of beach and trudged with her head down. All the seaside lights of the buildings were turned off, and it was almost possible to believe she was walking along a deserted beach in the middle of nowhere, miles from civilization and the people who came with it.

She reached the sea turtles' nest and paused, as she always did, to see if the nest had emptied since the last time she'd looked.

What she saw made her hold her breath. The sand was moving, shifting as something beneath it moved. The babies were hatching!

Suddenly enthralled, everything else forgotten, she sat cross-legged on the sand to one side of the roped-off area to await one of nature's miracles.

"Are you all right?"

Jake's voice startled her, and her head jerked up to find him standing just behind her.

"What are you doing here?" she demanded in a loud whisper.

He squatted down so he could hear her over the pounding surf. "Are you all right?" he asked again.

"Shh! Don't scare the turtles!"

"The tur—" He broke off and looked at the nest. "Oh, my God," he said with quiet wonder. He plopped down beside her, sitting Indian style. "Are they really coming out?"

She nodded and put her finger to her lips. He took the hint and fell silent.

The moon was still bright enough to guide them to the water, Rainbow thought, if they didn't take too long to emerge. If they didn't get out before it set, though, they might be confused and head toward the glow of the streetlights. She crossed her fingers.

She drew a sharp breath as the first little dark form began to emerge above the sand. So enchanted was she that she barely noticed that Jake reached out and took her hand. Besides, even if he was an idiot, it was nice to be sharing this miracle with someone else.

The next minutes were tense as the little turtle struggled out of the loose sand that confined it, but at last it made it, then hobbled slowly around as if seeking company, or trying to decide which way to go.

Then another head appeared above the sand. This turtle climbed out more easily, as if its predecessor's efforts had loosened the sand and blazed the trail. Free at last of the nest, it too wandered for a few moments before beginning its slow, laborious walk to the sea.

Then, in a few breathtaking moments, as if the

sand had suddenly come alive, dozens of little turtles burst free of their nest, climbing out three and four at time, crawling over one another in their eagerness. Apparently the first two had only been waiting for their brothers and sisters, because as soon as they burst free, all the turtles began marching toward the sea.

One tried to head the wrong way. Rainbow hesitated a moment, then rose and went to pick it up. Taking it down a little closer to the water, she set it among its brothers and sisters and watched with pride as it found its way.

By the time she sat beside Jake again, the last few turtles were climbing out of the nest.

"How many eggs do they lay?" Jake asked, whispering in her ear.

"Around a hundred, I think."

"Incredible."

In what seemed like only a few minutes, it was all over. Except for a couple of stragglers, the baby turtles vanished into the waves. The stragglers weren't far behind, though, and soon the beach was silent and still, except for the eternal lapping of the waves.

"Wow," Jake said.

She looked at him. "Wow," she agreed.

"I hope they all grow up."

"Only ten percent will make it to adulthood."

He shook his head, apparently not liking the odds.

Rainbow turned away from him, focusing her attention on the water and setting moon, hoping he would just go away. But he didn't move, and finally, unable to find the serenity the sea usually gave her, she faced him. "Why are you following me?"

"I'm not. Well, not exactly."

"Right."

He shook his head impatiently. "I'm just making sure you get home safely."

"I'm not your responsibility."

"I don't quite see it that way. I invited you out, and until you're safely home, I'm responsible."

"God, what a male attitude!"

He stiffened. "What do you mean by that?"

"What makes you think I need you or any other man to protect me?"

"I don't think that's what I said."

"No, but it's certainly what you implied! I'm perfectly capable of finding my own way home, thank you!"

"I never said you weren't. It's just that—well, whether you want to admit it or not, it's dangerous for a woman to be out alone at night, especially this late at night when there are no other people around. So whether you like it or not, I'm going to escort you home."

She longed to argue with him, but angry or not, she was still rational enough to realize she would have only made a fool of herself. He was right, after all.

But she was in no mood to admit he was right. So, head high and mouth firmly shut, she began walking up the beach, leaving him to follow or not as he chose.

Apparently he chose to accompany her, regardless of her response to him. She could hear his feet crunching in the seashells right behind her.

She was behaving badly and she knew it, but she couldn't quite bring herself to be friendly after what had just happened between them. He had no business acting as if she were too stupid to know what she had seen with her own eyes, and in her opinion he was adding insult to injury by insisting on escorting her home.

It didn't matter if he was right about the dangers to her out here. His actions clearly shouted that because she was a female, he considered her weak and in need of protection. True or not, she didn't have to like it.

Finally, however, her sense of courtesy overcame her resistance, and she slowed down until they were walking side-by-side. For all he insisted he had to escort her home, he wasn't making any effort to mend fences between them, and that bothered her. Reviewing what had happened, she was sure her reaction was justified. What did he have to be annoyed about, other than the fact that she hadn't liked having her judgment and memory questioned so bluntly? He had been the one who'd behaved badly.

But she had the definite feeling that he felt otherwise, and she began to wonder if he was one of those people who felt they should be able to say anything, however insulting, with immunity.

But no, that didn't seem like Jake. He had, after all, apologized for his remarks at their first meeting. What was he so miffed about?

But there didn't seem to be any answers forthcoming. She didn't want to broach the subject, because it would simply get them into another argument.

But with each step she took, she felt less annoyed and more sad. Walking always calmed her, and in times of upset she practically wore a path in the beach or in her living room carpet. Unfortunately, the calming effect this time was merely leaving room for the sorrow.

What might have been had once again proved to be an illusion. She had made a minor attempt to break out of the cage in which she seemed to be living, and for her efforts had merely had another lesson in the folly of hoping.

Well, she would never hope again, she promised herself. She'd get a cat or a dog—surely they were more trustworthy than men—tend her garden, see her clients, and make herself be content with her life.

Anything else only led to trouble; she ought to know that by now.

Jake walked her to her door, waited until she turned the key in the lock, and pushed it open. Then he said good night and walked away without another word.

What had barely begun was over.

Fifteen

IN THE MORNING, ROXY TOOK ONE LOOK AT RAINBOW and said, "I knew it! You should have listened to me. That man is nothing but trouble."

Rainbow, who had hardly slept at all, was huddled over a mug of coffee. The last thing she wanted was a lecture from her mother, so she kept her head down and didn't say a word.

"Men!" said Roxy, in a tone of utter disgust. "They're after only one thing, and if there's the least little complication, they bail out like rats deserting a sinking ship."

Despite her resolution, Rainbow replied. "Deserting a sinking ship is *wise*, Mother."

"Wise? Are you saying Walter was *wise* to treat you the way he did?"

"Apparently so. I'm a mutant, Mother. A weirdo. A freak."

"Oh, good Lord!" Roxy sat with a thump and regarded her daughter worriedly. "I don't want to hear you talk like that."

"Why not? It's true."

"It's *not* true! My dear child, you're blessed with a wonderful gift."

"Really? It doesn't seem to be doing me much good lately. I can't read the cards, I can't sense what's coming, and I scare people away. I wouldn't call it a blessing."

"*Some* people run from you," Roxy corrected her. "Others run *to* you. Think of all the people you've helped."

"I'm not sure I ever helped anyone."

Roxy frowned. "You sound depressed."

"I'm just being realistic."

"You *are* depressed."

Rainbow didn't bother to answer. If her mother couldn't see the difference between realism and depression, then no argument was likely to change her mind.

Unfortunately, Rainbow's silence didn't silence her mother.

"Rainbow's depressed," she announced to Gene, when he walked into the kitchen. He had evidently been out for his morning run, because he was hot and sweaty, and the first thing he did was hit the refrigerator for some Gatorade.

"Rainbow doesn't get depressed," Gene said. "She has an unquenchable spirit."

"See how unquenchable you think *this* is: she's decided she's a weirdo, and a *mutant*, and that she scares people. She's also decided that she's never helped anyone with her talents."

Gene looked at his niece. "She's depressed," he said.

"Hah!" said Roxy, triumphant. "What did I tell you?"

"I'm just being realistic," Rainbow said.

Gene sat across from her at the breakfast bar. "I take it the date last night didn't go well."

"It was a disaster." Although, Rainbow admitted privately, it hadn't really been that bad. In fact, most of it had been wonderful. It was just those last few minutes . . . she shook herself, trying not to minimize what had happened. "We had a fight," she said, deciding to forestall the inevitable inquisition from her mother. "He's a domineering, superior male chauvinist pig."

"Ah," said Gene, as if much enlightened.

Roxy saw it differently. "Well, of course he is. That's the way all men are."

"I beg to differ," Gene said.

Roxy waved him to silence. "Gene always thinks he's the exception to every rule," she told her daughter.

"Well, he is," Rainbow said, standing up staunchly for her beloved uncle.

"You see?" Gene said to his sister.

Roxy ignored him. "Rainbow, if your only problem with him is that he's a male chauvinist, then you're never going to get married. Men are *born* believing they're superior."

"I resent being treated as if I'm too stupid to know what I've seen with my own eyes."

"Well, of course," said Roxy. "But that's the way men treat women."

"Not necessarily," Gene interposed. "What happened, Rainy?"

"I saw a man staring at me in the restaurant last night. When we got to Jake's apartment—"

"You went to his apartment last night?" Roxy said in horror. In her case, what was sauce for the goose was not sauce for her daughters. She had lived a freewheeling, eclectic lifestyle and had had many affairs. The lesson she had learned from all this was that she didn't want her daughters to follow in her footsteps.

"Shut up, Roxy," Gene said. "What happened when you got to his apartment?"

Rainbow shrugged. "There was a picture on the table of the man I had seen at the restaurant. Jake didn't believe me."

"Did he *say* he didn't believe you?"

Rainbow thought back over it. "He said I was mistaken."

"That's a big difference, Rainy."

"No, it's not! He was essentially saying that I didn't have the sense to know what I'd seen with my own eyes."

"Actually," said Gene, "he was saying that he couldn't imagine that someone he knew would have sat in a restaurant staring at you without saying a word to him. He was surprised."

Rainbow made a face at him. "So? Why didn't he just say that? Why did he have to accuse me of being wrong?"

"An unfortunate choice of words."

"Quit making excuses for him," Roxy said. "You men always stick together."

"I'm not sticking with Jake. I'm just pointing out that this all may have been a misunderstanding."

"Then he should have said so!" Rainbow looked down at her mug, trying to conceal sudden tears.

"Did you give him a chance?"

"He walked me all the way home and never said another word about it."

Gene frowned at that.

"Beast," said Roxy.

"There's something more going on here," Gene decided.

"Of course there is," Roxy announced. "He's a *man*. That's what's going on here. Rainbow got mad, and he didn't get laid."

"Mother!"

"Roxy!"

She shook her head at both of them. "I know men.

That's all they want, and if they don't get their way, they act like spoiled brats."

"In all honesty, Mother," Rainbow finally said, "I don't think that's what happened." Because if he had wanted her that badly, he could have had her on his couch yesterday afternoon. But there was no way she was going to say that.

Gene nodded, as if he understood what she wasn't saying. "I'm sorry, Rainy."

She shrugged. "The story of my life."

"You see," said Roxy. "You *see*? She's depressed."

"I'm not depressed! I'll be fine. I just need to wake up and get on with life."

Needing to escape her mother, she carried her coffee into her bedroom and started dressing. She had a nine o'clock reading, which would keep her safely out of the way, but after that she was going to have to find something to do so she could hide from this excess of familial concern.

And tonight was the seance Roxy had agreed to hold for Mary Todd. The thought gave her a twinge. It wasn't that she doubted either her mother's sincerity or her intentions, but it was plain to her that Mary Todd was up to no good. And Rainbow had to live in this town. If something unpleasant happened tonight, Roxy could go on her merry way back to Sarasota, and Mary wouldn't give a damn, but Rainbow would be tarred with the brush of whatever happened because of her mother's involvement.

She smothered a groan and stood looking out her back window at her garden. It looked as if it was going to rain soon. The clouds were low and gray, and moving swiftly. Maybe they were getting a tropical storm.

She ought to check the Weather Channel, or turn on her weather radio. Even at this distance from the water she sometimes got some flooding from a storm.

Unlike her mother, who dressed flamboyantly, Rainbow made a point of dressing conservatively to meet her clients. This morning she wore a blue voile dress with a short-sleeved jacket that she felt was both feminine and businesslike.

Her client, though, was an old and favored one. Christine Morgan wouldn't have minded if Rainbow had greeted her in a T-shirt and jean shorts.

Christine lived at the Towers with her husband and their two Yorkshire terriers. Her primary concern at these readings was the welfare of her children and grandchildren, and so far Rainbow had had nothing but good news to give her.

This morning was different, though. Rainbow felt a heaviness the instant she touched Christine's hand in greeting, and felt a growing reluctance to do the reading. Much as she would have liked to suggest that Christine come back another time, she didn't dare. Feelings like this shouldn't be ignored.

They sat at the table in the reading room, and Christine shuffled the tarot cards. Then Rainbow took them and laid them out face down in a simple T pattern. She had a feeling she wasn't going to need many cards this morning to get to the root of the heavy dread that was filling the air around her. Flipping the cards over quickly, hardly seeing them, she felt her impressions spiral rapidly into images and feelings.

"Water," she heard herself say. "There's a lot of water . . . flood? No, no, not that . . . I see a boat . . ." Her voice trailed off as she reached through the dark for a clearer image.

"We were thinking about taking a cruise," Christine said helpfully.

"That's it. Fire and water." Rainbow yanked herself out of the well of concentration. "Don't take the cruise you're thinking about, Christine. Something bad will happen. I see fire and water and feel terrible fear. Take a different cruise. But don't take the one in . . . December. You were thinking of December, weren't you? Over Christmas. Please don't take that cruise."

Christine nodded, looking disappointed. "I always wanted to take a Christmas cruise. Oh, well. We can do something else and take the cruise next year, I guess."

Rainbow reached out and touched her hand, feeling again the sense of heavy darkness. "This isn't the cards talking, Christine. I'm deadly serious."

"I know you are." She gave a little smile and a shrug. "Ben will probably be relieved. He wasn't all that keen on the idea anyway."

After Christine left, Rainbow felt a desperate need to get outside and breathe some fresh air in the hopes she could shake that terrible feeling of doom.

Premonitions like this were rare, but they were the reason she kept using her talents for other people. If her talent helped prevent just one tragedy, everything else would be worthwhile.

Which was why she wasn't going to call herself a freak again. She might be a freak, she might be the mutant and weirdo she called herself, but that was nothing next to being able to help someone avoid a tragedy.

Of course, there were always questions that plagued her. If something was destined, how could you avoid it? What if by telling Christine and her husband to avoid this cruise, all she did was postpone the trouble she foresaw?

And what if, by encouraging Christine not to take the cruise, she actually changed the future somehow? How would Christine feel about her if there was no fire on the cruise?

Such questions could give her a headache, so she decided to just leave them alone. There weren't any answers, so why worry herself about it?

The wind was blowing too strongly to allow the use of an umbrella, and the day was too warm and humid for a raincoat, so she changed into casual clothes, evaded her family in the kitchen, and darted out the front door before anyone could stop her.

She didn't hear thunder or see lightning, so she felt it was safe to go down to the beach and walk.

The huge waves were pounding the shore, dragging the sand away in great chunks. The tide was high, cutting the usually wide expanse of white beach to half its width. The churning waters had turned up piles of seaweed, abandoning them on the shore to die.

Surfers were rarely seen along the Gulf Coast, but today there were two young men carrying their boards out into the water to take advantage of the waves. She wondered if they had left their brains at home. The undertow out there would be fierce, and the water was full of all kinds of flotsam as the currents tossed the sea floor to the surface.

Other than the surfers, the beach was empty except for seagulls who hunkered in the sand and pelicans who seemed to be playing on the wind.

The rain had soaked her, plastering her clothes to her skin, but she didn't care. It was a warm rain, and despite the wind, the air was warm, too, keeping her from getting chilled.

When she reached the area where the turtle's nest had been, she stopped, but no sign of the nest was left. Even the poles that had held the plastic yellow tape that marked off the area had vanished, carried away by the hungry waves.

She hoped the baby turtles could survive this storm. At least they had hatched before the waves had torn open the nest. Would they have drowned otherwise? Probably.

The clouds were still low, and there was no sign of relief in sight from the weather. All the way out to the horizon, the sky was a dark, leaden gray.

She resumed her walk, eyes down to watch for shells the waves might toss up, or for a pretty piece of driftwood. When she looked up again, she had reached the Towers.

Just then, lightning flickered in the sky out to sea, and a short while later, a hollow roll of thunder reached her. Time to go home. Most especially time to get away from the Towers. She didn't want Jake to see her out here and think she was mooning over him.

Which, of course, she absolutely was not. She wouldn't moon over any man ever again.

The waves seemed to have grown even higher, and the tide had risen. Her footprints in the wet sand were gone, and large puddles were forming in the hollow behind the highest point of the beach. She definitely should have headed back sooner.

"Rainbow!"

She turned, her heart sinking, and saw Jake running down the beach toward her. She wanted to keep walking, but her feet seemed to have become mired in the sand.

He caught up with her. "You shouldn't be out here," he said. "You could get hit by lightning."

"There wasn't any when I started out," she replied, her chin lifting defiantly. "Do you always tell people they're idiots?"

He swore and looked out to sea, his hands clenching and unclenching. Finally he looked at her again. "I'm sorry. I was in the rec room trying to fix a leaky faucet when I saw you out here. Then I saw the lightning."

"You should have taken your own advice and stayed inside, where it's safe."

"Apparently so." He brushed his wet hair back and looked at her through the rain. "Look, I'm sorry. I saw you, saw the lightning, and got worried."

"Why were you fixing a faucet? Doesn't the building have a handyman?"

"Yeah, but it's his day off, and the dripping was driving the Wednesday Morning Bridge Club crazy."

In spite of herself, she almost smiled. "Life as the association president isn't all it's cracked up to be, huh?"

He gave her an unexpected grin. "Frankly, it's a headache. Listen, can we continue this discussion indoors? Or in my car? I'd be happy to drive you home."

She looked down, and was horrified to see that not only was she soaked, she might just as well have been wearing plastic wrap. Very little was left to the imagination.

"I'll just soak your car. I can run home in just a few minutes." She started to turn, but before she could step away, he reached out and lifted her right off her feet. With one arm beneath her shoulders and one beneath her knees, he carried her toward the Towers.

"Just put me down this instant, you arrogant creep!"

He flashed her another grin. "Sorry, lady, but I can't let you risk getting yourself killed."

"This is battery, you know! I could have you arrested!"

"Go ahead. But for now, quit wiggling so I don't drop you."

"Put me down this instant!"

"Sure. If you agree to come inside or let me take you home."

"This is extortion!"

"Probably."

She gave serious thought to popping him in the jaw, but decided that he could get her arrested just as easily as she could get him arrested. Besides, if he dropped her, she was apt to break something. "Jake, please. Just put me down."

"Sure. Like I said, just as soon as you agree to show some common sense."

"Common sense? You're a fine one to talk about that! People with common sense don't go around acting like cavemen!"

"Aw, gee, I thought women liked cavemen."

Then she *did* come very close to popping him. "I do not like being manhandled."

"I wonder if there's a gender-neutral form of that word."

She gaped at him, not comprehending. "What?"

"Yeah, you know. Like 'personhandled.' And what if it's a woman doing the manhandling?"

She absolutely, positively did not want to stop being angry with him. She was clinging to the shreds of her fury with all the determination of a drowning woman grasping at straws, but laughter was threatening to overwhelm her, because despite everything else, she had a great appreciation of the absurd, and this whole situation was absurd. "Jake, please."

"Sure. Anything your little heart desires, as long as it involves getting you out of this storm immediately."

"Okay, okay! You can drive me home."

He set her on her feet at once and held her hand as they jogged up to the building.

Almost the instant they stepped under the awning

at the entrance, between one gust and the next, the wind's breath became icy. Turning back to look out at the sea, they saw a wall of heavy rain approaching, so thick it obscured everything behind it. Lightning forked down from the sky, striking the water, and thunder cracked deafeningly.

"Just in time," Jake said. He turned to look at Rainbow. "You're shivering!"

"The temperature just dropped fifteen degrees."

Another gust of wind struck them, this one strong enough to cause the awning to flap wildly and the supporting poles to bend ominously.

"Let's get inside," Jake said. "This is going to be bad."

She didn't argue. They made their way through the storm-darkened lobby and took the elevator up. Jake unlocked his door and threw it open to let her enter first.

I shouldn't be doing this, she thought, as she stepped across the threshold. Here she was again, in the lion's den, and such a short time after having been bitten. Maybe she ought to see a psychiatrist about why she was so incapable of staying away from people who hurt her.

Jake's apartment was gloomy, turned into near-darkness by the storm. "You know," Jake said, as he closed the door, "this is downright spooky. If I were a ghost, I'd rattle some chains right about now."

"But it's so much more impressive in broad daylight, don't you think?"

"Well, of course. But mood helps a lot, too." He hit the switch for the lights, but nothing happened. "Great. No power. Hang on a minute, I'll get you some towels."

"Thank you."

The wind gusted, rattling the windows, and Rainbow could have sworn she felt the building move.

The walls creaked eerily, and she found herself longing for the safety of her ground-level cottage. At
least there she wouldn't have far to fall if the wind
blew the house away.

Jake returned, handing her a thick towel. "Listen,
if you want, there's a terrycloth robe hanging in the
bathroom. You can change into it, and I'll throw
your clothes in the dryer. Up to you. Me, I'm going
to go change right now."

He disappeared into the bedroom, leaving her to
stand in the middle of his living room dripping and
shivering as she tried to dry her sodden hair. The
wind rattled the windows again, and even in the
gloom she could make out debris blowing past in
the rain.

She decided a dry terrycloth robe sounded too
good to pass up, especially when she felt as if she
was turning into an icicle.

In the bathroom, she peeled off her clothes and
wrung them out over the bathtub. Jake's robe, which
probably came only to his knees, nearly reached her
ankles, and enveloped her in warmth.

Carrying her wet clothes, she stepped out into the
living room. Jake was already there, wearing jeans
and a sweatshirt.

"I just realized," he said, sounding sheepish, "no
power, no dryer."

She had to laugh. "I didn't think of it, either."

"I can't even offer you a warm drink, unless you
want hot water out of the tap."

"That's okay. It's just nice to be in something dry.
The power shouldn't be out long."

"Probably not."

He crossed to the window. "It looks vicious out
there."

"Well, unless it's a tropical storm, it'll blow over

quickly," she said, hanging her wet clothes over the kitchen sink.

"That would be good."

She perched on the couch, being careful to keep the robe wrapped around her legs, and felt the tension in the atmosphere. Neither of them really knew what to say after last night, she realized. And maybe Jake didn't really want to say anything at all. Maybe he was just one of those overly protective men who would have rescued any drowned rat from a storm. Maybe he'd be glad when she could leave.

She ought to be feeling the same way, she realized. Only she didn't. Part of her desperately wanted to mend their fences and restore them to where they had been before their argument. Some of her apparently still believed in fairy tales.

Don't be stupid, she told herself. The fairy tale got it wrong; the prince *always* turned into a frog.

"I love storms," Jake remarked, his back still to her as he looked out through the sliding glass doors. "I've seen some real humdingers around the world. They can cause a lot of damage, I know, but they're always so beautiful anyway."

As he spoke, the wind whistled and the glass in the doors bent visibly.

"You'd better get away from there," Rainbow said. "If that glass shatters . . ."

"You're right." He stepped away. "Actually, if glass is going to fly, we'd be better off in the bathroom. Or the hall."

"I don't think I want to go into the hall wearing your robe."

"Of course not." He stuffed his hands into his pockets. "Maybe you'd better call your family and let them know you're safe?"

Rainbow had thought of the same thing, but she really, *really* didn't want to talk to her mother right now. *Hi, Mother. I'm sitting in Jake's apartment wearing nothing but his bathrobe.* Yeah, right. No matter what she said, Roxy was probably going to give her an earful. "They know I'd have taken shelter somewhere."

"I'm not so sure of that." In the gloom his face was unreadable. "When I saw you, you were planning to jog home."

"That was before it got this bad. I could have gone into any store or restaurant on the street."

"True."

Well, for once he wasn't disagreeing with her. "Besides," she said as thunder rolled again, "it's not safe to use the phone in an electrical storm."

The lights flickered briefly, and the refrigerator clicked and whined as it tried to start, but then the power went off again. There was a thud from outside, as Jake's cast-iron patio furniture moved a few inches in the wind, and a planter tipped over.

"That poor ficus," said Rainbow.

"Well, I'm not going out to rescue it until this lets up a little."

"Of course not."

Another tense silence. They might have been two strangers meeting for the first time.

After a bit, while the wind continued to whine and the thunder continued to roar, Jake came to sit at the other end of the couch.

"About last night . . ." he said.

She looked away, reluctant to discuss it. "Forget it."

"I can't forget it. I spent all night thinking about it when I should have been sleeping. I got up this morning and tried to work, but it was all I could think about. Actually, having to fix that faucet was a welcome relief from obsessing about you."

"I don't want you to obsess about me," she said, feeling strangely irritated by the word.

"Too bad. I seem to be doing it anyway."

She didn't know what to say to that.

Just then there was a knock at the door. Jake looked at her, and she looked at him.

"I'll just go into the bathroom," she said.

"I don't have to answer it."

"It might be important. Maybe somebody's had some storm damage." She rose and darted into the bathroom before he could contradict her again. He was the most contradictory man she had ever met. If she said the sky was blue, he'd probably claim it was green.

She left the door open a crack, but could hear only the murmur of voices, Jake's and a woman's. A couple of minutes later, she heard the door close.

"You can come out now," Jake said.

She came back to the darkened living room. "Storm trouble?"

"Actually, no. Trixie Martins says Harvey Little was banging on her wall again last night, so she called the cops. By the time they arrived, the banging had stopped, but they spoke to Harvey anyway, and he claimed she was doing it."

"Fun."

"Anyway, Trixie wanted me to know the cops can't do anything about it anyway, at least not unless they hear the banging."

"So what now?"

"God knows. The guy owns the unit. It's not like I can throw him out."

"Violating the rules . . ."

"Would undoubtedly be cause to start legal action, but first you have to prove he's doing it, then you have to get a lawyer and file suit, and God knows what else. Something tells me this is going to be a royal pain in the butt."

"It sounds like it." Feeling sympathetic, she sat on the couch again. "Maybe it's just the ghosts."

"Maybe it's just the ghosts?" He repeated the words disbelievingly, then sat beside her and laughed. "Just the *ghosts*."

She started to take umbrage at his response, but before she could work up a full head of steam, he stopped laughing and spoke.

"I'd rather it was Harvey doing the banging," he told her seriously. "At least I can get rid of him, convoluted and painful though the process might be. But I don't seem to be able to do anything about these damn ghosts!"

"So you believe they're really here?" Hope lightened her heart.

"I don't want to," he admitted, "but I'm running out of excuses for that furniture on my ceiling."

"Do you know Christine Morgan?"

He nodded. "I think so. She hangs around with Nellie Blair."

"I did a reading for her this morning, and I gave her a warning. Every time I warn somebody like that, I get left with this uneasy feeling. Maybe I made a mistake, for one thing. Or maybe by warning them, all I've done is postpone something. Or what if I've changed the future somehow, and the disaster I foresaw never materializes? How can I ever be sure I was right?"

He nodded. "I can see that. But what does this have to do with the haunting here?"

"Sometimes," she said, "you just have to believe."

He nodded slowly. "Maybe," he said slowly. "Maybe."

She didn't say anything more, just gave him the space to think about it.

He turned to her suddenly. "Rainy, about last night . . ."

She braced herself, and refrained from telling him not to call her Rainy. Somehow, on Jake's lips the pet name didn't sound like a transgression.

"Did you really see the man in the photograph at the restaurant?"

Remembering what Gene had said about misunderstandings, she refrained from getting annoyed. "Yes."

"You're *sure* it was the same man?"

"Of course I'm sure." She couldn't quite control her irritation at being asked to repeat herself.

"Do you know who he is?"

"Of course not. I asked you about him, remember? Although I did have the feeling there was something familiar about him. I've probably seen him around town before. Why? Is he a friend of yours?"

"You could say that."

"Well, how very rude of him not to stop and talk to you!"

"I don't think he could."

"Why not? It's merely common courtesy."

"I know." He shrugged. "Last night when you stormed out of here, I very nearly had myself convinced that you were scamming me."

She drew a deep breath, ready to tell him to take his butt to hell and park it on some brimstone, but before she could explode, he continued.

"I know you're not," he said almost gently. "I know you wouldn't do that. That's what I realized at four this morning. I keep toying with the idea because it's easier than giving up the things I've believed in all my life. It's safer."

"What do you mean?"

"Rainy, the man in that picture is my Uncle Joe."

Sixteen

THE LIGHTS SUDDENLY WENT ON, BUT RAINBOW hardly noticed. She stared at Jake, not disbelieving him, but thoroughly stunned. She had never before seen an apparition, and she had always assumed they would look like patches of fog. At the very least, they ought to be translucent. The man she had seen at the restaurant had looked every bit as solid and real as Jake.

"Maybe," she said hoarsely, "maybe your uncle has a twin. I've heard we all have twins somewhere."

Jake shrugged. "I don't know. It's possible, I guess. But you're the one who believes in ghosts. Are you telling me you can't accept this?"

"He didn't *look* like a ghost."

"I gathered that. I mean, if he *had*, you'd have said you saw a ghost."

Thunder boomed, sounding as if it were right over head. Rainbow jumped, feeling surprisingly edgy. "Silly as it sounds," she said, "while I'm comfortable with the idea of premonitions and psychic intuition, and while I believe that my mother really does channel messages from beyond, and while I can readily

believe that ghosts put your furniture on the ceiling
. . . I'm not happy about seeing a ghost that looks as
solid as you or I."

"Believe me, I can identify with that."

"I mean, when my mother channels, it's so . . . *re-moved*. If you know what I mean."

He nodded. "This was up close and personal."

"Too personal. That ghost was looking right at
me. He smiled at me and nodded. I've heard of such
things—in fact, my mother worked on a haunting a
couple of years ago that involved her ex-husband—
but I never expected to see it myself."

"Some things are easier to accept in theory than
in actuality."

"Exactly. The only ghostly manifestation I ever
saw was a basketball."

"A *what?*"

"Oh, one of my mother's guides got a little peeved
and materialized a basketball and dribbled it down
the table, scaring everyone half to death."

"Man!" said Jake. "Remind me not to annoy your
mother's guides."

"You don't have to try very hard. They get pee-
vish all on their own." She sighed. "It's silly. I know
it is. I hear voices, I feel premonitions, I get intuitions
and feelings from beyond, but I freak out just because I actually see what I've been talking about and
believing in my entire life. Stupid."

"Not stupid," he said. "Hey, look. I've been living
with furniture on my ceiling, and it's taken me all
this time to admit something paranormal must be
going on here. But it struck me last night that I was
fighting it to the point of being ridiculous. I mean,
I've got *furniture on my ceiling*! Why the hell should
it be so impossible for me to believe that you saw
Joe? If he can levitate the furniture, he can certainly
materialize himself."

As one, they looked at the chair, table, and lamp on the ceiling in the corner.

"I wonder," Rainbow said, "how long he's going to leave it there."

"I wish I had a clue." He turned to her. "What I'm saying is, I don't have any trouble believing you saw Joe last night."

"*I* do."

"And isn't that weird?" He gave her a rueful smile. "Our positions seem to have reversed."

"Yeah." She looked at the furniture, then reached for the photo of Joe that was lying face-down on the coffee table. She turned it over and felt again that electric sense of shock. There was no doubt in her mind that this was the man she'd seen in the restaurant.

"This is a very powerful manifestation," she said finally. "The furniture, and now this. It's extraordinary."

"You won't get any argument from me."

"There has to be a reason for it . . . Perhaps something he's trying to tell us."

"Maybe it's just a wake-up call to me," Jake suggested.

"What do you mean?"

"Well . . . toward the end of his life, Joe's letters to me started to change. He always wrote once a week, but usually he talked about the things he'd been doing and what he was planning to do. The last few months he started to talk about all the mistakes he'd made with me."

"Mistakes?"

Jake shrugged. "I couldn't really understand what he was trying to get at. Except that once he said he'd taught me to value logic above feeling, and that he'd been wrong."

Rainbow felt an ache of sympathy. "Did he?"

"I don't know. Yeah, he used to say things like, 'Boy, use your head. It's the best tool you've got.' And he used to preach that a real man is in control of himself at all times. But I don't see what's wrong with that."

"Me either. Not really. Except . . . if you go too far?" She said the last tentatively, not wanting to offend him.

Jake sighed and looked at the upside-down furnishings. "Yeah," he said after a while. "Maybe."

"Well, I don't see anything wrong with you," she told him firmly. "You were a little pigheaded about paranormal stuff, but that's not unusual or even wrong. It's not wrong to want proof, Jake."

"But it's wrong to ignore the proof when it's right before your eyes." He shook his head.

"It just took you a little while to accept it. You had to be sure there wasn't any other explanation."

He smiled at her. "Are you defending my asininity?"

"Is that a word?"

"Damned if I know." His smile deepened, and something seemed to leap and sparkle in his eyes. Thunder rumbled loudly, and lightning flashed so brightly that it seemed to flare in his eyes.

Suddenly nervous, and reminding herself of all her vows to stay away from men, Rainbow jumped to her feet and walked over to the balcony doors. "I guess I ought to put my clothes in the dryer, now that the power's on."

"Sure. I'll do it."

She kept her back to the room as she listened to him get her sodden clothing from the kitchen and dump it into the dryer. She heard the dryer door slam closed, heard it turn on.

And then she felt his hands on her shoulders and his heat right behind her.

"Are you all right?" he asked.

"Fine. The storm doesn't seem to be letting up." She was looking out the window at sheets of rain and the tops of palm trees swaying in the violent wind, but she hardly saw them. All she was aware of, suddenly, was how close he was. How heavy his hands felt on her shoulders, and how welcome.

"No, it doesn't."

His hands tightened a little, and her heart leaped in response. She felt a growing heaviness deep inside her, a softness that made her feel like she was melting. She had to put a stop to this now, before she got hurt.

But she was torn, utterly at war with herself, because she wanted Jake so very much she almost felt that walking away would hurt as much as staying eventually would. Truly, she thought with a moment of wry insight, she was on the horns of a dilemma, and no choice seemed good.

But then, gently and slowly, he turned her to face him, and need triumphed over caution. Indeed, caution vanished, vanquished by the hungry way he looked at her. That hunger was like a balm to her battered soul, assuring her of something she had long ago lost: the realization that she was a desirable woman.

His hands moved, sliding down slowly from her shoulders, grazing across the peaks of her terrycloth-covered breasts. The sensation, light as the whisper of a moth's wing, caused her to draw a sharp breath as lightning streaked through her in a jagged bolt of aching passion.

Before she could draw another breath, he tugged at the belt and the robe fell open, revealing her to him.

"Rainy?" he said, his voice husky and thick.

"Oh, yes," she whispered, giving in to the glorious need that pulsed within her. "Oh, yes!"

"Joe," Lucy said, "mind your own business. I never took you for a voyeur!"

"I'm not looking, I swear," Joe said, his expression hurt. "I'm watching you-know-who. The wall-banging doesn't seem to be having the desired affect, Lucy."

"Then we'll have to think of something else. But you keep your eyes on me, you hear?"

He gave her a sheepish grin and moved away from the edge of the cloud. "At least Jake seems to be coming to his senses."

Lucy suddenly smiled. "That part is working, dear. I'll grant you that. So now, what can we do about *him*?"

Jake drew Rainbow into his arms, holding her snugly against him and feeling a deep-seated tension easing away. Oh, Lord, it felt so good to have her in his arms again. So good!

"Tell me," he whispered. "Tell me we're alone. Please . . ."

Rainbow struggled against the tidal wave of desire that was sweeping over her, and lifted her head just long enough to test the psychic ether. "We're alone," she said, then, with a strangled sigh, leaned into Jake, giving herself over to his care.

"This ghost thing has unexpected complications," he muttered, as he bent and lifted her high into his arms. Her robe gaped, exposing one rosy breast, and he had to force himself to concentrate on first things first. Like getting her to his bed immediately.

"Your uncle wouldn't . . ."

"I don't put anything past Joe," he said, almost

grimly. "After all, he put the damn furniture on my ceiling!"

Turning, he eased them sideways through the bedroom door, then kicked it closed behind them, as if that would make any difference. Outside the storm continued to rage, windows rattling and thunder roaring.

The bedroom was dim, dark enough to feel like a warm cave safe from the furies without, but with enough light to let him see his way to the bed. As he laid Rainbow down on the sheet, lightning flared, showing him her beauty in stark relief.

The image of her was branded on his retinas, and on his soul as well. He was never going to forget this woman, he realized. No matter where he went, no matter who he loved after her, he was going to remember Rainbow Moonglow lying on his navy blue sheets as lightning forked through the sky outside.

Standing beside her, he stripped away his sweatshirt and pants. Another flare of lightning brightened the room, and he saw the smile curve her lips as she looked at him.

Then he stretched out beside her and helped her ease her arms out of the robe. He tossed it somewhere, not caring where it might land, feeling suddenly like a sailor in a storm-tossed ship who needed to find safe harbor.

He needed to be inside her with every fiber of his being, but he also wanted this to be as good for her as he could make it. Whether this was the only time they'd be together, or just the first of many times, he wanted her to leave him with a smile and only good memories.

So he restrained himself, holding his own desires in abeyance until he had satisfied all of hers.

Reaching out, he ran a gentle hand along her

length, from shoulder to upper thigh. She was so smooth and satiny, so delicate compared to him, and it seemed almost wrong that anything as large and rough as his hands should touch her.

But she seemed to like the caress, for she arched upward as if reaching for more, and a soft sigh escaped her.

Exquisite, he thought. She was exquisite.

He dared again, stroking her almost as if she were a cat, watching her curl in response, taking her sighs to his very heart. When he bent and kissed her lips, she welcomed him eagerly, wrapping her arms around him and holding him close as if she never wanted to let go.

He had never tasted anything sweeter than her mouth, and he might have drunk there forever, except that he was being called by other delights. Lifting his head, he smiled down at her in the gloom, and received an answering smile from her swollen lips. Then, as if he had all the time in the world, he began to trail kisses downward, over her chin, along the delicate line of her collar bone, and lower yet, until he reached her puckered rosy nipple.

The instant his mouth touched her there, she arched as if a shock had run through her and clutched at his head, holding him closer still. Triumph filled him, quickly drowned in the rising waves of his own need. He had passed the point of simply wanting to please her and reached the place where her needs were his.

His tongue flicked at her nipple, teasing it to hardness, and as she responded he hardened, too. When he filled his mouth with her, it was almost as if all of him was filled with all of her. Her sighs seemed to be his, her moans might have come from him.

And never, ever, not once in his life, had he felt so completely close to another person.

He teased her mercilessly, lapping at both nipples, sucking strongly until soft moans escaped her on every breath. Her legs parted, spread wide, and her hips arched upward, begging for him, but still he continued to tease her and taunt her, loving the ecstasy he was building in them both.

But his hands had desires of their own. One of them wandered downward, across the smooth hollow of her stomach, and found its way into the tight curly hair at the top of her thighs.

She froze, and for a horrifying instant he wondered if he had shocked her or hurt her, but then her hips arched upward, pressing hungrily against his hand, demanding stronger, deeper caresses.

He was only too glad to oblige. Panting like a runner at the end of a long stretch, he slipped his hand further down, parting her dewy folds and finding the nub of her desire. A soft cry escaped her, and she writhed against him, beckoning, begging, demanding more.

He stroked her, guiding her gently on her journey to completion, promising himself that later there would be more, that later he could explore every soft curve of her with his eyes, hands and mouth, that later he could memorize her every contour, and take his time over each hill and hollow.

But he was aching now, aching with a need as intense as any he had ever felt. His whole body was throbbing, driving him to find his own pleasure in her.

But wait, he told himself in a ragged moment of clarity. *But wait.* Make sure she's satisfied first. He didn't think he could bear it if she didn't wring every ounce of pleasure out of these stolen moments. His own pleasure was not in doubt; he would find it. But hers . . . hers he needed to be sure of before he could take his own.

His touches deepened, and her moans grew wilder. She cried his name over and over, as if calling him to come with her. In a moment, he thought, in a moment. He clung to the promise as he refused her pleas, determined she crest before him.

His finger slipped inside her warm, silky depths, and the sensation was like an explosion in his head, nearly carrying him past all thought. Just when he felt he couldn't take it anymore, she climaxed with a low, keening moan.

Before her moan had died, he slipped over her, entering her fully. Her body welcomed him, making a special place for him, and her hazy eyes opened momentarily as a smile of sheer pleasure curved her lips.

Then he forgot everything as he drove himself to the summit, rising higher and higher, and to his own amazement, carrying her with him.

She cried out again, digging her nails into his shoulders, and in astonishment he felt the ripples of another climax all around him, and then, in an instant, he exploded in the ultimate moment of pleasure.

Moments later, still joined among the tangled sheets, they drifted off to sleep.

He was going to kill someone. Some loud, noxious buzzer kept ringing, dragging him up from the depths of a beautiful dream in which he and Rainbow played on a sunny deserted beach.

It sounded again, insistently, and he rolled over, losing his last connection with her. He wanted to groan from the sense of loss, from the return to the real world where two were not one, but only two after all.

The dryer, he realized groggily, as the buzzer sounded again. Her clothes. They were dry, and the machine was telling him to get them before they wrinkled. The way he felt right now, he could have let them stay, but the buzzer would wake Rainbow, and anyway, she'd look awfully funny going home in wrinkled clothes.

He turned his head and looked at her. A small frown knit her brow, as if she resented the buzzer, too. He didn't want to leave her, but he wanted to let her sleep. He had a feeling she'd been up all night, too, and right now, the fatigue seemed to have melted from her face.

Sighing, moving carefully so as not to disturb her, he climbed from the bed and padded through the apartment to the utility room. There he pulled her clothes out of the dryer and carried them to the living room to fold them.

Such tiny panties, he thought, as he held up a small pair of turquoise bikinis. Such a tiny bra, just a scrap of turquoise lace to hold breasts he had found to be perfect.

He tucked them under the folded T-shirt so she wouldn't be embarrassed, then went into the kitchen to make coffee. He was up; he might as well do something useful and wake himself up all the way.

Someone started hammering on his door. He dashed to it, trying to answer it before the noise woke Rainbow. The hammering stopped when he was halfway across the living room, then started again while he struggled with the locks, which for some reason were sticky.

Remembering at the last instant that he was naked, he stopped himself from flinging open the door, and instead peered around the edge of it. He found Trixie Martin's husband standing there.

"That asshole is banging on the walls again," Martin said. "Damn it, Carpenter, *this has got to stop*. Bad enough he keeps us up all night, but now we can't even take a nap to make up for it."

"Uh . . . yeah. I was . . . um . . . napping myself. Let me get dressed and I'll come on up."

"Well, hurry," Martin said. "It'd be just like him to stop before you get there, and unless somebody *else* hears it, he's going to be able to keep on doing it until he drives me over the edge."

Jake had to bite back a sharp retort, reminding himself that Martin wasn't trying to be a pain in the ass, that he had a valid problem that needed attention. "I'll be right there," he said again, and closed the door, locking it. This time, for some strange reason, the lock didn't stick.

He hurried to the bedroom, figuring if he didn't get dressed and out of here quickly, Martin was apt to hammer on the door again and disturb Rainbow.

But it was already too late, he realized, as he stepped through the bedroom door. Rainbow was sitting up on the edge of the bed, looking adorably tousled and drowsy, her face still soft with sleep.

"What's wrong?" she asked.

"Harvey Little is apparently banging on the Martins' wall right now, so I've got to run up and read him the riot act."

"Oh."

Life wasn't fair, Jake thought with an internal groan. What he wanted to do was crawl right back into bed with Rainbow and love her senseless. She looked so sweet and tempting right now, and she wasn't awake enough yet to have marshaled all her defenses. She would be warm and languid and oh so receptive right now. He ached with yearning and felt an uncharacteristic impulse toward murder. Right now he could have cheerfully killed Harvey Little.

"I'll come with you," she said, as she watched him pull on his jeans.

"No," he said hastily. "Just go back to sleep." *Please go back to sleep*, he thought desperately. *Be here for me when I get back.*

"No, really, I need to get up." She rose, depriving him of breath with the unencumbered sight of all her feminine glory. "My clothes?"

He gave up, and railed silently against the unfairness of the universe. "They're folded on the couch."

He watched her go, and realized that for the very first time in his life, he was actually regretting the sight of a woman leaving his bed. *Uh-oh.*

He found his sweatshirt, a wrinkled heap on the floor, and his Top Siders, and shoved his bare feet into them as he yanked the shirt over his head.

When he stepped out into the living room, Rainbow had already put on her panties and was struggling to fasten the catch on her bra.

"Let me," he said, glad of any excuse to touch her. He stood behind her and fasted the two little hooks, then watched with disappointment as she pulled on her T-shirt and shorts. She slipped her feet into her sneakers without even untying them, then smiled at him.

"Let's go," she said.

He didn't bother to tell her that her hair was a wild, tousled mess. She looked as if she'd been caught in the storm, and that was okay. Besides, it was sexy as hell.

Thinking of the storm, he glanced out the window as they were leaving. The sky was still dark, but the rain had stopped. Maybe it was almost over?

He hoped not. The storm was as good an excuse as any to keep Rainbow with him.

She yawned as they rode the elevator to the Martin's unit. "Thanks for letting me sleep," she said.

"You're more than welcome. I just wish you could have slept longer."

She smiled. "Me, too. But that's okay. I'd really like to know what's going on with this banging."

He hoped it was Harvey Little doing it. It would give him an excuse to vent some of the frustration he was feeling right now. But how could you vent on a ghost?

When they stepped off the elevator, they could hear the thumping the Martinses were complaining about. It wasn't very loud in the hallway, but it was definitely audible.

"I'm going to knock on Little's door," Jake said. "Do me a favor, please, and stand back, in case he's in a rotten mood, okay?"

She shook her head. "Sure. But I think you're being overprotective. If that guy tried to hit anyone, he'd probably wind up in cardiac intensive care."

He gave her a half-smile. "Maybe. But if I need help, I want you to be able to get it for me."

Her pride salved, she didn't seem to mind being asked to stay out of the way. He was learning, he thought. He was finally learning how not to say the wrong thing to this woman.

He banged on Harvey Little's door loud enough to ensure that his knock would be heard over whatever was going on inside. There was no immediate answer, so he hammered again.

The door flew open, and Harvey Little glared up at him. "What the hell do you want?"

"You're banging on the wall again."

"I am *not*. I'm sick of those friggin' people! They're throwing stuff against the wall and claiming I'm doing it just so they can get me thrown out! What the hell did I ever do to them?"

"Do you mind if I come inside to check it out?"

"Check what out? You go look at *their* wall! It's

got to be dinged up all to hell. Half the time it sounds like he's throwing *her* against it."

"May I take a look at your wall, please?"

Harvey stepped back, flinging the door wide. "Be my goddamn guest," he said sarcastically.

Rainbow started to follow, despite Jake's warning to stay out of the way, but Little barred her bodily. "I don't want no freaking witch in my unit."

Jake felt his simmering temper rise to the boiling point. He had a strong urge to flatten the man's face, but quelled it. "She's not a witch, Little. She's a psychic."

"What's the goddamn difference?"

"I'd also appreciate it, if you'd watch your mouth in the presence of a lady."

"*Lady?*" Harvey sniffed. "She's a witch."

But Jake noticed he didn't curse again.

"I don't want her in here," the obnoxious man said again.

Jake looked apologetically at Rainbow. Little was within his rights.

"I just wanted to sense the psychic atmosphere, Mr. Little," Rainbow said pleasantly, with a friendly smile. "There are some ghosts in the building, and they might be causing—"

"I ain't got no goddamn ghosts!" Little shouted, "and I don't want no witch in my place comin' up with stories about how I got 'em and how they must be after me for somethin' I done. Now, get lost!" He slammed the door in Rainbow's face.

"Now look," Jake said sternly, "that rudeness wasn't called for!"

"It's my home and I say who comes in here. Now, get your ass in there and look at the damn wall, then get the hell out!"

Jake had to exercise great restraint not to tell this jerk exactly what he thought of him. With hands clenched, he marched into the bedroom to check the wall.

That was when he realized that the pounding had stopped. Well, he thought, that was probably evidence in itself. When had it stopped? Right about the time he'd knocked on the door?

There were no marks on any of the walls. Repeated hammering on drywall would at least have left some dents, especially if it was as loud on the other side as the Martinses claimed. There was, after all, a concrete firewall between all of the units.

Little followed him, practically breathing down his neck.

"You see?" Little demanded. "They're the ones making the noise."

"I doubt it," Jake said. "I seriously doubt it."

"You are gonna check their walls, aren't you?"

"Yes, of course. But I think it would be wise of you to let Ms. Moonglow come in here and see what she can find out. If you have a poltergeist—"

"I ain't got no chicken guests!" Little shouted. "And no ghosts, neither!"

Jake had had enough. "Listen, Little," he said, "what you've got is bats in your belfry! If you don't want to get to the root of this problem, then you can damn well live with the banging until the ghosts drive you insane! See if I give a damn!"

"Ghosts! It's a bunch of crap, I tell you! I thought you was a reasonable man, Carpenter. Guess the little coos got to you, huh?"

Jake gave serious thought to decking the disgusting little man, then decided he wasn't worth it. Without another word he stalked out and listened to Little slam the door behind him. Almost at once the banging resumed.

Rainbow looked at him. "What happened?"

"Harvey Little came within an inch of becoming

a ghost himself. Other than that, nothing. There are no marks on the walls. If he's making that ruckus, I can't imagine how."

He knocked on the Martins' door, and it was opened by Trixie. Her face looked haggard, and there were dark circles under her eyes. "He's going to drive me insane," she said, letting them in. "Do you hear it?"

He heard it. Without waiting for an invitation, he marched into the bedroom on that side of the apartment. The walls here were just as unmarked as Harvey Little's. And the banging was going on right now, sounding as if the man on the other side of the firewall was beating on it with a sledgehammer.

"Harvey Little isn't making that noise," he told the Martinses. "I'm really sorry, but he couldn't make that kind of racket without damaging the walls."

The couple exchanged unhappy looks. "Then what do we do?" asked Martin. "We have to sleep sometime."

Jake looked at Rainbow, throwing thirty years of scientific training out the window. "What do you suggest?"

"Could I have just a few minutes alone in here? Would you mind?"

The Martinses were agreeable, so Jake joined them in the living room while Rainbow remained in the bedroom. The banging continued unabated.

Trixie, wearing a skin-tight fluorescent green tank top that revealed a significant amount of cleavage, brought out a plate of fresh-baked cookies and offered Jake some coffee.

He was glad to accept; his much longed-for wake-up cup was still sitting in the coffeemaker in his unit, probably growing more bitter by the minute.

"That Harvey Little is *such* an unpleasant man,"

Trixie said, as they all sat gathered around the coffee table. "He's always so rude when I speak to him."

"In fairness," said Jake, who really didn't want to be fair to Little at all, "he probably isn't getting any more sleep than you are."

"Do you really think it's the ghost?" Trixie asked, her eyes wide. Her husband shifted uncomfortably; clearly he was one of the people who didn't like the ghost idea at all.

"I'm beginning to think so," Jake admitted, "and it isn't easy for me to say that. Everything I've believed up to this point in my life argues against it. But then, I've got that furniture on my ceiling."

"I heard about that," said Martin. "I'd like to see it, if you wouldn't mind. Although, to be honest, I'd rather have furniture on my ceiling than someone or something banging on my wall every time I try to go to sleep."

Jake nodded. "I can see your point."

"Do you think Rainbow will really find out what's going on?" Trixie asked.

"If anyone can, she will." He spoke with more confidence than he felt, partly because he still wasn't fully comfortable with the idea, and partly because he had the distinct impression that Rainbow was floundering right now as much as any of them. He'd been expecting glib dictums from her in her capacity as psychic, and instead had discovered she had as many questions and doubts as any of them.

And that had somehow endeared her to him even more.

They were eating cookies and drinking coffee and talking about plans for a condo association yard sale when Rainbow at last emerged from the bedroom. Jake noticed at once that she looked disturbed, but she managed a smile.

"What did you find out?" Trixie demanded immediately. "That awful man killed someone and they're haunting him now?"

Jake had to smother a smile at Trixie's blood-thirsty imagination, but he noticed Rainbow looked pained.

"I'm not really sure," she said hesitantly. "I need to . . . think about it some more before I say anything. Maybe get a few more impressions."

Trixie looked severely disappointed. "You mean we have to keep listening to the banging?"

"I don't know," Rainbow said honestly. "I really don't know. There's something going on, and I'd have to say the ghosts are involved in it, but until someone can figure out exactly what it is, they may keep banging. I wish there were something more I could do."

"Just keep working on it," Martin said, looking uncomfortable. "I'll take any help I can get. Maybe Trixie and I will take a trip in the meantime. We need some sleep, and if that obnoxious Harvey Little isn't responsible for this—well, then, I guess we'll have to find a way to get through it."

Rainbow nibbled disinterestedly at a cookie, declined an offer of coffee, and just generally indicated that she wanted to go as soon as possible.

Jake did, too, but he figured his chances of taking Rainbow back to bed were about nil. She certainly didn't look like a woman who wanted to make love.

As soon as they could do it gracefully, they made their escape and went back down to Jake's apartment. Once there, he drew her into his arms and hugged her.

"What's wrong, sweetie?" he asked.

She shook her head. "Nothing, really. I'm just confused. You know, I was standing in that bedroom, trying to feel what was behind all that banging, and I got the same impression I got from one of my clients this morning—fire and water and doom. Now, how could I get the same impression from the ghosts? And what does it mean?"

"I don't know."

"You know . . ." Involved in her thoughts, she pulled away from him and started to pace. His arms felt empty, but he let her go. "The very first time I met Harvey Little, I felt death around him. I thought for sure he was on the edge of a heart attack."

"He looks it."

"But what if that's not it? What if it's someone else's death I was feeling?"

Until then, such simple words had never caused a chill to run down Jake's spine. It was as if Rainbow had spoken some great truth, and he knew it at a level beyond conscious thought. Not yet ready to put *both* feet on the psychic bandwagon, however, he said noncommittally, "I don't know."

She gave him a rueful smile over her shoulder. "Me, neither," she said.

With great reluctance, but feeling somehow compelled, he pursued the conversation. "Are you sure it's the *same* feeling you're getting? Or could they be different but similar?"

She cocked her head, thinking about it. "I don't know for sure. This morning I told my client not to take a cruise in December because of that feeling. But then I got the same feeling when I was standing there concentrating on the cause of the banging. Yes, I'm sure it was the *same* feeling."

"Well . . ." The words wanted to stick in his throat, but he forced them out anyway. "Well . . . Joe was killed in that boat explosion. Fire and water and doom."

She nodded. "I know. But what would that have to do with my client?"

"I don't know, but it could sure as hell have something to do with that banging. If it's Joe making that ruckus." He couldn't believe he was saying these things. Worse, he was appalled that they actually seemed to be making sense.

Rainbow didn't look as if she thought he'd lost his mind, though.

"It's Joe and Lucinda," she said. "*That* much I'm sure of."

"So where does this get us?"

She shook her head and gave a tired laugh. "I don't know, Jake. Maybe Joe and Lucinda don't like Harvey Little. Or maybe they don't like the Martinses. Or maybe for some crazy reason, that's the only wall they can pound on. Ghosts have to follow rules, you know."

"Rules? *Really?*" The idea caught his attention, striking him as at once ridiculous and brilliant. "What kinds of rules?"

She shrugged. "I don't really know. It's not as if they're posted anywhere. But look at us, Jake. There are rules we have to follow just to participate in this reality. Physical rules. The things you call the laws of physics. Naturally, in their realm, ghosts have to have similar limitations."

Jake suddenly felt as if he were standing on shifting sands. He had always assumed that physical laws were immutable, but he hadn't taken that assumption and looked at it the way Rainbow just had. He had never thought of himself as *following* those laws. That implied a certain amount of volition where he had thought there was none.

Stricken, he sat on the couch and stared up at the furniture on his ceiling. "Damn, Joe," he heard himself murmur, "that's a hell of a message."

And right then, he wouldn't have been the least bit astonished to see the furniture start dancing a polka.

Seventeen

"**D**ON'T TELL ME YOU WERE OUT WITH *HIM!*" ROXY said, as soon as Rainbow stepped through the door. Jake had brought her home when she insisted that she had to get back. The storm had turned to a steady drizzle, and she'd been perfectly willing to walk, but he had refused to hear of it.

Consequently, Roxy, who seemed to have the eye of an eagle, had seen him drop her off. Now she stood looking at her daughter with her hands on her hips and her turban askew.

"He just gave me a lift because of the rain, Mother." Which was true enough, although far from the whole truth.

"After what he did to you last night, I'm surprised you'd give him the time of day."

"It was a misunderstanding. We talked it over."

"Oh, really?" Roxy asked ominously.

Gene looked up from the script he was reading. "Roxy, please. Let Rainbow run her own life, and let me have the peace to study my lines. I start filming next week, and I still don't have a grip on my character."

Roxy sniffed. "You don't have a grip on *anything*

if you don't care that your niece has just spent time with a man who hurt her badly last night."

Gene sighed and closed his script with a snap. "I care, Roxy. I *care* that it's her life and she's entitled to do as she sees fit without your interference!"

"I'm her *mother*!"

"Somehow when you say that, it sounds like a threat!"

Rainbow stepped forward, taking her mother's arm, and trying to divert the coming explosion. "Shouldn't you be resting for your seance tonight?"

Roxy rolled her eyes. "As if I can rest when I'm worried sick about you. You walked out into that awful storm, and I had no idea whether or not you were lying dead on the beach!"

"Oh, for Pete's sake," said Gene in disgust. Putting aside the script, he rose and announced, "I'm getting the hell out of here. And if you're wise, Rainy, you'll get out, too. She's in a real mood."

"I was worried!"

"Well, there's no need to worry now," Rainbow said firmly, steering her mother toward the kitchen. "I'm safe and dry, and I'd really like a cup of hot tea. Mother, are you sure you should do this seance tonight?"

"Well, of course," said Roxy, diverted. She never liked to have her judgment questioned. "I said I would, and so I must."

"But Mary Todd is up to something."

"Well, of course she is. *I* know that."

"But I have to live in this town, and if something outrageous happens tonight—"

"If something outrageous happens, Rainbow, you can hardly be held responsible. After all, you'll have no part in it."

"I was thinking that I ought to come along—"

"No!" Roxy was quite definite on that. "You stay

clear. If you're not there, no one can blame you."

"But, Mother, if you feel that way, you shouldn't be going either!"

Roxy filled the kettle and put it on the stove. "Ah, but I'm curious to know just what that woman is up to."

Rainbow sighed, realizing she wasn't going to be able to prevent this. "Just be careful, all right?"

"You're worrying too much about it, dear. The spirits rarely cooperate, you know. They have their own agendas. Mary Todd is apt to get a great big disappointment." She spooned tea into the teapot and set out cups, then joined her daughter at the breakfast bar.

"You look troubled," she said to Rainbow. "Did that man do something else?"

"No! No," she repeated more calmly. "It's just that—Mother, have you ever gotten exactly the same psychic impression from different sources?"

Roxy tilted her head, frowning. "I don't understand you."

"This morning I had a very strong impression of fire, water, and doom from one of my clients. Then I had the same feeling when I was at the Towers a little while ago, investigating the banging that some of the residents are complaining about."

"The banging? You looked into that? What is it? A poltergeist? It would be so unusual in a building where there are no children!"

"It isn't a poltergeist." Rainbow sighed and wished the kettle would start to boil. She was *dying* for a cup of tea. "No, the banging has the same source I've been feeling all along."

Roxy nodded. "That poor man who died when his boat blew up. Well, that certainly explains the fire, water, and doom impression."

"Of course. That's obvious. But it doesn't explain

why I got the same impression from my client this morning. And why I keep feeling that death hovers around one of the building's residents."

"Which one?"

"That unpleasant man who was hiding behind the ferns yesterday."

"Oh, him. Well, it's hardly surprising that he'd have an unpleasant aura. It goes with the rest of him."

"But it isn't just an unpleasant aura, Mother. It's that feeling of death. And today, I got the feeling that it's not *his* death I'm sensing."

"Oh." Roxy lifted both of her plucked eyebrows. "Oh!"

"Indeed."

"You want to be careful about saying things like that, dear. You could get sued. This man, unpleasant as he is, would certainly not like it if you were suggesting he caused someone's death."

"I'm not saying he did! I'm just saying—oh, I don't know what I'm saying. It just seems like entirely too much coincidence to have all these feelings associated with that building and some of the people in it."

"Maybe the building is about to collapse."

Rainbow shook her head. "No, that's not it. The feeling wouldn't be attached to just a couple of people."

"And the haunting," Roxy reminded her. "It's attached to the ghosts."

"And that's why it's so confusing."

Roxy nodded. "Well, there's nothing else for it. I'll have to hold a seance at the Towers."

And this time Rainbow didn't disagree. "I think so, Mother. I'll let Jake know, so he can announce it. I think we ought to invite anyone who wants to attend so they can see and hear for themselves. It'll cut down on rumors and problems later."

"Well, I can't say I'm thrilled at the idea of trancing in front of a huge crowd, but I suppose you're right."

The kettle started whistling, and Roxy went to pour the boiling water into the teapot. "If the ghosts at the Towers really *do* have a message for someone there, we might as well give them an opportunity to deliver it. But if we're going to have a crowd, at the very least they must agree to be quiet. It's hard enough to go into trance with a half-dozen people stirring and whispering. A roomful of them would make it just about impossible. It requires *concentration*, dear. Intense concentration."

"I know, Mother."

"Of course you do. I have a terrible habit of repeating the obvious for emphasis. It's just that I want you to make sure *they* understand the difficulties."

Roxy sighed and carried the teapot over to the bar, where she sat down and faced her daughter. "The most frustrating part of being psychic is that it is not under our complete control."

"Tell me about it." Rainbow sighed. "A few weeks ago I started to get the feeling that my life was about to undergo a major change. But no matter how hard I try, I can't discover anything else."

Roxy reached out and patted her daughter's hand. "Actually, that's a blessing. Life would be so boring if we knew what was around the next corner. Most of us who have abilities are gifted at helping others but are blind when it comes to ourselves. You just have to trust that everything will work out as it should."

Which was a remarkably optimistic statement from Roxy, who was forever predicting doom for her daughters if they didn't take her advice.

But it comforted Rainbow nonetheless. It would

all work out. And as long as she didn't think about Jake, she could almost believe that.

Mary Todd was the ringleader of a group of senior citizens who called themselves the Hole in the Sea-wall Gang. This small group—never larger than seven and currently at an all-time low of five since the death of one of their members, and the recent defection of David Dyer to Fort Myers—gathered at Mary's house for dinner that evening.

Mary had years ago given up cooking, so she served Chinese takeout and pizza on paper plates. It was an eclectic menu, but Felix Crumley, the city attorney, claimed Chinese food gave him indigestion, and Luis Gallegos, a retired restaurateur, claimed it was too bland. Mary shuddered as she watched them eat heartily of the pizza while she delicately picked at her lo mein with a fork. The two others used chopsticks, but only Hadley Philpott, a retired philosophy professor, seemed to have any real skill at it. Arthur Archer, a local minister, finally gave up halfway through the meal, realizing he was apt to starve if he didn't resort to his fork.

After dinner, Mary swept everything into a trash can and passed around the liqueur glasses and a bottle of Tia Maria. The fortune cookies were dessert.

"So, Mary," asked Arthur, "have you called us together to discuss replacing our two lost members?"

Mary shook her head. "I don't know that I'm ready to do that, Arthur. I was considering breaking our traditional rule and asking someone younger to join us, but—" Mary shrugged. "She married the chief of police. Entirely too close to the law for my comfort."

"Well, I'm an attorney," Crumley reminded her.

"But a sensible one. No, I realized that asking Jillie

Corrigan would put her in an untenable position. She hasn't been married long enough to want to keep secrets from her husband."

"True," Luis agreed.

Arthur looked shocked. "A woman should *never* keep secrets from her husband."

"Really?" Mary asked. "And is that a two-way street, Arthur?"

He reddened faintly.

Mary's grin was evil. "I rather thought you weren't telling your wife about some of our hijinks."

Hadley Philpott cleared his throat. "It seems to me you didn't call us together to discuss the ethics of marital secrecy."

"No, of course not, Hadley. How brilliant of you to realize it."

Hadley frowned at her but didn't bother to retort.

"I thought we should discuss the strange events at the Paradise Towers."

Silence greeted her announcement. Arthur, she noticed, looked down at his liqueur glass, betraying discomfort.

"What is it, Arthur?" she demanded. "It has always struck me as supremely odd that ministers, who spend their entire lives insisting on life after death, are the first to become disturbed when the subject of ghosts arises."

He lifted his head. "My conception of the afterlife doesn't include ghosts roaming the earth, rattling chains. They have far better things to do."

"Such as singing in the heavenly choir until the end of time?" Mary's tone was dry. "Pardon me, but they'd all die of boredom. Regardless, the ghosts at the Towers aren't rattling any chains. They're rattling crockery. Putting furniture on ceilings. Creative little things like that."

"I don't think God would allow—"

"Excuse me," Mary interrupted. "There are a great many things going on in this world that we would both agree God wouldn't allow, yet they still happen. Perhaps we shouldn't attempt to speak for God, but instead address what is actually happening."

"Quite," said Hadley, feeling his pockets for the pipe he always carried. Mary wouldn't let him light it, but he could chew on the pipestem, which was a great comfort when these discussions began to get hairy. "The Deity is, and always has been, inscrutable. But ghosts, Mary. The implications!"

"They are fascinating, aren't they?" Her dark eyes sparkled.

Hadley cleared his throat again. "Basically, what ghosts suggest is the intersection between separate universes with different physical laws."

Mary nodded. "And where these universes intersect, the physical laws of both are altered."

"Well, possibly. To an extent, I suppose that would have to be true. Otherwise, there would be no manifestation." He found his pipe and popped the stem between his teeth.

"But where does this get us?" Luis asked. He was an eminently practical man. "We can't expect to solve the mysteries of the universe over liqueur."

"Certainly not," said Mary. "But there is the question of the haunting at the Towers. Assuming—what is that phrase you always use, Felix?"

The lawyer swallowed a mouthful of Tia Maria. "*Arguendo*," he supplied. "Assuming *arguendo*, for the sake of argument."

"That's it. Assuming *arguendo* that the ghosts exist, what do they mean, and what can we find out about what they're up to?"

Hadley frowned. "Why should we do any better than anyone already working on the case? Didn't the residents already call in Rainbow Moonglow?"

"Yes. And now her mother has arrived as well. Roxy Resnick is a trance channeler. She's going to hold a seance for us tonight."

Now every face at the table except Mary's looked appalled.

"Now, really," said Hadley. "So many of these people are frauds."

"Not Roxy. I hear she's actually quite good. But I figured we'd give her a trial run tonight."

"I don't think I want to be part of this," Arthur said into a prolonged silence. "This could seriously damage my reputation."

"No one has to know about it," Mary reminded him. "But if anyone should hear about it, you can always dismiss it as a parlor game."

Arthur shook his head. "In my capacity as a minister, I can't be involved in such things."

"I'm not asking you to participate as a minister. Besides, this is just a test of the woman's talents. I feel we owe it to the residents of the Towers to check her out. And what better way than to test her on something we already know."

There was another long silence, this time broken by Felix Crumley. "I don't much hold with this psychic stuff, Mary, but I *do* like Rainbow. She's a sweet young woman, and if you set about proving her mother is a fraud, she could be seriously hurt."

"Did I say her mother was a fraud? In fact, Felix, I seriously doubt it. I am absolutely convinced the woman believes in what she does. But she might be *wrong*. And before she holds a seance for the Towers residents, *someone* ought to check her accuracy."

"Why does it have to be us?" Arthur asked.

"Because we're here," said Mary. "And who else is going to bother?"

*   *   *

Gene had rented a car so he could get to his filming sessions for the environmental group that had hired him as spokesman. He dropped Roxy and Dawn off at Mary Todd's house and then headed out for an evening with Nellie Blair. Rainbow was charged with hanging around to wait for her mother's call to come get her.

It was enough to drive her nuts. For one thing, she was worried about what Mary might be up to. In spite of the fact that she loved Mary, she wasn't blind to the older woman's faults, among which was her being meddlesome.

And she couldn't stop thinking about Jake. Their time together that afternoon had been like a fairy tale come true, and now that she was facing an evening by herself in her empty cottage, she was paying the price for her weakness. It was going to hurt worse than she had ever imagined, she realized. Far worse. Why didn't he at least call?

And then there was that impression of fire, water, and doom that she'd had three times now. That seriously worried her, and she kept thinking about it, trying to make sense of it, recognizing its importance but unable to unravel the mystery. What if everyone at the Towers was facing some kind of threat?

Finally, ten minutes after her mother had left, unable to stand it any longer, and despite all her resolutions, she called Jake. She wanted to be angry that she'd had to call him, but the instant she heard his voice, she melted.

"Hi," she said shyly, when he answered the phone.

"Hi." His voice turned warm and welcoming. "I've been sitting here staring at my computer, wishing you would call."

"Really?"

"Really. I wanted to call you, but I didn't want to

stir your mother up. Can we do something together
tonight? Go out for dinner? Take in a movie? Walk
on the beach?"

"I have to stay here and wait for my mother's call.
She's doing that seance for Mary Todd, and she'll
need a ride home."

"Then how about I come over there?"

"Really?"

"Really. Is it okay?"

"Oh, yes," she said, her voice turning breathless.
"Please."

As soon as she hung up the phone, she started
wondering where she'd left her brain. Not five
minutes ago she'd been feeling miserable, recognizing that the closer she got to Jake the more it was
going to hurt when they separated, and instead of
heeding her own common sense, she'd invited him
over here!

She was out of her ever-loving mind!

But that didn't keep her from running to the bathroom to comb her hair and put on a touch of
makeup. She almost changed into something pret-
tier, then decided that was going too far. She'd already let him know how eager she was to see him.
Why compound the problem?

Jake made it over in record time. Almost before
she'd finished putting on her lipstick, he was knocking at her door.

Her heart was hammering as she opened it, and
when she saw him, she couldn't prevent the wide
smile that creased her face. He was here, and suddenly all the rest of it didn't seem so important.

She invited him in, and as soon as she closed the
door, he reached for her, sweeping her into his arms
and giving her a deep, devouring kiss.

She felt herself melting into that warm, soft place
he seemed to take her to without any trouble.

He lifted his head suddenly, looking down at her. "How long does a seance take?"

"It varies . . ."

"Well, what's the minimum time?"

She shook her head. "Well, assuming she can get into a trance . . . maybe an hour?"

"Let's assume she can." Then he lifted her right off her feet. "Where's your bedroom?"

She could have been offended, but she wasn't. This was exactly what she wanted. No time for thinking, no time for letting ordinary things get between them. Just the two of them loving one another in the only way they could.

He carried her across the living room and into her bedroom, where he lowered her feet to the floor. "You make me crazy," he said huskily. "Absolutely crazy."

That would do, she thought, and found herself feeling as sexy and beautiful as she had ever felt in her life. In his eyes she could see herself as he saw her, and what she saw made her feel so very good.

He reached for the hem of her T-shirt, and pulled it up over her head. Then he tossed his own onto the floor beside it. Helpless to stop herself, she reached out and ran her hands over the broad, muscled expanse of his chest, loving the way he felt, loving the sensation of his skin against hers.

He smiled and tugged at her shorts until they fell to her ankles, and he steadied her as she stepped out of them. His jeans went the same way. Then her underwear and his disappeared into the corner and he drew her against him, crushing her to him so that they met from chest to knee.

She could feel his arousal against her belly, and the sensation sent spears of delight shooting through her.

It was strange, she thought, as the haziness of passion filled her, but she felt as if she had been created for this moment and this man . . . as if she had been born to be right here.

"There are no ghosts here," he said.

"No." What was he talking about?

"Let's leave all our ghosts out of this, okay?"

She nodded, not quite sure she understood, but at this point she was willing to agree to anything if only he would keep on holding her and touching her.

Bending, he pressed his mouth to her breast and sucked strongly, a sensation so pleasurable that she felt her womanhood throb sharply in time to the movement of his mouth. Her knees turned watery, and she clung desperately to his shoulders, afraid she would fall and lose his kiss on her breast. Her nails dug into him and he groaned.

Wrapping his arms around her waist, he lifted her off her feet, keeping her breast available to his mouth. Throwing her head back, she wrapped her legs around his waist and pressed herself snugly to him, needing more, so much more.

Never had anyone made her feel this way, but Jake's touch was like a spark that turned into an instant conflagration. Just the look in his eyes was enough to make her feel weak, and his merest touch filled her with hunger for him.

Dimly, without realizing they had moved, she felt the bed beneath her back, and then he was lying on top of her, between her legs, his weight bearing her down in the most delicious way. His mouth moved to her other breast, renewing the assault on her senses, and she heard herself groan, a deep sound that was torn from her very depths.

She arched against him, needing the pressure of him between her legs.

Then, in the space between one instant and the

next, she came to her senses. She might want him with every cell in her body, but she needed more, far more than sex. Without something more, what they were doing became a meaningless, cheap act.

"No," she said, and pushed against his shoulders.

He lifted his head, looking down at her from heavily lidded eyes. His cheeks were flushed with passion and he was breathing at least as heavily as she was. "What's wrong?" he asked hoarsely.

"I don't want to do this, Jake." Her voice quivered, revealing that she was on the edge of tears, but she swallowed hard and blinked them back. "This isn't right."

He stared at her for long seconds, as if his brain were having difficulty grasping what she had just said. Then with a deep groan, he rolled off of her and lay beside her with his eyes closed.

She closed her own, unable to look at him, unwilling to read his expression. He was probably furious with her, she thought. And he had every right to be. She shouldn't have let things go this far before saying no.

"Rainy?" His voice was still husky, but so gentle it brought the tears back to her eyes.

"I'm sorry." Her voice was thick, her throat so tight it hurt.

"No," he said. "*I'm* sorry."

Astonishment forced her eyes open, and made her look at him.

"I *am* sorry," he repeated. He raised himself on one elbow and looked at her. "The way I barged in here and just carried you off to bed . . . well, it was disrespectful. I'm sorry if I made you feel cheap."

It took her a few moments to find her voice. The tightness in her throat and chest nearly smothered it. "It's . . . I'm sorry, Jake. I just can't be . . . casual about this."

He nodded. "Understood." He touched her cheek gently, then rolled out of bed to pick up their scattered clothing. He passed hers to her, then turned his back and donned his own.

Still blinking back tears, Rainbow pulled her clothes on quickly, with trembling hands. She had been a fool, she decided, a fool to let him get so close, and a fool to call things off so late. The sensible woman she believed herself to be was apparently a chimera.

"Hey." Jake spoke softly and crossed to her, touching her cheek again. "It's okay," he said. "I got carried away, and I apologize. You're right. There has to be more than sexual attraction. For both of us."

Which was, she thought glumly, as good as admitting that was all he felt. And right now, *she* felt as if someone had driven a stake through her heart. But somehow she managed to find a smile for him, wobbly though it was.

"Rainy?"

"Hmm?" She couldn't quite trust herself to speak.

"I mean it," he said quietly. "I want more than sex with you. Sex is wonderful—I'd be the last person on earth to deny it—but it's not enough. I'm losing my head over you in more ways than one."

Suddenly the pain in her heart was gone, and she was able to look at him steadily, her momentary fear vanquished.

"I keep promising myself to take it slow, so we can build the things that really count." He gave a rueful laugh. "I'm not doing too well in the 'slow' department. I'm sorry."

Then, before she could decide what to say, he hugged her and dropped gentle kisses all over her face. "Time, Rainy. Give me time. Please?"

She nodded, and was delighted with another kiss.

"Now," he said, "before I lose my head all over again, can we go into another room and talk about something safe?"

His pleading tone actually made her want to laugh. "Sure. How about some tea?"

"Sounds safe enough," he agreed. "With the counter between us, okay?"

Together they went out to the kitchen and started a pot of tea, the old emotional standby in Rainbow's family. Jake reminisced about some of the teas he'd drunk in various places, allowing as how his favorite was green tea.

When their cups were full, they sat side-by-side at the breakfast bar.

"My family does everything in the kitchen," Rainbow remarked. "It's like the rest of the house doesn't exist, at least when there's anything to be discussed."

"Must be nice. I never really had your standard family. My dad died when I was young, and my mother had to work. Uncle Joe was a great father figure, but it wasn't the same as having a whole family that could gather round to do things together, or discuss things." He shrugged. "Not that I'm complaining. My mom was wonderful, and Uncle Joe was as good a father as any kid could ask for. He just didn't live with us."

"It must have been hard on you, though."

He flashed a crooked grin. "Oh, there were advantages. There was no one to check up on me after school, for one."

"Did you get into a lot of trouble?"

"Nah. I was always one of those geeks, you know? The most trouble I ever got into was mixing chemicals from my chemistry set that weren't supposed to be mixed. I'm probably lucky I didn't start a fire or asphyxiate myself. And I was always a rock hound. I started when I was about eight, with a hammer from Joe's toolbox. I never did tell him I'd heisted it, but I figure he probably knew anyway. So I'd go out after school, instead of doing my homework, and wander around, chipping off chunks of rock in the woods and hills around the house."

"You lived in a little community?"

"Northern New Jersey. We had a house on what used to be a farm, so I had plenty of room for exploring."

Rainbow smiled. "That sounds really nice."

"Had a stream out back, too, a creek that was deep enough for swimming and good for fishing. Joe got me my first rod and reel, to replace the cane pole I'd been using, and I thought I was such hot stuff for a while."

He smiled, his eyes growing distant with memory. "About the time I was thirteen, we had to move. The guy who was renting us the property decided he could get more money elsewhere, so we moved into town. Boy, what a change that was. But it helped me develop what social skills I have." He gave her a rueful look. "Not that I seem to have too many, lately."

"You're doing just fine." She felt a tug on her heart for the little boy he must have been. She was sure his childhood had been more difficult and lonely than he was letting on.

"Anyway," he said, "to continue with a long and boring story, I had my first girlfriend when I was sixteen. It lasted about four weeks, but I was pretty proud of the accomplishment. Somebody liked me well enough to go steady with me for a whole month."

"At that age, that really *is* an achievement."

"Yeah." He laughed quietly. "Then came college, and that's where I got a *real* education. I went right back to rock hounding and met another geology student. I have to tell you about Annabelle. She was a real free spirit, willing to pack up a tent and sleeping bag and head into the hills on weekends to look for rocks. I thought that made her just about perfect. By junior year, we were engaged, and we lived together in this ratty little apartment off campus that we shared with about ten thousand cockroaches and our friends. It was great fun for a while." He sipped his tea and shook his head.

"What happened?"

"I guess you could call it a personality conflict." He looked straight at her. "I'm telling you this so you'll understand my initial reaction to you. Annabelle was New Age when the term was new. She lived and breathed enough kooky ideas to start a zoo. It started to get to me after a while, particularly when she planned every day according to her horoscope and mine."

"Horoscopes?" Rainbow wasn't too fond of them. Like the cards, they could be used to focus psychic intuitions, but like the cards they could be equally useless or abused.

"Horoscopes. At first it was the ones in the paper every morning. Then she was buying books that promised to give more accurate ones. And finally she was casting them herself. Every night she'd settle down and do our charts, and if they warned of an accident the next day, she'd insist we stay home. Or if they said it was a good day for financial gain, she'd hare off to spend money on something she thought was a good investment. I mean, those things controlled her. Finally I just couldn't take it anymore, and I left."

"I'm sorry."

"I'm not." He smiled at her. "Annabelle had other wacky ideas, of course. Overnight she decided to become a strict vegetarian, and she started talking about chakras, and trying to even out the flow of mine. I began to get the impression that she thought there was something seriously wrong with me but didn't have the guts to say so."

"I can see why."

"So anyway, to get to my rather roundabout point here, I tend to react negatively to anything that reminds me of her. So you got flack for Annabelle as much as anything when we met. And I'm sorry. My behavior was inexcusable."

Rainbow shook her head. "There's no need to apologize, Jake. We're both guilty of that."

"Walter, you mean?"

She nodded. "Walter. And others. Apart from my client base, I guess I've developed a very distrustful attitude toward people. Uncle Gene says I need to break out of my shell."

"I can sure as hell see why you've developed one if other people react to you the way I did on our first meeting."

One corner of her mouth lifted, and she felt a trickle of amusement. "Other people aren't usually quite so blunt."

He winced. "I deserve that."

"Oh, don't feel bad about it. I can deal with bluntness a lot better than two-facedness. At least I know where I stand." Her expression grew shy. "Is that what you meant about leaving our ghosts out of it?"

It apparently took him a minute to remember what she was referring to. His brow knitted, then cleared. "Oh! Yeah. That's what I meant. Maybe if we can leave our ghosts out of it . . ." He hesitated.

Rainbow leaned forward, hardly daring to hope, afraid that the least little sound would prevent him from continuing.

Then, startling her, the phone began to shriek jarringly.

She gave him an apologetic look. "That must be my mother."

"Go ahead. Don't mind me."

It was Roxy, and all she said was, "Come get me this very instant!"

"Mother? What's wrong?"

"I don't like being deceived. And Mustafa hates being tricked."

"What happened?"

"Just come get me! At once." *Click.*

Rainbow looked at Jake. "Something happened. I'm almost afraid to imagine what. I need to go get her."

"I'll drive."

She reached for her purse, but before she made a step toward the door, the phone rang again. She snatched at the receiver, hoping against hope that something else dreadful hadn't happened.

"Rainbow? This is Pat Webster. You have to come up here right away! Terrible things are happening."

"I may take a few minutes, Mrs. Webster. I need to rescue my mother and sister."

"All right, but please hurry! The ghosts are going nuts."

Eighteen

"So tell me," Jake said, as they drove over to Mary Todd's house, "do the tarot cards tell you what to do?"

Rainbow looked at him. Hadn't they already discussed this? She wasn't sure, but she understood why he needed reassurance. "No . . . the cards aren't magic. They don't have any power at all. And frankly, I'd say the same about horoscopes and any other method of divination."

"Really? So what are they?"

"Guides. A means of focusing. Divination tools are really just a way to tap into your own subconscious—or your own psychic intuition. They don't have any power of their own."

"So you wouldn't read a horoscope or the cards and let them control you?"

Rainbow shook her head. "Absolutely not. But I *do* let my intuition guide me, especially when it's clear."

He nodded and let the subject drop. Two minutes later they pulled up in front of Mary Todd's house, a large clapboard structure with the grandeur of another era. Roxy and Dawn were waiting on the veranda and came down the walk to them before they had even pulled to a complete stop.

"Him!" Roxy said disapprovingly, when she saw Jake.

"*Mother*," Rainbow said warningly. "What happened?"

"Oh, Mustafa decided to have a little fun. Would you believe those people wanted to *test* me? To see if I was a fraud? Well, you can be absolutely certain they'll never question it again!"

Rainbow and Jake exchanged looks. "Maybe I'd better check on Mary," Rainbow said.

He nodded. "Wave from the door if you need me."

"You're not going in there!" Roxy protested. "Rainbow . . ."

Rainbow ignored her mother and walked up the seashell-paved sidewalk to the house. When she knocked on the door, no one answered, so finally she opened it and stepped in. "Mary?" she called. "It's Rainbow."

"In the library," Mary called back.

Rainbow walked down the hall and into the second doorway on the right. Mary Todd and four gentlemen were sitting in a circle facing the chair that must have recently been vacated by Roxy.

"Are you all right?" Rainbow asked. She didn't like the looks on the gentlemen's faces. They all looked pale and on the edge of shock.

But Mary Todd cackled her dry laugh. "I'm sorry I offended your mother, gal, but by George, that was some show!"

"It was a demon," Arthur Archer said, his voice strained.

Rainbow took offense. "My mother doesn't deal with demons, Reverend. Ever. Her guides are simply souls who have passed on."

The look he gave her was hollow.

Mary cracked another laugh. "Don't mind him, gal! He's just learning that he doesn't know as almighty much as he thought. Now, me, I think I'm going to *enjoy* being a ghost!"

Rainbow shuddered at the mere idea.

Hadley Philpott pried the pipestem from between his teeth and cleared his throat. "It's fascinating! Absolutely fascinating! The ramifications—well, I'll need some time to explore them thoroughly, but the intersection of two separate universes . . . the manifestation of powers that boggle the mind . . ." He trailed off, resuming his contemplation.

"They'll be all right," Mary told Rainbow. "Don't worry about 'em. Never hurts anybody to have their preconceptions smashed. They may be old dogs, but they can still learn new tricks, or I wouldn't hang around with them. Just give them some time to get over the shock."

Rainbow nodded, still feeling uneasy. "My mother—"

Mary interrupted without apology. "Tell her I'm sorry. I didn't mean to make her so angry. I just wanted to know what she could do. Where's the harm in that?"

"I think she thinks you thought she was a fraud."

Mary shook her head emphatically. "Never crossed my mind, gal. I know she believes in what she does. But that doesn't mean she can do it, if you follow me."

"Maybe." Rainbow felt a stirring of anger on her mother's behalf.

"I just wanted to make sure she can deliver, before those people at the Towers get a whole lot of poppycock fed to 'em." Her dark eyes grew hard. "Now you don't have to like that, and you can call me an old busybody if you want—and I certainly am! But

I'm not going to apologize for looking out for my friends. Never have, never will."

Rainbow's face felt frozen, but she nodded.

"Anyway, if you can forgive Carpenter for what he said, you can forgive me for giving your mother a simple test." She suddenly grinned. "A test which she passed with flying colors, by the by." She cackled. "Hee-hee! It was worth it just to see the look on Arthur's face when the stuff started flying through the air!"

Rainbow turned to leave, but Mary pushed herself out of her chair and hobbled over to her without using her cane.

"Child." Mary reached out and touched her arm. "Really, I'm sorry I upset your mother. And to be quite frank, I expected her to wow us. I never would have done this if I had thought there was any real chance she'd be humiliated."

Rainbow felt her face softening, and nodded. "I'll talk to her, Mary."

Roxy and Dawn were already in the backseat of Jake's car. Rainbow climbed in the front. "Mary apologized, Mother."

"It's too late for that. I am not some sideshow freak to be trotted out for the entertainment of her friends."

"But that's how you make your living, Mother! Not everyone who comes to see you believes in what you do. Some of them just come for entertainment. I see it every day in my business."

"Really?" said Jake.

"Really. I see people all the time who think it might be a fun and interesting way to spend a half-hour."

Roxy sighed. "All right. All right. But I'd have felt a whole lot better about if she'd just been honest with me."

"Well, I can understand that. But in point of fact, Mary Todd has a Machiavellian streak. She seems to enjoy manipulating people."

"I don't like being manipulated."

"No one does, Mother. I hear Mustafa put on quite a show."

All of a sudden, Roxy laughed. "Apparently so."

Dawn spoke. "He had things flying all over that room. It was really something. I think he was having a fit of pique."

Jake pulled up in front of Rainbow's house and braked.

"I'm going to leave you here," Rainbow told her mother. "Pat Webster wants me to come over to the Towers. She said something is going on."

"Then I'll go with you," Roxy decided.

Rainbow stifled a sigh.

"Mother," said Dawn, "she'd really rather do it herself."

"All right, all right," Roxy said irritably, pushing the car door open and climbing out. "I know when I'm not wanted!"

As Roxy stormed up the walkway to the door, Dawn leaned forward. "Don't mind her," she said to Jake and Rainbow. "Her only problem is that she wasn't treated with her usual deference. She'll survive." Then she climbed out and shut the door.

"Whew!" said Jake.

"She can be a handful," Rainbow agreed. "Although I have to admit I think Mary handled the matter poorly. But she *did* apologize, and Mary's as lovable as she is difficult."

Over at the Towers, they found many of the residents milling around in the lobby.

"Things were flying again," Abe Levinson said, as soon as he saw them. "Stuff was jumping out of cupboards and closets. Colonel Albemarle and his friends are checking the place out." He gave a grimace that might have been an embarrassed smile. "I don't put much faith in their Dustbusters."

The corners of Jake's mouth quivered as if he were suppressing a laugh. "They don't seem to have worked well so far."

"Anyway, there was apparently some heavy banging from your apartment, so you might want to check it out."

Jake nodded and looked at Rainbow. "What do you suggest?"

"I think we should hold a seance as soon as possible. I'll talk to my mother about it."

"Can't you do it?"

Rainbow shook her head. "That's her line. She'll do a far better job than I could."

"Tomorrow night?"

"I don't see why not, but let me call her just to be sure."

She headed for the pay phone, but he stopped her. "Come up to my place and use the phone. We can check out the banging and you'll have more privacy for your call. Easier to hear."

She nodded.

Jake looked at Abe. "Would you mind finding some volunteers to make up and print handbills for distribution? I'll know exactly when the seance will be scheduled when I come back down in a few minutes, but in the meantime, we'd better look into getting notices out quickly."

Abe nodded. "Somehow I think we'll have more volunteers than we can use. People are getting sick of this."

Rainbow and Jake rode up together in the elevator. When they reached his door, they stood listening for a minute, trying to hear the banging Abe had told them about. The unit was silent, though. In fact, the whole building was silent.

"Whatever it was," Jake said, "it's over."

Rainbow nodded. "I guess so, but . . ." She hesitated.

"What?"

"Well . . . I'm getting a very strong sense of presence from your apartment."

Jake looked down at her, his blue eyes unreadable. "Joe?" he asked finally.

She nodded slowly, still uncertain of how he would react to mention of his uncle.

He smiled faintly. "Well, maybe he's putting the furniture back."

"I have to say, you're getting better about this."

At that he released a short, humorless chuckle. "What choice do I have? Denying what's going on here will only make me a bigger fool."

He shoved the key into his lock and threw the door open. The unit was dark now, and quiet. Reaching in, he flipped the light switch.

"My God," he said.

Rainbow stood on tiptoe, trying to see over his shoulder. "What? *What?*"

He stepped aside and pointed. All the furniture was back on the floor in its usual position, as if it had never been moved at all.

"Wow!" Rainbow said quietly, and stepped into the apartment. She could feel Joe's presence strongly and sensed that he was there in the room with them, watching.

Jake spoke, his voice hushed. "Is he still here?"

Rainbow nodded.

Jake came further into the living room and turned in a slow circle, looking around almost as if he expected to see his uncle somewhere. "Close the door, please," he said to Rainbow. "I don't want anyone to . . . disturb us right now."

She complied and moved further into the room herself.

"Can he hear us?" Jake asked.

"Yes. I'm sure of it."

"So," he said. "Joe? What is it you want? Can you tell me?"

Rainbow held her breath, half expecting a voice to boom out of the ether. Nothing happened.

Jake looked at her. "If he can move my furniture, and materialize for you, why can't he just talk to me?"

"I don't know." And she honestly didn't. That was another one of the questions she had long tried to answer.

"Well, that settles it," Jake said decisively. "We're definitely going to have a seance, and if your mother doesn't want to hold it for the entire building, she can hold it here, for me. And I'll gladly pay her fee."

Rainbow looked at him, feeling something inside herself shift irrevocably. Her heart started to ache, and she had the worst urge to reach out and hug him.

Jake scanned the apartment again, as if seeking answers to the mystery, and suddenly drew a sharp breath.

Rainbow looked at him in concern and saw that he had turned nearly white. He sat with a sudden thump on the sofa.

"Jake? Jake, what's wrong?"

He pointed toward the writing desk near the wall. Rainbow looked, but didn't see a thing.

"Jake? What's going on?"

"I saw him," he said in a husky rush. "*I saw him.*"

"Who? Who did you see?"

"Joe . . ." His voice trailed off and he looked at

her. "Didn't you see him? He was right there, as clear as day!"

Rainbow shook her head and sat beside him. "No, I'm afraid not. But I've never seen a ghost. Well, except for the other night in the restaurant. So I guess that's not one of my talents."

"I can't believe you didn't see him. He looked as real as you do."

"I'm sorry I didn't. But I believe you."

And suddenly he smiled. "I believe *you*."

Her heart took a great leap, but she didn't dare ask him what he meant. If she had somehow misunderstood, there could only be embarrassment and pain, so she decided to leave it alone and hug her newfound hope as close to her heart as she could get it.

Jake said slowly, "But how come I couldn't see him before? I've kind of felt something or someone was here when I was alone, but I never saw him. Why now?"

Rainbow thought about it. "Maybe . . . maybe it's because you've started to believe. Maybe some door has opened in your mind and Joe can come through to you now, whereas he couldn't when you refused to believe it was possible."

He nodded slowly, accepting her assessment. "It makes sense to me." Suddenly, he turned and hugged her. "Thanks, Rainy. Thanks for helping me to see."

Her throat tightened again and she hugged him back, throwing out the last of her reservations about Jake. He was a good, wonderful man. But they had business to take care of, and with difficulty she pulled back and touched his cheek gently.

"I'll, um, call my mother now," she said.

Roxy was still in a snit. "I couldn't possibly do a seance tomorrow," she told her daughter. "After what I've been through this evening—no, there is no way I could be in the proper frame of mind."

"Mother—"

Roxy ignored her. "And Mustafa is in a terrible mood, too. He had a temper tantrum, you know. There is no telling what he might do if I call on him before he's had a chance to cool down."

"What about Red Feather?"

Roxy sniffed. "Red Feather has *always* been difficult and obnoxious! And unpredictable besides. Mustafa at least makes a sincere effort to help— when he's in a good mood."

Rainbow sighed. "Mother, things have been happening. The furniture is down off Jake's ceiling, for one. We came into his unit and it was all back where it belonged."

Roxy fell silent for a moment. "Really?"

"Really. And the other residents say things have been flying out of cupboards and closets. I get the feeling the ghosts are getting impatient to make a statement."

"Who cares what the ghosts want?" Roxy demanded. "What about *me*? You act as if it's easy to go into a trance and channel for a bunch of difficult spirits who have the personality and temperament of a bunch of prima donnas."

"I didn't say it was easy . . ."

"No one understands," Roxy said in distressed tones. "Even my own daughter. It is exhausting. *Fatiguing.* It leaves me feeling wrung out and near the edge of collapse. I couldn't possibly have my energy up by tomorrow."

"Jake says you can hold the seance in his place, if you don't want to hold it for the entire building."

Roxy hesitated. "No," she said finally. "No. Not tomorrow. The day after tomorrow. That's as soon as I can possibly manage it."

Jake whispered, "Tell her I'll pay her."

Rainbow covered the mouthpiece. "Money won't change her mind," she whispered back.

"Then try stroking her ego."

"Mother," Rainbow said into the mouthpiece, "the situation is getting really desperate. These people need help, and you're the only one who can help them."

"That may be," Roxy agreed with a heavy sigh.

"There's no question about it, Mother. What if these people get so desperate they turn to someone who doesn't have your skills and ability?"

"Then they're fools," Roxy said firmly. "It'll be on their heads, and they'll get exactly what they deserve. No, it will have to be the day after tomorrow. First thing in the morning. Say, nine."

"But, Mother . . . Jake is willing to pay you."

Roxy gasped. "Rainbow! As if I can be bought! I'm ashamed of you. No, absolutely not. The day after tomorrow at nine is my final word, and if you insult me again, I won't do it at all."

Roxy hung up with a loud bang, leaving Rainbow to listen to an empty line.

"So what is it?" Jake asked, when she hung up.

"Day after tomorrow at nine in the morning. That's final. She was insulted when I said you'd pay her."

Jake winced. "Uh-oh. I didn't mean to offend her."

"Well, it was worth a try. She's just in a very offendable mood tonight."

He sighed and leaned back against the couch. "I guess I need to get downstairs and see about getting notices out."

But Rainbow's thoughts were traveling along a different path. "Where exactly did you see Joe standing?"

"Right over there, in front of the little writing

desk. You know, that's a real antique. It belonged to my great-grandmother."

"It's beautiful."

"I've been thinking about getting it refinished. It's worn down to bare wood in a couple of places."

"That might be a good idea. Jake? What if Joe was trying to get you to look in the desk?"

He sat up suddenly. "What?"

"Maybe there's something important in it. Have you looked through it?"

"No, not really. I haven't had time. Mostly I've been trying to get a handle on life. You know—writing my book, solving all the problems of the building's residents, chasing ghosts, chasing one very reluctant psychic . . ." He grinned at her. "I always figured I could get to it whenever."

"Maybe 'whenever' is right now."

He nodded and rose, going over to the desk, pulled out the chair, and sat.

The top opened out to create a writing space, and revealed pigeonholes and drawers. The pigeonholes were full of papers, and he began examining them.

Rainbow came to stand behind him, looking over his shoulder.

Most of the papers seemed to be old bills and financial records, none of which probably mattered now. They gave a picture of Joe, though, as a frugal man who paid off his credit cards in full every month, and used them sparingly—except when it came to his boat. A stack of bills showed that he took good care of routine maintenance on the *Lucky Star*, that he'd even taken a course in motor maintenance and repair, as well as courses in navigation, safety, and first aid.

Jake looked up at her. "Not the kind of guy whose boat you'd expect to blow up."

She nodded. "He took better care of it than most people take of their cars."

"Well, I guess he might have overlooked something. And accidents happen no matter how careful you are."

He reached for another stack of papers and discovered that Joe had been making regular charitable contributions, and that he had "adopted" several children overseas and had corresponded with them regularly.

"He never said anything about this to me," Jake said, his voice thickening a little. "I didn't know he did so much. Hell, I didn't know he did anything *like* this."

"He was certainly generous."

He nodded. "A few stars for his crown, I guess. I need to see what I can do about these kids he was writing to. I wonder if anybody told them what happened. But maybe they don't really care."

The letters Joe had received from the children, though, seemed to indicate otherwise. Apart from the donations he made every month, he sent them other things, such as toys and cards.

"I don't know if I can keep doing this," Jake said finally. He looked away.

Instinctively, Rainbow reached out to touch his shoulder. "I'm sorry, Jake. I'm so sorry."

"Me, too." After a few minutes, he sighed and tucked the letters away. "I'll figure out what to do about these later. Let's just move on and get this over with."

Rainbow was certain that he had been avoiding this task since he'd moved in because he expected it to sadden him, and she certainly wouldn't have thought less of him if he'd been unable to continue now.

In fact, looking through all these papers seemed

like prying, even though Joe was dead. It was a terrible trespass, she thought, and went to sit on the couch, not wanting to intrude any further into the private affairs of Joe Krebbs.

Jake continued his survey, scanning papers and setting some aside, returning others to their original niches, sometimes smiling, sometimes frowning.

Then he came upon a stack of letters to Joe from his friends back in New Jersey, and a letter Joe had started writing to a friend but had never finished. It had been written the day of his death.

Jake couldn't handle it. He passed it to Rainbow. "Will you read it? I can't. I just can't."

She took the piece of lined paper. Joe's handwriting was strong and bold, and only a little difficult to read.

" 'Dear Bob and Mary,' " she read aloud, " 'I thought I'd let you know some really big news. I was thinking maybe I'd tell you after I did it, but I'm too excited to wait.

" 'In just a couple of hours, I'm going to take Lucy out on my boat. She's the lady I told you about in my last letter. Well, I'm going to ask her to marry me. Got the ring and everything.

" 'Funny, huh? Bet you thought I'd never do it. I know I sure did. I'm so old now, I figured nobody'd ever want me. I also figured I was a hard case, you know? One of those people it could never happen to.

" 'But it happened, and now the time just seems to be going too slow. Every time I look at the clock, it seems like only a couple of minutes have passed, but it feels like it's been hours. Tonight just can't get here fast enough. Guess I got it bad.

" 'Anyway, I got the ring, got champagne and a fancy dinner on order. I even bought a tablecloth. Bet you never thought I'd do that. I'm taking her out on a sunset cruise, and I'm going to surprise her with the ring.

" 'You know, this is the scariest thing I've ever done.' "

Rainbow looked up. "Do you want me to continue?"

Jake nodded, his face set in the hard lines of a man struggling with strong emotion.

"He goes on, 'I'm beginning to wonder if my memory is as good as it used to be. Guess I should tell Lucy about it before I propose, so she can bail out before it's too late. The other day, I was sure I left my boat keys on the peg in the kitchen, but when I went to grab them, they weren't there. Found 'em this morning when I went down to the boat to clean things up for tonight. Now, is that bad, or what?' "

"Christ," said Jake.

"What?"

He shook his head. "Just go on. Please."

She bent her head again to the letter and continued reading. " 'Then last week, I ran into this guy in the elevator. One of the new residents. I know his name. I know where he's from, but all of a sudden I ask him if he's got a brother back in Jersey by the name of Maroney. Guy looks at me like I'm crazy and says his name isn't Maroney.

" 'Now, I know that. I mean, would two brothers have different names? And besides, there was only a little resemblance. Now, why would I think there's a connection? It's been bothering me ever since, so I guess I ought to tell Lucy about that.

" 'It's a good thing this guy didn't ask me anything about Maroney. He probably would have popped me in the jaw. Mahoney was some minor mob guy who was—' " Rainbow broke off and looked up. "That's where he stopped."

Jake nodded and rubbed his chin with his hand.

His beard stubble rasped quietly, but he seemed not to notice. He was lost in thought, and Rainbow imagined he must be thinking about his uncle and how much he missed him.

But his thoughts seemed to be running along a different line. "That bothers me," he said.

"What does?"

"That Joe misplaced his boat keys. He wasn't the kind to do that. The last time I saw him, maybe six months before he died, he was just fine, as alert as ever. And there was nothing in his letters . . ." He trailed off, his expression growing miserable. "Does senility come on that fast?"

"I don't know. But I *can* tell you I'm the kind of person who doesn't leave her keys in the car, yet I've still managed to do it once or twice. That can happen to anyone."

"I know, but he seemed worried about it. Worried enough to think of telling Lucy."

"Maybe he was more worried than you or I would be because he was so much older."

He nodded slowly. "Maybe," he said finally. "Maybe."

She handed the letter to him and watched him stuff it back in with the others. Then he closed the desk. "Well, I guess I might as well go down and see about getting the announcements prepared so I can distribute them first thing in the morning. Do you want me to take you home first?"

Rainbow shook her head. "I'd like to help. Besides, maybe things aren't finished for the evening."

"Things?"

"The manifestations."

"Oh." He looked around quickly, as if half-expecting to see something floating in midair.

"He's not here now," she said, feeling braver because of the change in his attitude. "But that doesn't mean he won't return."

"I gotta figure out what he wants, Rainy. It must be important, or he wouldn't go to all this trouble. I mean, it must be tough to do the things he's done, don't you think? Otherwise, people would be seeing things like this everywhere."

Rainbow nodded. "I imagine it takes incredible effort."

Jake looked around again, then said, "Well, let's go take care of the flyers. If there's going to be any flack about this seance, I want to know *before* your mother shows up."

She hadn't thought of that, but considering Roxy's current state of mind, she considered it an excellent idea.

"Ho-ho!" said Joe, slapping his palm against his knee. "The boy's finally gotten the message!"

"He's quick, isn't he?"

"You bet." Joe beamed with forgivable pride. "Always as smart as a whip. More often than not he was two steps ahead of me."

"So he'll probably catch the guy," Lucinda said, allowing a sense of satisfaction to show. Much as she had argued with Joe that it didn't really matter anymore, she couldn't quite escape the feeling that it *did*.

"I hope so." Joe suddenly sighed and tilted his head backward, looking up at the clear blue sky above. It was a deeper, more beautiful blue than on earth, a blue that seemed to reach out and embrace him with warmth.

Then Lucy asked tentatively, "But what then, Joe? What happens after they catch him? What do we do?"

He looked at her, his entire face softening with love. "I don't know, Lucy. But I'm not worried about it. There's a plan. I absolutely believe there's a plan. Our dying when we did was for a reason, just like there's a reason for what we're doing now. When the time comes, we'll know."

She nodded, but the uncertainty didn't quite leave her expression.

He reached out and took her hand. "Have we been bored for one instant since we got here?"

She shook her head.

"And didn't we get a chance to meet all the people we've known who came here ahead of us? Well, maybe when we get done, we'll get together with them again and throw a party that'll rattle the clouds."

She had to laugh at that, and her concern vanished like mist before the morning sun.

"It's great here," Joe said. "And to be quite honest, honey, the only thing I regret about having died was that we never got a chance to make love."

She blushed brightly. "I'm an old woman, Joe," she protested.

"You were a *beautiful* woman, Lucy. The most beautiful I'd ever known. And you're even more beautiful now."

Her smile was both embarrassed and delighted.

He shrugged one shoulder and returned her smile. "Anyway, if there's one thing I'm sure of, it's that we'll have something to do when this is done."

She nodded. Joe was always one to make something happen. And she couldn't really complain or worry too much, because now she had all eternity with him. It was as much as anyone could ever want.

Nineteen

HARVEY LITTLE HAD A PLAN. FROM THE INSTANT he'd found the notice of the seance under his door that morning, his mind had been spinning plots, each increasingly more outrageous, until he at last settled on one that would work. Come hell or high water, he had to prevent the seance from taking place.

And the easiest way to do that, he figured, was to convince everyone that the haunting was a hoax.

He knew it wasn't, of course. He knew it for sure because the banging on his wall at night hadn't stopped when the Martinses had decided to go to Miami for a week just so they could get some sleep. They'd thought *he* was doing it. The jerks. If they'd used their brains, they'd have realized he wasn't getting any sleep, either. He'd have to be a total crazy man himself to stay up all night banging on walls just to annoy those two twits.

Now that he was sure the Martinses weren't doing it, he was absolutely, positively sure the ghosts were.

And he figured if they were banging on *his* wall, they had to be after *him*. Which was a kink in his life, and a serious threat to his safety.

He sure as hell hadn't gone into the witness protection program and escaped his old mob associates just to come down here and get nailed by a ghost!

He had to go all the way to Tampa to get some materials to carry out his plan. Because he was impatient by nature, and not too swift as a rule, he managed to get not one but *two* three-hundred-dollar speeding tickets on the way over.

They were peanuts compared to what he'd spent on the industrial magnet he'd bought at a junkyard. His credit card was nearly maxed out by the time he was done, but he wasn't worried. Skipping out on credit card companies was easier than skipping out on the mob.

As soon as he got back to Paradise Beach, he bought one of those white foam coolers for a couple of bucks, and hunted up some dry ice.

He also rented a hand truck, because moving that industrial magnet—which was about as big as one of those round stones those Yap Islanders used for money—almost as tall as a man—was next to impossible. He knew why he was lugging all this iron around, but he sure couldn't figure out why those stupid islanders wanted money that was so difficult to move around.

"Jeez," one of his mob friends had remarked, after he'd told Harvey about those idiots and their crazy money, "you couldn't *steal* anything that big! It don't make no sense!"

Which Harvey thought was a sensible remark from a guy who usually exhibited about as much gray matter as a snail.

Even with the hand truck, getting the magnet into the building was a bit of a challenge. He chose early afternoon, a time when most of the geezers were snoring in the middle of their afternoon naps, or out somewhere "enjoying their retirement."

Harvey wasn't retired. He still did an honest day's work for an honest day's pay—although he kind of figured the Feds might not think his work was honest. In fact, he was pretty sure they'd raise Cain about it, but you couldn't expect the government to be sensible. Making book was an honest profession. He'd never *forced* anyone to bet, and he always paid what he owed his clients. He was an *honest* bookie, and proud of it. The way he saw it, he was providing a public service.

What did they expect him to do, anyway? They'd changed his name, changed his nose and chin, given him a credit card which he had to pay *himself*, and found him a job in an auto repair shop—and then they had waltzed away, figuring their job was done unless he got recognized.

As if any self-respecting man of his talents was going to be happy fixing cars.

He figured they owed him a hell of lot more than that, anyway. After all, he'd had to give up everything to testify against the mob and avoid jail himself, and this was all they could do for him? Hell, he'd have been better off in prison. At least the mob wouldn't be looking to cut out his liver if they found him, and he'd still have his bank accounts waiting for a cozy retirement.

But for a guy who'd given up everything, he figured he'd done okay. He'd built himself a nice little operation, and he had enough credit to buy this damn magnet.

And all of this shit because that jerk Joe Krebbs had recognized him in the elevator. Sometimes life just plain wasn't fair!

The Feds hadn't been worried that Joe had almost recognized him. Harvey had called them right after his encounter with Joe in the elevator, and they'd said they'd look into it. After a week of unbearable anxiety, Harvey had finally heard back: the Feds believed that Joe was convinced that Harvey wasn't related to Herbie Moroney.

And Harvey was supposed to believe that? It had been a relief when Joe had been killed. He'd thought that everything was okay . . . until now.

Now he was scared to death that Joe, a spook, had figured out who Harvey really was and was planning to tell the whole world about it. And that was why he absolutely had to prevent this seance.

The first thing he did was take the cooler of dry ice up to Jake Carpenter's floor and stash it in the janitor's closet. That called for a little lock-picking, but he'd been picking locks since he was eight; this one was child's play.

Then he took the lid off the cooler, figuring that once the closet got cold enough, the cold would seep out into the hall. There was about a half-inch between the bottom of the door and the rug, plenty of room for the cold to get out, and he'd bought enough ice that it wouldn't be all gone for hours yet.

By the time he wrestled the magnet out of his truck and onto the hand truck, he was drenched with sweat and feeling a little dizzy. Christ, this place was hot! Here they were on the first day of September and it wasn't any cooler than it had been in July. When he left here eventually, he was sure as hell going to head back up north.

He managed to wheel the magnet in through the fire door and down the hallway without seeing a soul. He pushed it onto the elevator with a grunt, and hit nine, one floor above Jake Carpenter's. The unit directly above Carpenter's was vacant, waiting for the return of some Canadian snowbirds, and he only needed it for a few hours anyway.

Unfortunately, the elevator stopped on the third floor and the doors opened. He found himself look-

ing at Bill Dunlop. He tried to step in front of the
magnet to conceal it, but it was a little bigger around
than he was, and anyway, nosy Dunlop leaned
around to look behind him, as if it was any of his
business.

Dunlop hit the button for the twelfth floor. He
gave Harvey a friendly smile. "What in the world
are you going to do with that?"

Harvey thought desperately for an explanation.
"It's . . . uh . . . well . . . it's a modern sculpture!" he
blurted.

Dunlop looked faintly amused. "Really? It's . . .
rather unusual."

"I like it," Harvey said defensively.

"Oh, I wasn't criticizing your taste," Dunlop said.
"Don't you live on the tenth floor?"

Harvey gritted his teeth. "Yes."

Dunlop obliging pushed the button for the tenth,
and Harvey had to ride past the ninth and push the
damn magnet off the elevator.

Dunlop helped him. "Want me to help you get it
to your door? I'd be glad to."

Help like that was the last thing Harvey needed.
He'd only have to push it all the way back down
the hall again to the elevator. "Nah," he said shortly.
"I'll do it myself."

The doors closed and Dunlop was gone. Harvey
waited a few minutes, to make sure Dunlop got off
the elevator on the twelfth floor, then he punched
the down button. One floor. He just had to get down
one floor.

Three minutes later, the elevator doors opened
again, and he wanted to scream when he saw the
Levinsons inside. Christ, at this rate, everybody in
the damn building was going to know he had this
blasted magnet!

He stood there a moment, trying to figure out

whether he'd be better off riding this elevator, with people who'd already seen the magnet, or getting it on the next trip, and risking the chance that someone else might see him. Before he could make up his mind, Abe Levinson was stepping out to help him.

"That must weigh a ton," Abe said. "Let me help you get it on the elevator."

No choice. He and Abe pushed it onto the elevator, while Mrs. Abe squeezed back into the corner.

"Looks like an industrial magnet," Abe remarked.

Well, there went the art excuse, Harvey thought grimly. "Yeah," he said.

"What do you do with it?"

Harvey wanted to tell him it was none of his stinkin' business, but he figured that might be a stupid thing to do. "Health," he said finally, remembering a flaky girlfriend he'd had once. "Magnets are good for health."

"I'm surprised you can run it off the building current," Abe said.

Harvey thanked his lucky stars when Abe and Mrs. Abe got off on the fourth floor. That meant he didn't have to ride all the way down to the lobby and maybe get off the elevator again.

And what was this about running it off the building current? He looked down at his monstrous purchase and for the first time wondered if he'd made some kind of mistake.

He hit the up button for the ninth floor, but Abe had already pushed the lobby button—damn all these helpful neighbors, anyway—so Harvey had to ride all the way down before he could go back up. But this time nobody interfered.

And he consoled himself that it didn't really matter if everyone figured out he was behind the magnet; all that mattered was that they didn't hold the seance, even if they rode him out of town on a rail.

Which nobody did anymore, so he wasn't really worried about it.

Every muscle in his body was screaming by the time he pushed the magnet down to the snowbirds' apartment on the ninth floor, but he managed it. The lock was easy enough to pick, and finally, he had the thing safely inside with the door locked behind him. He pushed it into the kitchen, then knocked it over.

With a loud thud, it landed on the floor, probably dinging the linoleum. He didn't care. All he had to do now was plug it in. But first, he thought, he was going up to his place to get a beer.

Jake heard the terrible thud on the ceiling. He was in his office, but hurried out to the living room to see what was going on. Nothing. Not another sound.

The ghosts, he decided. It had to be the ghosts. "Joe," he said to the empty room, "you'll get your chance tomorrow, okay? Just let me work in peace for a little while. Please?"

Nothing and no one answered him.

Joe fumed to Lucy, "I don't want to be blamed for anything that turkey does!"

Lucy patted his arm consolingly. "Jake will figure it out, dear. He's a very bright young man."

Harvey had more than one beer. He figured he'd worked hard enough that he was entitled to more than that, so he had three. By the time he went back down to the ninth floor, he was feeling a whole lot better about everything. He also couldn't feel his aching muscles anymore, which was fine by him.

He returned to the snowbirds' unit and felt the heat slap him in the face when he entered. Jeez, it was hot in here. The unit was like an oven. The snowbirds had turned off their air conditioning.

That was when he had his second qualm. What if they'd turned off their power, too? The thought gave him butterflies in his stomach, and he started cursing himself for a jerk, but switched to congratulating himself when he was able to turn on a light.

The three beers probably had a lot to do with the fact that he decided to wire the magnet directly into the wall, even though he didn't know a whole lot about electrical wiring. But, he told himself, he hadn't been known in his former life as Herbie "The Brain" Moroney for nothing.

The plug was too big to fit the wall outlet, so naturally it only made sense to take the plug off the magnet and the plate off the wall and connect the wires directly. At his first attempt, he got a shock that threw him backward.

Cursing, he figured out that he'd probably be safer if he turned off the circuit breakers first. He couldn't figure out which one to throw, so he threw them all—which made it a little difficult to see what he was doing in the shadowy kitchen that didn't have even a little window.

But he finally managed it, twisting the wires together to make a direct connection. Then he flipped the circuit breakers and went back to turn on the magnet.

It made a brief hum, and then with a slam he heard all the circuit breakers blow as the kitchen light went out.

"Damn," he said, kicking the magnet, then yelping at the pain. "Oh, shit, I broke my toe!"

He hopped around on one foot for a minute, swearing through his teeth, until the first slicing pain eased and the beer in his system anesthetized him again.

"Shit!" he said one last time.

Duct tape. He needed duct tape. That necessitated a trip back up to his apartment, but this time he didn't run into anyone else.

He taped the circuit breakers in the on position, so they couldn't blow again, and turned on the magnet.

There was a long, loud hum, almost like a purring engine, and he laughed gleefully as he imagined everything metallic in Jake's apartment below gluing itself to the ceiling.

Then, bam! The light went out and the magnet fell silent. Anything which the magnet had levitated in Carpenter's unit had just fallen to the floor.

A check of the circuit breakers showed they were still taped into position.

That's when his beer-fogged brain remembered the main circuit breakers for the building.

He swore again and darted out into the hallway, limping because of his broken toe. He jabbed the elevator button, but nothing happened. Of course not. Power to the whole building was out.

Muttering nasty words, he hit the stairs. Nine flights. *Christ.* At least when the power came back on, he'd be able to take the elevator.

He was two floors down when he remembered that he'd left the magnet turned on and the circuit breakers taped. He wouldn't be able to throw the main. It would just keep blowing.

By this point, he was very close to giving up. But he'd spent all that money, and he was damned if he was going to just throw it away. Growling, and panting like a winded runner, he climbed the two flights, let himself back into the unit, and switched the magnet off.

That was when the dim lightbulb of his brain came on. The only way he was going to get this to work was to wire the magnet into the 220 dryer outlet.

"You're a genius, Herbie," Harvey told himself. "An absolute genius." And just in case somebody reached the main downstairs before he did, he'd turn off the circuit breakers here so he wouldn't get fried.

Man, it was nice to be so brilliant.

Jake's computer screen winked off, along with his desk lamp. The unit was suddenly utterly silent, as even the air conditioning shut down. He waited a couple of minutes, thinking it was just a brief power outage, but finally he went to check his circuit breakers. They were all on.

He waited another few minutes, then decided maybe he'd better go check the mains. He opened his door to find Abe Levinson standing there, hand raised as if he were about to knock.

"Power's out in the whole building," Abe told him.

Jake nodded. "I was just going down to check the mains."

"The super ought to do that," Abe said.

He was right. Jake decided to wait another few minutes, especially since the elevators wouldn't be working. "Did you want something?"

"No, I just wanted to tell you I saw the weirdest thing."

"What's that?"

"Harvey Little. He was in the elevator with a huge industrial magnet."

Jake felt surprised. "How big is huge?"

Abe gestured with his hands.

"That would lift an entire car!"

Abe nodded. "I know. He said it was for his health."

"His *health*?" Jake had run across his share of New Age wackiness in his life, but he couldn't remember any of it needing an industrial magnet.

"That's what he said," Abe repeated. "*However*. The wife and I were downstairs visiting the Addingtons when it suddenly struck me that an industrial magnet might explain some of the goings-on around here."

"It wouldn't explain the furniture on my ceiling."

"Of course not. But maybe some of the other stuff. Maybe Harvey's been behind a lot of this."

The idea appealed to Jake. While he'd come to accept that Joe had put the furniture on the ceiling, he couldn't imagine why his uncle would want to scare the other residents half to death. And he really relished the possibility of being able to explain away some of the other stuff. It would vindicate him, just a little.

No, he decided, it was just too easy. Too much had happened to be blamed on a single industrial magnet. And no magnet could have lifted that plastic watering pot and dumped it on his head.

So what was Harvey Little up to?

Just then the power came back on, and the air conditioning kicked in with an audible *thunk*.

Jake spoke. "Where was he taking the magnet?"

"Out of the building, I think. At least, he was headed down on the elevator."

"I still don't know how much he could have done with it. Besides, how could he run it off the building current?"

"I wondered the same thing myself."

The phone started ringing, and Jake glanced at it over his shoulder. Maybe it was Rainbow. "Come on in while I get that, will you, Abe?"

"Sure." Abe stepped into the unit. "It sure looks

better with all the furniture off the ceiling. How'd you manage it?"

"I didn't. It just came down all by itself and went back to where it's supposed to be."

Abe shook his head. "Well, no magnet could have done that."

Jake picked up the phone and said, "Hello."

But it was not Rainbow's voice that answered him. "Jake, this is Millie Cartera down the hall from you."

"Hi, Millie. How's it going?"

"I think you ought to go check out the hall near the janitor's closet. I came up in the elevator just a short while before the power went out. When I passed by the closet on the way to my unit, I felt . . ." She hesitated. "I wasn't going to call you because I felt silly, but the more I thought about it . . . anyway, could you walk by there yourself? I think you'll see what I mean. Are you sure we can't have the seance any sooner than tomorrow?"

"Roxy Resnick is adamant about that, Millie. Not before tomorrow morning."

Her sigh was audible. "Well, I just hope nothing else happens before then. I'll meet you in the hall by the closet. I want you to see this for yourself!"

"I'm on my way."

He hung up. "That was Millie Cartera."

"What's wrong?"

"I'm not sure. She seems awfully nervous about it, whatever it is. She wants me to meet her by the janitor's closet."

Abe raised an eyebrow. "That's a strange place to meet."

Jake shrugged. "Whatever is going on is apparently happening there."

"I'll come with you."

They didn't have to walk far. The problem wasn't visible from Jake's door, because the janitor's closet was in a little dogleg in the hallway, but as soon as they rounded the corner they could see what had unnerved Millie. There was a faint, white mist hovering there, and the closer they got to it, the colder the air grew.

"Whoa," said Abe, uneasily.

Millie's door was right across from the closet, and it opened now as she peered out. "You see?" she said. "I don't want any ghosts and cold spots right outside my door."

"Me, neither," said Jake sympathetically. He walked closer to the mist, and felt a definite chill on his skin. "Boy, that's cold."

"It gave me goosebumps," Millie told him. "And I almost couldn't bring myself to walk through that fog." She shuddered. "I was afraid I'd . . . feel something."

Jake stuck his hand into the thickest part of the mist. "Just cold. Very cold." He stood there considering this phenomenon, every instinct telling him it had to have a logical explanation. He looked down, trying to see what it could be coming from—and that was when he noticed the white fog seemed to be swirling from beneath the closet door.

"Does anybody have a key for the closet?" he asked.

"The super," Abe said. "He should have it."

"Go back to my unit and call him, will you?" Millie lived alone and Jake didn't know if she'd be comfortable letting them into her apartment.

"Sure thing."

"I'm going to stay right here and make sure nobody runs off with the evidence."

Abe, who had already started back toward Jake's, paused and looked at him. "Evidence?"

"I'd bet fifty bucks right now that this is a hoax."

And he had a pretty good idea what they were going to find when they opened that door.

"A hoax?" Millie repeated, as Jake disappeared around the corner. "But who on earth would want to frighten me this way?"

"I don't think it's directed at you, Millie."

"Then what could be the point?"

"I wish I knew."

But right then, a loud humming seemed to fill the building. Millie gasped and looked around wildly as the hall lights flickered. "Oh, my God," she whispered, "what's that?"

"You stay here and make sure nobody opens that door until I get back."

"But . . ."

He didn't wait for her protests, he ran down the hall, noting that the noise grew louder as he approached his place. And he had a damn good idea what was causing it.

He reached his door and stepped inside. Here the humming was loud enough to make his ears hurt, and he saw Abe standing by the phone, watching as silverware jumped off the counters and plastered itself to the ceiling.

"Neat effect," Abe remarked. "The super's on his way up."

"And I bet I know what's going on here."

Abe grinned at him. "Harvey Little," he said. "Where do you suppose he stashed it?"

"The unit above mine is empty."

"Shall we go see?"

They decided to take the stairs, figuring the magnet must be drawing so much power that the mains were likely to blow at any instant, and they didn't want to be in the elevator when it happened. Abe lagged only a couple of steps behind as they loped up to the next floor.

Here they found residents in the hallway, looking around worriedly. The noise was louder than ever. Jake headed straight for the empty unit and tried the door. It wasn't even locked.

He threw it open, and across the living room saw Harvey Little looking like a madman as silverware and pots came flying out of cupboards toward him. Jake walked over and looked down at the magnet, which was covered with kitchen utensils.

Just then, a can of tuna popped out of a cupboard and attached itself to the magnet with a clang. Harvey jumped.

Wires in the laundry room off the kitchen were spitting sparks, and Jake didn't wait to see any more. He headed for the circuit breakers and ripped the tape off them, allowing the 220-volt line to shut down.

"Damn it, Harvey," he said sharply, "are you trying to burn the building down?"

Harvey, still a little stunned by what had happened, didn't answer. He stood all hunched up, with his arms wrapped around himself, as if he expected the silverware to attack him again.

"I think he got more than he bargained for," Abe said.

"Looks like it." Jake supposed he ought to be angry at Harvey, but all he felt was amusement bordering on laughter. The guy looked so silly standing there, as if he expected to be assaulted, and the wiring job he'd done—well, it would have made excellent fodder for the Three Stooges.

On the other hand, Jake reminded himself, the guy had broken into someone else's apartment and had risked burning the place down with his jury-rigged wiring.

"I guess we'd better call the police," he said.

That seemed to wake Harvey up. "No!" He turned, looking almost wildly at Jake.

"Why not? This isn't your unit, so you're guilty of breaking and entering. God knows what that magnet did to the floor, and you tore up the wiring in here. I imagine you broke a whole bunch of laws."

"I'll fix it," Harvey said. "I'll fix it all. And I didn't take nothin'."

Jake looked at Abe. "What do you think?"

"I think I want to know what the hell he was trying to do."

"Me, too." Jake looked at Harvey, raising a questioning eyebrow.

"If I tell you, do you promise not to call the cops?"

"Maybe. If you pay to have everything in here fixed."

"I *said* I'd fix it."

"No, you'll *pay* to have it *properly* fixed," Jake said. "Judging by what you did to the wiring, I wouldn't trust you to repair anything."

Harvey scowled. "You don't have to be so nasty."

"I'm talking to a criminal, remember?"

Harvey's frown deepened, but fear crept into his eyes. "I was just making a haunting."

"Oh." Jake exchanged looks with Abe. "Why do you want to do that?"

"Because I don't want no seance tomorrow!"

"Why not?"

Harvey had already considered this question and had a ready answer. "Because it's wrong. It's evil."

"Well, you don't have to participate."

Harvey wasn't yet ready to let go of his original plan. "But you don't *need* a seance now," he said eagerly. "Because it was *me*. I did it. And I won't do it anymore, so you can forget all this ghost stuff."

Jake rocked back on his heels, thinking that Harvey was entirely too eager to cancel the seance—

eager enough to do a number of things that could get him arrested. And that whetted Jake's curiosity considerably. "Well . . ." he said slowly, "I can see you did the stuff with this magnet. But you want to tell me how you put the furniture on my ceiling?"

Harvey hadn't thought about that, but he had an answer anyway. "Trade secret."

"Mmm. And what about all the *other* stuff that's been happening? You sure didn't use a magnet to dump a plastic watering can of water on my head?"

"Wires," said Harvey, having the sense not to elaborate.

"Really." Jake was unimpressed. "I didn't find any wires."

"That's the trade secret," said Harvey, who had suddenly realized that he was walking on thin ice. He had the distinct feeling that his explanations weren't doing the trick.

"And why did you do this to begin with?" Jake asked. "What was the point?"

They hadn't called him "The Brain" for nothing. Harvey hadn't even considered that question, but he had no doubt he'd come up with something. His thoughts scurried frantically around, looking for a suitable excuse, and finally produced one. "Um . . . to lower property values?" It came out as a question, and that was when he realized he was doomed.

"Tell you what, Harvey," Jake said pleasantly—too pleasantly. "You come to the seance in the morning, and pay for the repairs to this unit, and I won't call the police. But if you *don't* show up tomorrow morning, I'm going to lodge a complaint against you. And don't forget that Abe is a witness to what you did in here."

Harvey whitened, terrified. "I can't do that," he said hoarsely.

"Why not? It's just a seance. What do you have to be afraid of?"

But Harvey couldn't answer. It had finally dawned on him that there was no way out. Either way, he was a doomed man.

And for the first time in his life, Harvey Little, a.k.a. Herbie Moroney, considered the possibility that he wasn't as brilliant as he'd thought.

Twenty

"**I'M GETTING MARRIED,**" GENE ANNOUNCED AT breakfast. He was wearing a shirt that proclaimed, "I'll stack my memories up against your toys any day."

Three women, all hunkered over their teacups and looking as if the morning had come hours too soon, turned their heads and gaped at him.

"I'm getting married," he repeated with a big grin. "Nellie said yes last night."

Roxy groaned. "Gene, don't do this to me!"

His grin faded. "Do what to you? *I'm* the one who's getting married!"

Roxy put a hand over her eyes. "I can't handle this! First that Mary Todd woman, now this!"

"Mother," Rainbow said, "I hardly think Gene's announcement is in the same category."

"Yes, it is! Now he'll want me to be happy for him! I couldn't be happy for anyone this morning. I'm still too drained from that fiasco, and I need every ounce of energy I have if I'm to get through the seance this morning!"

"Mother," said Rainbow, "it really doesn't take

any energy to be happy for someone else. Happiness *expands* your energy."

She rose from the breakfast bar and went over to give her uncle a big hug. "I'm thrilled for you, Uncle Gene. Don't mind Mother. She's been drowning in self-pity ever since Mary Todd's seance. Are you and Nellie going to live here? I hope?"

He hugged her tightly and smiled down at her. "Part of the time. We've decided to keep both our homes and shuttle back and forth."

"Wonderful!"

Dawn agreed. "I'm so happy for you, Uncle Gene."

"He's a traitor," Roxy said. "After all these years, he's going to get married. He swore he never would."

"That was before I met Nellie. Come on, Rox, be happy for me."

"Well, I am. Or I will be when I get this awful seance behind me. I can't imagine how I was so foolish as to agree to it! A room full of people—oh, it's *never* going to work!"

Still moaning, she went to get dressed for the big event. When she emerged from the bedroom a half-hour later, she was wearing a purple silk caftan, and a spangled matching turban, carefully pulled down so that it covered every last wisp of her orange hair.

"Well, let's go," she said impatiently. "I want to get there early enough to get a sense of the building's aura before the people start crowding around me."

After putting Dawn's steno equipment in the trunk, they all piled into Gene's rental car, which was bigger than Rainbow's, and headed for the Paradise Towers. Rainbow had to hand it to her mother—the woman's mood improved with each block they drove, and by the time they arrived, Roxy

Resnick was fully on her mettle. No one would have guessed that less than an hour ago she had been depressed and complaining.

Jake was waiting for them in the lobby. Ignoring Roxy's glare, he gave Rainbow a hug and a quick kiss in greeting. The brief, chaste embrace and kiss left Rainbow feeling as if she were floating on a cloud. She felt a silly smile stretch across her face.

"I set things up in the rec room," Jake said. "It's over here."

The room was large, with one wall of windows giving a view of the beach and the Gulf. Bridge tables filled nearly half the room, and ping-pong tables had been folded up and pushed to the walls to clear the other half. The chairs had been set up as for a theater, all facing a dais with a long cloth-covered table.

"I thought Roxy could sit at the table," Jake said. "But I wasn't sure. Don't you need everyone to hold hands?"

Roxy sniffed. "I'm a channeler, not a table tipper."

"Oh." Jake clearly didn't understand the difference, and Roxy didn't bother to enlighten him. "Dawn, set up your machine wherever you like. Rainbow, will you sit with me?"

Dawn set her stenography equipment up right in front of the dais, and pulled a chair over to sit on. Rainbow obeyed her mother's summons to sit at the table beside her, giving Jake an apologetic look. He returned a rueful shrug.

Roxy folded her hands in her lap and closed her eyes, drawing deep, slow breaths as she centered herself. Rainbow waited patiently while Roxy sought calm. Minutes ticked by and the Towers residents began to find their way into the room. They moved with surprising quiet, Rainbow noticed, as if they were in church. One by one and two by two, the seats filled nearly to capacity.

Roxy's breathing had grown very slow and shallow, indicating to Rainbow that her mother was going into a trance. It was too soon! They hadn't even given the usual introductory speech. She looked at Dawn and saw that Dawn recognized it, too, and was looking worriedly at their mother.

Just then the Dustbuster brigade arrived, all five of them, under the leadership of Colonel Albemarle. Since their last gathering, they had a adopted a uniform similar to the colonel's: khaki shirts and shorts. Only Albemarle wore a pith helmet, and he removed it as he led his men into the room.

He formed them up and faced them. "Men," he said, "ghosts are going to be called on today. I want you to station yourselves around the room—"

"Quiet!" Roxy barked, in a voice far deeper than her own.

A shiver ran through the assembly, and looks were exchanged.

"I beg your pardon," Albemarle started to say stiffly, but he was silenced again.

"Be quiet," said the low, booming voice that issued from Roxy's mouth. "The woman is in trance! Don't disturb her!"

Rainbow recognized the British accent of Mustafa, one of her mother's guides. Mustafa was an Oxford-educated Lebanese who had been killed by a bomb in Beirut. He was the most helpful of her mother's guides, but he could also be a pain in the neck when he chose. She hoped he wasn't in a contrary mood today.

Colonel Albemarle positioned his men more quietly. They stood in the corners of the room, Dustbusters at the ready.

Jake suddenly spoke. "Rainy? Can you ask your

mother to wait a couple of minutes? We're missing someone who promised he'd be here."

Mustafa answered. "Go get him," he said imperiously. "He will be the focus of today's session."

Jake froze a moment, looking at Rainbow for explanation. She shrugged.

"Back in a minute," he said. "If he hasn't already left town."

"He's in his flat," Mustafa said. "He won't want to answer the door, so I suggest you threaten to call the police."

"I never would have thought of it," Jake said drily. He left the room.

Mustafa/Roxy looked at Rainbow. She felt the chill she always experienced at the way her mother's eyes seemed to change in trance, becoming darker. "Give your mother the blue crystal," he said. "It will help her focus."

Rainbow thought Roxy was doing quite well without any assistance, but she opened Roxy's handbag and took out the large silk bag that contained her mother's crystals. Drawing forth a sapphire one, she put it in her mother's hands. The woman's fingers immediately clamped around it.

"That's better," Mustafa said. "Now we wait."

Jake returned five minutes later, holding Harvey Little by the collar of his shirt. Harvey looked terrified, and kept saying, "Please, please, anything but this!"

Jake shoved him into a seat in the front row. As soon as he let go, Harvey jumped up and tried to run. Jake grabbed the back of his shirt and returned him to his seat.

"Need some help there?" Albemarle asked. Pointedly, he swatted his swagger stick against the palm of his hand.

"He's going to sit right here. Aren't you, Harvey?"

Jake said. "Because if you try to get away again, I'm calling the police."

A murmur went up from the assembled residents.

"Don't you think you're being a bit too harsh?" someone asked. "You really can't force the man to come to a seance."

"Oh, yes, I can," said Jake. "Call it one of the terms of his probation."

Harvey blanched even more, if that was possible, and scrunched down in his seat.

"But he hasn't done anything!" a woman in black said.

"Yes," said Abe Levinson, rising to his feet, "he certainly has. And if you ask me, Jake is letting him off easy."

"But what did he do?"

Jake shook his head. "I promised not to tell if Harvey behaves."

Harvey shrank even more, but managed to say defiantly, "I don't believe in this crap. It's all bullshit."

"Language, language," Jake said warningly. "There are ladies present."

"Just a bunch of old biddies," Harvey grumbled, ignoring the glares from the other residents.

"If I were you," Jake said pleasantly, "I'd shut my mouth before I got ridden out of here on a rail."

Harvey scowled at him, but subsided.

"We are ready," Mustafa said.

Every eye in the room fixed on Roxy.

"Joe and Lucy are here," Mustafa announced, after a pause.

A murmur passed through the room like the sigh of the wind in the trees.

A man stood up. "How are we supposed to know you're not lying?"

Rainbow tensed, wondering if Mustafa would

take offense. He was usually so easily offended.

"He's not lying," said a stentorious voice from the door. Mary Todd toddled into the room, leaning on her cane, an evil smile on her face. "Take it from me. You don't want to piss off this ghost."

An uncomfortable laugh spread through the room.

Mary went to the front, taking the vacant chair next to Jake. "Sorry I'm late, Mustafa," she said to Roxy. "My golf cart battery died and I had to call a cab."

Roxy inclined her head. "Good morning, Miss Todd."

"I take it you're not as annoyed with me as Roxy is."

"By no means. I enjoyed the party at your house. My hostess, however, is still in a snit."

"Can't say as I blame her," Mary said with a laugh.

"It's usually unwise to practice deception."

"Well, I can't say I won't ever do it again." Mary's head bobbed in emphasis. "I take my kicks where I can get them."

But Roxy's head was sagging, and her breathing was growing deep again. Rainbow glanced at her sister and saw that Dawn was watching their mother attentively. Impatient rustlings began to fill the room as the silence lengthened, and Rainbow wondered if her mother was going to continue, or disappoint everyone by coming out of trance.

But just as the impatient audience began to whisper among themselves, Roxy's head lifted.

"Well," said the familiar voice of another of her guides, "a crowd of white oppressors."

"Red Feather!" said Dawn in dismay.

A smile stretched across Roxy's face. "I don't get out nearly enough," she said in the easy, slightly accented voice of her Indian guide. "I used to be Roxy's favorite. Then that stupid Mustafa showed up."

"You'd get out more if you'd behave yourself," Dawn said sternly.

"I told you it was all bullshit," Harvey grumbled. "She got nothin' to say."

"Shut up," said Jake.

Rainbow looked at him, her heart sinking. Red Feather's interruption of Mustafa was hardly likely to convince Jake that her mother was anything other than a fake. He'd come a long way in his attitude toward these things, but that didn't mean he couldn't regress if this seance dissolved into a circus.

Even as she felt her stomach sinking, a shimmer began to appear in the air in front of Harvey Little.

"I am not bullshit," Red Feather said.

"Men!" Colonel Albemarle barked. "Get your weapons ready."

Harvey stared at the patch of shimmering air in front of him and leaned as far back in his chair as he could.

"Red Feather, no," Dawn said. *"Please don't!"*

But Red Feather was on a roll. The shimmering air began to glow with a purple light.

"Weapons?" Red Feather repeated. "If you want weapons . . ."

The purple patch of light grew suddenly, shifting and changing like an amoeba until it finally resembled a large Dustbuster, at least four times as big as any carried by Albemarle's cronies. Moments later a purple hand grew out of it, holding the handle.

"No," said Dawn.

"Yes," said Red Feather.

The ghostly Dustbuster floated in the air, then began to move toward the colonel.

"Shall we duel?" Red Feather asked.

"Men!" the colonel barked, his voice cracking into an undignified squeak. "Turn on your machines!"

At once five Dustbusters whined to life, all of them directed toward the glowing apparition.

"Close in," the colonel ordered.

The five men began moving toward the glowing Dustbuster that seemed to pulse with an unearthly power. Meanwhile, residents began scrambling out of their chairs to move to the farthest reaches of the room.

"Somebody's going to get hurt," Dawn said. "Red Feather, you have to stop this!"

"This spook is a man right after my own heart!" Mary Todd said.

The ghostly Dustbuster turned toward her and bobbed, as if nodding.

Meanwhile, the Colonel's brigade moved in.

All of a sudden, the glowing Dustbuster charged toward one of the men. He jumped back instinctively at the same moment his Dustbuster died. Red Feather's booming laugh filled the room.

"Your puny weapons are useless," Red Feather chortled.

"Red Feather," Rainbow said sternly, rising to her feet, "you stop this right now, or I'm going to wake Mother up!"

The ghostly Dustbuster paused in midair.

"You heard me," Rainbow said. "Cut it out, or I'll wake her!"

"You're no fun," Red Feather complained, but the manifestation was dissolving in air, vanishing even as he spoke. Then it was gone.

"Now let Mustafa come back," Rainbow continued sternly. "We're here for information, not games."

"Yeah, yeah, yeah," said the ghost impatiently,

but Roxy's head dropped to her chest again, and her breathing slowed.

"It's all right," Rainbow said to the group. "You can go back to your seats. He likes to show off, but he can't hurt anybody."

"I don't know if I can believe that," said one man. "Not with the way things have been flying around my condo. I even got beaned by a pillow."

"He's gone," Rainbow insisted. "It's safe now."

In small groups, everyone returned hesitantly to their seats. The men with the Dustbusters shrank gladly back to the edges of the room and turned off their machines.

Colonel Albemarle looked uneasy. "I guess they don't work, after all."

Harvey snickered, but shut up when Albemarle glared at him.

Jake spoke. "Everybody, settle down, okay? Let's just see what happens."

"Easy for *you* to say," Harvey muttered.

But then Mustafa spoke again, silencing everyone else in the room. "Joe and Lucy are here. They want their friends to know they are well."

Harvey groaned. "How dumb can you get? Anybody could say that."

Mary Todd reached around Jake and poked Harvey with the end of her cane. "Be quiet, boy. Some of us would rather listen to the spooks than you."

Harvey rolled his eyes.

"Joe and Lucy are well and happy," Mustafa repeated, emphasizing each word, as if impatient. "They were called before their time, but they have no regrets."

Nellie Blair stood up. "I hope that's true. Before she died, Lucy was happier than I'd ever seen her."

"And she's still happy. She says she would send you another vase full of dried flowers if she could.

But it was she who played the games with your watering can."

"Really?" Nellie brightened.

"What I want to know," said Zach Herschfeld, "is why they've been driving us crazy with all this stuff."

A murmur of agreement arose from the assemblage.

"It was all planned so that you would bring in a psychic," said Mustafa.

"Yeah, right," said Harvey.

"And it was particularly planned because of *you*," Mustafa said sharply.

"Me?" Harvey almost squeaked the word. "I don't even know these ghosts you're talking about."

"Yes, actually you do, since it's because of you that they're ghosts."

Harvey blanched. Every eye in the room fixed on him, and none of the looks he got were particularly kind. Jake turned toward him, his face taking on a dangerous expression.

"I didn't kill no one!" Harvey said quickly.

"I wondered about that explosion," said Olive Herschfeld. "Joe always took such good care of his boat."

"And the key," said Jake. "The key was missing when he went to look for it. He found it on the boat and was worried that he had Alzheimer's. Joe wasn't a forgetful man."

"I just borrowed it!" Harvey said. "That's all I did. I just wanted to go fishing. I was lucky I didn't get blown up!"

"You borrowed his boat?" Jake looked like he was ready to leap out of his chair and strangle the man. "Borrowed it without telling him, I suppose! That's theft. And what the hell did you do to it, anyway? You're probably the reason it blew up!"

"I didn't do nothing to the boat! I took it out on the bay, but I got seasick so I brought the damn thing back. Didn't even ding the paint."

"Yeah, right," said Jake. "Why don't you 'fess up like a man?"

"I told you, I didn't do nothin' to the boat!"

"He didn't," said Mustafa's booming voice, cutting across the room and silencing everyone. "He didn't hurt the boat."

"See?" said Harvey, suddenly glad to have someone speaking for him, even if it was a ghost.

Jake turned toward Roxy. "Then why is this seance about Harvey?"

"Because," said Mustafa, "he was the one who was supposed to be killed in the explosion."

A gasp went through the room.

Jake shook his head. "Do you want to explain that?"

"I would be glad to," Mustafa answered. "Harvey Little is here under the Witness Protection Program."

"I knew it!" Suddenly Harvey was on his feet, stabbing a finger in Roxy's direction. "I knew it. I didn't want this spirit crap from the beginning, because I knew you idiots were gonna expose me! Do you want to get me killed?"

"Sit down!" Jake grabbed Harvey's sleeve and jerked the man back into his chair.

"Let me finish!" Mustafa's barked command had the effect of freezing the entire room. "That's better. Now, to return to Mr. Little, or Mr. Moroney, as he used to be known . . ."

Harvey's face turned as white as fresh-fallen snow. "How did you know that?"

"I know a great many things that are hidden to mortal eyes," Mustafa said, with forgivable smugness. "I know, for example, that you were found out nearly a year ago."

Harvey's color didn't improve. "The boat," he said, in a strangled voice.

"Precisely," Mustafa agreed. "The bomb was meant to kill *you*. Your acquaintances in the mob tracked you here to Paradise Beach and saw you getting on Joe's boat that day. They boarded later that night and left a little present, intending to surprise you. When they saw the boat blow up, they thought they had killed you. Instead, they had killed Joe and Lucy."

"My God," said Jake quietly.

"They have since realized their mistake," Mustafa continued. "They're looking for you again, Herbie."

"*Herbie?*" Jake said.

"Herbie Moroney," Mustafa explained. "Also known as the Brain, although a bit sarcastically, I must say."

Jake looked at Harvey. "Apparently."

"Hey, I'm no dope!" Harvey protested.

"You were the one who tried to hook an industrial magnet into house current," Jake reminded him. "Not exactly Einstein."

Rainbow interjected, "Why does the mob want to kill Mr. Little?"

"Because he testified against a mob boss, and sent him to prison for life. They have long memories."

"And why does Joe care?"

Mustafa replied, "Because he and Lucy fear that some of their friends may get hurt in the mob's next inept attempt to kill Herbie Moroney."

An appalled murmur spread through the room, but Harvey Little looked most frightened of all.

"You've got to get out of here," Abe said, looking at Harvey. "No one else here should be hurt because of your misspent life."

"I don't have any money," Harvey said. "I spent it all on the magnet. I don't have any place to go—" He broke off as fear made him shudder. "I never hurt anyone," he said plaintively. "I was too stupid to hurt anyone. Except the boss. I was too scared to go to prison . . ."

Gene stood up. "I'm sure you've got a contact in the Witness Protection Program. Somebody you can call."

"I was supposed to be safe! They promised me I'd be safe!"

Jake looked at Gene. "One thing is for certain: we've got to get him out of this building as soon as possible."

Gene nodded. "I couldn't agree more."

Harvey wailed, "But nobody will help me! Nobody's gonna believe I'm in danger because a *ghost* said so!"

"I can do something about that," Gene said firmly. "I still know some people. But the first thing we have to do is get this slimeball out of this building, and make it clear he's not going to come back."

Everyone looked at Harvey, who was too busy being afraid to have anything to say.

It was Rainbow who came up with an idea. "Let's fake an arrest."

Gene's, Jake's, and Harvey's heads all snapped around to gape at her.

"Splendid idea," said Mary Todd, tapping her cane for emphasis. "Chief Corrigan is a reasonable man."

"He'll help," Rainbow agreed. "I'll call him right now."

"I don't want to be arrested!" Harvey looked as if he wanted to crawl out of his skin.

"We're just going to pretend," Jake said. "I doubt they'll come after you if you're in police custody."

"No, they'll kill me like a goldfish in a bowl while I'm locked up in some jail cell!"

"Nobody's going to lock you up. We're going to find a way to get you out of Paradise Beach."

"Why?" Harvey's color was coming back, along with his big mouth. "Why should you help me?"

"So nobody else gets killed, you jerk!"

That seemed to reassure him.

Rainbow went out to the lobby to use the pay phone to call Chief Corrigan. She tried not to think how this information was bound to affect Jake, once he had a chance to think about it. Her heart ached for him, though. How awful it was to know that his uncle's death had been caused by a murderous attempt on the life of another person, far worse and more meaningless than an accident would have been.

Blaise Corrigan always took her calls readily, so she wasn't surprised when she was put straight through to him.

"This is going to be a little hard to explain," she said."

"It usually is, when *you're* involved," he said with friendly humor. "Just tell me the basics."

"I don't know if you're aware of it, but one of the people at Paradise Towers is in the Witness Protection Program."

"Really?" The humor faded from his voice. "How'd you find out?"

"One of my mother's guides told everyone, and the man didn't deny it."

"It's true, then. This isn't good. Having his identity announced that way could cause him a lot of trouble."

"He was already in a lot of trouble. My mother's guide said that the mob blew up Joe Krebbs's boat last year because they thought it belonged to this man and they were trying to kill him."

"Oh, my God!"

"Anyway, Mother's guide says they've discovered they killed the wrong people, and they're coming back after Harvey Little. So in order to protect the other residents, we need to get him out of there in a way that makes it clear he's not coming back. We thought maybe you could pretend to arrest him, and keep him under watch while my Uncle Gene calls some people he knows in Washington to see what they can do about getting Harvey out of here."

"Sounds like a good plan to me. The more noise we make about getting him out of there, the safer the other Towers residents will be."

"That's what we thought."

"I'm on my way."

He had believed her, Rainbow realized suddenly. For all he had sometimes seemed uncomfortable with psychic powers while they dated, he hadn't questioned her or treated her like a lunatic.

It was a revelatory experience for her, and she felt the shackles of old fears beginning to let go. Not everyone was like her former fiancé, she realized. Maybe her relationship with Corrigan had died simply because they didn't click, and not because she was psychic. Maybe it was possible that every unfortunate thing in her life wasn't directly related to her abilities.

When she returned to the rec room, everyone was still gathered, as if uncertain if they dared to leave and go back to their units. Roxy was emerging from her trance, looking drained.

"What happened?" she asked faintly.

"Mustafa was wonderful, Mother," Dawn said reassuringly. "He solved the mystery for us."

Roxy wailed, "Why do I always have to miss the exciting things?"

"Because you're the medium, Mother."

Roxy was not appeased.

Rainbow reached Jake and Harvey Little. Mary was still sitting beside them, fondling the head of her cane and looking vastly entertained by the morning's events.

Jake looked at Rainbow. "Any luck?"

"Chief Corrigan is on his way over. He's going to pretend to arrest Harvey, and them keep him under guard until someone figures out how to get him safely away."

"Great," Jake said.

Harvey didn't look as if he really thought so, but apparently he couldn't think of any alternative.

"Why is someone getting arrested?" Roxy wanted to know. "What did I say?"

Rainbow looked at Dawn. "I'll explain it to her," Dawn said.

In the distance, they could now hear the sound of sirens. Rainbow smiled as she realized that Chief Corrigan was going to make this "arrest" in as high a profile way as possible.

"I don't believe this," Harvey said. "I spent my whole life staying away from cops."

"Cops are good," Jake said drily. "They can actually help you sometimes."

"Yeah, right."

Jake shook his head. "Look, guy, it's like this. You can either leave here with police protection, or you can go on your own, but either way, we both know you're not going to be hanging out here."

Harvey scowled but shut his mouth, which to Rainbow's way of thinking was a good thing, since she was finding his attitude very tiresome and was feeling very little sympathy for his plight.

The Dustbuster brigade, she noticed, had vanished into the woodwork. She thought they were probably humiliated by Red Feather's reaction to their weapons, and she felt sorry for them. Silly or not, they were all nice old men who had been trying to help their neighbors. When things calmed down a little bit, she resolved to find a way to make them feel better. Maybe the Towers could throw a thank-you party for them.

Chief Corrigan and three other policemen walked in just then and made a show of arresting Harvey. Three minutes later, moaning all the way, he was led out in handcuffs. Rainbow hadn't a doubt that this would make the evening news, which ought to hold the mob off long enough to allow somebody to spirit Harvey away.

"Thank goodness he's gone!" Mary Todd cried. "What an obnoxious little man!"

But it all seemed anticlimactic to Rainbow. The residents were drifting away, apparently so uncomfortable with what had happened that they weren't even stopping to thank Roxy.

This omission was not lost on Roxy, who finally wailed, "Rainbow, take us home right now. To Sarasota! I have had enough!"

Rainbow nearly sighed, realizing she was going to spend the next hours bandaging her mother's wounded ego.

Jake reached out and caught her hand as she started to join her mother and sister. "Come see me as soon as you get back?" he asked. "We need to talk."

She felt his hand tighten around hers, and she squeezed back. Suddenly the day seemed bright and cheerful. "Sure. It won't take me all that long."

And even less time, now that she knew he'd be waiting for her.

Twenty-one

It was eight o'clock that evening before Rainbow knocked on Jake's door. The lateness of the hour was an indicator of the state Roxy had been in. It took only an hour to get to Sarasota from here, but Rainbow hadn't been able to just drop her mother off and return. Instead, she'd been obliged to sit with her for hours, assuring her she'd done a wonderful job and probably saved lives.

Roxy had finally quieted, but swore she would never again channel for anyone in Paradise Beach.

Rainbow could well understand why.

Then Jake was opening his door, and all of that seemed incredibly far away as he smiled, drew her inside, then swept her into his arms for a long, hungry kiss.

Before she could do anything but register delight and a deep, warm sense of satisfaction, his hands were sweeping over her body, carrying her to those pinnacles of delight where only he could take her.

"I've missed you," he said, when he came up for air. "God, I wouldn't have believed it was possible to miss someone so much when they'd only been gone a few hours."

Rainbow felt something deep inside her bloom, like a flower reaching for the sun. She looked up at him from heavily-lidded eyes and released a long sigh of satisfaction. "I missed you, too."

"Good." And he sounded as if he meant it. "I don't want to be crass and carry you straight off to bed. I should tell you all the news first."

"Be crass," she suggested, a laugh of sheer joy rising from the pit of her stomach. She ought to be afraid, she realized. She ought to be terrified that she'd become too attached to Jake, but inexplicably, she felt safer than she'd ever felt in her life. The pain would come later, of course, but right now the anticipation of it couldn't touch her.

"No," he said, looking regretful. "I will *not* act like an animal, even if I feel like one. You must be hungry and tired, so I'm going to feed you first while you put your feet up and relax. We'll share the news—and then I'll drag you off to my lair."

"Promise?"

His blue eyes sparkled with heat. "Believe it."

He released her in stages, as if letting go of her was very difficult. But at last they stood apart, though it felt to Rainbow as if the tension between them crackled in the air.

"Dinner," Jake said finally, shaking himself as though coming out of a Roxy-like trance. "I made dinner for us. Let me go warm it up."

She watched as he crossed the room, and tried to find some shreds of common sense to hang onto before she became utterly lost in the sea of yearning he created in her. But it was too late, she realized. Too late to save herself. There was nothing she could do now except ride the waves.

"I made lo mein because it heats up well," he said over his shoulder, as he walked into the kitchen. "I hope you like it."

"I love it. You made it yourself?"

"Absolutely. I even went out to an oriental grocery to get the noodles. Made from scratch, my love, earlier today, with these two talented little hands."

She followed him, feeling a thrill at being called his love, even as she tried to remind herself he didn't really mean it. "They certainly are talented hands," she managed to say lightly.

"And I intend to prove just *how* talented . . . later. Once I've taken care of *you* properly."

She was touched. "You don't have to take care of me, Jake."

He looked at her. "I don't *have* to . . . I *want* to."

She wrapped her arms around herself, hugging the delicious feelings he was giving her as close as she could, as if afraid that they might slip away.

He popped the bowl of lo mein into the microwave and turned it on.

"News," he reminded himself. "Gene managed to get hold of a contact in Washington. Don't ask me which contact. He's a very cagy man, your uncle."

Rainbow nodded. "There's a lot he won't talk about."

"Well, I get the feeling he knows some very powerful people. Anyway, the gist of it is, sometime in the next twenty-four hours, Harvey Little, a.k.a. Herbie 'The Brain' Moroney, is going to be swept away to parts unknown by the Witness Protection Program. Or by somebody. I'm assuming it's Witness Protection. He also found out the whole damn story. You know, your uncle would make a great inquisitor. I gather he got Harvey to sing like a bird."

"What *is* the story?"

He pulled the lo mein out and replaced it with a bowl of fluffy short-grain rice. He turned the micowave on again.

"Harvey was evidently a minor hoodlum with

some mob connections up north in New Jersey. He was an idea guy, or thought he was. Anyway, somehow, in some way, he got his bosses interested in some kind of scam for disposing of garbage. Which is why my uncle felt he might have met him somewhere. Joe was in the garbage business."

"Really? But Harvey didn't actually try to kill him?"

Jake shook his head. "Apparently not. After Joe recognized Harvey in the elevator, the Feds checked it out and decided Joe had believed Harvey when he said he didn't know any Moroney. Apparently Joe had merely seen him around somewhere, when Harvey was nosing out the business—if you'll pardon the pun."

Rainbow gave an obligatory groan and he grinned at her.

"Anyway, not being too bright, Harvey readily accepted that Joe had simply mistaken him for someone else."

"But how did the mob find Harvey?"

"No one knows, although they suspect there was a leak somewhere along the way."

"Obviously."

Jake shrugged. "I'm just glad I'm not relying on the Witness Protection Program. I'd be having the willies."

"Me, too."

The microwave beeped and Jake pulled the rice out. He carried the steaming bowls to the already set table. He'd done a nice job, Rainbow noticed. Crystal and china gleamed on a white tablecloth, and a vase of red roses made a beautiful centerpiece.

They sat and Jack served them. Rainbow was surprised to discover that she was famished, and Jake's lo mein was the best she had ever tasted.

"You can cook for me anytime," she said appreciatively.

"I intend to."

The warm look in his eyes nearly left her breathless. For a moment, she just stared at him, until she realized that she was gawking like a lovelorn teenager. A blush suffused her cheeks and it was all she could do to return her attention to her meal. It was a painful moment of awareness for her as she realized how vulnerable she was.

"Anyway," Jake said, picking up the thread of the story, "Herbie's garbage scheme wound up costing the mob some money and trouble. They were after him, so he turned state's evidence in exchange for being put in the Witness Protection Program. The mob boss and a couple of his henchmen got sent up for a long time. Harvey apparently knew a lot more about what was going on than just what he was involved with."

"So he isn't a killer, or anything?"

Jake shook his head. "Small-time con man, and not even a good one. The Feds apparently figured he wasn't worth bothering with, until he offered to testify."

"I could almost feel sorry for the guy."

"*Almost* being the operative word," Jake agreed. "He sure is irritating."

"So Mustafa was right."

Jake nodded. "The mob thought Joe's boat belonged to Moroney. They'd been watching him, looking for a reasonably good way to wipe him out. The boat seemed ideal."

"I'm sorry, Jake."

It was a moment before he looked at her. "So am I. But what's done is done, and it just as easily could have been a mindless accident. Or worse, he could have gotten really sick and suffered for a long time.

I've been thinking about it a lot this afternoon, and I decided this really wasn't so bad. He died when he was happier than he'd ever been. We should all be so lucky. I'll always miss him, but . . . well, Mustafa said he was happy."

"So you believe that Mustafa is real?"

He put his fork down and looked straight at her. "If I ever doubt you or your mother again, I will personally cut out my own tongue."

She was nearly overcome by a hysterical urge to laugh. And it was purely hysterical, because what he was saying was unlocking the floodgates behind which she'd been trying to dam her feelings. "That's . . . that's quite a change in attitude," she said finally.

He shrugged. "When you see your deceased uncle as large as life, and an ectoplasmic Dustbuster in broad daylight, it's kind of a wake-up call."

But she had to press him. She had to know if this was for real. "It could have been faked."

"Not in broad daylight. Not in a room full of people. Not right in front of my nose. I know what I saw. I know what I heard. I'm convinced."

Her appetite was gone now, as her heart began a slow, heavy beating. She waited, hardly daring to breathe, feeling as if she stood on a pinnacle between possible futures, where one move could send her tumbling down the wrong side.

"Are you through?" he asked.

She managed a nod, her gaze following him as he stood and reached for her hand.

"Rainy?"

Somehow she managed to rise on legs that felt like water, clinging to his hand as the world seemed to whirl out of control around her.

"You're psychic," he said. "I can live with that. I can live with tarot readings, and premonitions, and your mother and her crazy guides. In fact, I think

I'll even enjoy them. What I want to know is, can *you* live with *me*?"

She blinked, hardly daring to believe what he was saying. "Why shouldn't I be able to live with you? You're perfectly *normal*."

"So are you," he said softly, drawing her closer. "Extraordinarily normal. You're kind, generous, level-headed, gorgeous, sexy—and psychic. I used to think that was weird, but it finally struck me that the only thing that's weird is that you can sense what I can't. You have a gift, and I don't. Can you live with someone who can't share that part of your world? Can you trust me to trust you?"

That was when she realized that trust really was the issue. The past had taught her not to trust people, to fear that they would be unable to accept her gift. Could she trust Jake to accept her?

It was a dangerous step, and she felt as if she hovered at the edge of a cliff—one foot extended out, into empty air—having to trust that when she moved forward, something would be there to catch her.

The psychic ether offered no answers. This was one she was going to have to decide herself, with no guidance but what was in her own heart. If she was to break out of the shell she was living in, she was going to have to take this chance.

She looked up into Jake's eyes, eyes as blue as a midsummer sky, and felt her heart open wide, felt herself take that frightening step.

"Yes," she said. It was the rightest, truest thing she had ever said. She felt it all the way to the tips of her toes.

Then she took that step, and his arms were there to reach out for her, to catch her and lift her high against his chest.

"Thank God," he said, his voice shaky with emotion. "And now I'm going to be crass."

"Please," she said breathlessly, "be very crass."

He laughed and turned to carry her toward the bedroom when a voice, seeming to come out of the thin air, said, "Oh no, you don't!"

Jake froze. Rainbow felt the hairs on the back of her neck rise.

"Who's in here?" she asked in a whisper.

Jake pointed with a jerk of his chin, and she turned her head.

Standing in the bedroom doorway was the man she had seen in the restaurant. Jake's uncle. And with him, wrapped in his arms, was a lovely woman of about sixty, with steel-gray hair and bright, dark eyes.

"Uncle Joe?" Jake said, as if he didn't quite know what to make of this.

"You two go somewhere else," Joe said. "This is *our* home, Lucy's and mine, and we're not ready to give it up yet. This is where *we* were supposed to live."

Then, before Jake could say another word, the two ghosts vanished on a whisper of chilly air.

Jake swallowed and looked down at Rainbow. There was something very like laughter in his gaze. "I think we're intruding on their privacy."

She nodded, feeling an absurd desire to laugh. "So it seems. I don't know about you, but I'd rather not have an audience, either."

Gently he set her on her feet. "Right. Let's go to your place. As far as I'm concerned, they can have the condo for as long as they want. I think we ought to get our own place anyway, someplace we pick together."

Rainbow felt her breath catch in her throat. "Our own place?"

"Isn't that what married people do?"

"Married?" She was feeling stunned, as if too much was happening all at once for her to absorb.

Jake smiled down at her. "Yes, married. Will you marry me, Rainbow Moonglow? And have little children with me in our very own bungalow by the sea?"

Astonishment turned to joy, as belief settled in her heart as gently as down. "I guess I don't have any choice."

His brow creased. "Why not?"

"The tarot said my life was going to change dramatically."

He cocked a brow. "So you'll marry me because of what the tarot said?"

She shook her head, beginning to smile. "I'll marry you because I love you."

He caught her around her waist, and swung her in circles. "I love you! Love you, love you, love you!"

Finally he set her on her feet again, grinning from ear to ear and holding her hand like a schoolboy. "Let's get out of here," he said. "Let's go someplace private."

She nodded and walked with him to the door.

As they were stepping out together to start their new life, they heard a voice from behind them say, "Well, it's about time!"

Laughing together, they closed the door behind them and walked away.

Dear Reader,

If you're looking to put more romance in your life, then don't miss next month's romantic selections from Avon Books, starting with the return of those irresistible Cynster men in Stephanie Laurens' *Scandal's Bride*. Richard Cynster, known to his family as Scandal, has decided he'll avoid the fate of most Cynster men—he'll never marry. But then he meets beautiful Catriona Hennessy. Will Scandal soon be headed to the altar?

Next, it's the moment many of you have been waiting for—the next contemporary romance from Susan Andersen, *Be My Baby*. I know that Susan's *Baby, I'm Yours* is a favorite of her many, many readers, and if you haven't yet experienced the pure pleasure of reading one of Susan's fast-paced, sexy contemporary love stories...well, now is the time to start! It's contemporary romance at its finest.

Eve Byron has charmed countless readers with her delightful heroines and strong heroes, and in *My Lord Stranger* she gives both. It's a Regency-set love story you're not likely to forget.

Margaret Moore is a new author to Avon Romance, and *A Scoundrel's Kiss* is sure to please anyone who loves a rakish hero tamed by the love of a woman. Here, our hero makes a bet with his friends that he can seduce any woman in England...even the prim-and-proper heroine.

Enjoy!

Lucia Macro
Lucia Macro
Senior Editor

Avon Romances—
the best in exceptional authors and unforgettable novels!